Other books by
JENNIFER L. ARMENTROUT

The Titan Series
(New Adult Paranormal)
The Return
The Power

Wicked Trilogy
Wicked
Torn

Covenant Series
(Full series completed—Young Adult Paranormal)
Daimon
Half-Blood
Pure
Deity
Elixir
Apollyon
Sentinel

Lux Series
(Full series completed—Young Adult Paranormal)
Shadows
Obsidian
Onyx
Opal
Origin
Opposition
Oblivion (Daemon's POV of Obsidian)

The Gamble Brothers Series
(Full series complete—Adult Contemporary Romance)
Tempting the Best Man
Tempting the Player
Tempting the Bodyguard

For details about current and upcoming titles from
Jennifer L. Armentrout,
please visit www.jenniferlarmentrout.com

The Struggle
Published by Jennifer L. Armentrout
Copyright © 2017 by Jennifer L. Armentrout
All rights reserved

Library of Congress Cataloging-in-Publication Data
The Struggle/Jennifer L. Armentrout—First edition
ISBN: 978-0-9979691-5-3

Interior Design & Formatting by:
Christine Borgford, Type A Formatting

The
STRUGGLE
A TITAN NOVEL

#1 *New York Times* and International Bestselling Author
JENNIFER L. ARMENTROUT

The STRUGGLE

A TITAN NOVEL

For my sister-in-law Jerry . . .

1

*D*oing the right thing had never felt more wrong than it did right then.

Maybe that was how it always felt.

I wouldn't know.

It was so rare when I actually did the right thing.

My knuckles ached from clenching the steering wheel. Every cell in my body demanded that I turn the vehicle around and go back—go back to Josie, because she was *mine*, and I belonged with her, in her and beside her.

But I couldn't.

Everything had changed now.

Heady, deadly power churned deep inside me, and it was nothing like what being an Apollyon felt like. Oh no, this was like the Apollyon on steroids. I had a feeling that the unexpected awakening, the even more surprising subsequent ability to kill Atlas, was just the beginning of what I was capable of, because the entire world was different to me now.

The sky was a shade I'd never seen before. The sea off the Pacific Coast Highway was a dizzying kaleidoscope of blues.

Skin sensitized, I could feel the dampness in the air. I inhaled and it tasted of sea and salt. I was going damn near a hundred in this SUV, and I felt like I could still go faster—that I should be going faster.

And I was *hungry*.

Not for food.

For what lived and breathed inside of the pures and the halfs, the demigods and gods, and inside of Josie.

I couldn't be around her.

It was too dangerous.

Miles were between Josie and me now, and soon there'd be thousands, and it had to stay that way, but I . . . I could still feel her body beneath mine, her skin soft against mine, and I could still hear her soft cries echoing in my ears.

I love her.

Pressing my boot down on the gas, I knew where to go. A place far from here, far from everything. A place where I could think and plan, because I was going to take out every single motherfuc—

"You're making a mistake."

"Shit," I cursed as I jerked the steering wheel to the right. The tires squealed. Dust along the embankment flooded the air as my gaze flew to the passenger seat.

That godsdamn nymph was sitting beside me.

He was shirtless, as usual, wearing his doeskin pants, and he was as glittery as a damn disco ball.

"What the hell?" I exploded, straightening the wheel before we careened off the highway. A crash wouldn't kill me, but I really didn't feel like testing out how indestructible my skin could be. "You could've caused me to wreck."

"As if your life isn't already a wreck?" he replied, smiling slightly. "The answer would be yes—yes, your life is a wreck."

I gripped the steering wheel. "What in the fuck of all fucks do you want?"

"We need to talk."

Anger rippled under my skin. "There is nothing we need to talk about."

"Oh, there is." The nymph waved his hand, and the engine cut off without any additional warning.

Cursing in every language I knew, I was able to coast the SUV to the narrow side of the road, between two large boulders. I dropped my hands and twisted toward him. "You know I could kill you with a snap of my two fingers."

"You could. And maybe you will one day." Those purplish eyes glimmered. "But not today."

"I don't know about that." Akasha crackled over my skin, casting a whitish-amber glow over the interior of the SUV. It came to me so easily. I barely even had to think about it. "I'm really not in the mood."

"Because you left Josie?" he replied.

Exhaling roughly, I worked a kink out of my neck. "Careful, nymph."

"You've chosen to leave, correct? Even though she's unprotected?"

"She is not unprotected." Unease brewed deep in my gut, because even though she was with the incredibly happy duo known as Alex and Aiden, and even though she was a demigod, the Titans were dangerous. However, I knew from previous experience that the Titans would retreat for a while. After losing Atlas, they wouldn't come after Josie for a bit, giving me time to search them down and end them.

Besides, I was more dangerous to her.

There was something inside me, and it was cold and cruel. I could taste it. I could feel it, and it wanted to devour Josie.

"You've made your choice, God Killer?"

About to tell him that he could dive head-first out of the window, something occurred to me—a memory from when he magically appeared at the Covenant and warned about what was inside of me. "You knew."

"Knew what?"

"That I was the God Killer."

"That you could *become* the God Killer," he corrected. "We all knew there was a chance. After all, it became your destiny when the other passed."

I shot him a quick look. "What destiny crap are you talking about?"

A secretive smile curved the corners of his lips. "There is so much you do not know."

Why I hadn't blasted the glittery fuck-face out the window yet was anyone's guess.

"She loves you," he said quietly. "Do you even realize what that means?"

My throat closed off. Within a traitorous heartbeat, I could see Josie in my mind's eye—her stricken face when I'd admitted to feeding on her. I saw her after I'd taken out Atlas and was about to turn Aiden into a Slurpee. Her and all that hair, all that blonde and brown hair flowing around her beautiful face as she'd nicked me with the blade tainted with the blood of a Pegasus.

I saw her staring at me like she had no idea what I was.

And then I saw what a dark part of me knew I was capable of doing to her. Closing my eyes, I swore under my breath. I didn't want to see her.

"No," he murmured. "No, you do not." There was a pause. "But you will."

Scrubbing my hand across my jaw, I opened my eyes and

stared out at the ocean as cars raced past us on the highway. "I'm only going to ask you one more time. What do you want?"

"Do you understand what it means to be a God Killer?"

"That I can pretty much kill anything?"

"That was an unintelligent response. And I mean that as no insult. The knowledge of what you are capable of exists deep inside of you. It is what led you to force the awakening."

It was that thing inside me.

"You have made your choice," he stated again.

"Yes," I answered. "I can't . . . I can't be around any of them."

The leather seats crackled as the nymph leaned toward me. I didn't need to look at him to know he was way too close. "And you know where you want to go?" When I didn't answer, he asked, "Why would you need to drive there?"

Looking over at him, I raised my brows. "Because I figured I'd drive and then I'd have to fly there."

The nymph's ultra-bright red lips curved into a smile. "You are the God Killer. You merely need to picture where you want to go and go there."

I stared at him. "You're shitting me."

"Try it." He sat back, his eyes like jewels. "And you will learn you are not just capable of death. You are capable of so much more."

My first inclination was to simply throat-punch him right through the car door, but I decided to humor him. "Like what?"

"Like creating life."

A harsh laugh burst out of me. "Yeah, you're about a second away from ceasing to exist."

"Try it," he cajoled, completely unafraid. "Picture where you want to go. Try it just once."

Glaring at him, I shook my head, but I did it. I don't even know why, but I did. I pictured the rocky coasts and blue-green seas, and I could almost feel the golden sun on my skin, but it was more than that. There was another voice that sounded like mine, but wasn't. It told me where I needed to go.

Andros.

Warmth soaked into my skin, and my eyes flew open. "Holy . . ."

Shock nearly bowled me over. I was no longer sitting inside the SUV. Stumbling back a step, I realized I was staring at the frothy sea—the sea I hadn't seen in years. My jaw unhinged. Impossible. I had to be hallucinating.

"See," the nymph said, and I jerked to the side. He was also beside me. "You are capable of a lot, God Killer."

I shook my head. "I don't . . . How is this possible?"

The nymph turned to the ocean and then his lifted his hands, spreading his arms out. "Everything is possible."

This couldn't be real, but as I turned around, I knew . . . Dear gods, it was real, and I was half the world away from Josie in less than a second. I could barely process it.

We stood on the thin strip of white sand and rock of Andros, the northernmost island in the Cyclades. Mountainous and full of water-fed valleys that bore the fruit I used to sneak as a child, it was barely tame.

The weirdest damn sensation itched under my skin as I took in the path leading to the stairs climbing the steep hill. Taking a deep breath, I lifted my gaze to the sprawling sandstone home that was perched atop the highest peak. It was a monstrous building, three stories with several wings that, if it were the same, contained nothing more than marble statues and oil paintings depicting the gods. Balconies surrounded the upper two levels, with many nooks and crannies to hide in.

The veranda wasn't empty.

"What the . . . ?" I trailed off.

There were people out on it, scores of them staring down at

where we stood, and I could sense the aether in the pures and the fainter traces in the halfs.

The house should've been vacant. There was no reason for any of the staff to have remained after Mother had died.

"Who are these people?" I demanded.

The nymph inclined his chin. "Some were your mother's staff, her servants . . . her confidants. They are now yours. Others came when you awakened. They are also yours."

What the hell? "I don't want them here."

"Their master has finally come home."

Master?

"Did you think it would be different?"

"Yes." I frowned as those on the veranda, one by one, lowered themselves onto their knees and bowed their heads. Oh hell. "I thought it would be empty, for starters."

The nymph chuckled.

Crossing my arms, I exhaled roughly. "I have no use of them."

"Oh, you will find use of them, I am sure."

I slid him a sidelong glance. "I'm really going to get tired of repeating myself. I have no need of servants. Gods. Those halfs should be freed."

"Those halfs are here of their own volition. They are here because it is where you are, as I am here because of you," the nymph said. "I am here to help you."

"Why? Why would you help me?"

The nymph smiled. "My kind has walked this realm long before man—before the gods from Olympus overthrew the Titans. We were here even before the Titans ruled."

Well, that sounded like a really long time ago, in a time period called I Don't Give a Fuck. "What does that have to do with anything?"

Those odd eyes twinkled. Actually twinkled, like a pair of

tiny stars. "We believe that the time for change has arrived once more."

The question of what kind of change was due to arrive died on the tip of my tongue. I wanted no part of whatever the nymphs believed in or wanted. I had my own goals. I would ferret out whatever foxhole the Titans were hiding in and I would gladly destroy each one. They would be no threat to Josie.

"What is your name?" I did ask.

One eyebrow rose. "Ewan."

I snickered. "Ewan the Ewok."

The nymph frowned.

"Never mind," I sighed and started forward. "Goodbye, Ewan."

"Do you want to know about love?" he asked.

Rolling my eyes, I kept walking.

"Love is the root of all that is good, and the root of all things that are evil," he called out. "Love is the root of the Apollyon."

The fine hairs on my arms rose, and I stopped. The pures and halfs on the veranda waited, the women's pale blue and rose-colored dresses billowing in the breeze. Something about what the nymph was saying rang eerily familiar.

"Fate is afoot," he continued. "Things cannot be undone. Fate has looked into the past and into the future. History is on repeat."

Slowly, almost against my will, I turned around. The nymph stood where I'd left him, but there was something ancient and wise in his gaze.

"Know the difference between need and love." Ewan's voice carried on the salty breeze. Those amethyst eyes rolled back, revealing all-white pupils.

"Oh hell no," I muttered, actually wanting to take a step back to stop what I knew was coming.

The nymph glided forward and spoke the words that had been meant for the first Apollyon—for Alex—and brought life to a prophecy once unfinished.

"For what the gods have feared has come to pass. The end of the old is here and the beginning of the new has been ushered in." His voice rose, carrying out to sea and over the cliffs. "For the sun child and the new god will give birth to a new era and the great creators will fall one by one, reshaping our homes and hearths, reaping man and mortal alike."

Oh, fuck me sideways.

Sun Child? New God? Give birth, and reapings? Yeah, I wanted no part of this. "You know, you can—"

"A bloody path has been chosen," he went on, because of course. There apparently was no stopping this. "The Great War fought by the few is coming, and in the end, the sun will fall and the moon will reign until the new sun rises."

My brows rose. Sort of sounded like a normal day to me.

"Know this," the nymph seemed to bellow. "The strength of the sun will be needed to conquer, for the strength of war and cunning will not be enough. Love and need must be reconciled. If not, the great land will perish, for the bull is in the house of the lion."

Well.

I officially had no words. At all. None.

Ewan the nymph dropped to one knee. "Goodbye Seth, the God of Life . . ."

A shiver blasted down my spine as a bolt of lightning struck off the coast, slamming into the ocean.

The nymph bowed its head. "The God of Death."

2

*T*he floor of the massive mansion that belonged to Gable's mother shook and rattled like it was nothing more than a piece of cardboard.

Shooting off the couch, I let the thin, soft-as-a-dream blanket fall to the floor as the rumbling became sound, a building roar that shook my chest and raised tiny goose bumps along my arms.

Eyes wide, I turned in a slow circle as books tumbled from shelves, smacking off the floor. Above me, a crystal chandelier, one that probably cost more than a car, trembled and clanked. Teardrop-shaped crystals fell to the floor, shattering into pieces. A tall, slender lamp toppled over, smashing its pale gray shade. Behind me, more books hit the floor.

"What in the world?" I whispered, voice hoarse and tired—tired from the tears that had been burning up my throat.

Something—something big was happening, and it could be *anything*. A horde of daimons. Another ticked-off, supercharged Titan. A wave of shades that had escaped from Tartarus. It could . . . it could even be Seth.

No.

He wouldn't be doing this, whatever this was, no matter what Alex and Aiden believed about him. He wouldn't put me in danger of the house caving in on me.

Snatching my titanium dagger off the end table, I darted around falling books and tore open the door, hitting the brightly lit hallway just as an explosion of thunder deafened my pounding heart. Glass shattered at the end of the hall, no doubt a priceless vase rendered to nothing more than shards. The house shook again. Art canvassed slipped from the walls as I raced into the grand atrium, my gaze immediately zeroing in on the scorched spot where Atlas had once stood.

The spot where the Titan had died.

And not too far from there, Solos had taken his final breath. That space on the floor was clear, wiped clean of blood, but for a split second I saw him staring down at his chest, at the gaping hole where his heart had been before his knees had given out. He'd been dead before he hit the floor, and he hadn't deserved that. Solos should still be here.

Swiping the memory aside, my gaze flew to the glass double doors. They were closed, but the way the panes of glass shook I doubted they would stay intact much longer.

I gasped as another quake hit the house. The floor rolled and rippled under my feet like water, lifting me up. I stumbled to the side, throwing my arms out to steady myself.

Somewhere in the house, doors slammed open and someone shouted one word.

"Earthquake!"

Earthquake!

Relief punched me so hard in the gut that I laughed— laughed loudly and a bit crazily. Just an earthquake.

Duh.

I was in southern California.

Not everything had to be supernatural.

Lowering the dagger, I turned to the spiral staircase. Several half-asleep people stood there, and of course, I was using the term "people" loosely.

There wasn't a single mortal in the house.

The shaking subsided as Deacon ran his fingers through his messy blond curls. "I hate California," he grumbled.

Behind him, Luke was scrubbing a hand over his eyes. His bronze-colored hair was sticking up in every direction. Standing beside them was Gable. Poor Gable. We'd literally plucked him off a beach, told him that his father was Poseidon and that he was also a demigod whose powers were bound, and then he witnessed up close and personal what a Titan was capable of.

The fact that he was standing there and not rocking in a corner somewhere was admirable.

"We haven't had one that bad in a long time," Gable said with sleep clinging to his voice. "We'll definitely get an aftershock from that."

Deacon's pale gray eyes widened. "Aftershock?"

Gable nodded. "Or that could've been a foreshock. You never really know."

"What is that?" Deacon lowered his hand, frowning. "Like an uncircumcised earthquake?"

Aiden, his older brother, lifted his chin and stared at the ceiling, slowly shaking his dark head. There were no two brothers less alike. Well, maybe Lucifer and Michael. They were brothers.

My lips twitched into a tired smile as Gable explained exactly what a foreshock was. Aiden reached out, draping an arm over the shoulders of Alex Andros. Her hair was a mess, but a sexy mess. When I woke up, my hair looked like I'd stuck my fingers in an electrical outlet, but not Alex. Hers was a tumble of wavy locks.

She was beautiful in a wild, unfettered way, and while we'd tentatively bonded over our shared time with evil psycho gods and our truly weird relation to Apollo, I wasn't nearly as close to her as Deacon and Luke were.

She and Aiden were legends, actual *legends*.

And they were so in love with one another that there was no doubt in my mind that they'd spend eternity together wanting no one else.

Aiden placed a hand on the railing as he stared down into the atrium, his silvery gaze seeming to go to the spot mine had when I'd first entered, to where the Titan Atlas had stood, holding Solos's heart in his meaty grip—to where Seth had gone all God Killer on everyone, tapping into all our powers, our aether, and killing Atlas.

Something Seth should not have been able to do.

God, that felt like forever ago, but it wasn't. Only about a day had passed since Atlas had come through those very doors and snuffed out Solos's life in a heartbeat. Only the night before when Seth had become something so feared that the Olympian gods had ended Alex's mortal life to prevent her from becoming it. Only *hours* since I'd done what Medusa had warned with the blade dipped in the blood of the Pegasus, knocking Seth out long enough for him to at least calm down. And it had only been this morning when Seth had escaped the panic room, found me in the library, made love to me, held me in his arms, and finally, *finally* told me he loved me.

Just seconds in a lifetime, and Seth had become a thing so powerful, so deadly that he'd left us, left *me*.

An ache lit up my chest as I blinked back tears I refused to allow to fall. I would not cry, because there was no time for that. As soon as Hercules got back from communing with the gods or whatever he'd left at dawn to do, I was out of here, gone from this house that pretty much dripped the kind of money I couldn't even begin to wrap my head around.

Locating the other two demigods was what my father—Apollo—had ordered me to do, but that had fallen way down my priority list, and I didn't even care. Didn't give a flying Pegasus about what that said about me, because no one, *no one* had ever fought for Seth before.

And I would.

I would fight till my dying breath for him.

Besides, it wasn't like no one would be gathering up the other two bound demigods and brutally introducing them to a whole new way of life. The Army of Awesome, dubbed by Deacon himself, had promised to retrieve the demigods. One was somewhere in Thunder Bay and the other was living in some town in Britain.

I'd promised Alex and Aiden that I would wait until Herc returned before I left to find Seth. I had a strong suspicion of where Seth had gone, and getting there, all the way to an island in the Aegean Sea, was not going to be easy.

"Josie?" Aiden called.

I blinked, refocusing on him. He was standing only a few feet from me, his hand wrapped firmly around Alex's. Everyone was downstairs. I hadn't heard them move. "Sorry?"

"I asked if you've slept at all?"

Nodding, I smoothed a hand over my head, catching the thin wisps of hair. I pushed them back from my face. "An hour or so."

Those startling silver eyes told me he knew I was lying, but it was Alex who spoke next. "You really should rest, Josie. Herc will be back soon, and we'll have a better grasp on everything."

Herc had been planning to go to the gods to see how Seth

could be contained, but since that was no longer an issue, I wasn't quite sure what the point was now.

Sighing, I glanced back to where one of the artworks had fallen to the floor. "I don't think I'm going to be able to sleep after an earthquake."

Gable shuffled past us, heading toward the kitchen, mumbling about checking the Internet to see if there was anything about the earthquake. I'd vaguely remembered seeing a MacBook on the counter in there earlier.

Luke lifted his arms over his head, stretching as he eyed the direction Gable had gone.

"I'm kind of hungry," Deacon announced.

The corners of Luke's lips tipped up. "You're always hungry."

"Yeah, but the earthquake has made me even more hungry." Deacon grinned as he folded an arm around the taller man's waist. "Not sure how that works, but I could really go for a bowl of nachos." He glanced over at the three of us. "Too bad none of you have cool powers."

"Cool powers?" murmured Aiden.

"Yeah. Like two of you are made demigods." Deacon nodded at his brother and Alex. "And you," he said, talking about me, "are a legit real demigod, and none of you can whip up a plate of nachos out of thin air. What good is being a demigod if you can't do that?"

Alex laughed as she leaned into Aiden. Without looking at her, he let go of her hand and draped his arm over her shoulders, urging her closer. "Well, I guess we're pretty useless." She grinned.

"That's what I've been saying for a long time." Deacon smiled when his brother rolled his eyes. "What time is it, anyway?"

"A little after two." I glanced down at the dagger I still held. What was I planning to do with it? Stab an earthquake with it? The slight weight in my hand, though, was a reminder of how different things were now from a year ago. Back then, if the ground had trembled, I would've known immediately what it was even in a land not accustomed to rocking and rolling, but now? Now I expected and prepared for a battle.

My fingers tightened around the dagger.

Though, for a moment, everything almost felt normal. Well, as normal as anything could be now. And I could almost pretend that Seth was going to walk through those fancy glass doors or out from one of the many hallways. He'd come to me, and we'd stand side by side, much like Alex and Aiden.

Except that wasn't going to happen.

With a loud yawn, Alex looked around the grand room. "I wonder if there is any dam—"

Under our feet, the floor rolled once more, throwing all of us in different directions. My knees cracked off the tile, and I dropped the dagger. It skittered across the floor as I planted my hands, steadying myself as Aiden cursed under his breath. I was frozen for a second and then I moved. Pushing to my feet, I threw my arms out as the floor, the walls—*everything* shuddered.

Gable burst out from the kitchen, his face pale. Fear pierced my heart, because he lived here—lived where the ground shook often—and if he was freaked out, we should be freaked out.

My wide gaze met Alex's.

"Holy shit!" Deacon grabbed the banister, holding on as the entire house seemed to shake from its foundation.

Dust plumed into the air. A light above the door popped. Sparks flew. The thick, reinforced glass of the double doors slipped free and broke into pieces on the floor.

"This is bad, so bad." Alex gripped Aiden's arm as pieces of plaster dropped from the ceiling, smashing onto the tiles.

I darted to the side as another large chunk of the ceiling came down. The opulent, sparkling chandelier crashed into the floor and shattered.

Then the floor split right open.

Luke shouted as he hooked an arm around Deacon's waist, yanking him away from the staircase. I swallowed a scream as a deep rift split the grand room, from the broken doors straight across the atrium, cutting through the scorched spot where Atlas was laid to waste. A chasm in the floor formed, several feet wide.

The shaking eased off and then the world stilled again.

"Gods," muttered Aiden, keeping one hand on Alex's shoulder as he knocked back several strands of wavy dark hair.

Heart pounding, I turned to the rift in the floor and took a slow, small step toward it.

"Be careful," Gable warned. "The floor is unstable—this entire house is probably unstable right now."

"Is this . . . is this normal?" I asked, lifting my gaze to his. "Earthquakes do this?"

Before I could answer, a strange scent filled the air. Not propane or the burning smell of electricity—scents that would be expected. No. I wrinkled my nose. It was a musty, damp, and dank smell. Like rich, undisturbed soil and decaying roots.

My heart tumbled over.

It reminded me of the way the shades smelled.

"I have a *really* bad feeling about this," Alex said.

Aiden took a step back from the rift, pulling her with him as Deacon gasped out, "No shit."

"I think we should leave," Gable announced, walking backward, toward the kitchen. "I really think we should just leave."

Movement stirred from the break in the ground. It sounded like rocks falling, bouncing off one another. Air caught in my lungs as a faint shiver skated over my skin, and instinct roared to the surface, forcing me to step back before I even realized what I was doing.

Silence fell, and the only thing I could hear was the pounding of my heart. A dirt-stained hand appeared, reaching out from the chasm and smacking down on the broken tile.

3

*S*omething or someone was hauling itself out of the hole in the floor and that had "nope" written all over it. Nothing good could be climbing out from deep within the ground. I'd seen enough horror films to know that.

Spinning around, I scanned the floor for the dagger I'd dropped and couldn't see it in the mess that covered the tiles.

Crap.

Alex stepped to the side, blocking Gable, and her stance widened, shoulders squared. Even though she wore nothing more than leggings and a tank top, she looked badass and ready—prepared for anything. Alex was a demigod now, but she was first and foremost a Sentinel.

The same went for Aiden and Luke. They took up the same stance, effectively continuing to force Deacon and Gable behind them.

I saw all of this because somehow I was on the other side of the chasm.

Another hand appeared and then a head—a dirt-covered bald head broke the surface, and I distantly heard someone gag.

"Oh my gods," I whispered, eyes widening with horror.

Ripped and flayed skin peeled back from the head. Entire

chunks of skin were missing from the hollowed cheeks. The skin on the arms was no better. Strips of flesh hung from the chest. One of the eyes was nothing more than an empty, rotten socket, and some kind of cloth was wrapped around its hips, a cloth that might've been white and pristine at one time, but was now covered in mud and singed with soot.

The scent of sulfur misted the room.

The one good eye met mine, and its iris was a milky blue.

"Holy daimon babies," whispered Alex. "Is that a zombie? Like a real zombie?"

"That wasn't an earthquake." Aiden reached to his hip, but he was empty-handed. They'd been sleeping and had come downstairs with no daggers.

"I think that's obvious," Deacon muttered from behind Luke.

All of us were immobile with disbelief.

The head on the thing swiveled from me to the other side, and then it pulled itself out, hitting the crushed tile on its hands and knees. A great shudder rolled through the wrecked body and it doubled over, opening its mouth and coughing violently, spewing clumps of soil and small pebbles.

The thing spoke, rocking onto its knees, back bowing as it threw its arms out. "Δωρεάν."

It was a tone of voice so guttural that it sounded like its vocal cords had been destroyed, spoken in a language I didn't recognize at first, and wouldn't have if my demigod abilities hadn't been unlocked.

"Free," I repeated, looking across the rift. "It said 'free.'"

Upon my voice, it turned its head at me again.

"Free from what?" Deacon asked. "The set of *The Walking Dead*?"

Any other time I would've laughed, but that thing was rising to bare feet that were nothing more than gnawed muscle and bone. It took a step toward me.

"Don't come any closer," I warned, having no idea if it understood a single thing I said.

The thing shuffled another step forward.

"I think it likes you," commented Alex, from the *other* side of the room.

Power built in the center of my chest, right behind the mark of Apollo, reminding me that I didn't need a dagger to fight. I lifted a hand, hoping that whatever this thing was, it was a friendly and would listen to me. "Stop."

Stretching out a gnarly hand in my direction, it opened its mouth in a lipless snarl, revealing ragged, broken teeth.

Okay.

Probably not friendly.

I reacted, tapping into the power—into akasha. Summoning the element of air, I felt the energy whip down my arm. A gust of wind hit the thing in its chest.

It flew backward.

Alex let out a strangled sound as she and Aiden dropped to the floor. The thing shot across the chasm, slamming into the opposite wall in a way that reminded me of a fly hitting the windshield of a car going about 100 miles per hour. A gruesome sound burned my ears as it exploded like a tick full of blood.

"Oh my gosh." I dropped my hand.

"I think I'm going to be sick," Gable moaned. "Seriously. I might vomit."

Alex and Aiden rose, their eyes wide as they looked over the rift at me. Aiden's dark brows rose halfway up his forehead. "Whoa," he said.

"I . . . I didn't mean to do that," I said, swallowing hard. "I mean, I meant to stop it but not make it go splat."

"I guess it's a good thing you didn't accidentally set one of us on fire," Luke commented.

My head snapped in his direction. "I only did that, like, once!"

Luke grinned.

"That was kind of impressive." Alex looked over her shoulder, cringing. "I can control air, but not with that kind of force."

"Well, that's because she's a real demigod," Deacon said.

Alex rolled her eyes. "We're real demigods—"

"Guys. I think we're about to get more visitors." Luke pointed at the chasm. More hands had appeared. "Let's argue about being real demigods later."

They came out of the rift faster than the lone one, all in the same rotting, decaying shape. Their bare-boned feet clicked off the pieces of tile.

There were almost a dozen.

I'd never seen anything like this.

Their jaws snapped, exposing ragged teeth that could easily tear through skin.

"Zombies are all fun and games until they're standing right in front of you," Deacon said.

One of them, a tall one, broke free from the pack, lurching toward Alex. She hopped back as she threw out her arm. A second later, the zombie-looking thing skidded backward, falling into the fissure.

"Deacon," Aiden said calmly. Smoke drifted off the tips of his fingers. "Get Gable into the kitchen. Keep him there."

For once, Deacon obeyed without argument. Whipping around, he grabbed the stunned-into-silence Gable and hauled ass to the kitchen, slamming the door behind them just as one of the so-very-dead-looking things howled a sound of rage and blood, sending a shiver down my spine.

They attacked.

There was no time to figure out what was happening, what these things really were, or why they were coming after us. The things could move fast. Half went toward Alex and the guys. The rest raced in my direction, and for a split second, fear punched through my gut. I was immobile with it. I may be a demigod, but these things were terrifying looking, and I was just a mortal girl about to get her flesh torn off her bones.

But I wasn't a mortal girl.

Far from it.

Instinct took over, forcing my body to move. I darted to the left as I tapped into the powers stirring inside me. Reaching the raised dais, I spun around. A small ball of flames hit one of the creatures in the back. Fire erupted, swallowing its body.

"Holy crap," I whispered.

On the other side of the chasm, ultra-bright flames danced over Aiden's knuckles. Then he turned, taking out another as Luke brandished a dagger. Apparently he'd been the only one who came out of his bedroom prepared. Overachiever. Jumping forward, he slammed the dagger into one of the eye sockets and jerked his arm back, his lip curling in disgust as maroon-colored blood spurted out at him. The thing shrieked as it fell to the floor, shattering upon impact.

"That's so gross," he muttered, flipping the dagger. He twisted, eyeing another creature. "So freaking gross."

Tapping into the fire element, I welcomed the lava now coursing through my veins. My right arm heated, and a bolt of fire shot from my palm, smacking the closest creature to me in the chest. It went down in flames. I spun, hitting another creature. The third zigged and zagged on me, getting close enough that the smell of rot and death turned my stomach. I danced back a step, tapping into fire once more. Flames swamped that creature as it fell forward. I turned, throwing out my arm. Fire crackled over my fingers, and I let it go just as another creature shot forward. The fourth creature took the hit in the shoulder, spinning it around. I turned as the fifth one jumped—jumped like a jackrabbit, landing no more than a foot in front of me. I reared back, but it wrapped a bony, fleshless hand around my forearm.

Fiery pain erupted, robbing the air out of my lungs. The touch seared my skin, forcing out a hoarse scream. The creature laughed, spewing dirt into the air. Rearing back, I tore my arm free just as a dagger sliced through its face from behind.

It didn't jerk or spasm—simply fell to the floor, exploding into a pile of clumpy ash.

I was standing face to face with Luke.

"Looked like you could use the help," he said, twisting at the waist. "Are you okay?"

Breathing through the pain, I looked down at my arm. Four marks the size of fingers burned my arm. "I'll be okay."

Luke didn't get a chance to respond, because those on fire were rising from the floor. The flames receded, revealing charred skin and bone.

"What the hell?" I gasped out, pressing my wounded arm to my stomach as I scanned the atrium.

Aiden and Alex were backing up, both with the same stunned expressions on their faces. "This isn't good," she said. "I thought fire killed zombies."

"Yeah, I don't think these are zombies, babe," Aiden replied.

"Head shots seem to work," Luke called out. "So they're kind of like zombies."

"We don't have daggers." Aiden stepped to the left, halfway in front of Alex. It seemed like an unconscious, protective move. "We could push them back into the crevice."

As soon as he finished saying that, as if the gods were laughing at us, several more climbed out of the hole in the floor.

"I don't think that's going to work." Alex sighed.

My dagger was nowhere to be found among the broken tiles. It could've even fallen into the chasm. If fire didn't kill these things, then . . .

I only knew of one other thing.

Instead of pushing away the pain, I used it to fuel me, and I reached deep inside, tapping into the very center of my being. Akasha roared to the surface, and releasing the supreme power was like a flower opening up to the sun. It was a *release*—a burst of white light powered down my arm like a cyclone.

I let it go, sending it straight to one of the charred creatures lumbering toward Luke and me. The pale light shrouded the creature for a half-second, and then it exploded into ash.

"Well, that works, too." Luke grinned, obviously having way too much fun with this, and I had to wonder how he ever thought he could stop being a Sentinel.

Following suit, Alex and Aiden summoned akasha, while Luke was more hands-on, using the dagger. We took down nearly a dozen, but they streamed out of the crevice like an unending *Night of The Living Dead*.

Exhaustion was already settling into my bones as I released another bolt of akasha. It might've been the lack of sleep or the battle with Atlas and how Seth had . . . how he had fed off of all of us, but we couldn't keep this up forever.

Akasha rippled down my arm as the smell of sulfur deepened. The ground shook once more, tossing me backward. I grunted as I hit the floor on my bad arm and my akasha faded out. Shifting onto my back, I dragged in air between my teeth.

"Josie!" Aiden shouted.

One of the creatures was right at my side, reaching out with those painful, super-gross hands. I rolled onto my side and pushed up. My left hand dragged across the floor, slipping over something smooth and cold. I glanced down, spying the dagger. Wrapping my fingers around it, I shot to my feet, screaming as I brought the dagger down. The sharp blade cut through skin and bone, sinking deep into the skull. Wrenching the dagger free, I stumbled back a step as the thing fell to pieces.

The house trembled as the rift in the floor widened, and through the charred bodies and the fresher ones that now rose, a horse head appeared.

"Am I seeing things?" I asked just as one of the creatures reached for me. I brought the dagger down and whipped back toward the opening. There was another horse head and then another.

"What in the world?" Akasha faded from Alex's arm.

An undercurrent of power rippled through the room, coasting over my skin. I had no idea what was happening at this point, but three horses rose up out of the ground, dark as night and covered in black armor, and they held riders. The two on the outside were dressed head to toe in black, and the one in the middle wore leathers—leather pants and a leather, sleeveless shirt. A golden band wrapped around his well-muscled upper arm, and an aura of power surrounded him. He had a head full of wavy black hair, and his face was brutal in its beauty, as if his features had been carved out of granite.

The two men unhooked the silvery lassos attached to their waists. With startling reflexes, their wrists snapped and the lassos shot out like lightning, slicing through the creatures like heated knives through butter.

My brows shot out as I watched the two men make short work of the creatures. The lasso thingy would've been real helpful about five minutes ago, because within seconds, the creatures were all gone. Nothing more than soot and ash on the floor.

Aiden exhaled heavily. "Nice of you to join us, Hades."

Luke stepped back, bumping into me. We exchanged looks.

Hades?

The Hades?

Oh my *gods*.

"Sorry, mate." Hades spoke, his voice accented. "Was in the middle of entertaining Persephone when literally all hell broke loose."

"They're yours?" Alex gestured at the pile of ashes.

Hades smirked. "Were."

"What in the world is going on?" Alex demanded, resting her hands on her hips as she stared up at Hades—*the* Hades. "The ground split open and these things came crawling out like cockroaches."

"You don't know?" Hades sighed as he forced his horse to turn around. Dismounting, he stood next to the massive beast, and I saw just how tall Hades was. Like, *giant* kind of tall.

"Yeah, we're a little in the dark here," Aiden replied. "We thought it was an earthquake until they started coming through."

The kitchen door cracked open and Deacon stuck his blond head out. "Is it safe . . ." He trailed off, eyes widening when he spotted the horses, the men, and Hades. "Yep, I'll just keep Gable distracted a little longer."

The door shut.

Hades's smirk grew as he surveyed the room, his all-white eyes beyond eerie, and I just stood there, arms dangling at my sides. The dagger was forgotten in my hand. There were dead things reduced to ashes on the floor—the floor that was currently split wide open. There were horses—giant warhorses I was pretty sure were not of normal size, and Hades—the god of the Underworld—was standing a mere handful of feet from me.

"Should we bow or something?" I whispered to Luke.

Luke slid me a sidelong glance and murmured, "I'm just not going to move or draw any attention to myself."

"Too late," Hades said, turning to us. "A half-blood and Apollo's daughter. I figured we'd be meeting under different circumstances."

I shivered, thinking "different circumstances" probably meant our deaths.

"What were those things?" Aiden asked.

Hades nodded up at the men. They hooked their super-special lassos to their waists but did not dismount. They sat upon their horses, eyes straight ahead and as silent as graves. Turning in unison, their heels dug into the sides of their horses and turned to stand sentry by the rift.

Understanding dawned, and my stomach dropped. I realized who the two men were—Hades's servants. *His* men. They were what Seth had pledged himself to become upon his death, to serve under Hades, taking Aiden's place.

I suddenly felt sick.

"Those creatures were held in the pits of Tartarus, deep within the fire caverns," Hades explained, swiping his booted foot through the pile of ashes. "They were once daimons."

I needed to sit down.

Even Alex paled.

"Did you believe when daimons die they simply cease to exist?" Hades queried, tone smug. "No matter what they tell you, everything is sorted out in the end."

"Kind of like Hogwarts?" Alex asked.

Hades inclined his head to the side.

Alex sighed. "Never mind."

"The daimons spend eternity being burned alive and then

put back together, only to suffer the same fate nearly at once."

I *really* needed to sit down.

"Sometimes I change it up. Burying them alive in just enough lava to sear the skin away and then let them dig their way out of rock and soil is fun," Hades continued with a shrug. "The torture drives them insane." He paused. "Then again, they were daimons. Not much going on between the ears anyway."

Oh my.

"Okay. Could've lived forever without knowing all of that," Alex said slowly. "But what were they doing up here?"

A fissure of energy rolled through the room, followed by a blinding bright, golden light. Electricity poured in, pure power, lifting the tiny hairs all over my body. The light receded and in its place were two forms.

Hades sighed. "Always have to make a grand entrance, don't you?"

Apollo stood by the staircase, and beside him was Hercules. The sun god—my father—stepped forward, and his all-white eyes sparked. When he spoke, fury sharped his tone. "What have you all done?"

4

My father looked like he was only a few years older than me, which was as weird as it sounded. He wasn't dressed like Hades or how I'd ever imagined any god to look.

Apollo was wearing faded jeans and a tight black shirt.

I'd first met him when I was a young, lonely girl, and he was just a strange man who went by the name Bob, who gave me candies and dolls. Looking back, I totally got how incredibly creepy that was, but for a short summer, he'd been my only friend.

And now he was my father—my absentee father who randomly appeared and disappeared within minutes, and I hadn't been around him long enough to see him like this, truly angry.

I sucked in an unsteady breath as he stepped forward, the all-white eyes giving way to irises as blue as mine. "Do you all have any idea what you've done?" he demanded.

I opened my mouth, but Alex responded before I had the chance to even figure out what to say. "You're going to have to be a little more detailed. We've done a lot of things."

Apollo's eyes narrowed on what was his great-great-great-great-times-a-thousand granddaughter. "You killed Atlas."

"Um, *hi Dad* . . ." I kept my expression blank as Apollo's

golden head swung in my direction. "And how is that a problem?"

Hades chuckled darkly. "Luv, look around and you should be able to answer that question."

Aiden's frown was severe.

"You weren't supposed to kill Atlas or any of the Titans. " Apollo's voice was as harsh as a violent windstorm. "You were supposed to *entomb* them."

"Okay. Sorry?" A prickly feeling along my skin grew. I was *so* not in the mood for this.

"Sorry?" Apollo repeated. "Perhaps my instructions were not clear enough when I explained that the Titans needed to be entombed."

Alex barked out a cutting laugh. "Your instructions are *never* clear."

His eyes snapped blue fire and he looked like he was gearing up for a major rant I really didn't want to listen to. "He was going to kill us," I said, and I felt that should've been explanation enough. "He *was* killing us. Look at what happened to Solos. If it hadn't been for Seth—"

"I really don't want to hear that name right now," Apollo interrupted, and yep, he was ticked off.

"Sorry, but we're going to need to talk about him." Aiden's voice was level and calm, but I tensed all over. "Because we all have several questions about what happened with him."

Neither Hades nor Apollo answered.

"How did Seth become the God Killer?" asked Alex. Her arms were folded across her chest and her hip was cocked to the side. She was all attitude. "As far as we knew, that wasn't possible. I was the God Killer and when I died my mortal death, that was that."

Impatience flooded Apollo's expression, tightening his jaw.

"I'm not sure if you remember how unordinary that entire event was?"

Alex raised a single brow.

"We had no idea what truly would happen to you or to Seth. Making you a demigod—who also happened to be the Apollyon and the awakened God Killer, while there was another Apollyon alive—had never been done before. I warned you—all of you—that anything was possible," Apollo shot back, but he hadn't warned *me* about any of this. Then again, he didn't really tell *me* much. "Anything was possible."

"So you're telling me that you really had no idea Seth could tap into all of us and somehow become the God Killer?" Disbelief colored Alex's voice.

"That is what I am saying," Apollo replied sharply.

My frustration grew, as did the ache in my arm. "Okay. Even if all the super-special gods in the world had no idea that Seth could somehow become the God Killer, that still doesn't explain how he killed Atlas. We were told—*he* was told—that only the demigods with their unlocked abilities could kill them."

Apollo's jaw flexed. "They could *entomb* them."

Whatever.

"We were not sure if the God Killer could," Hades stated after a moment. We all turned to him. He looked particularly bored with the conversation. "God Killers did not exist when the Titans were in control. We felt it was best to not put it in that unstable cretin's head—the possibility of him being able to take out a Titan."

"He is not an unstable cretin." My hands curled into fists.

Hades smirked. "That's a matter of opinion, luv."

I exhaled heavily. "Basically, you guys knew there was a chance Seth could become this. After all, didn't you have Alex and Aiden watching him?"

"Well . . ." Alex trailed off.

"And you knew there was a chance he could kill a Titan, but you said nothing," I continued. "And now I'm assuming the earthquake and the charbroiled daimons had something to do with Atlas's death?"

"Just like with Ares's death, there was a weakening in all of us, allowing the Titans to make their escape." Hades's boots clicked off the crushed tile as he walked to his horse. "With Atlas, the ripple effect was much more severe." His large hand moved along the side of the beast. "It punched a hole straight through the earth, through Olympus and my realm. Unfortunately it damaged the fire caverns, allowing for openings here and several other places."

My knees felt weak. "Punched a hole . . . a hole straight through Earth?"

Hades nodded. "He *was* Atlas, after all."

The kitchen door opened once more and Deacon drew up short. His gray eyes widened as he spotted Apollo.

Gable bumped into him from behind. "Who's that?"

"Nope," Deacon said, turning right back around. "That is all kinds of nope right there."

And Deacon pushed Gable back into the kitchen.

"Gods," Luke muttered under his breath as he scratched his fingers through his hair.

Anger tightened Aiden's jaw. "Okay. Did it ever occur to any of you that if you just told us that there was a possibility that Seth could become the God Killer and that he could kill a Titan, we might've been able to prevent him from killing a Titan?"

"And exactly how do you think you would've stopped the God Killer?" Herc spoke, shrugging out massive, muscular shoulders. "Even I, the Hercules, would've been unable to stop him. He could *kill* me."

"Oh, the tragedy," murmured Hades.

"I will probably never say this again, but Hercules is right," Apollo admitted. "Your knowledge would've changed nothing."

"That is . . ." I shook my head in wonder. "That is the absolutely stupidest thing I've ever heard. Knowledge is everything. Knowing what he could possibly be capable of ahead of time could've given us a chance to stop him—could've given *him* the chance."

Apollo said nothing, because how could he deny that? To do so would be foolish.

"This is not our fault," Aiden said. "Like always, you all deem it necessary not to tell us everything and like always, everything goes sideways fast."

"We tell you what you need to know when you need to know it," Apollo snapped back.

Herc rolled his eyes. "Trust me, you've only had what? A few years of dealing with a need-to-know basis. I, the Hercules, have lived—"

"I am done with you." Apollo waved his hand, and Herc just disappeared. There one second, gone the next.

My mouth dropped open as I stepped over the dais. "Did you kill him?"

Hades laughed.

"I wish," muttered my father. "I sent him back to Olympus. I have no need of him now. *We* have no need of him."

I shook my head. "We still have to find the other demigods."

"You already know where they are, and we have bigger problems." Apollo turned to Alex and Aiden. "We have a God Killer who is obviously AWOL—a God Killer who is a threat to all of us."

"He's not a threat to you." I walked toward the crevice,

steering clear of Hades, his men, and his horses. "If he was, he wouldn't have done what he's done."

Alex glanced at me and then agreed. "He left here without harming anyone."

"He did hit me," Luke added dryly. "But he didn't kill me and he could've easily done so."

"I know what he did," Apollo growled, and I felt heat creep into my face. Did he really know what Seth had done before he'd left? Because, ew. "Seth cannot be trusted. Not now."

Closing my eyes, I tried counting to ten. I only made it to three. "He has given you no reason not to trust him. He has done—"

"You do not know him as well as you think you do," Apollo responded, his back to me. "You do not know him at all."

Tears of anger and frustration filled my eyes. "I know him better than any of you."

Apollo's back stiffened. "You need to find the other demigods now. The Titans need to be entombed—" He held up a hand. "—and *not* killed. We will deal with the God Killer."

Aiden and Alex exchanged looks.

Ice drenched my veins. "What do you mean, deal with him?"

"Once you locate the other demigods, bring them to the Covenant," Apollo ordered.

I stepped forward. Pieces of tile fell into the gaping crevice.

"Careful," Luke murmured as he stopped a few feet behind me. "I so don't want to go down there after you."

Neither did I. "What do you mean by 'deal with him'?"

"What do you think, luv?" Hades asked as he mounted his horse with the kind of fluid grace I imagined only gods had. "We may not be able to kill him. Yet. But we can neutralize him."

The iciness spread, seizing my stomach. "How?"

Hades didn't answer, but he gave me a faint, mysterious smile, one that caused my stomach to dip unpleasantly. Guiding his horse around, he nodded toward Alex and Aiden. "I'll be seeing you two soon."

Then with a flick of his wrist, his horse turned again, toward the tear in the floor. His men followed, and all three disappeared into the smoke whirling from the floor.

Any other time I would've been shocked and awed by all of that, but not today.

"How?" I demanded once more.

"It doesn't matter," Apollo responded. "What you need to be focusing on is locating the other demigods—"

"I know what I need to be doing," I cut in.

"And what is that? Running off after him?" Anger filled every word Apollo spoke. "As if what I've ordered you to do is not more important?"

I took a deep, even breath. "Alex and Aiden have agreed to—"

"I know what they've agreed to do. It does not matter." Apollo turned his head to the side, but didn't look in my direction. "You will locate the other two demigods and then wait for me at the Covenant in South Dakota."

I almost laughed. "Oh, I don't think so."

"You'd disobey me?" Apollo queried in a voice too soft for comfort.

Across from me, Alex and Aiden looked like they wanted a bucket of popcorn, but both remained quiet as I stared at my father's back. "I will do what I feel is right, and finding Seth is what I need to do. I love Seth. I love him when no one else believes in him and I will still love him when everyone realizes who and what he truly is. That will never change. And there is nothing you can say that will change my mind, so you might as well not even attempt it and just tell me how you plan to neutralize Seth."

"You won't love him when he drains you dry."

I sucked in an unsteady breath. "He would never do that."

"He wouldn't? Because I'm pretty sure he has already fed from you."

My gaze shot to Alex and Aiden. Had they told him? No. They hadn't seen Apollo since I had. Or at least I didn't think so.

"You don't understand, Josie. You approach everything with Seth as if it is a black or white issue, as if there is not gray. You don't know him like I do—like all of us do. Whether you want to admit it or not, we do not know what Seth is capable of. We never have and you did not know him when he worked alongside Ares."

While a part of me recognized that Apollo had a point, he was still wrong. I didn't know Seth then, but I knew that was a different Seth. People could and did change. "Since you seem to be watching from afar like a total stalker, then you know he stopped and he told me what happened."

Apollo tipped his head back. A moment passed and then he said, "You sound like a foolish child in the middle of a tantrum."

"Oh geez," Luke murmured from behind me, and Alex's eyes widened.

For a moment I was consumed with the skid mark his words had left behind. Just for a few seconds, and then I shed that hurt like I'd done so many times in the past whenever I thought about my father, where he was and why he hadn't been a part of my life.

There was a time when I saw Apollo that I wanted to rush to him. That all I wanted was for him to hold me like I'd seen Alex and her father embrace one another. That I wanted him to talk to me like he did when he spoke to Alex and Aiden.

But right now, I wanted nothing more than to punch him in the throat.

Anger filled me, squelching the exhaustion and the pain in my arm. "How would you know what a child sounds like in the middle of a tantrum? Like you're actually around children enough to know that? I mean, you weren't there for any of my tantrums. Or my birthdays. Or holidays. Or any of the hundred times my mother had a relapse and I was scared to death that she would accidentally hurt herself."

My words struck their mark. I knew this because the room suddenly filled with electricity. Alex and Aiden shifted uneasily, and I had a feeling Luke was slinking away.

"You think that's what I wanted?" Apollo asked. "That I chose to not be there for you?"

"Right now you choose to not even look at me when you speak to me, so yeah, I'm going to go with you chose not to be there for me."

Apollo whipped around so fast I barely saw him move. I couldn't read the emotions in his face. I didn't want to.

I spoke before he could. "You barely speak to me when you do decide to appear. Hell, you seem more happy to see them than you are to see me, your daughter." I gestured at Alex and Aiden across the rift. I don't know what exactly had tipped me over the edge. It could've been everything and anything at this point, but there was so much raw hurt building inside of me. "You won't even tell me anything about my mother. You always disappear before I can even ask."

His chest rose and those large hands opened. "Sometimes it is best to not be given the chance to ask a question that will lead to an answer you will not want to hear or need to know." Regret flickered across his face the moment he snapped his mouth shut.

Everything in me stilled and slowed. Even my heart. "Why . . . why would you say something like that?"

Apollo's gaze shifted away, and I . . . I knew. I just knew. My heart dropped to my stomach and a hole opened up in my chest. "I want to see my mom. Now."

"That is not possible," he answered quietly.

I drew in a breath and then another, and it did nothing to help the sinking feeling spreading throughout me. "Because she's in Olympus, right? I'm not allowed to go there?"

Apollo, my father, said nothing.

Behind him, Alex and Aiden blurred out of focus. "That's what you've been telling me this entire time. That she's *safe* in Olympus. So I want to see her."

"Josephine . . ."

"I want to see my mother," I stated again, clearly and slowly just in case he didn't understand my request.

"You can't." His voice as strained as his expression.

"If you do not take me to see my mother, I will go myself."

Surprise filled his ocean-blue eyes.

"I know where there is a gateway to Olympus," I said, and then I bluffed big time, because I didn't know if Medusa would allow me or if I could get past her. "And I can and will get through that gateway."

A heartbeat later, Apollo was standing right in front of me. "You must understand that I've told you what I have because I felt it was best at that time. You'd just learned that you were my daughter and that a Titan was coming for you. You'd just discovered that your grandparents had been murdered. I told you what I did because I did not feel you could withstand the truth."

Nothing was still in me anymore. I was full of trembling cracks and shattered pieces barely held together.

Apollo's voice lowered. "I tried to stop Hyperion when he

went to your grandparents' house, but I didn't get there in time. Your mother was . . ."

"No," I whispered.

His eyes closed. "Your mother was already dead."

5

Apollo was talking and I was hearing what he was saying. I heard those words and I felt them on my skin like a thousand pricks of a burning needle.

Mom was dead?

I opened my mouth and a cry of denial erupted from me, building into a scream. Rage and heartache blanketed every cell in my body. I screamed and screamed as fury and horror mingled with all the aether in my veins.

Apollo's ocean-blue eyes widened a second before the irises faded into white orbs. He reached out a hand toward me. "Josie—"

Pure power erupted. I exploded like a volcano. Bright light had poured out from me, crackling and snapping. It filled the room until there was nothing but light and power and all the pain that was tearing through my insides, ripping me apart. It went on and on until my throat turned raw.

My scream gave out and the light flickered once before falling to the broken floor like shimmery paint thrown into the air.

Alex and Aiden were on their backs. So was Luke.

And my father was gone.

* * *

I didn't remember leaving the house.

The next thing I knew I was standing on the rocky cliff that overlooked frothy, white-capped waves.

My knees shook as the sun crested on the horizon, turning the waves from blue to pink, and then my legs gave out. Knees cracked off the hard soil and I fell back, landing on my butt.

Too exhausted. Too shell-shocked. Too . . . too *everything*. I didn't move. Couldn't. My eyes stung. They were so dry, yet so full of tears burning straight through the sockets. Slowly, I lifted my gaze to the deep blue sky.

Apollo had lied to me.

He'd lied to me this entire time. He'd tried to explain himself to me in those blurry moments after he'd told me my mom was . . . that she was dead.

He'd claimed that the lie had been necessary. For my own good. He'd said that I'd been under a lot of stress. That I needed to keep it together so I would be safe. He even said that when he'd looked at me in the dorm room for the first time as my father, he couldn't bear to see me hurting more than I already was.

He promised me that she was in paradise.

These were the words that felt like my skin was being tattooed with. None of those words made up for the lie, because this whole time, for months, I'd been living as if my mother was alive and safe. I believed I would see her again, and I would hug her. I would get to tell her that I now believed those stories she'd used to tell me, the ones that I'd attributed to her sickness. Now I wouldn't.

Squeezing my eyes shut, I pressed my lips together as another roar of rage, another scream of pain built in my chest. I was here and my mom . . .

She was gone.

She'd been gone for a long time now, and I had no idea. I went on with my life and hers had ended. How hadn't I known? How could that even be possible?

Shifting forward, I planted my hands in the soil as my chest ripped open once more. The pain was so potent it was tangible, a bitter coating in my mouth and throat.

Everyone was gone now.

My grandparents. Erin, my roommate who also happened to be a furie. Solos. My mother. Seth.

A tremble rattled my arms as my fingers dug into the soil, scratching up nothing but dust. He should be here. The moment those words entered my thoughts, I couldn't push them away or forge them. Seth should be here for this—for me, because I needed him.

I *needed* him at this moment more than I ever had.

"Josie?"

Inhaling sharply, I opened my eyes at the sound of Alex's voice. I didn't look or speak, and after a few moments, I felt her draw close.

Alex sat beside me, drawing her knees to her chest. "I'm not going to ask if you're okay. I know you're not."

Lowering my chin, I lifted a shaky hand and pushed a few loose strands back from my face. I opened my mouth, but I couldn't find any words.

Silence stretched between us, and then Alex said, "I had to kill my mom."

That got my attention.

My head swung sharply in her direction. She was staring out over the ocean, her pretty face pensive. Maybe I'd heard this story before. In that moment, I couldn't remember if Deacon had told me. "Why?" I managed to croak out.

Smoothing back her deep brown hair, she rested her chin

on her knees. "My mom had pulled me out of the Covenant when she learned that I was to be the Apollyon. We lived as ordinary mortals until a group of daimons found us. They attacked, and I had to run away, you know? I thought they'd killed my mom. Aiden and Apollo—well, Apollo was known as Leon back then, but anyway, they found me and brought me back to the Covenant. I didn't really let myself process what I believed to be her death."

Faint sunlight touched her cheeks. "It was easier just not to think about it. After all, I had a lot going on. Probably wasn't the smartest thing, but I learned later that my mom wasn't dead. She'd been turned into a daimon, and she was hunting us—hunting *me*."

"Why was . . . why was she doing that?"

She pressed her lips together. "She knew what I was. She retained all that knowledge after she was turned into a daimon. It changed her. Made her evil. She thought if she turned me, she could control the Apollyon." Alex drew in a stuttered breath. "Once I knew she'd been turned, it became my duty to kill her."

I shook my head. "And you did?"

She nodded as she looked over at me. "She never would've wanted to become what she had, and I couldn't let her be that way. I found her and . . . and it was the hardest thing I'd ever done."

I couldn't even wrap my head around it.

"I know what you're feeling," she said quietly. "I've felt it twice. The anger. The pain."

My lower lip trembled. "Something else we have in common."

"Seems like we have some of the worst things in common," she replied, a wry grin on her lips. "I know there is nothing I can tell you that's really going to make you feel better except that I *know* your mother is in a better place."

A flash of anger surged through me. "How do you know that?"

"Because I've been there." Her eyes met mine, and for some dumb reason, I had forgotten that Alex had died a mortal death. "I'm there six months out of the year," she continued. "I one hundred percent agree with whatever violent thoughts you have when it comes to Apollo, but no matter what, he would've made sure your mother is in the Elysian Fields. Anything she wants, she will have access to, and she is not alone. She's most likely with your grandparents right now."

If what Alex said was true, and I guessed it had to be true, I didn't have to think of her as just . . . just ceasing to exist or being alone. Mom hated to be alone. Hope sparked alive. If Mom was in the Underworld, couldn't I visit her? "Can I see her?"

A sad smile tugged at her lips. "To get into Elysian Fields when you do not belong there is not easy."

"But I'm a demigod."

"That doesn't matter. You'd need Hades to cross you over or you'd have to enter through one of the gateways, and that isn't simple. You'd have to travel through the Underworld to get to Elysium," she explained. "And with you being a demigod, there are things down there that would sense you right away." She paused. "Maybe one day, once everything settles down, Hades would allow you to visit her, but it is not something often allowed. Your mom is safe and most likely happy, but she is dead and the living do not visit the dead."

Hope fizzled out. I bit down on my lip as I turned my head. "Except for you."

"Except for Aiden and me," she agreed.

Technically I'd died a mortal death when my powers had been unlocked, but it hadn't been the same as Alex. I was simply a mortal one moment and a demigod the next. I wasn't sent to the Underworld. I wasn't sure I was even technically considered dead during any of it. "Do you visit your mom there?"

She hesitated. "Yes."

That was something we didn't have in common. I cast my gaze out over the ocean, wondering if what Apollo had said about Erin was true. For all I knew now, she could also be dead.

My chest hollowed out.

"It gets easier," she stated. "It really does."

I was going to have to take her word for that.

Dawn arrived as we sat side by side, and the sky turned a calm shade of blue, cloudless and endless. "Apollo is a shit father," Alex said so suddenly that a harsh laugh escaped me. A small grin appeared on her face. "No. Seriously. He is."

"Yeah," I forced out, closing my eyes briefly.

"I think he tries. Like, he really probably thought he was doing the right thing by not telling you about your mom. The gods . . . they have a very messed-up view of things." Alex straightened out her legs. "Nothing we do will ever change that."

I gave a curt shake of my head. "He doesn't try hard enough. He barely speaks to me when he's here. He talks more to you and Aiden, and I know how that sounds. Like I'm jealous—" I exhaled raggedly. "I *am* jealous. You have a better relationship with him."

"I've known him longer and we've fought side by side."

Throwing up my hands, I cursed in exasperation. "Exactly. I get that he wasn't supposed to know me before and that being around me now weakens him, but I . . . I don't care," I spat the last three words out. "I just . . . The time he's here, he could try to get to know me. Try to be a father. And he lied to me, and I don't care what his reasons are." On a roll, I kept going.

er warned us that Seth could become the God Killer and might actually kill a Titan? We needed to know that."

"Agreed." Alex twisted toward me, her brown eyes sharp. "Aiden and I were told to keep an eye on him, and I know you don't like to hear that," she added when I opened my mouth. "You were right when you told Apollo that no one knows Seth like you do."

I snapped my mouth shut.

"You know *this* Seth, and I'm not sure who or what he really is now, but we know the old Seth too, and because of that, we have to be cautious. The gods had to be cautious." Her lips curled on one side. "And they were cautious because apparently they kind of knew more than what they told us."

"He's not evil," I said for what felt like the thousandth time.

Alex's brows furrowed together as she turned back to the ocean. "I think . . . I think you're right."

"I am," I said vehemently.

She nodded again and a moment passed. "I *am* sorry about your mother."

The next breath I took hurt. "Thank you."

Alex dragged the tips of her fingers through the crab grass and dirt. "If you ever need to talk about it, I'm here."

Pressing my lips closed, I nodded. I ran out of words along with the desire to find them. I didn't say anything else. Neither did Alex. We just sat there in silence, shoulder to shoulder, joined in a way by the terrible things we'd experienced, the heartache we'd felt, and the shared dread of the unknown we faced.

6

*T*he house was as quiet as a ghost as I stood in the room I'd sworn I would never return to. I'd only made it a few feet inside the door when my feet stopped moving.

I couldn't even believe that I'd walked into this damn house and I sure as hell had no idea why I'd come up here, to this room. It was the last place I ever wanted to be, but I was here, and had been standing here for what had to be hours.

Hours.

The people in the house—the staff or servants or whatever—had given me a wide berth as I'd entered. All except one. He was a male half-blood. He'd stayed back as I climbed the stairs, but I knew he was out in the hallway. Whoever the half was, he possessed major common sense and an admirable amount of instinct, because he'd known not to follow me into this room.

If he had . . . ?

The coldness in my chest spread like a vortex of ice and wind. If anyone had followed me in here, it would've been the last thing they'd done.

My hands open and closed at my sides as crackling power seeped out of my pores. The room was just like I'd left it all those years ago. A neatly made bed stood in the center of the spacious quarters. The nightstand by the bed only had a lamp positioned in the furthest corner. How many times had I moved that lamp closer to the bed and then found it the following evening pushed back to the farthest corner of the nightstand? Every single godsdamn day. There was a narrow dresser across from the bed with the same damn TV sitting on it, and that was it. Nothing else was in the room but a fine layer of dust covering the dresser and nightstand.

This had been my bedroom.

I wanted to burn this room.

Why did I want to come here? This wasn't a place of happy, happy memories.

Emptiness poured into my chest as I surveyed the cold and lifeless bedroom. Coming back to this house meant I'd be near only a few thousand people. Andros wasn't heavily populated. Coming here was a smart move, but walking into this room was a mistake.

I rubbed my palm over my chest, but nothing filled the gaping hole there, because that void had nothing to do with this house or this bedroom.

Exhaling roughly, I walked toward the heavily shrouded window and pulled the curtain back. Dusk had begun to settle over the courtyard down below. I closed my eyes, and instead of being sucked back into those long nights and mornings of staring out this window, watching my mother, I saw Josie's face and I wanted to be there. I wanted to see her—

And then it happened.

My heart took a beat and every cell in my body scattered. One second I was in my old bedroom and the next I was standing in a small room that appeared to be a hotel. I took a step back as my gaze swung around the room. Heavy curtains were drawn, blotting out the sun. I caught a glimpse of blonde hair splayed out across a pillow.

Shit.

I hadn't meant to do this.

But I had.

I'd brought myself to Josie.

Holy shit.

It had only taken a second, a freaking second, and I was suddenly within feet of her, and she was right there, lying on a bed, curled onto her side. Her back was to me, but I knew that was Josie. I knew the line of her body, even under a thin white blanket. That was her curve of the hip and waist. That was my Josie—that was *psychi mou*. My soul.

Only hours had passed since I'd left her, but it felt like a fucking eternity. I took a breath and it got stuck somewhere in my chest.

She was *right* there.

I didn't move or dare to breathe too loudly. She couldn't wake up. If she did and she said my name—if she looked at me, I couldn't walk away again.

I shouldn't be here.

Seconds slid by in a slow succession as a hundred questions rose in my head. Where was Josie? This didn't appear to be the house we'd been in. Were they still in Malibu or had they left? If I concentrated hard enough I swore I could hear the ocean outside. Where was everyone else? Alex and Aiden? The boys and Poseidon's son? How in the hell had I come all this way without realizing I was doing it?

The gnawing in the pit of my stomach rumbled like hunger pangs.

I needed to be gone from here. Josie wasn't safe with me.

One foot followed the other and then I was at her back. My heart thundered in my chest as muscles along my back and shoulders tensed. All thought processes were clicking off and common sense dive-bombed off a cliff. My fingers grazed over her soft, silky hair. I lifted a thick strand and curled my fingers around it. My gaze crawled up over the slope of her bare shoulder and the thin strap of one of those tank tops she was always wearing. I laid the strands of her hair down on the pillow as my gaze tracked the deep rise and fall of her chest. Lowering my hand, I snagged the edge of the thin blanket and drew it down, revealing the deep dip of her waist. The tank top she wore had ridden up, showing off a section of skin and the lacy edges of her panties.

Josie squirmed in her sleep, shifting halfway onto her back. I held my breath as those thick lashes fluttered. Any second she could open her eyes, and I'd be lost. I'd be found. And there would be no going back.

Those eyes didn't open.

Her hand fell to the side, slightly brushing my arm. It was like a jolt of electricity, lighting up every cell.

Wake up.

That order whispered in my thoughts. It was wrong, so very wrong, but if she opened her eyes and saw me, I . . . I couldn't walk away.

I wanted to wake her up. I wanted to touch her—hold her. I wanted to curl my body around hers. I needed to feel her skin flush against mine. I needed to hear my name on her lips. My gaze flickered to the swell of her breasts, and the hunger raging inside me mixed with stark arousal. I needed everything about her.

Everything.

Fear punched through my gut—fear for her. I dropped the blanket. Struggling against instinct that was primal and raw, I forced myself to take a step back and then another. The back of my throat burned. My knuckles ached from how tightly I was now clenching my fists.

I could not be here.

Closing my eyes, I pictured the house on Andros and I felt the tugging. Within a second, I was back to the house, to the old bedroom.

"Gods," I growled.

Shaken, I pivoted around and left the bedroom, slamming the door shut behind me. I passed the half in the hall and took the steps two at a time. On the main level, I headed for the study and straight for the liquor.

Fuck.

What I'd just done was leveling up on the whole stalker thing. And it had been so damn dangerous. The hunger for her, for what was inside her, was a monster clawing its way out of me. I couldn't do it again. There was no way. I hadn't even made it a full fucking day without searching Josie out.

The cabinet door opened before I reached it. With a trembling hand, I grabbed the first square-based crystal decanter. Popping the lid, I lifted it to my mouth and drank until my entire body burned. I drank until the decanter was empty, then I reached for another. Amber liquid swished, and I drank until there were no thoughts of Josie.

Until there were no thoughts of anything.

Josie

Opening my eyes, I found myself staring at the unfamiliar bedroom walls. My heart was pounding and as I inhaled deeply, I caught a woodsy scent. Jerking up, I threw the cover off and swung my bare legs off the bed.

"Seth?" I said his name before I could stop myself.

I turned around, scanning the darkened room. Of course there was no answer. He wasn't here. My stomach hollowed as I backed up, plopping down on the edge of the bed. Running my hands through my hair, I tugged the strands back as I exhaled roughly. My head thumped and my eyes burned. I didn't know how long I'd slept, but I knew it couldn't have been more than a few hours. I hadn't wanted to fall asleep. There was too much to do, but my body had given out to sorrow-tinged exhaustion the moment we arrived at Gable's uncle's house. Or was it his aunt? Grandmother? I had no idea. For all I knew it could've been a second home.

Rich people had those kinds of things.

After Alex and I had gone back inside, we'd discovered that the guys had everything packed up. It was obviously no longer safe at Gable's home. Too weary to argue, I climbed into the back of the SUV and rode several miles down the coast to yet another sprawling mansion.

I'd expected there to be more damage from the Atlas-induced earthquake, but a block away from Gable's home, the large palm leaves were swaying in the breeze and cars zoomed up and down the roads.

The mortals obviously believed it had been an earthquake and nothing more.

When we got to the house on yet another cliff overlooking the sea, I followed Gable to a guest room, stripped off my jeans, and climbed into the bed. I hadn't wanted to sleep, but at the same time I did, because then I wouldn't have to think about my mom or Seth or my father.

But now I was awake.

Swallowing down the bitter knot of emotions, I stood and

walked over to where my jeans were lying on the arm of a dark brown chair. I dragged them on and then toed on my flip-flops.

I left the bedroom and made my way down a wide spiral staircase. The house was quiet, but as I entered what I guessed was a massive living room, I could see Luke and Deacon on a startling white couch. Luke was on his back, head resting on the arm. Deacon was curled on his side, his blond head on Luke's chest. An arm and leg were thrown over Luke's waist and legs as if he were ensuring that Luke was actually getting some rest. Both were asleep, and staring at them caused a twinge of hurt to spike my heart.

A soft-looking gray blanket was draped over the back of a chair. Picking it up, I carefully laid it over the guys. Neither stirred. I figured only another earthquake, hopefully one that didn't include scorched daimons, would wake them.

Finding my way through the house, I opened French doors that led out onto a heavily shaded patio. It wasn't empty. Alex was sitting in one of the outdoor chaise lounges. Of course, it was white. The people who lived here apparently had a thing for white furniture.

She tipped her head back and smiled up at me. "Hey."

"Hey." I stopped in the middle of the patio and crossed my arms. "What are you doing out here?"

"Can't sleep," Alex said, running her hands over her thighs. "I mean, I did for about an hour, but I woke up and couldn't fall back. I came out here so I wouldn't wake anyone else up." She paused. "You should still be sleeping."

"Yeah," I murmured, spying a rocky path in the dirt and crabgrass. "Do you think that leads to cliffs or the beach?"

"Don't know. Want to find out?"

A weary smile tugged at the corners of my lips. "Sure."

Alex popped up faster than I would've expected, but then

again, she was like the Terminator on crack. We hit the worn path in silence. A couple of minutes later, we discovered that it led to a cliff. Not a sheer one like back at Malibu. The path continued down the slope to a patch of sand and rock.

Eyeing the hill, I decided I really didn't want to climb back up. So, I found a boulder and sat down. "It's really beautiful here."

"Yeah, it is." Alex's hair lifted off her shoulder as she stared out into the sea. "I think I could live somewhere like this. You know, Aiden and I have been talking about a place we'd like to settle down when we're topside. Right now, it's wherever Deacon is, but we'd like to have our own place eventually."

"You're thinking it might be in California?"

One shoulder rose. "Maybe. Aiden would love some place in the mountains, though."

"And you?"

Her whiskey-colored eyes met mine. "I'd love wherever he's at."

My heart turned over heavily. She really meant that, and God, I . . . I would've felt the same way with Seth. Wherever he was, I would be happy. I still felt that way. I just needed to get to the islands and hopefully convince him to stop being so . . . so damn stupid.

"So, what's your game plan, Josie?" she asked. "You let us know if it's changed. We'll do whatever—"

The sky cracked behind us, and we both moved in unison. Every muscle in me protested, but I pushed through it. Springing to my feet, I spun around, having no idea what to expect and preparing myself for anything.

Anything except what I saw.

7

My heart stuttered as I recognized the massive man standing before us. An eternity could pass, and I would never forget the curved pitch-black eyes, the shaved head, or the shade of skin that was neither black or white or tan.

I'd never forget Hyperion.

"Oh crap," Alex muttered.

Fear exploded in my gut as everything clicked into place. My wild gaze gauged the distance between him and the house where Gable was resting. Bone-deep knowledge told me that, even if the home were only a few feet away, it wouldn't matter. There was no safety in the house, and I'd used the Pegasus blade on Seth. The remaining blades were most likely inside the house, with Gable who could not be seen by Hyperion. And I had no idea how to entomb a damn Titan.

The same bitter knowledge also told me we would not win this fight.

"Miss me?" Hyperion asked.

Shimmery white light powered down my right arm. "Like I'd miss a gunshot wound."

Hyperion laughed darkly. "Oh, but I've missed you."

Terror trickled down my spine as I tapped into the aether.

Power flickered inside me, weakened from the overuse and no real rest. "Run," I urged Alex.

Brandishing blades she must've had hidden on her, she widened her stance. I noticed one of them was the Pegasus blade. "Never."

"You should listen to her," Hyperion warned.

"And you should stop talking," she spat back.

His lips curled into a cruel smile as he focused on me. "I have a bone to pick with you, Sunshine. After our last well-spent time together," he said, and I flinched, "I had to piece myself back together, and that was not pleasant."

My heart was pounding fast. "Can't say I feel bad about that."

"Well, you will know exactly how it feels by the time I'm done with you. Told you I'd be back." His chin tilted toward Alex. "And your idiot friend there is going to be an amazing snack. A made demigod. So thoughtful of you, Sunshine."

Alex's eyes blazed. "Oh, I am so not a snack."

Hyperion sniffed the air and laughed again. "You're not much of anything except soon to be very, very dead."

I sensed the moment Alex was about to attack. Her rage was palpable, and I struck first, releasing the bolt of akasha. It slammed into Hyperion's shoulder.

He laughed.

Laughed.

His smile spread as he stepped forward, and the ground trembled under his bare feet. "You're going to have to do better than that."

Alex launched forward, spinning in air. Her right leg extended, about to make an impressive dropkick as I tapped into the aether again.

Hyperion's laugh was like a blast of icy wind. Stepping into her kick, his hand snapped out as fast as lightning. He caught her by the ankle and flung her—flung her like a Frisbee.

"Alex!" I shouted as she flew backward, slamming into a boulder.

She hit the ground and rolled, pushing up to her knees as she threw her head back, knocking the long strands of brown hair out of her face. The blades were still held tight in her hands.

So badass.

I let go of akasha, this time hitting Hyperion in the chest. He jerked back a step as Alex yelled my name. I turned just as she tossed one of the blades at me. It wasn't dipped in Pegasus blood, but it would have to do.

Spinning back to Hyperion as Alex jumped to her feet, I tapped into the element of air. Loose strands of hair lifted off my shoulders and a gust of wind shot across the distance.

Hyperion powered through it. Gasping, I shot to the side and spun, thrusting the blade out. The fun end hit its target, sinking through his skin and embedding deep into his chest.

I lifted my chin.

Hyperion *tsk*ed softly.

Everything happened so fast.

He didn't even look behind him as Alex came down on him, the blade raised high. Wrapping one hand around mine, which was still clenching the handle, he threw out his other hand, catching Alex in the chest. He swatted her back like she was a gnat.

I drew on the power of fire, heating the dagger until the skin of my hand was scalded.

Hyperion wretched my wrist hard enough that a cry of pain parted my lips. His other hand flew around, connecting with the side of my face. Black starbursts exploded behind my eyes.

I tore my arm free, blinking to clear my vision as I stumbled back several steps. Hyperion reached down, tearing the blade from his chest.

The blade disintegrated in his grip.

"Oh crap," I gasped out.

He whipped around, catching Alex's arm, snapping it like it was nothing but a dry limb. The tainted blade fell to the ground. Her scream of pain blistered my ears, and pure stark terror hit me as he wrapped his other hand around her neck.

Hyperion would kill Alex.

He would do it without a second thought.

I sprung forward, slamming my heel into the small of Hyperion's back. He moved an inch forward, and I dipped down, reaching for the blade Alex had dropped. Between his tree-trunk-sized legs, I saw Aiden pounding up the sandy hill, his expression furious. Hyperion laughed as he threw Alex to the side like she was nothing more than a ball of paper. I caught just a glimpse of Aiden veering off to the side, going for her.

A deep voice shouted, and then a stream of fire went up, circling Alex and Aiden. Hyperion turned, kicking the blade several feet away. My gaze followed his and I saw Luke and Deacon racing toward us.

"Oh, even more things to play with." Hyperion flicked a finger—*a finger*.

Luke was lifted off the ground without warning. He flew through the air like a bullet, slamming into the base of a palm tree. He hit the ground. Deacon didn't stop.

My eyes widened with horror as Deacon threw up his hand again. Smoke wafted from his fingertips. Oh no, no. He could not face Hyperion. What was he thinking?

Popping to my feet, I took off as Hyperion shifted toward Aiden's brother. I ran, ran faster than I ever had. Darting in front of Hyperion, I skidded to a stop and spun around, planting myself between them.

"Josie!" Deacon yelled.

"Go," I demanded, breathing heavy. "Dammit, Deacon. Get the hell out of here!"

"Now don't listen to her and ruin all my fun," Hyperion taunted.

I stepped back, forcing Deacon backward as the wall of flames around Alex and Aiden dropped. Alex was on her feet, cradling her arm. Aiden's gunmetal-gray eyes widened when he saw his brother.

I couldn't let Hyperion get to him—get to any of them.

Pushing off my back leg, I spun out, preparing to deliver a viscous kick. Hyperion swung out his arm, catching me around the waist. I shouted as he lifted me. My arms flailed as he slammed me into the ground. The impact rattled every bone in my body.

Hyperion grabbed a fistful of my hair. Shouting as he lifted me up, my hands grabbed at his as fiery pain erupted over my scalp. My feet left the ground, and I was suddenly eye to eye with Hyperion.

"I have spent days and weeks and months fantasizing about what I'm going to do to you." His was voice was soft, but the words hit me like a sledgehammer. "I cannot wait to get started."

I drew in a short breath.

Then I was flying backwards, and I didn't have the chance to brace for impact. Hitting the ground, I gasped as the air was knocked out of my lungs. Stunned, I couldn't move for several seconds. Holy crap. I had to dig deep, summoning akasha as I started to lift myself up, but I couldn't find the strength. All I had was instinct, a drive to survive. I put one hand in front of the other and moved my knees. I crawled—*crawled* along the dusty ground, fingers digging through thin blades of grass.

Get up. Get up. Get up.

Lightning struck across the sky, filling the air with electricity. Dumbly, I watched the sky rip right open. Wings—all I saw were wings. Wings that spanned eight feet, attached to long, lean bodies. They circled at dizzying speeds. Screams—screams of fury ripped through the air, raising the hairs all along my body.

"Furies!" someone shouted. Maybe Aiden?

Erin. *Erin!*

Backup was here. Finally. All I needed to do was to get up. Just get—

Pain exploded along the side of my ribs as I was flipped over. My back hit the hard dirt as the air wheezed out of my lungs.

Hyperion loomed over me. "Time for us to go."

I opened my mouth, but another burst of pain robbed me of breath and sight, and then there was nothing but darkness.

* * *

A shiver woke me.

The first thing I became aware of was the fact I was lying on my side and there was a hard, damp floor under me. It was cold, too cold. Blinking my eyes open, I bit back a moan. I could barely see anything as I gingerly lifted myself up, planting one hand on what turned out to be a cement floor.

Where in the world was I? Where was everyone? The furies?

Moving a hand to my wrist, I jerked my fingers back when a faint shock traveled up my arms. There was something wrapped around my wrists. Bracelets—thin bracelets.

They most definitely hadn't been there before, and I had a bad feeling about them—about all of this.

My ribs hurt as I sat up. The steady throbbing in my temples caused my head to swim as my eyes slowly adjusted. There was a small window high up. Dust danced in the faint light that trickled in. Taking small breaths, I lowered my gaze along the wet cement walls. A dank, musty scent filled my nostrils, reminding me of how the shades from the Underworld had smelled.

I shivered again.

Turning slightly, I bit down on my lip as my body protested the movement, and then gasped. I wasn't alone.

There were two people in the room with me. Both were lying on their sides. One was female. Dirty, bedraggled hair that appeared to be somewhere between brown and black shielded her face. She was only wearing what appeared to be a tank top and underwear. Even in the pale light, I could see that her thin legs were covered in either bruises or dirt. Near me was a shirtless male, his chest and stomach sunken in. Horror gave me strength to sit up fully as I stared at them.

I had a horrible suspicion of who they were and where I was. "Hello?" I croaked out.

Neither body moved. I had no idea if they were alive. Forcing myself to move, I winced as I managed to drag myself the few feet to the closest body. The closer I was, I could make out some of his features. He had high cheekbones and full lips, but that was all I could see. His jaw was bruised and dirtied. I placed my hand on his still arm, sucking in air as I felt his cool, clammy skin.

And his eyes opened.

Drawing back, I stared into dull, vacant eyes. I opened my mouth to speak, but terror closed my throat off, because I knew—*I knew* there was barely any life in those eyes.

He was almost a shell, a dried-out husk of a person, and they . . . these two people were the missing demigods. The ones we were headed to find.

I sat back—fell back on my butt and I felt no pain as I stared at him. "Oh my god," I whispered. "No. No way."

This couldn't be happening. I couldn't be *here*. Panic unfurled in my chest. My gaze swung around the room as my pulse pounded erratically. Oh god, I couldn't be here. I would wake up and—

No. This wasn't a nightmare. I was with the Titans and that could only mean one thing for me. No one would be coming. Seth didn't know I was captured. He was *gone*, and I didn't know what had happened to Alex and Aiden or Deacon or Luke. I had no idea if they were alive or in here, wherever here was, or somewhere else if the furies had protected them.

My fingers curled in, nails digging into my palms.

I dragged in a halting breath.

I was so screwed.

And I was scared—*terrified*. I didn't want to be. I wanted to be like I was sure Alex would be if she were in my place. Scared but strong, confused but plotting a way out from the moment she awoke. But I wasn't her. I hadn't trained since birth. I was just a mortal less than a year ago, and I knew—oh *gods*—I knew what was going to happen to me. All those horrid, whispered promises Hyperion had made me before Seth had arrived the last time. He was going to carry through with them. I *knew* it.

Pressing the back of my hand to my mouth, I squeezed my eyes shut. Tears burned as the panic infiltrated every vein. I couldn't—

Voices and footsteps echoed outside the chamber, and I froze, unsure of what to do as I tried to decipher the language they spoke. Moments passed and I began to understand.

A woman was speaking. "You are a fool, Hyperion. You are not the one in control here."

"I did not ask for your council."

She made an exasperated sound. "Her? He will come for her and he already—"

"Close your mouth or I will rip your tongue out, Tethys," Hyperion warned. "You know I will."

My heart stopped and there was only silence for a few seconds, then I swallowed hard, eyes widening as I heard the locks turning on the door. There was nowhere for me to go, and it didn't matter, because the door swung open, and light leaked into the room, revealing a narrow tunnel and Hyperion standing in the center of it.

The male beside me suddenly moved. He scuttled back against the wall and hunched over, curling his forearms around his face as he began to rock.

"Good." He strode forward, legs encased in leather. "You're awake. Now the fun can really begin."

I threw up a hand. "Don't come any closer."

He stopped, and I could hear the smile in his voice. "Or what?"

There was no point in replying. Concentrating, I reached deep inside of me and searched for aether and . . . and found nothing.

"What . . . ?" I pressed a hand to my stomach, to my core, and felt *nothing*.

Hyperion chuckled. "There is nothing you can do. You see, Sunshine, nothing is simply absolute. There is always a nullifying factor. Those bands around your wrists were once around ours."

Lifting my arms, I stared at the thin bands.

"They were forged in Olympus with the blood of Zeus and Cronus," he explained. "Titan blood is powerful, and if you mix it with the Olympians? It was what allowed our children to entomb us. Those bands nullified our powers long enough for us to be placed in those tombs. They were removed when we did the whole deep-sleep, never-wake-up gig. Luckily, we were able to find a few."

I couldn't breathe.

"Do you know how the gods maintain their power, their immortality?" he asked casually, like we were discussing how to spruce up the place.

"No," I grunted out, heart thumping. "But I guess you're going to tell me?"

"No, Sunshine. I'm going to show you."

"Yay," I muttered, lifting my gaze to his.

"Your bravado is false. The stench of terror seeps from your pores."

I shuddered.

"But that's okay. Pretend you're brave. It will be so much more fun breaking you, and I will this time." Hyperion crouched in front of me. "But back to the more interesting part of the conversation. For the gods to live outside of Olympus, we must . . . feed."

My stomach hollowed as I trembled.

"We can make it feel good or we can make it feel like your skin is being flayed from your bones, but you . . ." He reached out, folding his hand around my jaw. I winced at the touch, and he smiled. "You already know that."

Breathing raggedly, a scream built in my throat as the male demigod whimpered.

"And it's time to feed."

8

"You need to feed, Kýrios."

Lowering the glass, I raised a brow as the amber liquid swirled along the crystal. At some point, I stopped drinking straight from the decanter and bottle. That was an improvement.

Night had fallen, the sky was blanketed with stars, and until Basil had spoken, I'd been alone on the balcony. It had only been the sound of waves crashing against the shore and my thoughts.

Thoughts only of Josie.

Every spare moment was consumed by her. How was she feeling? Did she still mourn the death of Solos? Was she okay? Angry? Hurt? I assumed she was furious at me, and I hoped for that, because anger was better than pain—pain I'd inflicted upon her. And when I wasn't thinking about that, I was remembering what she felt like—her silky skin, her soft hair, and her plush lips. I recalled her throaty laugh and breathy moans. Sometimes, when it was quiet in this massive tomb of a home, I'd hear her calling out to me.

I was fucking losing my mind.

My lips curled up on one side as I lifted the glass. At least I hadn't unintentionally willed myself to her again, but my head was a relentless one-way train I couldn't get off of. Three days had passed since I'd arrived here, since I last saw her sleeping, and the only thing I'd done was pop out of one room and into the next.

Well, that wasn't the only thing I'd managed to do.

I was making an impressive dent in the liquor stock. The liquor here was blended precisely for our kind, mixed with only the gods knew what. One shot would probably knock a mortal flat on their ass. Maybe even kill them.

I was pretty sure I'd spent the last three days in what most would consider a drunken stupor.

"Kýrios?"

Gods, this man did not give up.

"I've already eaten." I took another drink, lips peeling back as the burn cascaded down my throat. Each evening, a feast that could feed an army was prepared. Duck. Cow. Pig. Chicken. Tonight there'd been a random pizza in the mix of the roasted hen and grilled fish. "And how many times have I told you not to call me master?"

"Yes, Kýrios," he replied in thickly accented English.

My eyes rolled as my fingers tightened on the glass. I glanced over to where the dark-haired Basil stood. He was maybe a decade older than me, dressed in all-white linen. He was a half-blood.

A servant.

He didn't have the mark of servitude on his forehead, though.

When I realized there were over a dozen halfs in service, I told them to leave. Released them from service or some bullshit. None of them left. I'd ordered the pures to hit the road. None ɟf them left. According to Basil, they were pleased to serve their *theós*.

I was the God Killer, but I was no god.

At least that was what I kept telling myself. Kind of hard when the half and pures bowed whenever they saw me. Or the fact that the men and women here who wore cloth the color of amber were priests and priestesses, for shit's sake.

And they were chock full of aether. Not like a demigod or a god, but more potent than a pure or a half.

Just because I was the God Killer and could pull an Apollo, randomly poofing into rooms, didn't mean I was a god. It didn't matter what that nymph had said when he'd finished the prophecy given to Alex all that time ago.

I was not a god.

I also recognized I was surfing the mad river of denial.

But what the fuck ever.

"You must feed, Kýrios. It is the way of your kind," Basil tried again. A medallion hung from his neck. Engraved in the center was an "S" closed at the end. The invincibility rune. The priests and priestesses wore the same symbol. I was currently not acknowledging what that medallion symbolized.

I knew what Basil was getting at with the whole feeding shit. Yeah, he wasn't talking about consuming calories.

Real fucking weird around here.

I could leave. Even considered it on the second day when I entered the large bedroom facing the sea, the one I'd decided would be mine, and found a priestess waiting for me. On my bed, completely . . . nude.

Males across the world probably hung their heads in shame when I'd ordered her from my sight. Hell, the Seth before Josie would've been all halle-fucking-lujah, but when I saw the woman, all I saw, all I wanted, was Josie.

Screwing Josie out of my system would probably speed along the process of detaching myself from her, but I couldn't bring myself to do it, to even entertain the idea.

I was beginning to wonder if the odd urge to return here had meant something else. Something that obviously had to do with Ewan, the servants, the priests and priestesses, and the damn medallion.

Closing my eyes, I tipped my head back against the chair as I bent one knee. A low, simmering burn in the pit of my stomach rode me hard. It was a burn that no food would satisfy. Liquor dulled the need a little. Not a lot, but some.

Basil snapped his fingers, drawing my attention again. Opening my eyes, I saw a woman step out onto the balcony. Her golden gown billowed around her legs.

I stilled.

She was a blonde and tall like . . . I sucked in a sharp breath. The gown did very little to hide the curves of her body.

"Lydia would be honored to serve you," Basil said softly, so quietly I thought I was hearing crap.

The pure-blood came forward, and my brows rose as she lowered herself onto her knees before me. "Please," she said, staring up at me with eyes as blue as the sea at the shores. "We can help you."

"Help me?" I repeated dumbly.

She nodded.

"You're blonde," I croaked out, wondering why all the damn priestesses that I'd seen so far were blonde.

A look of confusion marked the woman's face as her hand floated to the long strands. "Do you . . . do you not like blondes?"

I really didn't have a preference to be honest, and Josie's hair wasn't just one shade of blonde or brown. It was an odd mixture I'd never seen before.

I also couldn't believe I'd said that out loud.

Irritation rose. "I'm done." I waved one hand as I looked over at Basil in warning. "This is not going to happen."

The priestess hesitated and then looked over her shoulder questioningly. When he nodded, she rose. She hurried from the balcony.

"Go," I ordered roughly.

Basil bowed stiffly and then exited through the archway, entering the house. I was alone once more.

What in the hell happened to this place?

Not that this wasn't an improvement from when my mother ran this house. There'd been beatings and parties and beatings and guests. There hadn't been priests or priestesses.

Or staff that actually wanted to be here.

There most definitely hadn't been a pillared temple at the end of the honey-scented, wild thyme-filled courtyard. The really weird part of that? The thing had to have taken at least a year or so to build. It didn't just appear in the last couple of weeks.

I'd seen the temple on the first day. Above the entryway, the invincibility rune was carved into the sandstone. Two priestesses in amber-garbed gowns had waited outside.

I hadn't gone in.

I would not go in.

This place was fucking bizarre.

For what the gods have feared has come to pass.

"Hell," I muttered, lifting my gaze to the starry night. "You out there, Apollo? Eavesdropping? You hear what that nymph had to say?"

There was no answer, but I laughed anyway. "Out with the old and in with the new, eh? Does that mean your time has come?"

Still no answer.

Not that I expected any of the gods to come within a mile of me now.

I sat for a while and a while turned into maybe an hour or three. Tossing back the rest of the Metaxa, a native liquor, I held the glass up and watched as the crystal folded into itself, evaporating into dust with just a mere thought and an even smaller push of aether.

That was new.

Standing, I swayed a little to the right, my foot knocking into an empty bottle of the spicy brandy. The other was only half empty. I swiped that one off the floor and took a deep drink. Who needed glasses anyway?

I started to walk back through the doors and then remembered that walking was for losers. Smirking, I decided I wanted to go to the room I chose, and I felt my body shift—actually, it felt like all the cells in my body were buzzing apart and coming back together.

Strangest damn sensation.

A second later, I was inside the cavernous room my mother used to reserve for *special* guests. I still hadn't gone to my mother's old chambers. If I went to that room, I'd probably set it afire.

I opened my eyes and cursed. "You've got to be kidding me."

Another priestess was perched on the ornate bench at the foot of the bed, her hands folded primly in her lap. This one was older, probably somewhere in her mid-thirties. Still beautiful. Her hair was pulled back from her face and left hanging down the center of her back.

And holy shit, she wasn't a blonde.

Fisting the bottle, I raised it to my mouth. "You have about five seconds to leave this room or you won't be leaving it in one piece."

The priestess rose slowly, unlocking her fingers. "Please hear me out first."

I swallowed the fiery liquid. "Four seconds."

"My name is Karina."

"Three seconds."

A small smile appeared. "I am the head priestess of the Temple of the Appointed."

Basil may have mentioned at some point that the Temple was called that, and I may have immediately disregarded that piece of information. "Two seconds."

"And you, Seth the Appointed, are a god."

My lips twisted into a smirk as I raised the bottle once more. "I might've been told that a time or five hundred before."

A perplexed frown pinched her face. "I do not jest, Kýrios. When you awakened, you fulfilled the prophecy decreed by the Delphi oracles many, many moons ago. You are now a god and no longer bound to mortal whims or obligations. You've risen above."

I stared at her, eyes narrowed. There was something different about her. I might have been slightly intoxicated, but there was a humming to her that wasn't present with the other priestesses.

"You will usher in the new," she continued, taking a tentative step forward. "But you must learn what it means to be a god."

"Is that so?" I murmured, walking past her. Finishing off the rest of the brandy, I set the empty bottle on a dresser.

"You may drink and be merry as much as you like," she advised. "You may indulge in any manner of entertainment you seek, but you *must* feed."

Turning, I lifted my arms and leaned back against the dresser. "What is it with you people and the whole feeding shit? This place is like the opposite of AA."

She inclined her head to the side. "You do not understand.

Did Basil not inform you?"

I exhaled raggedly. "He might've been talking and I might've been drinking."

Karina took a small step toward me, and she must've read something in my expression because she stopped and stiffened. "You can eat as much mortal food as you'd like, but it will not sustain you now. Gods must feed on aether. *You* must."

Aggravation filled my tone. "I am not—"

"You are a god," she said, green eyes flashing. "And if you are a smart god, you will stop lying to yourself."

My brows shot up. "Did you just say I was stupid?"

"I said no such thing." She clasped her hands together.

Rubbing my hand across my jaw, I eyed the massive bed. "You need to go."

"I cannot."

My head turned to her slowly. Whitish-amber light crackled over my arms, across my bare chest. The room tinted. "You really do not want to test me."

Her chin lifted as her nostrils flared. Stupid of her, but brave. "I understand."

"You understand nothing." My voice pitched low as I took a step toward her. Only a foot away, a knot formed in my gut. The aether inside her sang to me. My head was already dizzy, but now the room seemed to tilt.

"You are confused. You did not expect any of this even though we've been watching and waiting. Preparing. This has all been foreseen."

Waiting? The humming in my core grew, and the empty hole inside me spread.

"And you are in pain." She lifted her hand, placing it between her breasts. "Here. You are in a lot of pain in your heart. I understand."

How did she know? Oh, the whole waiting and watching part. Nice.

"But you still must feed."

The buzzing cleared long enough for me to say, "I can't do that." The back of my throat itched and burned. "It makes me . . ."

Makes me . . . crazy. Out of control.

"You are no longer the Apollyon. You are no longer the child of a half-blood and a pure-blood. You are a god," she said, taking another step forward. She had to tip her head back to meet my stare. She was short—short as Alex, and she wasn't blonde or tall or full of curves.

I looked at her and I didn't see Josie.

Her eyes searched mine. "The Apollyon can feed, but was never meant to do so. When pures feed on one another, it is a taboo and dangerous thing, because they were never meant to do so. That is how a daimon can be created, but for the gods . . . For them, they are surrounded by aether in Olympus. They breathe it. For you, a god existing outside of Olympus, you will need to feed."

I flinched as she placed her hand on my shoulder.

"You must, and then you will understand," she said, and her voice echoed in my head, drilled down my spine, and . . . and she looked nothing like Josie.

"You must feed," she urged, reaching down and wrapping her cool fingers around my wrist. She raised my hand and placed my palm against her sternum. "Now."

The tightening in my gut lashed out. I moved, curling one hand around the nape of the woman's neck and my palm pressed in. Every part of my body came alive, like the desert during a rare rainstorm.

I did it.

I *fed*.

9

Josie

Breathe in.

Breathe out.

Lying on my side, I focused on simply making it through the lingering pain. The burn of feeding had eased, but with every breath I took, pain lanced my ribs and shot across the back of my head.

Breathe in.

Breathe out.

I had no idea how much time had passed since Hyperion had brought me here. A day? Longer? Shorter? My empty stomach rumbled. I was hungry, but the mere thought of eating twisted my insides.

Forcing my eyes open, I wearily scanned the dark room. I could see the forms of the other two prisoners. I wasn't alone. Letting out a shaky breath, I placed my palm against the dirt floor and winced as I pushed myself up into a sitting position. It felt like my ribs were on fire as I scooted back and leaned against the wall. I'd barely moved, but I felt out of breath and disoriented as my vision adjusted to the low light.

I cleared my raw throat and it hurt. "Hello . . . ?"

Each time I was awake, each time I was alone, I called out to the other two. I never got a response. I honestly didn't expect this time to be any different. But it was.

Something in the shadows stirred. Clothing rustled against the floor. The form slowly, painfully pushed into a sitting position. "Who . . . who are you?"

It was the male.

Relief nearly made me cry out. He was alive and could talk. That was . . . good. Gingerly tipping my head back against the wall, I swallowed hard. "I'm . . . I'm Josie. You?"

A few moments passed. "Mitchell. My name is Mitchell Cousins."

I repeated his name in my head.

"Do you . . ." His breath hitched. "Do you know what they are, why they have you?"

Resting my arms in my lap, I focused on the shadowy outline of Mitchell. "They're Titans and they . . . they're feeding on us."

He coughed out a broken, dry laugh. "So I'm not crazy, and what's been happening is . . . is really happening."

"Yeah. It's really happening. You're a . . . a bound demigod," I told him, flinching as sharp pain stabbed the back of my head. "We were looking for . . . you guys. We knew you two had been taken—"

"You knew about this before they got you?" Surprise colored his tone.

"I . . . I found out what I was about a year ago." I wasn't sure how much I should tell or how much even sounded believable to a guy who had been in here for nearly a year. "My father sent someone to protect me, but Hyperion found me. We fought him off, and we couldn't find you two."

Mitchell didn't respond for a long moment. "Will . . . will someone be looking for you?"

My chest ached. "Yes."

"Will they find us?"

"They . . . they will try," I said, hurting for him and the girl who hadn't moved once since I'd been here. I'd told the truth. Alex and Aiden would try to find me. So would Deacon and Luke, and if Seth knew, he'd try. I believed that. I really did. But I had no idea how they could find us. I strained to see him through the muggy darkness. "Do you know who the other person is?"

"That's Lauren." His voice sounded like sandpaper. "I don't know her well."

Glancing at where she lay, I didn't see a single part of her move. "Do . . . you know how long you've been here?"

He shuddered. "I don't know. It's been . . . a while. She was here before me, and they . . ."

"They what?" I whispered.

Mitchell didn't respond right away. "The big dude . . . Not the one who brought you in."

"Hyperion?" Just saying his name made me want to vomit.

"Yeah, not him. There's another. He's got a mohawk. Blue hair, I think." Mitchell paused and seemed to rally up the strength to continue. "He comes for her. Not so much anymore, but in the beginning, it was like . . . every time I was awake he was in here and he'd . . ."

Part of me didn't want to hear it, but I didn't stop him.

"He'd drag her out of here and I don't think they'd go very far. She would scream, and I could tell she'd fight him . . . or she used to. I could hear the things he was doing to her." His voice cracked, and my breath caught. "He . . . he would *hurt* her. He would do things to her. I could *hear* it."

Oh *gods.*

Horror robbed me of the ability to speak as my heart thundered against my chest. All those horrible things Hyperion had said to me had been repeatedly carried out on her.

"I tried . . . I tried to stop him when he would come for her. You have got to believe me. I tried. I really—"

"I believe you." Tears burned my eyes as I tried to see the girl in the shadows, lying against the wall. "I believe you."

When he spoke, his voice was hoarser than before. "He . . . he just feeds off her now. Does it right here, and I . . . I can't stop him."

I dragged my right leg up, bending it at the knee. I couldn't even begin to fathom what she had been going through—what he had been going through. "Who comes for you?"

"The woman—I can't pro-pronounce her name."

Maybe he was talking about the one who was with Hyperion—the one who was arguing with him. I remembered how he'd curled away from them.

"Can you . . . can you do something for me?" he asked, and I had no idea what I could do for him. "Can you see if she's still alive? She hasn't moved since they brought you in . . . and they haven't come for her. I can't . . . I don't have the strength to move."

My stomach dropped as my gaze skittered from him to the other shadowy form. I tried to speak, but my voice got lost for a moment. It took a few seconds for me to croak out a yes, and then I pushed away from the wall.

It was easier to crawl over to where I saw her lying. Standing up and walking required too much effort and stress on my ribs, so I slowly made my way over to her. Dusty dirt coated my palms as I reached her still legs. A knot formed in my throat as I inched up to her waist. She was facing the wall. Hand shaking,

I brushed long, clumpy strands back from her face. It was too dark to make out her features beyond the dirt covering her face.

Please don't be dead. Please, please, please.

A tremble coursed through my arm as I pressed my fingers against her neck. I gasped at the touch of cool skin. I moved my fingers, feeling for a pulse. I didn't feel—feel anything. Jerking back, I tried to swallow.

"Is she . . . ?"

Carefully, I shifted her onto her back—or tried to. Her body was stiff and one arm appeared stuck to the floor. Her hair fell to the side and I saw her eyes were open, fixed and empty. She was—

I fell back and then scuttled backward, putting distance between us—between me and this poor girl. My brain couldn't even process the ramifications of what this meant—what this meant for us and for the world.

"Josie?" Mitchell whispered.

Moving until my back was against the wall, I ignored the pain in my ribs and head. "She's . . . I'm sorry. She's dead."

"Oh God."

My eyes were peeled wide, staring at where she rested.

"This has to be a nightmare," he cried. "Oh God. Oh fucking God. What . . ."

Another tremble rocked me, and this time, it didn't stop. I pulled up my knees and wrapped my arms around them. She was dead. That girl—that bound demigod was dead, and she was lying there with us.

"She's dead," Mitchell gasped. "She's dead and we'll be next."

10

*B*ack out on the balcony, I watched the sunrise and the ocean became an array of blues, lavenders, and pinks.

I'd slept like a baby last night.

Sleep hadn't come to me easily since I'd left Josie. The all-consuming thoughts of her had kept me up, as did the constant struggle to stop myself from going to her. The blood alcohol content I'd been rocking for days probably also didn't help when it came to getting a restful night, but after I'd . . . I'd fed and Karina had excused herself, I was out like a stoned kid in a game of dodgeball.

Feeding was different this time around.

Before, I'd be all over the place. Buzzed. Full of high-octane energy like I'd just smoked crack or something. Not this time. Yeah, I could feel the power in me, stronger than it had been before I'd fed, but I was . . . I was *leveled* out. Energized but calm when I woke minutes before dawn.

It had never been like that before.

But if I was to believe what everyone was saying, I was truly different now.

Bending at the waist, I rested my forearms on the stone railing and stared out over the ocean. Kernels of guilt had sprouted in my chest. There hadn't been a damn thing sexual about the feeding, but there was no denying the level of intimacy it required. Obviously, I had to be physically close to do it. I had to touch the other person.

I closed my eyes, remembering how I'd taken from Josie what was not mine to have. A hand pressed just below Josie's breasts. I'd done it out by the graveyard at the Covenant.

I'd done it the same way with Karina, minus the orgasm, the kissing, and all that other stuff.

Leaving Josie meant I wasn't with her anymore, but I'd rather set my nuts on fire than be with another woman. Maybe one day that would change, but I doubted it. Just like I doubted I'd ever be okay with the idea of her being with someone else, even if that someone else deserved her.

Anger snapped alive at the mere thought of her being with someone. I'd kill the son of a bitch that touched her, and yeah, that was wrong. The whole "I can't be with you, but you can't be with anyone else" was another way I was leveling up in the whole stalker biz, but I couldn't change how I felt.

Exhaling, I straightened and was about to head back inside when a door farther down opened and Karina stepped out.

"Good morning, Kýrios." She stopped, clasping her hands together. "You appear well rested."

"I am." I rested my hip against the railing. "But I have a feeling you expected that."

Her chin inclined as her dark eyes glimmered in the faint morning light. "I did." She glided forward, and I wondered if her feet even touched the ground. "I sense that you have questions, and I find that knowledge is more easily accepted when the sun has just begun its journey."

I arched an eyebrow at that, but she was right. I had questions. Lots of them, and while there was still a part of me that just wanted to give zero fucks, something inside me, something new and strong, refused to allow me to walk away from this—from what I was.

"I do have questions," I answered finally, folding my arms across my chest.

Her smile was oddly relieved. "Ask away."

"What are you, exactly?"

The smile slipped. "What do you mean?"

"You're a pure-blood who is a priestess. I get that, but you're no normal pure. The aether in you is stronger, almost like what I'd feel in an Apollyon," I explained, easily recalling what it had felt like to be around Alex before and after she'd awakened. "But I was unaware that priestesses still served the gods and I have no idea why the aether is stronger in you than an ordinary pure."

"We have been around since the dawn of time serving the gods. Just because they have retreated to Olympus does not mean we stop our service. We are just more . . . quiet in our service now."

"You mean, you just don't sacrifice virgin mortals anymore?"

Her lip quirked up on one side. "There is that, but those who serve the gods are chosen at birth. The gods we serve mark us all with their icons, and since we are chosen, we are simply more *pure*. We are more godly, which is how we have more aether in our blood. It has been that way since the beginning and will be that way to the end."

I didn't miss the fact she hadn't really denied the whole sacrificial virgin question. I probably should check out the temple soon and make sure they weren't hoarding virgins. Adding that to the to-do list.

"And you bear the icon of what god exactly?" I asked.

She tilted her head to the side, and it was pretty impressive that the elaborately coiled hair didn't topple her right over. "You already know the answer to that."

Maybe I did, but I waited.

Unclasping her hand, she reached up, curling her fingers along the folds of her dress. She pulled it aside, and for a moment, I thought she would expose her breasts, and well, that was going to end this conversation real quick, but she didn't, thank the worthless gods.

She exposed only the upper swell of her right breast, and there it was, a rosy-colored birthmark in the shape of the invincibility rune, the same as above the temple.

A muscle worked in my jaw.

"It is the mark of the God of Life and Death. The one who is absolute," she explained, smoothing the sleeve of her dress. "The Appointed God."

"That's a lot of names for one god," I said dryly. For some reason, a weird memory poked free. It was when Alex had been hauled before the Council under the false pretenses of discussing the daimon attacks her mother had been a part of. The reasoning had been a ruse and Minister Telly, who had been part of a secret group of dickheads hell bent on taking down the Apollyon, had used the stage to try to get her cast into servitude. During the questioning he'd called her something that suddenly raised the hairs on the back of my neck.

He'd called her the Harbinger of Death.

Except it had never been Alex any of them had to worry about. It had been me.

"A god we've waited a long, long time for." She folded her hands together once more. "The prophecy speaking of the

Appointed One was written into the void many centuries ago, and for hundreds of years, those born to serve the Appointed One have waited eagerly for their god. Twenty-two years ago, that god was finally born. The prophecy was finally set into motion, and we answered the call to come to Andros. You are the Appointed One, the God of Life and Death."

I stared at her for too long. "It sounds unbelievable. It feels unbelievable."

"Just like two Apollyons born within the same generation would've sounded unbelievable a handful of decades ago, correct?"

She had a point, but . . ."It doesn't make sense."

The "why me" went unspoken, but it was clearly out there. Why would I be raised to a true god status when there were far better suited people out there? I mean, come on. Even with just the control over akasha, I would go on a smiting spree for the fun of it.

"There is a lot of information that exists deep within you. All that the Apollyons who came before you have learned exists within you. That knowledge is what enabled you to awaken and become the God Killer."

"I get that, but I wasn't the first God Killer."

"Alexandria was, but her fate had also been written, and her destiny was never meant to be yours." Karina turned, resting small hands on the railing. "She was to destroy the god who sought to embroil the world in war and that was all. Because her creator, Apollo, still existed, he was able to stop her from becoming the true God Killer. She was always to become what she is today, a demigod."

"And I was what? The enabler to it all?" Old anger resurfaced. "So, everything I've done, I was fated to do?"

"Yes. Everything you have done, you were supposed to do."

Disbelief thundered through me. "No—no way. I can't believe that. I did horrible things, and if you know me as well as you all claim you do, then you know what I've done."

"I know what you've done."

I stepped toward her, arms lowering to my sides. "You're actually telling me that all of that shit was predestined and that I would become this ... As what? A reward?"

"I wouldn't consider it a reward." She focused on the ocean. "But it was predestined. You were to be created by Ares and to be used to awaken the true Apollyon—Alexandria. You were destined, along with your friends, to release the Titan Perses, who would then free his brethren. Everything that has happened since then was fated. Even the death of—"

"Don't say it," I warned. "I do not want to hear how watching someone die was meant to be—happened because of *my* destiny."

"Their destinies are only a small part of yours. What happened to them does not mean your fate is responsible." She lowered her chin. "But everything has been leading up to this, to what you were always destined to be."

"A god?" Derision dripped from my tone.

"Alexandria was meant to be the Apollyon and you were always meant for so much more." She looked over at me. "That may be hard to accept, but accept you must."

"You fucking sound like Yoda," I muttered.

"Excuse me?"

"Nothing." I sighed, and refocused. "Has this ever happened before? A god randomly created?"

She patted the railing. "The Olympians were birthed by the Titans. The God Killer was created by the gods as an absolute measure against any one supreme being. When Alexandria awakened, she did so to end Ares's rule before it could begin.

When you were awakened, it was done so to usher in the new age."

"The new age?" I laughed harshly. "What the hell does that even mean?"

She angled her slim body toward mine. "That everything we know is about to end, and a new era will begin."

"Well, other than that sounding like a parade I can't wait to see, it doesn't really tell me anything."

Karina smiled faintly. "That is not important right now. Josie is a part of your—"

"No," I cut her off. "She is no longer a part of anything that has to do with me."

"Why?" Her brows knitted together. "You fear yourself around her? That you will hurt her? Have you not realized anything? Feeding is—"

"I do not want to speak of her with you. That is the only warning I will give you." My hands closed into fists. "What I do from here has nothing to do with her."

"So your desire to seek vengeance against the Titans is driven by some other need?"

My eyes narrowed. "Careful."

She raised a shoulder and then turned back to the ocean. "You are the first," she said after a moment. "You are the only god to be risen, to be appointed with all the godly abilities. Do you know why the gods fear the God Killer so much? It is not just because you have the ability to kill them, but because you are absolute when only three others are. Zeus, Hera, and Cronus. They feared you, because they knew you could become them."

"And what exactly does absolute mean?" I asked. I'd never understood why the gods had created the God Killer in the first place. Apollo had tried to explain it once before in the vaguest terms possible, claiming it was a checks and balance system. Ares had never explained either. It made no sense that they would create something that could ultimately destroy them.

Then again, the gods seemed to excel in bad life choices.

And mortals consistently created things that would lead to their ultimate destruction.

So, hey, what did I know?

"You have the abilities of the gods, but you wield the ultimate power to destroy a godly being," she explained patiently. "Since Ares's destruction, there is no natural end to your beginning. The only true threats to you now are Zeus, Hera, and Cronus."

My brows flew up. "Wait. I get that Cronus could take my ass out, but how can Zeus or Hera do it when they weren't able to when I was the Apollyon?"

"*Because* you were the Apollyon. It added some measure of protection for you, but trust me when I say they would've found a way to destroy you, because they knew what was possible." She paused. "They've always known."

Of course they'd known and failed to mention all this shit. "So I'm guessing they're absolute?"

"Only absolute beings can kill absolutely. They could fight you and perhaps they would win," she said. "But you are the God Killer, the Appointed. They would not be wise to seek to do battle with you."

Huh.

Well, I was more badass than I originally believed.

"You're immortal, Kýrios. You are a god."

Those words finally, *finally* sunk through and it hit me then. Thunderstruck, I couldn't speak. I'd long accepted that I had no future. That once the gods had figured out how to end me, they would, and that my afterlife meant I'd be Hades's bitch. It wasn't until I met . . . I met Josie that I ever regretted making the deal that took away any real chance to have a long, happy life. But now?

I had a future.

I had an eternity.

It didn't matter what deal I'd made. The gods could no longer control my actions or my future. They could no longer control *me*.

I shook my head, still bewildered by all of this, but I could no longer deny the truth. "I'm a god."

"Yes." Karina pushed away from the railing and faced me. "And there is so much you need to learn."

11

I was going to die.

I *was* dying.

Standing among tall elm trees—trees so thick and full that only sporadic streams of light had broken through their bushy limbs—I could feel the life slipping out of me.

Cool air raised tiny goose bumps along my bare arms. I tried to draw in a breath, but the air went nowhere as I looked down at the beautiful white gown that tickled the tops of my feet—the gown I'd been so happy to wear.

Blood poured out of my chest, spilling down the front of the gown, ruining it. Pressing shaky hands against my chest, it did nothing to stanch the blood flowing from between my fingers.

Oh *gods*, I was going to die.

My knees gave out, but I didn't hit the ground. Arms folded around me, easing me down, holding me close. I blinked, trying to focus as I pressed against the warm, hard chest. Amber-colored eyes stared back into mine.

"Seth," I whispered. "Don't let me go."

"No." His face contorted. Tears filled his eyes as he lifted my head, pressing his mouth to my forehead. "I'll never let you go, Josie. *Never.*"

My hands slipped away, falling to the sides. I tried to speak once more, to tell him that I loved him, that I'd always love him, but I couldn't force the words from my tongue.

"Josie." His voice cracked as he rocked us back and forth. "I love you. I love you and I won't let you go. I will never—"

Gasping for air, I jerked upright and my eyes flew open. Darkness greeted me, and my body protested at the sudden movement. Every part of me ached—muscles, bones, and skin. Probably even my hair. Everything hurt, but I was alive.

"It was just a dream," I whispered hoarsely, gingerly leaning back against the hard, cold wall. "Just a dream . . ."

But there was something different about it, something too clear and crisp, too real. I could feel the fresh air on my skin, smell the metallic scent of blood, and I heard Seth—felt him against me.

But he wasn't here.

It was like those dreams I had while at the Covenant in South Dakota. The ones that had warned me that he was coming, and the voice had turned out to belong to Atlas, and he had come. They had been . . . prophetic in their tone, and I had the same ache in my temples as I did then. I wondered if they were dreams at all, and if they hadn't been simple dreams, was the one of me bleeding rivers in a white gown a warning?

None of that really mattered now.

Weary, I closed my eyes and pressed my lips together to stop the bitter sob swelling in my throat. Fuzziness clung to my thoughts, and I stilled for several minutes until it passed.

My throat was dry and my stomach empty. I was so incredibly thirsty and hungry, and I couldn't remember the last time I'd had a glass of cool water or food that wasn't stale hamburgers or possibly rotten fries.

The Titans tended to forget to feed us, and when they did, it was like they purposely found the most disgusting things to eat, but when hunger gnawed at our insides, we didn't really care what we put in our mouths. We became desperate.

I was that desperate.

Opening my eyes, I squinted into the darkness. I was alone again. I hadn't seen Mitchell in a while, and I had no idea if he was alive or if he was like . . . like that poor girl.

Before I'd been taken away, the girl had begun to . . . to decompose. The stench had been choking. The female Titan—Tethys—had finally removed the bound demigod's body and had done so without an ounce of care or respect for her. The Titan had grabbed her by the shoulders and dragged her body out of the room. Dragged her.

A shudder racked me.

I was now kept in a smaller room with a packed dirt floor that smelled of roots and mold. There might be mice in here, but I tried not to think about that.

I tried not to think about a lot of things.

I had no idea how many days passed since Hyperion had snatched me off the cliffs in Malibu. There'd been at least three, because I had been allowed to spend time in the sun three times when Hyperion had taken me above, and it had felt like days had passed between those times, but I couldn't be sure other than that there was a pattern emerging to his visits.

Hyperion would feed.

Another shudder worked its way through my body as I pulled my legs up to my chest. Sometimes he'd do it like Seth . . . like Seth had done—like when Seth had fed off me and I hadn't even noticed, but Hyperion made damn sure I knew exactly what he was doing. He'd press his hand into my sternum until the skin bruised, and I'd fight until the pain took over and all I could do was breathe through it.

It felt like every cell in my body was being scattered and the skin sliced off the muscles with a rusty butter knife, and I couldn't fight that. No matter how strong or brave I tried to be, the pain was all-consuming, and all I could do was shrink away from it, pray for an end, for the blissful nothingness that eventually followed.

Other times Hyperion . . . he was like a daimon.

He used his *teeth*.

Resting my head on my knees, I folded my arms behind my calves. There was one bite mark along my right wrist, just below the gold band. Wasn't exactly deep, but it was bruised and raw, and it was healing. At least, I thought it was. The other on my left arm was rougher and fresher. The skin didn't feel right and it still oozed blood, or maybe some other kind of fluid I didn't want to think about.

Could demigods get infections?

I had no idea.

Wasn't like there was anyone I could ask.

Once Hyperion was done, I'd be left alone for what I guessed was a day, maybe longer, to give my body time to replenish the stolen aether, just like a mortal body replenishes lost fluids and cells. That's what Hyperion had explained . . . or taunted. It wasn't like he actually conversed with me. Neither did the female Titan.

She was as cruel as Hyperion, perhaps even more so, but she was also afraid. That much I could tell, but Hyperion wasn't. Not at all.

It felt like a lot of hours had passed since I'd seen Hyperion last, and that meant Hyperion would be returning soon.

And I knew what would happen.

He'd order me to follow him, and if I didn't, he'd drag me from here. Literally. Then he would take me through what had turned out to be a warehouse, out through the loading docks and into the empty parking lot. He didn't just let me sit out there and soak up the sun.

Oh no.

He had to talk.

And then he'd haul me back inside. I would fight at first, no matter how pointless it was, because I had to. He always won those battles, but I had the bruises to prove I didn't go softly into the night or whatever.

I wasn't sure if I could go through it all again.

I didn't want to.

A raspy moan escaped me, and I lifted my hands, sliding them through the dry, matted hair, tugging it back from my face. My hair felt coarse and gross, as did the clothes I wore.

I hadn't showered since I came here. I knew I stunk, and I was okay with that, because I preferred to look as unappealing as possible to Hyperion.

Lowering my hands, I let them fall to my sides. My body tensed as I thought I heard footsteps. Air catching in my throat, I lifted my head and strained to hear more.

Hope that someone, anyone, was going to rescue me had fizzled out and died after the second time Hyperion had fed on me, because I . . . I had screamed for my father.

I'd screamed for Seth.

Tears of humiliation burned my eyes. I'd screamed for him until my voice gave way, and Hyperion laughed.

Apollo never came.

And Seth . . . he never answered.

He'd left me, and even though I'd planned to find him, to prove that I loved him and to show him that he was worthy of that love, he'd left me and I . . . I was here.

I knew Seth didn't know I'd been taken. Every part of my being knew that if he had known, he would've come for me. I knew that, but being here was like an open wound in my chest. It festered and rotted, breaking my heart every time I thought of him. Every time that I knew he wasn't going to swoop in and save me.

No one was coming.

It was solely up to me to survive this, to escape.

The only chance I had was when he took me outside. Hyperion once said that it helped replenish the aether, and I guessed it had to do with my father being the whole god of the sun thing.

Running was the only chance I had now. Wasn't the best plan, but it was better than accepting this was my future, my life, until there was nothing left of me to give.

And there wasn't just me to think about. There was Mitchell, and if he was still alive, he was here somewhere. He was beyond helping himself. I had to get him out of here before it was too late.

I rubbed at my eyes, wincing since I was too rough on the raw skin. Resting my cheek against my knee, I closed my eyes. I must've dozed off, because the next thing I knew my head was jerking up as the door opened.

Hyperion filled the doorway. "Good afternoon, Sunshine."

"Fuck you," I spit out, tensing.

He chuckled as he crossed the short distance. "So elegant. Want to try again?"

I swallowed hard. "Go fuck yourself?"

"Not necessary." He loomed over me. "Get up."

Part of me wanted to refuse, but if I didn't, he'd put his hands on me, and I didn't want to deal with that, so I rose on weak legs and stepped around him. I started forward on my own, making it halfway across the room before he slammed his hand into the center of my back, shoving me forward.

I nearly lost my balance, catching myself with a hand thrown out. "That . . . that was rude."

"You're too slow." His fingers dug into the flesh of my shoulder. "You walk like an overfed cow."

I bit the inside of my lip as we entered the narrow stairwell. He all but pushed me the whole way up.

"You actually remind me of a cow," he said as we went through a doorway where the double doors had fallen off the hinges. "A fat, spotted cow."

"You have such a way with words," I gritted out as we walked past wooden crates and empty, dust-covered work benches. "My heart is all aflutter."

His fingers dug in deeper, causing me to wince. "I'd think you'd have lost some weight by now. Your body must be holding on to the fat for dear life."

"Wow," I muttered. Truth was, I *had* lost weight. My jeans barely stayed up.

Hyperion reached around me, opening up the gray door. Sunlight poured in, and I squinted at the brightness. He led me down the ramp. The parking lot was vacant with the exception of two empty delivery trucks that had been there since I'd first been brought outside. They were older models. The words MILL AND SONS INC. were painted in faded red paint on one of the trucks. Weeds poked through the cracked cement. Several yards away, trees crowded the edge of the parking lot.

There was nothing else around here.

I knew this, because I had never seen any buildings or heard cars off in the distance, and no one had . . . no one had investigated the screams.

My knees wobbled as I walked ahead of Hyperion, the cement blistering hot under my bare feet. I had no idea where we were, but I imagined we were somewhere in the south, if we were still in the States.

"Sit," he ordered, dropping his hand.

Drawing in a deep breath, I started to do just as he said, but at the very last second, I sprung forward, forcing my legs to move. I took off.

"Really?" Hyperion laughed. "You're going to try to run from me?"

Legs and arms pumping, I ignored the stiffness and pain, and ran—ran as fast as I could. Tiny rocks dug into the soles of my feet, slicing my skin, but I kept running. I cleared the parking lot, darting through the trees. My lungs burned, and my head thumped. I didn't know how far I could run, but I would run as—

Fire erupted in front of me, swallowing a tree in a flash. Shrieking, I skidded and slipped. Arms pinwheeling, I whirled around just as pain erupted along the side of my stomach. My legs gave out, and I crashed into the ground.

"That was actually kind of fun." Hyperion reached down, wrapping his fingers in my hair. He jerked my head back. "I was beginning to wonder if the fight had gone out of you already. If I'd broken you that easily."

Panting through the pain, I forced my gaze to his all-black, soulless and endless eyes.

He smiled down at me. "That would've disappointed me."

"I wouldn't want that to happen," I gasped out.

"No, you wouldn't." His grip tightened as he knelt, wrenching my head back. "Guess what I did, Sunshine?"

I grunted as he tugged on my hair again. "I don't know. Walked an old lady across the street?"

Amusement flickered across his face. "I went back to visit your friends."

I stopped breathing.

His lips curved up. "They weren't there."

Air rushed into my lungs. "They're alive?"

"For now." He reached out with his other hand and cupped my jaw. "I tracked the little group all the way back to the Covenant. We can't get in there. Yet."

Relief coursed through me. Deacon and Luke, Gable, and Alex and Aiden were all safe for now. That meant something—everything.

"You know what I'd like to know?"

"How you're going to die?" Painful tension built along the nape of my neck.

"Charming." He smoothed a thumb over my lower lip, and I resisted the urge to bite his finger. "Where did your little God Killer go off to? He wasn't with them."

I held his gaze as I exhaled roughly. "I don't know."

"And I don't believe that." He let go of my hair and I dropped about a foot. Pressure eased off my neck. "Not for one second."

I said nothing.

Hyperion's thumb made another hard sweep along my lip and then he leaned in. The muscles along my back stiffened painfully. "You know there are many ways I can make you tell me."

My heart thumped against my ribs.

"Ways I haven't even begun to show you." His cool breath drifted over my mouth, and I had a horrible idea of what kind of ways he was talking about. His hand slid to my chin and his fingers dug in, bruising the skin. "Where is the—?"

"Hyperion."

A muscle flexed along his jaw, and then he rose, dropping

his hand. "What, Tethys?"

I slumped forward, catching myself with my hands. Unsure if I should be grateful for her interruption or not, I stayed quiet.

"What are you doing out here with her?" she asked, and I peeked up through the clumps of hair.

Tethys was gorgeous. Close to six and a half feet tall, she had long sable hair and features that somehow managed to look delicate and fierce all at once. She wore leather pants like Hyperion did, but she didn't run around topless. A tight, black tank top covered her chest and stomach.

"Did you seriously interrupt me to ask that question?" Hyperion replied.

She strode forward. "So what if I did?"

"I wouldn't like it, Tet."

"Does it look like I care about what you like?"

A coarse laugh sneaked out before I could stop it.

Tethys's eyes narrowed, and Hyperion whipped around and moved so fast, I didn't have a chance to dodge his blow. His fist caught my jaw, and I went down, hitting the ground on my side. Stunned, I lay there for a moment as my head rung.

"You and I both know you do," Hyperion said as he turned back to Tet.

Anger flashed across her face as she raised her hand. Hyperion was faster, though. He snatched up her arm, yanking her against his chest as he grasped her hair in his other hand. He pulled her head back sharply. The gasp of pain was cut off by his mouth. He kissed her in a way that didn't really seem like a kiss. More like an act of punishment and brutality, but Tet seemed to enjoy it, because his mouth couldn't silence her moan or stop her from slipping a muscular arm around his neck.

Oh man.

Weren't they, like, related? Gross. But they were distracted, busy shoving their tongues down each other's throats, so I pushed myself up and glanced over my shoulder. The fire that had engulfed the tree was out. My heart raced as I took a step back and drew in a deep breath.

"Don't even try it," Tet ordered.

My head whipped around. They were done making out, and both were focused on me. The chance to escape was gone. Defeat swamped me, giving way to desolation. Hyperion alone was bad enough, but with Tet involved, it would surely get worse. I folded an arm over my waist and waited.

"Why are you here?" Hyperion asked again.

Tet raised a dark eyebrow. "You're really not going to like why."

Hyperion sighed as he twisted toward the female Titan. "Get on with it."

She smiled tightly. "Cronus is aware of her. He wants to see her. Now."

12

Hyperion's grip on my arm was eventually going to snap the bone. Not that he particularly cared if he did.

He'd done that god transport thing that I guessed was only reserved for the super-cool gods. One second all three of us were standing in the forest, sweat coursing down the side of my face, stinging in all the raw abrasions, and then the next second, we were standing in cooler air, in front of a massive mansion built into the side of a mountain.

I was dizzy and off-kilter as Hyperion started dragging me toward a sprawling front porch. I almost didn't notice them at first. They were just immovable objects on the ground until I got closer.

They were bodies.

Horrified, I stumbled and would've fallen if he hadn't had such grip on me. There were dozens of them, and flies buzzed around their bodies. Bile rose into my throat, but there was nothing in my stomach to throw up. I clamped my jaw shut and focused straight ahead, on the front door of the home. There was a human male leaning against the house, but as we climbed the steps, the scent of decay and dankness grew stronger.

The male grinned as shadows poured into his eyes, eclipsing

his brown irises.

He was a shade.

Pushing away from the wall, he opened the front door for us. Tet stalked ahead, and I had no choice but to follow.

Cronus.

I was being taken to Cronus.

Numb with dread and fear, I was barely aware of the walk upstairs or down the narrow hall. Tiny, wheezing breaths left me as double doors opened to a large bedroom. I didn't want to go in there. Instinct screamed out, but I had no choice.

Two Titans were standing, one on either side of the bed. They were both males. One was bald and dark-skinned. The other was fairer and had shocking, bright blue hair, and I immediately thought of what Mitchell had told me. It was him—the one who'd done all those horrible things to that girl. Nausea hit me hard, and I had to look away. My gaze landed on the center of the bed, and then I wasn't thinking of the other two Titans.

My mouth dropped open.

He was all white hair and wrinkled skin. A gnarly beard covered half of his face. His shoulders were slim and his chest was sunken in, as was his stomach. Propped up by a mountain of pillows, this man looked like he couldn't lift his spaghetti arms, but he was Cronus.

This was *the* Cronus.

"Closer," the old man gasped out. "Bring her closer."

Before Hyperion could step forward, the dark-skinned Titan moved. "I will do it," he said, taking my other arm in a much looser, kinder grip.

Hyperion didn't let go. "She belongs to me, Perses."

My eyes widened. Perses? Wasn't he the one that Alex and Aiden and Seth had broken free from Tartarus to fight Ares? He'd escaped afterward and had been responsible for freeing the rest of the Titans.

Perses chuckled darkly. "You've played long enough. For a week, to be exact."

A week? It had only been that long? Felt longer. Pain bit into my arm, and I gritted my teeth. For a second I thought Hyperion was going to rip my arm right out of its socket, but then he let go and stepped back, joining Tet.

I glanced up quickly at Perses, but he wasn't looking down at me as he walked me around the bed to where he'd stood. As I drew closer, Cronus slowly lifted his chin. His black eyes were dull.

"Am I not what you expected?" He coughed out a dry, brittle-sounding laugh. "You see only an old, frail man before you?"

I didn't know what to say.

Cronus's fingers twitched against the duvet. "I'm not like them." His pale lips peeled back, revealing surprisingly white teeth. "It takes more than a few pure-bloods and a bound demigod to feed me. I'm older and more powerful. I need more." Pausing, he exhaled heavily. "A few days with a demigod should . . . it should do it."

Oh no, no, no.

My skin began to crawl. I thought about all those bodies outside and realized they weren't mortals. They'd been pures. He'd drained them dry and they'd been tossed aside as if they were nothing more than trash. I thought about Mitchell. Was he now tossed aside like Lauren, the girl, and those pures?

Would I eventually become one of them?

"We need to be careful," the other Titan spoke, the one with the blue, spiked hair. "She cannot stay here for long periods. It will not be safe for you. Not until you are fully restored."

"That is why I have not brought her here until now, Oceanus," Hyperion said.

The blue-haired Titan smirked. "And we're supposed to believe that? We know who she is. We know what you're about. All you concern yourself with is a personal vendetta."

Hyperion said nothing.

"He thinks she will draw Apollo out," Perses stated, still holding my arm like I was going to run. I wanted to, but I wasn't stupid. There was no place for me to go. "The only thing he will succeed in doing is bringing the God Killer to his door."

Air whooshed out of my lungs at the mention of Seth.

"He will not find her," Hyperion argued. "We are warded."

"Wards are not permanent," Perses retorted. "And you do not know him. I do. He will get through the wards. He will find a way."

"He hasn't yet." Smugness crept into Hyperion's tone. "I will find him first."

Oceanus sneered. "He killed Atlas, you fool. He is a god, capable of killing us."

Seth was an actual god now? I guessed that made sense since he was the God Killer, but Apollo hadn't called him that. Neither had Hades.

Hyperion rolled his eyes. "I am not afraid of him."

Perses cocked his head. "Perhaps you should be. We all need to be cautious."

"He will not be able to end me once I'm fully restored," Cronus said slowly, painfully lifting his hand. He crooked a finger. "Bring her."

Panic exploded in my chest, and I dug in, but Perses was strong, and my bare feet slipped on the hardwood floor. I threw up my hand, grasping the edge of the bed.

"Why?" I gasped out. "Why are you doing all of this?"

I'd asked Hyperion that and never gotten an answer beyond his hatred for Apollo entombing him, so I didn't expect Cronus to answer.

He did. "We want what our children took from us. We want to repay them for what they've done."

Revenge? This was all about *revenge*?

Holy crap, lives were being destroyed and lost all over something that happened back before time was probably even being recorded? And they accused Hyperion of having a personal vendetta? Didn't seem any different to me.

Oceanus moved toward the bed and slid an arm behind Cronus, easing him upright. "We must be quick."

"Closer," urged Cronus.

Fear overtook the panic. I fought—fought as best as I could, and the fight was over before it ever began. Perses lifted me up like I was nothing more than a struggling kitten. Pressed onto the bed and held down, panic consumed me. This was it. This was going to be it. I knew it. The dream had been wrong. I would die here. I would die being used as a universal power adapter—

"Don't be afraid," Cronus rasped, his eyes lighting up as he placed a bony hand against my sternum. "The pain is only temporary."

Seth

Basil stood beside where I sat, his hands clasped together in front of him. There wasn't a speck of dust on his white clothes. He waited in silence. The damnable chair I sat in was almost the size of a throne. Actually, if I was being honest with myself, which was what I was trying to do, it *was* a throne. It was the only chair in what used to be the sitting room. A dais had been built at some point and that was what the chair sat upon.

So, yeah, a damn throne.

My hands tightened on the titanium-plated arms and I tried

again. Eyes closed, I pictured Hyperion's face and let myself slip into a void. Opening up all my senses, I searched for him in the darkness.

This is almost like when Professor Xavier uses Cerebro, I thought with a smirk. I was looking for the imprint the Titan left behind. It was how Apollo seemed to always know where we were and could appear wherever we were at any given time.

Once I'd put the bottle down and started listening to what Basil and Karina had to say, I was figuring out there was a whole hell of a lot I could do. Karina had explained how all of this was possible, how I'd become what I was. A little part of me still almost couldn't believe it.

But the proof was in the Pegasus.

For starters, if I could picture the person or the place, I could easily transport myself there. I'd already figured that out when I'd popped in on Josie. Calling forth akasha or any of the elements required a mere thought, and if I was very still and quiet, I could feel the power humming under my skin.

I had to . . . I had to feed, though.

It wasn't like before—like it had been with Alex all those years ago or like it had been with Josie. There was no confusing need with want. I *needed* the aether Karina offered. I did not *want* it from her.

That was the difference between feeding from her and Josie. I wanted it from Josie, because I wanted her, everything about her, but I couldn't do that to her.

I also, frankly, didn't really care when I fed off Karina and she was several shades paler or when she immediately excused herself and barely made it to the temple to rest. I only felt the barest flicker of remorse when she had shown up last night and there were dark shadows under her eyes.

But if I didn't feed off her, then it would be one of the tall, blonde priestesses and I couldn't do that.

What in the hell did that say about me?

Nothing good.

Luckily, I did not need to feed every day. I started to recognize the signs—weariness, hunger for mortal food, and irritability. All signs that it was time to recharge.

It blew my mind that no one had ever known that all this time this was how the gods had maintained their power.

Exhaling roughly, I searched the abyss, but like the time before, I found nothing. Frustrated, I opened my eyes. "I can't find him."

"Then he must not be on the move," Basil replied. "That has to be good news."

I wasn't so sure about that. Just because Hyperion wasn't roaming around didn't mean the other Titans weren't, and Josie . . . She was still out there, maybe even still in Malibu. Or they'd left to find the other two demigods.

Unrest filled me, and it had nothing to do with aether. There was an odd sensation in the center of my chest. Had been there when I woke up. Almost like when you walk in the room and forget something. I couldn't shake it.

Something didn't feel right.

Thrusting my fingers through my hair, I narrowed my eyes as I stared across the narrow, empty room. "I tried seeking out Apollo this morning. Couldn't locate him either."

"He must be in Olympus, Kýrios."

I'd given up on telling the bastard to stop calling me master. I couldn't pop myself into Olympus. Since I'd never been there, I couldn't seek it out, but I knew of gateways that would let me in. Finding one would be . . . interesting.

And probably fun.

But once I made it to Olympus, they would not be able to

stop me from entering whenever I wanted, and that would be even more fun.

Standing, I walked across the raised floor and stepped down. I started across the room when Basil said, "You should bring her here, Kýrios."

I stopped before I was even realizing what I was doing.

"I know you do not like to speak of her," Basil continued cautiously. "Perhaps your heart no longer feels the same for her, but even if you no longer want to be with her, it is not safe for her to be out there."

Slowly, I turned around and faced him. Power rippled over my skin. "My feelings for her have not changed. They will never change."

Basil tilted his head to the side. "So you still care for her deeply?"

Part of me wanted to tell him to mind his own damn business, but I didn't. "She is *psychi mou*. I love her. I will always love her."

Confusion marked his face. "If she is your soul, then how do you not trust yourself with her? That alone would ensure her safety."

I opened my mouth to respond, but I found myself without words. Basil didn't understand. I hadn't been able to stop myself before. *But it is different now*, whispered the voice in the back of my head. Listening to that voice, caving to it, was too risky.

Spinning around, I stalked out of the door and passed several servants who were dusting or doing whatever the fuck they always seemed to do in the many rooms. They, of course, practically kissed the floor when they bowed.

I ignored them and went outside. Stopping under the shade, I scanned the horizon. Several small boats floated in the sea. I rubbed my hand against my chest, under my heart. I knew what the problem was. I needed to know if Josie was okay. I could do that without her knowing since I'd done it before. I could keep watch over her from afar.

After all, I was a damn god.

I could do that.

I should have already done this—checked in on her after I'd seen her sleeping. Basil was right. It wasn't exactly safe, even if she could protect herself or if the people she was with could throw down. But if I saw her again, could I really leave her again?

Lowering my gaze, I closed my eyes and pictured her face. A smile tugged at the corners of my lips. Her features pieced together so quickly and perfectly it was almost like she was standing right before me. Holding onto her image, I searched for her.

I found nothing.

"What the hell?" I opened my eyes.

Heart rate kicking up, I tried again, reaching out into the void, searching for her imprint and there was . . . there was nothing.

Confusion rose swiftly. That didn't make sense. No matter where Josie was, I should be able to find her. Mentally backtracking to the last place I knew she'd been at, Gable's house, I pictured the home and felt myself shift.

A second later, I was standing in front of the home Gable lived in.

"Hell," I growled. Immediately, I knew something had gone down here.

The driveway was cracked—not just cracked, but split wide open, creating a steep crevice. My head jerked up, and I rushed past the rift and pushed open the door. It creaked and fell from its hinges, crashing off the floor, but I didn't really hear it.

The house was utterly destroyed.

What had happened outside had continued inside and there were no signs of life, but I could feel it—a residue of power so potent that it was not from this realm. There was a coating that belonged not to just one god but many. Stepping back from the destruction, my hands closed into fists as knots of unrest formed.

Something had happened here.

Something bad.

And if I couldn't feel Josie, it meant one of two things. Her presence was being blocked, warded against me, or . . . or she was no longer in this realm.

13

I willed myself across the hundreds of miles, from the coast of California, beyond the Badlands, to the office of the Dean of the Covenant University.

Appearing in the center of the room, about three seconds passed before those in the room realized they had a visitor. Marcus was in the chair behind the large mahogany desk, reclining back, one leg hooked over the other, arms folded loosely over his chest as he listened to the two before him.

Deacon was sitting.

Luke was standing directly to his right.

Seeing them and not finding Solos with them was all kinds of wrong. That bastard hadn't deserved what'd happened to him.

Marcus was the first to see me.

Blood draining quickly from his face, he stood in a rush, bright green eyes wide. "Holy gods . . ."

Luke spun and stiffened, his expression locking down as he easily glided to the side, blocking Deacon, who was staring at me like he'd seen a ghost.

I smiled at the not-so-subtle protective move.

"Seth," Deacon breathed, coming to his feet. "You just appeared . . . out of thin air . . ."

"You know, there was nothing more annoying than Apollo

or any of the other gods just randomly popping up whenever they wanted," I said, my gaze flickering over them as I walked toward the desk. "But I've got to admit, being able to do it is pretty fucktastic."

Marcus continued to stare.

I smirked. "Yeah, spoiler alert. I'm kind of a god now." Pausing, I leaned forward, placing my hands on the smooth surface of the desk. "Isn't that scary?"

"Yeah," he breathed. "It is."

Raising a brow, I pushed away from the desk and crossed my arms. My gaze flickered to Luke. "Sorry about knocking you out. No offense meant."

A muscle flexed along Luke's jaw. "Not sure if I'm supposed to accept that or not."

I shrugged. "Everyone can relax. I'm not here to start a riot or bring the roof down."

"How?" Deacon breathed. "How are you . . . ?"

"Long story that I don't have the time nor the desire to explain." Out of the corner of my eye, I saw Marcus slowly sit down. Or his legs gave out. One of the two. "I'm not planning to stay."

"Of course not," Marcus replied.

I frowned slightly. "I went to the house in Malibu. Looked like some crazy shit went down."

Dark shadows were under Deacon's normally lively silver eyes. "Um, yeah. Apparently we were never supposed to kill a Titan."

"Oh, really?" I muttered dryly, using my "zero fucks to give" tone.

"Killing Atlas caused some major earthquakes," Luke explained, brows furrowed together. "You didn't know that?"

I raised a brow.

"It also punched a hole straight into Tartarus," Deacon added, leaning against the back of the chair. "Charred daimons escaped right into Gable's living room. It was like a scene out of a horror flick."

My stomach twisted. "What?"

"We fought them off until Hades and his men came up after them." Luke rubbed his fingers through his hair. "Then Apollo showed up. Things got . . ."

"What?" I repeated, the dread increasing.

A rare form of anger flashed across Deacon's face as he stared at me. "You weren't *there*. How could you not be there?"

My spine stiffened at the meaning to his words. When I spoke, my voice was deadly soft. "I like you, Deacon. I always have, so I'm going to say this once and only once. I *had* to leave."

"But you're here now," he said, pale cheeks flushing.

"Deacon," Luke warned, touching his arm.

"No." Deacon shook the half's hand off. "Josie stood up for you—defended you after you left us—left *her*. She stood up to Alex and Aiden who were afraid you had turned into evil Seth, hell bent on killing everyone."

My eyes narrowed.

"She stood up to her father—to Apollo when he showed up and started talking trash about you. She had *your* back," Deacon went on, his hands balling at his sides. "And you weren't there."

Anger rose to the surface and guilt snapped at its heels as I snapped, "I couldn't be there—be around her, Deacon. It's for her safety."

"Safety?" His laugh was harsh and so very unlike Deacon.

Akasha stirred inside me, and I pushed down the need to strike out. I liked Deacon and really didn't want to zap him through a window. "Look, I'm here to make sure she's okay since I can't . . . I can't sense her. That's all."

Deacon's mouth dropped open.

Behind the desk, Marcus briefly closed his eyes. "You don't know."

"Shit," muttered Luke.

As I stared at them, unease coursed through my veins like battery acid. "I don't know what?"

Deacon stared at me, but it was Luke who said, "After the daimons were taken care of, Apollo told Josie that her mother had died along with her grandparents."

"No." Disbelief flooded me. "Apollo said—" I cut myself off, suddenly understanding. "Apollo had lied to her this whole time."

Luke nodded. "Josie kind of lost it. A burst of akasha left her—knocked Alex, Aiden, and me flat on our asses. Apollo vanished at that point."

A wry smile tugged at my lips. *That's my girl.*

But my girl was hurting. Gods, she had to be hurting deep, because she'd always believed that she'd see her mom again, once everything settled down. She'd even planned to introduce us. It was such a mortal thing to plan, but that was Josie—that was *my* Josie. A powerful demigod, but still so very mortal. The urge to seek her out, to offer the comfort I knew she was so badly in need of, hit me hard, but Josie wasn't my girl anymore.

Something wasn't adding up, though. Apollo telling her the truth about her mother didn't explain why I couldn't sense her.

"That's not all." Marcus placed his hands on the desk. "You shouldn't be here. Seth, you should be home."

My arms unfolded as my frown increased. "My home?"

"The islands," Luke explained. "Josie thought you might go back to the islands you grew up in. That's what she was planning to do. She—"

"She went to Andros?" Surprise stowed my breath. How in

the hell did she figure out that was where I was going? I'd mentioned the islands only a few times.

Because she loves you, whispered that same voice in the back of my thoughts, and it was one hundred percent right. Because she loved me, she knew enough about me to figure out what my next steps would be, and she was going to come for me.

I needed to get back there. Gods, if she showed up and Basil found her—if she saw the temples and met Karina and—I could feel my form beginning to flicker out.

"Seth, wait." Deacon's eyes were wide as he called out to me. "Josie didn't make it."

I stopped. My heart. My lungs. Everything stopped, except for the earth, because it felt like it had shifted under my feet. "What do you mean by that?"

"Hyperion came after her." Luke's jaw tightened. "We'd left Gable's house and moved to one of his relative's houses so we could have time to plan what everyone was going to do. Josie was outside with Alex. They fought Hyperion—Aiden went out there, but he got her."

The edges of the room started to blur and turn white. "Hyperion has her?"

Deacon lifted his chin. "He got her and he's . . . he's had her for about nine days now."

Nine days.

Hyperion had had Josie for *nine days*.

Terror exploded in my chest as red-hot rage pumped through my veins. He had Josie.

Marcus was standing again. "Alex and Aiden left to find you, Seth. They've headed to the islands."

I was already halfway gone when I heard Deacon say, "You should've been there."

* * *

Nothing.

I couldn't feel a damn thing.

There was no trace of Josie, just like there had been no trace of the Titans. Panic clawed deep into my chest. There was nowhere to look—nowhere to truly begin.

He'd had her for *nine days*.

My stomach twisted, and I thought there was a good chance that I might be sick as I stood in the sand, several feet from the gently rolling ocean.

There was nothing stopping the steady stream of images flowing through my thoughts, invading every second. They had her, and I knew what they were doing to her.

Nine days.

You weren't there for her.

I hadn't been.

Not when she learned that her mother was dead, and not when Hyperion had come for her. If I had been, I could've comforted Josie. I would've made her forget all the heartache and pain. If I had been there, I could've stopped Hyperion.

If I had stayed a few days, Josie would be safely stowed away here, because now, when it no longer mattered, it was clear that Basil and Karina had been right. The only place Josie would've been safe from the Titans would've been here, with me.

"Fuck," I spat out. Centering myself once more, I searched for her, for anything, and there was still *nothing*.

Spinning around, fury pounded through me. I roared as a bolt of akasha slammed into a tall tree halfway up the cliff. Who knew how long the tree had been rooted precariously to the rocky slope? Probably centuries, if not longer, withstanding high winds and downpours and mudslides.

Akasha obliterated the tree in a second.

This couldn't be happening.

I was a god—I was the God Killer, and according to Ewan the nymph, Basil, and Karina, I was the Appointed God of Death and Life.

I was fucking *absolute*.

And I was standing here, blowing up trees, and I could do nothing to help Josie.

Lightning cracked overhead and the air sizzled as dark, tumultuous clouds rolled in, blotting out the sun. Turbulent emotions thundered inside me and into the environment around me.

Pacing, I dragged a hand through my hair, clasping the back of my neck. I had to find her. Now. Coming to a halt, I searched the skies. I'd been out here for hours, trying to hone in on Josie's whereabouts, and when that hadn't worked, I tried calling out to Apollo and he did not answer me. How could her father not have known?

How could I love her and have not known she'd been captured?

How was I any better than Apollo?

I wasn't.

That was a damn, sad truth. I'd lied to her. I'd put her in danger. I'd left her. I hadn't protected her. In a way, I was worse than her father, because at least he never got close to her, he never evoked a second of faith from Josie. She hadn't been planning to storm into Olympus to reconnect with her father. Josie had been planning to cross oceans to stand beside me, and I had fucking left her. It didn't matter now that it had been the right thing to do.

Stopping, I turned to the ocean and exhaled raggedly. Fear and anger battled with guilt. A streak of lightning lit up the sky once more.

I sensed Basil's presence. "You shouldn't be near me right now."

Basil, of course, didn't hightail his ass away from me. "Everyone is concerned. They fear something is wrong."

"Something *is* wrong." I turned around, finding Basil standing on the platform just above the sand, at the bottom of the stairs that led up the face of the cliff. "Hyperion has Josie."

His eyes widened. "I . . . I don't know what to say."

"I can't find her. I can't feel her at all."

Sympathy and concern flashed across his face. "There must be something we can do, Kýrios."

What I could've done was what I should've already done. That was the problem.

A priestess appeared at the edge of the cliff, her long blonde hair blowing around her in the increasing winds. It was the one I'd kicked out of my bedroom. She kept her chin and gaze down as she spoke, "A vehicle approaches the northern gate, Kýrios."

Having a pretty good idea of who was in the vehicle, I willed myself off the shore and outside the impenetrable, titanium gates that blocked the entrance to the house.

A sleek black Mercedes with tinted windows jerked to a sudden halt several feet in front of me. The purr of the engine quieted, and a moment later, the passenger and driver's doors opened.

Damn.

Alex and Aiden were here.

Josie

Cold water dripped and tiptoed down my brow. Water. *Water.* Blinking my eyes open, I blindly turned my head. Water glanced off my dry lips. I opened my mouth and then immediately gagged. The water tasted like spoiled eggs, but my throat was burning. I was so thirsty. I took in the tiny drops of disgusting liquid until my stomach churned.

Drawing in a shallow breath, I rolled onto my side. I was back in the cellar, and I had no idea how much time passed since Cronus had fed. I tensed as an aftershock of pain flared through my body, scorching bone and tissue.

I think . . . I think he took too much.

My hands and arms trembled uncontrollably as I stared into the shadowy cellar. Faint light trickled in front the small window. In the corner, near the door, I thought I saw something scurry across the floor.

I felt no fear or distress as I lay there. Before, the mere idea of being in the same room as a mouse had me seconds away from screaming. Now? I just . . . I just couldn't rally up the energy to be afraid.

I didn't feel much of anything.

Nothing.

Everything . . . everything had been stripped away. This was it. I understood that now. This was how it was going to end for me, because I really, really didn't think I'd survive another feeding with Cronus.

Or another one on one with Hyperion.

Hope . . . hope that I would find a way out of this had petered out toward the end of Cronus's feeding. The will to keep fighting, to keep existing, had plummeted out the window. It was weak—I was weak, but I . . . I couldn't do this anymore, and I . . . I just wanted to see my mom and my grandparents. That was all I wanted.

Footsteps sounded outside, drawing my weary gaze. A second passed and the door creaked open. It wasn't Hyperion or Cronus.

It was Perses.

A dull, distant part of me wondered what he was doing here. He'd never come before as far as I knew.

His booted feet stopped a few feet from me. "I'm not going to hurt you."

I didn't believe him. Not for one second.

Perses knelt in front of me. His cool fingers pressed under my chin, forcing my head back. "Well, you're awake. Can you stand?"

A huge part of me wanted to ignore his question, but I drew back a scant couple of inches. Drawing in a shallow, stunted breath, I planted my hands into the packed dirt and pushed myself up.

"Interesting," Perses said, rising. "I was beginning to wonder if you were dead."

"Not yet," I rasped out, getting my legs under me. I stood and I swayed. Wait—did I sway, or did the actual room sway?

I thought I took a step forward, but that's not what happened. My right knee gave out and then my left leg followed. I hit the ground, but didn't really feel the impact.

"Hell," Perses muttered as his gaze roamed over where I'd fallen. His face blurred in and out as I stared up at him. "You're worse off than expected."

Part of me wanted to laugh. What had he expected? Honestly? But the laugh never came. Air wheezed in and out of my lungs as black dots filled my vision. I couldn't get enough oxygen in my lungs. My muscles clenched painfully, and my heartbeat stuttered. Something . . . something was very wrong with my body. Like it was shutting down and there was nothing to stop it.

The last thing I heard before the darkness wrapped around me was Perses sighing and saying, "He's going to be so pissed off."

14

"So it's true?" Aiden stalked around the front of the Benz, coming to stand so he blocked Alex. "You're a god."

Any other time I would've laughed at his oh-so obvious act of protection, but there wasn't an ounce of humor residing in me. Only my rage and terror for Josie existed. "How could you let this happen?"

Aiden stiffened as if his spine had been hollowed out and replaced with steel. "How could *we* let this happen? Where in the hell were you?"

"I tried to stop him." Alex stepped out from behind Aiden, and I finally got a good look at her. A fading bruise covered the side of her face. Those bruises continued down to her right arm. "So did Aiden. He came out of nowhere, and we weren't pre-pared. We all were exhausted and—" She cut herself off. When she spoke again, her voice was hoarse. "We fought him, Seth. We did everything we could to keep him from taking Josie, but we couldn't stop him."

"He would've killed Alex." Aiden's voice was hard. "He was

going to kill all of us."

Exhaling roughly, I knew my anger with them was unreasonable and misplaced, because I was pissed at myself and I knew who was truly to blame. My gaze flicked back to Alex. "You okay?"

She nodded as she walked forward, stopping a few feet from me. Her gaze roamed over me. "You don't look any different." Her brows pinched. "I mean, if you're a god now, wouldn't you look more . . . I don't know, godly?"

"I think I've always looked godly."

Alex snorted.

Behind her Aiden rolled his eyes. "Can we talk?"

Stepping aside, I waved my hand and the heavy gates swung open silently. "I'll meet you inside."

Aiden opened his mouth to respond, but I willed myself to the receiving room, a large chamber to the right of what I now guessed was the throne room.

Basil appeared like a wraith. "We have guests?"

"Yes. Alex and Aiden." I walked over to the small fridge under the well-used liquor cabinet and grabbed a chilled bottle of water. "I'm guessing you know who they are?"

He nodded, "Of course, Kýrios."

"Could you stop with the 'Kýrios' stuff for a bit?"

"Of course, Kýrios," he answered, and I knew I was talking to a wall.

Basil pivoted around, and a couple of minutes later he escorted the shell-shocked pair into the room.

"Want something to drink?" I asked, gesturing to the cabinet area. "Help yourself."

Alex's mouth moved without words, and then she plopped down in the oversized chair, her heart-shaped face pale. "Are we supposed to, like, bow before you now?"

I coughed out a harsh laugh. "While I'd find that utterly amusing . . ." Pausing, I shot a pointed look in Aiden's direction. "Let's not do that."

Aiden placed his hands on the back of the chair Alex sat in, and then leaned forward. "How is this possible?"

Even though this was the last thing I wanted to talk about, I knew we wouldn't get anywhere until I gave them the Appointed God For Dummies breakdown. So I did, only leaving out the whole feeding thing. They wouldn't understand what I barely understood myself.

Alex continued to stare. "Holy shit, Seth."

"Yeah," I muttered, taking a drink of the water. "My sentiments exactly, but right now, I'm more concerned about . . . about Josie."

"We heard you went to the University to check on Josie and that's how you found out." Aiden moved, sitting on the arm of the chair. It was then I realized both were dressed as Sentinels—black tactical pants, black shirts. They could be killed, make deals, become demigods—but they were still Sentinels. "Deacon and Marcus called," Aiden explained. "They told us that you were a god and that you'd had no idea Hyperion had gotten hold of Josie."

"I've been trying to sense her out, but I can't." When they both stared at me with blank cow eyes, I sighed. "It's how I'm able to will myself from one place to the next. It's what Apollo and the other gods do, how they pop in and out. You have to either know the place or the person, but I can't feel her, or any of the Titans."

Aiden rubbed a hand across his chest. "We got Gable back to the University so he'd be safe. Deacon and Luke are going to try to locate the demigod in Thunder Bay. Then we headed here. Had a bit of difficulty finding you."

"I remembered you mentioning the whole Andros thing and my last name." Alex tucked a strand of her hair back. "But we got here as soon as possible to tell you about Josie. When you left . . ." Alex trailed off.

"You mean after I was rendered unconscious and you locked me in a panic room?" I finished for her.

She looked unrepentant. "As if you don't understand why we did that. We didn't know what we were dealing with. We had no idea that you could become the God Killer or that you wouldn't go all psycho on us. Hello! That's how it's worked in the past."

"Touché," I murmured.

"Josie was planning to come—"

"I know," I cut her off, disgusted with myself, with all of this. "I know what she was planning to do, and I know I shouldn't have left. I thought, after I destroyed Atlas, they'd lie low for a while. That I would have time to find them and destroy them."

Alex cocked her head to the side, brows pinching together. "It wasn't your fault, Seth."

I shook my head as I placed the water on the cabinet. "It was. I could've stopped Hyperion." My hand clenched into a fist. "And I will kill him for this. All of them."

"Well," Aiden drawled. "Supposedly we aren't supposed to kill them. It has certain ramifications. Apollo was none too pleased about you taking out Atlas."

"I don't give a single fuck," I growled, my skin growing itchy with impatience. "And I give even less than a single fuck when it comes to Apollo."

Aiden wisely changed the subject. "So, what's the plan? And before you even attempt to say you don't need our help, you're getting our help."

"Josie is one of ours," Alex chimed in. "I don't know her that well, obviously, but I like her and I want her to be safe and okay." Her gaze searched mine. "We need to help."

I appreciated their willingness. "Not sure how you can help when I can't do a damn thing. I keep searching for her, but I'm coming up empty."

"There's got to be a way." Aiden stood, widening his stance.

Walking to the glass wall that overlooked the ocean, I pushed down the blossoming panic that screamed what if I never found her? I focused. "Apollo and Hercules couldn't sense out the other missing demigods. Obviously wherever they are holding them is where they must have Josie."

"Okay. Then there has to be something," Aiden repeated, silver eyes flashing. "Alex and I have been tossing this back and forth on the way over here."

"It was quite the trip," she said dryly, and I knew there was a story there, but I didn't care enough to ask them to elaborate. "So we had a lot of time to think about this."

More time than I had, since I'd been busy drinking myself stupid and then finally learning about what I'd become. Shame was my middle name.

"The Titans need aether to regain their strength, correct?" Aiden stated. "Having two demigods and even Josie can't be enough for six Titans—seven, up until you eradicated Atlas. That can't be enough. So the next best thing would be purebloods."

Following where he was going with this, I swung around. "If we can find a cluster of missing pures, then we'd be closer to where the Titans are."

Alex nodded. "Unless they've been grabbing pures from multiple locations, then we're back at the starting line, but we can hope they aren't smart enough or they've grabbed more than the normal losses from one location."

"I've already made a few calls to some of the Guards I know

who protect pure communities," Aiden said. "I hope to hear something soon."

I should've been relieved that at least we'd have something to go off of, but every muscle in my body was tense, because what if . . . what if we were too late?

What if I was too late?

* * *

Night had fallen. I had no idea where Alex and Aiden were. The last I'd seen, they'd been transfixed by the priests and priestesses that they'd seen out by the temple after dinner. Now the house was quiet, as was the ocean. All I had were my thoughts, and they were full of Josie.

I'd tried sensing her out like I'd been doing all day, over and over. It had only been a day since I'd realized Josie had been taken, but it felt like a damn eternity of not knowing what was happening to her, what she was going through.

Smoothing a hand over my face, I squeezed my eyes shut. If we didn't hear back from the Guards Aiden had contacted . . .

"Seth?"

Lowering my hand, I turned. Alex stepped out onto the balcony. She'd changed in to jeans and a loose T-shirt. For a minute, she looked like any normal mortal out there.

"It's beautiful here," she said, her gaze bouncing from me to the dark ocean. "And you actually grew up in this?"

I didn't respond as she walked to the railing and turned her face up, closing her eyes to the sweetly scented breeze.

"How are you hanging in there?" she asked.

Smiling wryly, I leaned back against the warm sandstone wall. "I want to blow shit up."

She gave a soft laugh. "Understandable." There was a pause and then she lowered her chin and opened her eyes. "You're a god, Seth—and don't say something stupid—but you're an actual god."

"Bizarre, right?"

Her eyes widened. "Really freaking bizarre. We were talking to, um, Basil—is that his name? Yeah. Basil. He seems really nice."

"He's all right."

Glancing over her shoulder to the open archway, only a moment passed before she found my gaze again. "Can I just point out something to you?"

"If I tell you no, is that going to make a difference?"

A quick grin flashed across her face, and for a moment, I saw our past stretched out—I saw all the good and all the bad. I had been there for Alex when Caleb died, but I'd also tricked her many times. I'd used her to power up before she'd awakened. Yeah, my head had been a bit brainwashed, but that wasn't an excuse. In the end, I'd come through for Alex—for Alex and Aiden, but that didn't wash my hands clean.

Sometimes I had a hard time believing that Alex was actually standing in front of me and not trying to throat-punch me.

Alex's gaze met mine. "You said you want to blow stuff up, but you're not."

"I took out a tree earlier."

Her brows rose. "But the Seth I knew would be all over the place, blowing up more than a tree," she said. "You look the same, but you're a hell of a lot calmer."

I didn't feel calm.

"Being a god must have a weird . . . zen effect on you." She paused. "So I'm going to ask you another question. Why did you leave?"

My shoulders tensed.

"I have to ask." She reached up, twisting her hair into a rope, reminding me so much of what Josie did when she was nervous that I had to look away for a moment. "I mean, obviously, you're not out of control. You're not running around, doing evil deeds." Her nose wrinkled. "Like I've said, you're actually calmer than I've ever seen you."

My jaw locked down.

"And when you left, you didn't hurt anyone. Yeah, you knocked out Gable and Luke, but you and I both know you could've done worse. We *expected* you to do worse."

"Thanks for the vote of confidence."

She ignored that. "But you left after you saw Josie. That right there is a sign that you're okay. Well . . ." Her lips pursed. "Okay by your standards."

I shot her a droll look.

"And I'm going to be honest. We had sent Herc to get Apollo to find a way to keep you caged. Josie was all about finding you and being there for you, and she fought for you. I mean—"

"You don't understand, Alex." I pushed off the wall. "Or maybe if you think about it, you would understand. You of all people should understand."

She flinched. "Seth—"

"When I came to, knowing that something was vastly different in me, feeling what I was feeling, I didn't know what I was capable of. I left because I wanted to keep her safe, because I couldn't live with myself if I hurt her."

She tipped her head back, meeting my glare. "But now? Once you get her back, what are you going to do then?"

I stared at her a moment and then shook my head. I turned back to the ocean. "It's late, Alex, and I suddenly find myself with a case of shut the fuck up."

"I really would like to punch you right now."

"Get in line," I muttered.

She was quiet for all of five seconds. "I'm sorry. I really am. What you're going through? I can't even imagine it."

Pressing my lips together, I said nothing, which worked out perfectly because when I looked over my shoulder, I saw Aiden standing in the archway.

"Hey." He walked up to Alex, wrapping an arm around her shoulders. He drew her to his side. "Why don't you head to bed? I'll join you in a little bit."

Alex hesitated, because she rarely ever did what was asked or even suggested. So I nearly fell over when she said, "Okay."

Obviously I wasn't the only one calmer now.

After a quick kiss, Alex waved goodbye and slipped back into the archway. I saw that Basil was waiting in the wings and stepped out, immediately joining her. He was probably loving the fact that there were guests in the house.

"We picked the bedroom on the third floor, the one that faces the ocean," Aiden said, coming to join me by the railing. "Is that okay?"

"Fine with me. There are only a thousand unused bedrooms in this place."

"This is the home you grew up in?"

I nodded. "Until I was sent to the Covenant in England."

"You have a temple in the backyard then?"

My lips kicked up on one side. "No. That appears to be a more recent addition."

He crossed his arms on the railing and leaned against it. "This is a nice place though."

Raising a brow, I wondered what the hell Aiden was doing out here. Things had changed between all of us. Yeah, I gave up my afterlife so he could have immortality. I obviously wasn't gunning for Alex. We'd worked together a few times, but we did not like each other, and I knew that, deep down, Aiden hadn't forgiven me for a lot of things. Couldn't blame him for that. "Alex told me that you two wanted to keep me caged after what went down with Atlas."

"Do you blame us?"

"Nah." I watched him. "You have a reason for hanging around out here?"

"Maybe."

"So why don't you put your running shoes on and get to the point?"

Aiden laughed under his breath, but the faint smile disappeared when he looked over at me. "I know what you're going through right now."

"Do you really?"

"Yeah, I do." His gaze was unwavering. "When she was connected to you, it was like she was lost to me. A totally different person. That was tough to get through, but it wasn't the worst. When she was stabbed and actually died in my arms and there was nothing I could do? I held her and watched her bleed all over me and the floor."

A muscle started tapping along my jaw again.

"Then when Alex faced off with Ares at the University, and I could hear every single thing he was doing to her but I couldn't get in there to help her? I never felt more—more fucking helpless in my life. Every part of me was full of rage, but the terror consumed me when I finally entered that room and she was gone, taken to Olympus to heal. I was held immobile by that terror. And I don't think I need to explain how I felt when Alex died in your arms and I thought I'd never see her again."

I jerked a little.

"So, yeah, I get what you're feeling. I know that every second feels like an hour and every hour feels like a year. I get that you feel like you should be doing something, anything to get her back, but at the same time knowing there isn't anything you can do." He exhaled heavily as he straightened. "I still don't like you."

I laughed at that.

"But I don't wish what you're going through on anyone," he added, turning toward me. "We're going to get her back."

"I know." And I would gladly burn down every city to get her back.

Aiden clapped me on my shoulder. "As soon as I hear anything from the Guards, you'll be the first to know."

"Thank you." The two words were easier to speak than before.

"Get some rest." He stepped back. "Or at least try to."

I nodded, but as soon as he crossed the balcony, I closed my eyes and searched for Josie. There'd be no sleep tonight. Tomorrow . . . tomorrow I would need to feed, but that was something I didn't want to really think about at the moment. The void opened up and I didn't expect—holy shit! *There*! I felt Josie, felt her entire being, and I could catch the scent of pine and rich soil as if I was standing in the forest instead of by the ocean. I saw her imprint, and I knew I could latch onto it.

"Aiden." I spun, eyes wide. "I feel her."

"What?" He whipped around. "Josie?"

"Yes. I feel her. Holy fuck, I feel her. She's there." It was like a burning light inside me, calling out to me. "I need to go."

"Wait." Aiden hurried back. "Take me with you. You can do that, right? This could be a trap. You know that."

I supposed it could be. If it was a trap, I'd explode every single one of them, but I had to be smart about this. I could use Aiden. "If I get tied up fighting, you go to her. You get her out of there. Go anywhere. I'll find you and bring you back here."

He gave a curt nod.

Wrapping my hand around his forearm, I found the imprint of her again, and then willed myself to where she was, bringing Aiden along with me. It only took seconds to move from the balcony and discover that we were obviously on the other side of the world, under a canopy of thick elms that blocked daylight.

"Holy hell," Aiden grunted, stumbling back a step. "That doesn't feel right."

I stepped forward, scanning the trees and ground as my heart thundered in my chest. Senses were firing off left and right. We weren't alone. There was something very powerful here that wasn't Josie. Approaching a moss-covered tree that had been snapped at the trunk and had fallen over, I scanned the area and kept all senses on high alert.

My knees weakened, and fuck, I was about to eat dirt as I lurched forward.

I saw her.

I saw Josie.

She was lying on her side, back to me. Her hair was a tangled mess and the entire back of her shirt was covered in dirt. She was still, too still.

"Josie?" My voice broke, actually cracked when I said her name.

No movement. Not even a twitch.

Slamming a hand down on the fallen tree, I vaulted over it and landed in a crouch next to her. I placed my hand on her arm. Her skin was cold to the touch. I started to say her name again, but I couldn't find my voice.

Carefully, I eased her onto her back, gently brushing away the strands of hair plastered to her face, and I . . . I forgot how to breathe.

In that moment, I knew two things. I most definitely had a

heart. It was there, in my chest, and I knew that a heart could truly break, because mine shattered into jagged pieces.

"Josie," I whispered, her name pained and brittle.

Bruises of all colors mottled her pale face. A violent purplish contusion covered her right cheek and eye. The skin was swollen, and I doubted she could open the eye if she were awake. Another deep blue bruise marred her forehead. Her lips were chapped, the bottom one cut. Dried blood lined her temple. My gaze drifted over her. Bruises along her neck. Fingerprints clearly marked her skin. *Bite marks.* Even her feet were scratched and caked with blood. Every piece of skin I could see had been damaged.

But she was alive.

That much I knew, because her chest rose with shallow, uneven breaths.

"Is she okay?" Aiden called from somewhere nearby as I noticed there were two slim, goldish bands on her wrists that I hadn't seen before.

I tried to speak again, but I had to clear my throat. "I-I don't think so."

Aiden muttered a curse.

Sliding an arm under her body, I winced when she whimpered. Intense, blinding, burning rage filled me, a primitive fury that begged to be unleashed. The scent of burnt ozone filled the forest, along with a burst of power.

I sensed the Titan just as I gathered her in my arms. "Aiden," I warned, rising quickly. "We're not—"

"Alone," he answered. "I know."

Turning around, I spotted the Titan standing several feet from Aiden, and I recognized him immediately. "Perses," I growled. "It has been a while."

"It has." The dark-skinned Titan raised his hands as he

followed my movements with his all-black gaze. "I'm not here to make war."

Keeping my gaze trained on him, I stalked around the fallen tree and stood beside Aiden. His audible inhale when he saw the condition she was in sent nails drilling straight into my spine.

"I'm helping you." Perses lowered his hands slowly. "They had her warded. I figured that since you're now a . . . god," he sneered, "you'd been trying to sense her out. She needed to be removed from the wards for that to happen. This was the second time I brought her out. You're lucky."

"I am?" I said.

"I wouldn't have been able to get her out a third time," he added.

"Why?" Aiden demanded. "Why would you help her?"

I didn't care why he'd done it.

"You freed me from my imprisonment," Perses answered. "I figured I owed you. My brethren will not know how she escaped. It doesn't matter. They'll find the other demigods."

My gaze roamed over Josie's face, committing to memory the bruises, the torn red skin just under her bottom lip, the deep blue hues under both eyes. I saw the bite mark on her wrist. The torn skin on her upper arm. The *fucking* fingerprints on her jaw and throat, the contusions along her arms, the ragged and frayed soles of her feet. I felt her in my arms, knowing she'd lost too much weight in a short time to not have been starved.

This was my fault.

"And I figured that in the upcoming battle, because there will inevitably be one, you'll remember this," Perses added, speaking directly to me. "You'll remember what I've done for you."

"Of course," Aiden murmured. He touched my arm. "We

should go."

I didn't move. "Who did this to her?"

"Mostly Hyperion. He had her for a while." Perses folded his arms across his chest. "Then she was brought to Cronus."

"And?" I queried quietly.

Aiden shifted beside me as Perses said, "He fed on her. She screamed your name the entire time."

"Hell," Aiden muttered.

A black gulf opened up inside me, and there was nothing, nothing but icy, endless rage. And it was different this time. Akasha threaded itself within my fury. Slowly, I lifted my gaze. "You were there?"

"I held her down." Perses shrugged one shoulder. "I had no choice. I brought her out as soon as I could so you could find her."

Turning to Aiden, I said, "Take her."

Jaw clenched into a hard line, Aiden took her without question, holding her close to his chest. Then I turned back to the Titan I'd once helped free, the Titan who brought Josie out so I could find her.

"Thank you," I said, and then I summoned the purest power in me. The world tinted in bright whitish-amber light.

Perses opened his mouth, but it was too late. Throwing up my right arm, I let it go. The bolt caught him in the chest. His mouth opened, but there was no sound as shimmery blue liquid poured out. A network of veins appeared under his skin, lit white and gold. There was a loud pop and a flash of light. Then Perses was no more.

Only a scorched patch of earth remained.

15

Every so often, Josie's fingers would twitch or her brow would crease as if she were haunted by bad dreams. Her breaths were still shallow but more even. Other than that, Josie hadn't moved.

She hadn't woken up.

Sitting in the chair by the bed I'd placed her in, I hated to even blink, because an irrational part of me believed she'd disappear. She looked so incredibly pale against the dark blue sheets.

Only a few hours had passed since I'd brought her here and placed her in my bed. She was now safe. No one would get through me. No one. I would strike down anyone or anything that sought to do her harm without feeling a second of remorse, but she was in this condition because of my decisions—*my* choices.

Truthfully, it wasn't like I thought Josie couldn't defend herself. Josie was no damsel in distress. I'd seen her in battle. She held her own when we fought Atlas, but in the end, Josie was a demigod and they were Titans.

And I was a god.

When Alex had said that they'd fought Hyperion, I knew beyond a doubt that Josie had done everything in her power to fend him off. Her capture was not a representation of her weakness, just as my ability to keep her safe now wasn't a slam against her.

I just needed her to open her eyes.

Since she was a demigod, I figured she'd heal quickly. Even halfs healed faster than mortals, but I knew she'd been fed on. Gods only knew how many times. I could barely sense the aether in her, and that terrified me. Daimons were created when the aether had been drained from them. Could that happen with demigods? All the knowledge that resided deep inside me and I still had no useful answers.

My gaze roamed over her still body. She was absolutely filthy, but she was the most beautiful woman I'd ever seen. I'd wanted to bathe her, strip her out of the soiled clothing and wash her hair, erase the grimy dirt and the musty scent clinging to her, but I didn't want to disturb her. Other than trying to remove the bracelets, which I hadn't been able to do, and checking for more serious injuries, I'd left her alone, wary of even holding her hand, because it too was bruised.

"Come on, Josie. Open your eyes," I whispered to her. "Just open your eyes."

There was no response. Just like when I called for her father, and yeah, how screwed up was that? I'd actually tried to summon Apollo once more, and he did not come. How can he not know by now what had happened to her—what kind of condition she was in? Was he not checking in on his daughter at all? Like all the times before when I tried to sense Apollo and where he might be, there was nothing.

I was going to end that bastard.

Weary, I smoothed my hand over my face. Exhaustion had carved itself into my bones. I needed to feed. My control was shaky. I felt like a nuke about to explode.

Footsteps drew close and there was a soft knock on the

closed door. Rising, I walked over and opened it.

Alex stood in the hall. Her gaze immediately drifted over my shoulder. "How is she?"

I stepped aside. "She hasn't woken up yet."

"May I?" Alex asked, which was surprising, because she was more likely to act first and then ask permission, but I nodded nonetheless. She went to the foot of the bed, her lips pressing into a thin line. "Gods."

Returning to my seat, I scratched a hand through my hair. "I . . ." I could feel Alex's gaze on me. A punch of helplessness hit my chest. "I don't know what to do—how to help her."

"Being here with her is all you can do right now."

I dropped my hand to my lap. "Yeah, and what is that accomplishing?"

"She'll wake up, Seth. She has to."

Looking at her now, I wasn't so sure about that. If she was mortal, I seriously doubted that she'd be alive right now. My stomach twisted. "Have you seen bracelets like these before?" I gestured at Josie's wrists. "I don't see how they come on or off."

She frowned. "No. She didn't have them on before."

I had a really bad feeling about these bracelets. "I tried summoning Apollo."

Alex sighed heavily. "So did I."

I shot her a surprised look.

"I wasn't sure if you would—or if he'd answer you—so I called for him as soon as Aiden told me what kind of . . . well, how she was."

And he hadn't even answered Alex, his fucking chosen one? Yeah, he was done, so *done*.

Silence filled the room, and then I said what kept cycling over and over in my head, "Perses said she screamed my name when . . . when Cronus fed on her."

Alex stared at me.

"He said that Hyperion had been feeding on her. That he had her for a while." My jaw clenched. "He hates Apollo—hates him enough to really hurt Josie to get to him, and I thought . . . I thought I heard her calling for me a couple of days ago. Thought it was my imagination," I said. "Do you think it was her? That I was hearing her?"

She sat down on the bench pressed up against the foot of the bed. "I don't know."

"If it was really her?" My voice turned hoarse as I leaned over, my hand hovering above her cheek. "I didn't answer. I didn't stop any of this. She called for me and I didn't *answer*."

"But you wouldn't have been able to," Alex reasoned. "Not until Perses moved her outside their wards."

"I didn't even know she'd been taken. She spent all this time with—with gods know what being done to her, and I was here." Disgust . . . disgust for myself boiled deep. "I can't forget that."

Alex didn't respond for a long moment. "You love her." There was a hint of surprise in her voice. "You really are in love with her."

I coughed out a harsh, dry laugh as I leaned back against the chair. "You sound so shocked. Like I'm incapable of feeling such an emotion."

"No. I don't think that at all, but you . . ."

I raised a brow and waited.

A distant look crept into her features. "I asked you once if you'd loved anybody and you said to me, 'does loving yourself count?'"

I grinned a little at that.

Alex smiled too. "You're not the same guy. I know I keep saying that, but you really aren't. I think I said this before, but I'm going to say it again. I'm happy for you."

Oh hell. I stiffened, and the slight grin slipped from my face. "Alex—"

"You deserve happiness. You deserve someone like Josie." Her whiskey-colored eyes met mine. "I really mean that."

I held her gaze for a moment and then refocused on Josie. "And look what my love has done. I left her unprotected. I thought I was protecting her by leaving. I thought—it doesn't matter what I thought. In the end, I wasn't there for her."

"Seth," she said quietly. "You can't blame yourself for this. Don't go down that road. Actually, you've been going down that road for a long time now. You need to get off the 'I'm at fault for everything' road."

I really had no response to that.

Alex was quiet for a few moments. "What are you going to do now?"

"About what?" The possibilities of what she could be referencing were limitless.

She drew one leg up and planted her foot on the bench. "You love her. You've been in love with her, but you left her, and you kind of ended stuff with her before, right? When Aiden and I came up from the Underworld, you two weren't together. So you've kind of left her twice already."

"It's actually been three times, if I'm counting," I admitted, wanting to punch myself. "I've left her three times, and it still hasn't changed how I feel about her. If anything, what I feel has only gotten stronger."

"Well, that's how love works, dumbass."

I slid her an arched look. "You really going to talk to me like that, knowing what I am?"

"Do I really look like I'm scared of you just because you're a god now? You're still a dumbass. Obviously. You love her and you leave her. Over and over. It's like the definition of insanity, you know? Doing the same thing over and over and expecting different results."

My eyes narrowed.

"She's here," Alex pointed out the obvious. "And she really was planning to come to you, to prove how she felt about you—how much she loved you. She was going to fight for you. She was ready." She paused, appearing to let that sink in. "What are you going to do about that now?"

What was I going to do? Before I'd learned Hyperion had taken her, I'd planned on staying away, even once I learned what I was, why I'd always been drawn to aether in the first place, and the fact it appeared that I could control the need for it. But after I'd found out that Hyperion had her, I'd planned on bringing her here, but I hadn't thought beyond that or acknowledged that her presence was simply too much of a temptation for me to resist.

"I'm not good for her," I bit the words out.

She lifted her brows. "Then try *being* good for her. Have you ever thought about that? You know, fighting yourself to be with her?"

I opened my mouth.

Alex continued, "Love means you're going to be there for each other even when it sucks. Love means you're going to have each other's back and trust that the other person will be there for you. What you're doing isn't love. As soon as the shit hits the fan for you, you up and leave. You shut down and push her away. That's not the Seth I know."

Every muscle in my back stiffened. "Okay. First off, you're starting to piss me off. And secondly, do you really want me to be the Seth you used to know?"

"First off, I don't care." Her head cocked to the side. "And secondly, the Seth I used to know didn't run from anything that was difficult, even when he was super duper wrong. You need to man up, Seth."

My right hand curled into a fist as I stared at her in disbelief. "Did you seriously just tell me to man up?"

"Yeah." Alex shrugged. "And I'll say it again. Man. Up."

"Gods," I muttered, shaking my head. "Don't you have something to do? Like go annoy Aiden?"

"Nope." She paused. "Do you really think you can seriously let her go?"

My gaze fell back to Josie. She hadn't moved once during the conversation and that scared the shit out of me. Slowly, I leaned forward and placed my hand over hers. A jolt traveled up my arm and I inhaled sharply. Truth was, if Hyperion had never gotten her and she made her way here, I would've tried to resist her.

And I would've failed.

Because I did love her.

And if Hyperion hadn't taken her, and if I'd found her at the Covenant or on her way to find a demigod or on her way here, I wouldn't have been able to leave again. Because I loved her.

"No," I admitted in a low voice, drawing her limp hand to my mouth. I pressed a kiss to her palm. "Even if we weren't together, I wouldn't be able to let her go."

"Then maybe you should be with her then," she said. "Hell. Maybe you're too late. You _have_ pushed her away three times, according to you."

Unease exploded in my gut. The mere idea of Josie not wanting to be with me had never occurred to me. Yeah, that sounded arrogant as shit. I lifted my gaze from Josie and stared at Alex.

She grinned. "I had to point that out, but Josie loves you. She'll probably forgive you for leaving, but you can't keep doing that. You understand that, right? You can't, because eventually it's not going to be okay. You can't keep doing that to someone and not *ruin* them."

Fuck.

Alex was right, though. I'd told myself once that I would be the kind of man Josie deserved, even when we didn't have a future to speak of, but the first moment I felt out of control, I bailed on her. I did so to protect her, but I'd ended up doing the opposite.

The need for her, all that wanting, was endless, and it pounded through me relentlessly. There was no fighting it. I could leave a million times, but I would always come back. The truth of that would've swept my legs right out from under me if I wasn't sitting already.

And now we could have a future. We could have forever, and I could be the man she so rightly deserved.

That is, if she would have me.

Because I had pushed her away on multiple occasions and a person could only take that so many times.

But I could be awfully convincing when I wanted to be.

Kissing both sides of her hand, I gently laid her arm back down. I didn't answer Alex's question, but I think she got it. I think she understood.

"Aiden said you killed Perses," she said after a moment, changing the subject.

"He held her down while she screamed during the feedings. He was not going to survive that."

"Understandable. I think you did the right thing, but I'm guessing there might be some kind of earthly repercussions involved."

I shrugged one shoulder. "Were you pissed that we went to get her without you?"

She snorted. "A little. If something had happened, I would've had no idea."

"Nothing would've happened," I reassured her. "Not with me there."

"Yeah, you don't sound cocky at all."

"It's not cockiness. It's the truth and—" I halted when Josie's fingers moved restlessly at her side. Leaning forward, I held my breath and waited and hoped she'd open her eyes. When she inevitably didn't, I slumped back in the chair. I sighed. "Where is your shadow?"

"He's asleep."

"Shouldn't you be with him?" I paused. "Hint. Hint."

"Ha. I'm right where I'm supposed to be."

My gaze found hers, and yeah, once again, it was weird, the two of us sitting here after everything we'd been through. That she would be here for me, with Aiden asleep and not hovering over her after what I had put her through—what I'd done to them.

Alex smiled.

And it hit me then, almost doubled me over, that Alex truly forgave me. She really had, and I didn't know what to do with that forgiveness, how to process any of that. I cleared my throat.

Luckily there was another quiet knock on the door, so I didn't have to figure out how to respond.

Alex popped up from the bench and went to the door, opening it. Karina stepped inside the bedroom as she nodded at Alex. "I'm sorry to interrupt, Kýrios, but it is time."

Alex raised her brows at the word "Kýrios."

I knew what she meant. "Later."

"I'm sorry, Kýrios, but I do not think it would be wise to wait." The high priestess looked pointedly at Josie.

"He needs to be here with Josie," Alex said, folding her arms. Her eyes were narrowed in a way that said she was contemplating body-slamming Karina through a wall.

Exhaling roughly, I hated to do it, but Karina was right. Waiting wouldn't end well, and I needed to be fully charged for whatever might come this way.

"Stay with her," I said to Alex, rising tiredly. "Please."

Alex snapped her mouth shut and nodded as she eyed Karina distrustfully. I was going to have to explain all of that. Eventually. Karina backed out of the room and waited. I followed, closing the door behind me.

Josie

Waking up was like fighting through quicksand laced with sleep aids. I knew I needed to open my eyes. I thought I heard Seth begging me to do so, but that was crazy, because Seth wasn't here. I was in hell, waiting for Hyperion to bring me back to Cronus. Or was it Perses? Hadn't I seen Perses? I couldn't remember.

The cement floor felt . . . soft and warm.

I drew in a deep breath. The smell? I didn't immediately choke on the dank, musty scent. A tremble coursed through my body, and I thought I heard people speaking, voices I recognized.

Kýrios?

Master?

I seriously needed to open my eyes. Calling on every ounce of strength I had, I forced my eyes open. Well, one eye open. The right one kind of only cracked open. It was nearly swollen shut. I wasn't sure how that happened. The last time Hyperion had brought me out of that warehouse had been a blur. He'd fed on me before I was brought to Cronus, and they . . . it felt like they had taken too much.

Like they might've broken something.

My vision focused and I slowly realized I was lying on a bed—a huge, comfy bed, and I was staring up at a beige ceiling fashioned. There was a large ceiling fan gliding through the air silently, its blades shaped like petals.

Throat impossibly dry, I dragged my gaze from the ceiling to the foot of the bed. A girl stood with her back to me, arms crossed, staring at the closed bedroom door.

My heart started pumping. Could that be . . . ? I tried to get my tongue to work. Was I dreaming? Oh gods, if I was dreaming I wouldn't survive this once I woke up. I wouldn't be able to. I tried to speak again.

"Alex?" I croaked out.

She whipped around, her eyes widening with relief. "Josie!" She raced to the side of the bed, squeezing in between an empty chair and the bed.

"Is . . . is this a dream?" I rasped.

Her beautiful face contorted. "No. This is not a dream. You're safe."

Safe?

"Oh my gods, you're really awake." She practically shook like she was holding herself back from crawling on top of me. "How are you feeling?"

"I . . ." Mouth dry, I looked around the room in confusion. My hand floated to my throat and I winced.

Alex drew back from the bed. "Are you thirsty? Let me grab you something." She whirled and darted out of my line of sight. A second later she returned with a bottle of water, lid unscrewed. "Here, let me help you."

My body ached as she helped me sit. I planted my hand on the bed to hold myself up while she shoved a tiny mountain of pillows behind me. I eased back as she brought the bottle to my mouth. The first taste of the cool liquid on my tongue forced a moan out of my mouth, but it wasn't enough. It felt like a few drops.

I lifted my arm, cringing as pain shot down my side, but I wrapped my hand around the bottle, forcing it higher. More glorious water passed between my parched lips.

"Slowly," Alex eased the bottle out of my death grip. "You should probably drink this slowly."

She was right, but I hadn't had real water in *days*. My hand shook as I held onto the bottle just above her hand. Her lips pressed together and then she let me have another gulp. We went back and forth for a couple of minutes until there was no water left.

Alex lowered the bottle. "Oh my gods, we've been so worried."

I wanted more water, but my stomach felt weird. "You . . . Everyone okay?"

Her brows flew up. "My gods, we're fine. All of us. You shouldn't be worried about us."

There were so many questions, but my brain felt like it was full of cobwebs, and when I looked down at myself, I saw I was still wearing the same disgusting clothing. "Where . . . where am I?"

"Seth's house."

I jerked—my entire body painfully jolted. "Seth—Seth's here?"

"Yeah," She glanced at the closed door. "He actually just stepped out of the room. He's been sitting here with you. He went and got you—"

I started moving before she finished talking. Seth—I had to get to him. He was *here*. Pushing past the pain, I slid off the other side of the bed. The moment my sore feet hit the ground, I groaned. My legs gave and I fell, knees cracking off the floor.

"Josie!" Alex was by my side, bending down and wrapping an arm around my waist.

"I'm fine." I gritted my teeth as she helped me stand. "I need to see him."

"He'll be back shortly." She tried to guide me toward the bed. "I think you should wait for him."

Using everything I had, I pulled away from her and lurched across the floor, feet slipping. I reached the door, out of breath, and only managed to pull it open a few feet. Squeezing out, my wild gaze swung up and down a wide hallway. I caught glimpses of leafy plants and marble statues.

I heard Alex call my name.

Guided by some kind of primal instinct, I stumbled down the hall toward the gently rolling white curtains. I knew Alex was following me, but I didn't stop as I reached the archway that led outside. The scent of the sea grew strong, salt mixing with something sweet. Flowers? I wasn't sure, but it smelled nothing like the warehouse. The air was fresh here, clean and breathable.

Legs weak and trembling, I sort of wanted to lie down in the hallway, but Seth was here, and I needed him—*needed* to see him. I forced my legs to move even as tears of pain stung my eyes.

Placing my hand on the wall, I shuffled through the archway and out onto the balcony. Time seemed to slow down as I looked left and then right. That was when time stopped.

Just stopped.

I found Seth.

At first, I was struck immobile by the simple fact that I could see him. It felt like an eternity had passed since I laid eyes on him. Beautiful seemed like a silly word to describe him, but it was all I could think of, except he was more beautiful than I remembered.

His hair was the color of the sun, unruly and growing out, falling across a flawless forehead. Broad, high cheekbones. Strong jaw cut like marble. Skin golden. A face and body that had been perfectly sculpted. He was wearing dark jeans and a fitted gray shirt.

I could see his glyphs.

Stunning amber runes endlessly churned over every inch of exposed flesh. It was rare to see them.

He wasn't alone.

Oh gods, he was so not alone, not at all, and I thought for a moment that I hadn't truly woken up. I was having a nightmare, because Seth was embracing another woman.

16

My heart pounded painfully against my ribs as I stared at the man I loved—the man I was *in* love with—standing close, too close to another woman. And his hands were on her. One gripped the woman's small shoulder. The other was just below her breasts. Their eyes were closed, and the woman's tensed expression looked like she was in the throes of a—

Oh *gods*.

I tried to process what I was seeing. There was a part of me that recognized what was happening, but my thoughts were barely making any sense. One bounced off the other, and I couldn't grasp onto any of them.

This, after everything else, was too much.

Stumbling back, I threw my arm out, stopping myself from sliding down the wall like I was in the midst of a complete breakdown. Maybe I was, because I couldn't stop the gasp of surprise that sounded like thunder on the otherwise quiet balcony.

Seth's entire body jerked. He wheeled around and those beautiful amber eyes went wide when he spotted me.

Alex appeared beside me, and anger rolled off her in waves, but he wasn't looking at her. He was staring at me like he'd seen a ghost rise from a grave, like there was a part of him that never expected to see me again, and perhaps that was true, because he had left me.

And I guessed that did mean he hadn't expected to see me again.

Seth took a step toward me, the beautiful woman in the spun gold gown apparently forgotten. "Josie?"

The sound of his voice, my name spoken so hoarsely, was an explosion to my senses. This was real—all of this was real. My gaze darted between him and the woman. She smiled as she clasped her hands together. I sucked in a sharp breath.

I was suddenly on the move, unsure of what I was doing or where I was going. All I knew was I needed to be far away from right there. I needed a place to think, to straighten out the twisty thoughts and swamping emotions.

"Really?" I heard Alex say, disbelief dripping off her tone. "After everything we just talked about? Seriously?"

"Not right now," Seth snapped back, and I had no idea what they were talking about. "Josie," he called again. "Wait."

Turning, I stumbled back inside, each step as painful as the last. My breath was coming in pants. Tiny bursts of light dotted my vision. I squeezed my eyes shut as a wave of dizziness assaulted me.

"Josie." His voice was closer, and I stopped moving because I was seriously winded and needed a break. Walking was hard, but hearing his voice right then, that slight accent I could never place, was even harder. "Alex," I heard him say. "Can you give us some space?"

"I don't know if I want to give you space right now," she spat.

Gods, she'd seen him with that—that woman. Despite everything going through my head and everything that had happened to me, I felt my cheeks burn with embarrassment. I had no idea what was happening.

"Alex." His voice dropped low with a warning. "Go find something to do."

"Are you okay with me leaving, Josie?" she asked, and I wanted to disappear into the bushy potted plants. "Because if not, I'll make Douche Canoe over here disappear."

Seth let out an aggravated breath, and I opened my eyes. I could only look at Alex. Her face was flushed with anger, and I had a suspicion she would gladly throw down with him.

"I'm . . . I'm okay," I managed to say. "It's okay."

She hesitated, shooting one last glare in Seth's direction. "You're a dumbass—such a fucking dumbass." Turning to me, she gave a faint smile. "I'll check in on you later."

"Okay," I whispered, almost wishing I hadn't sent her away, because she was stalking off down the hall, and now Seth and I were alone. It was strange, because before Hyperion came, before I saw him outside, I'd wanted nothing more than to be alone with Seth.

"I can explain," Seth said after a moment.

An unbelieving hoarse laugh shook me. That was possibly the most incredibly cliché thing I'd ever heard.

"I know how that looked, but whatever you're thinking, you're wrong," he continued, and I heard him step closer. My gaze flew to his chest. "And I will explain everything to you, but right now is not the time."

I leaned against the wall, beside a statue of some dude missing half his arm. My head was spinning. I wasn't sure how Seth could explain away whatever had happened out there. She, whoever she was, was stunning and beautiful, and I was vomit-inducing disgusting at the moment. Covered in dirt and filth and dried blood, and who knew what else.

"I want to take you back to bed." He moved closer, reaching

for me.

"No." I held a weak, shaky arm up.

Seth stopped, and slowly, I finally lifted my gaze to his. The glyphs were gone. A muscle tapped along his jaw, but otherwise, his expression was void of any and all emotion. My heart squeezed. I'd seen that look before on him. Too many times before. "Josie, please let me help you."

He wanted to help me and there was nothing wrong with that. Right? My gaze dropped to my hand. A frown pulled at my lips. My fingers were covered with dirt, stained with blood. My arm was the same. Only patches of skin were clean, and that was really stretching the definition of clean. And those bracelets. Those damn bracelets were still secured firmly around my wrists.

"I . . . I need to shower." The moment I said those words, I knew how ridiculous they sounded, because even fresh and clean, I didn't look like *that* and a shower wasn't going to fix a damn thing that had gone wrong right now, but I still wanted to wash the dirt and the blood off.

His brows snapped together. "Let me take you back to bed. Have you eaten?"

Running a hand along the clammy skin of my arm, I shook my head when my fingers reached one of the bracelets. "I don't . . . remember the last time."

The empty stare disappeared. Something akin to grief twisted his striking features. "Then please, *please* let me get something for you to eat first."

Swallowing against the lump in my throat, I thought food would go a long way in easing the hollowed feeling in my stomach, but I needed a shower. "I just need to . . . to get clean first."

His eyes widened as his body jolted once more, and he opened his mouth to speak but seemed at a loss of what to say.

Then his chest rose sharply. "Okay. I'll help you."

I pushed away from the wall. "I can do it. I just need to . . . know where a bathroom is."

"Josie, stop. You can barely stand up." He reached out again, and this time he didn't stop. He carefully wrapped his hands around my upper arms. I winced and wasn't sure if it was because his touch hurt or because he was touching me. "Please let me help you."

We stood nearly toe-to-toe in silence. I was staring at his throat this time, and it was . . . was like we were suddenly two strangers. Two people who had split in life and gone in two very different directions, unexpectedly brought back together.

"I'm *going* to help you," Seth said after a moment. "There is no way that's not going to happen."

Too weak to really fight him on this, I nodded, and Seth moved so fast, I had no idea how I ended up in his arms, cradled to his chest, my cheek resting on his shoulder, and my heart went through the juice grinder again. There were so many times while I was held by Hyperion that I'd feared I'd never be in Seth's arms again, and now I was.

And he'd been holding someone else *minutes* ago.

Tears pricked the lids of my eyes. There was so much to worry about and so many things to cry and stress over, and now . . . now this.

He was striding down the hall and we were back in the bedroom within a blink of an eye.

Seth walked to a set of double doors across from the bed and nudged them open with his booted foot. He was quiet as he set me down on the rim of a tub that was the size of a small swimming pool. "Shower or bath?" he asked quietly.

Looking around the opulent bathroom, I felt sorely out of place among the white marble and lush, hanging bath towels.

"This . . . this is your home now?"

"It's where I grew up." Seth knelt in front of me, drawing my attention. There was no missing the fact he didn't refer to it as his home. "This used to be one of the guest bedrooms and baths."

Holy crap, what did the master bedroom look like then?

"Do you want me to draw a bath or a shower?" he repeated gently.

Soaking in a bath sounded wonderful, but the water would be so gross after a second of me being in there. "Shower."

Seth held my gaze for a moment and then rose swiftly. Turning, he walked over to an enclosed, step-down shower. There was no curtain, but with the high wall around it, there was no need. Well, for most people. I would most likely flood the bathroom.

As he turned on the water and the overhead rainfall shower came to life, it really began to sink in that I was free. That I wasn't going to wake up and find Hyperion looming over me. I wasn't going to be forced into another room. I didn't have to fight back every waking second. A shudder worked its way through me, and a small moan escaped.

"You okay?" Seth was immediately kneeling in front of me again, his hands on my knees. "Josie?"

"Yeah," I whispered, clearing my throat. "I'm just . . ." I was a lot of things. Scared. Sore. Confused. Relieved. Hurting. Exhausted. My heart felt like it had broken a thousand times in a span of a few days.

"That's not true. It was a stupid question for me to ask." Seth placed the tips of his fingers on my cheek. "I wish I could take the pain away. I would do anything to do that for you."

My breath caught. He sounded so genuine, but what was he doing out there? This whole time? How did I get here? Did he fight the Titans and free me? I had so many questions, but I didn't have the will to ask them at the moment.

I could only say, "You left me."

Seth's eyes slammed shut and he dropped his hand. Steam filled up the bathroom. He lowered his head until his chin almost touched my knee. "I know. Saying I'm sorry is never going to change that or what happened to you, but I am." His lashes lifted and he peered up at me through them, and his eyes looked oddly moist. "I have never been more sorry about anything in my life."

The twisting motion in my chest increased as I croaked out, "I need to shower."

Seth went as still as one of the statues out in the hall and then he exhaled unevenly. "Can you stand in there?"

It wasn't going to be easy, but I wasn't sure I could handle Seth helping me. Yeah, he'd seen *all of this* before, but I . . . I just couldn't. "I can."

He didn't look like he believed me, but he touched me again. Just the tips of his fingers against my cheek, and I fought the urge to press against his touch. "You're safe here. You will be safe from here on out."

There was the word again. *Safe.* That word rang as a falsehood, because if I had learned anything about my time with the Titans, no one was safe anywhere, but I nodded anyway.

Seth stared at me for a few more seconds. "I'll be waiting outside. If you need anything, call for me."

He lingered and then dropped his hand. He rose and left the bathroom, leaving the door cracked open so he could obviously hear me if I busted my ass, which was entirely possible.

I sat on the bathtub for a couple of minutes and then I got down to the painful process of stripping out of my disgusting clothes. I left them on the floor, never wanting to see them again as I walked toward the shower, moving like I was ninety years old and passing a fogged mirror on the way.

I couldn't make out much of how I looked, but I could see enough to know I was an utter mess.

Clutching the half-wall of the shower, I stepped in and under the warm stream of water. I gasped as the water hit my skin. My body simultaneously rejoiced and recoiled. Raw areas stung and burned like a thousand fire ants were gnawing on my skin, but I stayed under the stream, lifting my face up. The water washed away days of grime and dried blood as my knees wobbled.

It could be worse.

Those were the words I repeated over and over as I looked down and grabbed a bottle of shampoo. Pink and brown-tinted water swirled along the basin, cycling down the drain. It took two shampoos, one round of conditioner, and a complete, achy body scrub down for the water to run clear.

And I still stood under the shower, picking at the dirt under my fingernails, and when my nails were clean I washed myself once more. I soaped up my wrists and tried to work the bracelets off until my skin was red and hurt, and only then did I give up. The bathroom smelled like a botanical garden by that point.

I didn't allow myself to think through the whole process. Not until I was reaching for the faucets did the first real thought break through the haze and the simple joy of being clean again.

My mom was dead.

She was truly gone.

Through the whole time I was with Hyperion, I couldn't let myself think too much about, but now that I was here, I could see her face, the almost always distant glaze to her eyes, the sweet smile on her lips.

There would be no saving her.

No more looking forward to seeing her.

My father had lied and he had left me to rot with Hyperion, and I *had* rotted, from the inside out. The pain. The darkness. The constant fear. I'd lived in that for days and days, and it was still inside me, still haunting every breath.

And now I was here. I was with Seth. I was where I'd planned to be before I learned about my mother and before Hyperion had taken me, and it was all *wrong*. That had not been the reunion I'd anticipated, the one that had helped me keep my sanity in the long, dark hours trapped underground. It had just been *wrong*.

Clapping my hands over my face, I stepped back until I hit the cool tile wall. I slid down and curled into myself, drawing my knees to my chest. The position hurt. Tugged on raw skin. Pressed on bruised areas, but the tears started and it was like a floodgate opening up as I buried my face between my knees.

I don't know how long I sat in the corner of the shower. It could've been minutes or hours, but the tears didn't stop, and I couldn't move—couldn't force myself past all the pain and fear that festered inside me, the all-consuming, sucktastic realization that I was *weak*. I wasn't like Alex.

If I were stronger, I wouldn't be sitting here, in the shower, sobbing like a kid who didn't have anyone show up for their birthday party. If I had my shit together, I would already be out of this shower, ready to talk about what I saw, what I knew.

But I couldn't move.

Couldn't get my brain past any of this.

I was broken, truly, utterly broken inside, and the panic building in the back of my throat told me there was possibly no chance of fixing that, because I knew only I could repair this, and I wasn't sure I had it in me to do so.

Or maybe I did.

Maybe once I got all this messy emotion out of me, I could piece myself back together, because I had to. I knew I did, but right now, right this very second, I couldn't.

So caught up in my own head, I hadn't heard the door open or Seth call my name, but I suddenly heard his curse rip through the air. A few seconds later, the water turned off and then he was climbing in the shower, fully clothed, wrapping a fluffy, warm towel over my shoulders.

I lifted my head, barely able to see him through the tears. "My mom is dead."

He said something too low for me to make out, and then he was pulling me toward him. I was half in his lap, my legs between his, and water dripped off me, soaking through his jeans and shirt.

Seth didn't seem to notice. He wrapped his arms around me, holding me as tight as he could without squeezing me as I buried my face against his chest. One of his hands delved deep in the wet mess of my hair.

"It'll be okay," Seth said, his lips moved against my forehead, and he kept saying it, over and over, but the last time he'd held me and said that, it had been a lie.

17

*W*hen the tears ebbed and then stopped, all of the tension seemed to fade from Josie. Her body went limp in my arms. She was asleep, completely out of it.

Concern spiked when I lifted her and rose, and she made no sound or movement. She'd been unconscious when I brought her here and had only been awake for about an hour. Then again, unconsciousness was not the same as restful sleep, and I still had no idea what she'd gone through.

And why wasn't she healing?

Those damn bracelets drew my attention as I stepped out of the shower, my jeans now wet and clinging to my skin.

I shifted her in my arms, and the towel parted. Because I was the worst kind of asshole at the moment, I didn't look away quick enough to not catch a glimpse of the soft swell of her breast and a rosy peak. Lust punched straight through me, and the walk to the bed was not a comfortable one.

Using the element of air, I willed the blanket back and then laid her down, resting her head on the soft pillow. As I started to pull away, her hand fisted the front of my shirt. My gaze flew to her face. She was still asleep, but obviously, even dead to the world, she didn't want to be alone.

I couldn't refuse her.

Gently prying her fingers off my shirt, I stepped back from the bed and stripped off the wet shirt. The jeans went next. I grabbed a pair of loose sweats and pulled them on and then climbed into bed beside her. Josie was shivering from head to toe. I didn't think about what I was doing. I circled an arm around her waist and as carefully as possible, I drew her against my chest. She made a soft little sound, her lips brushed my chest, and that was all.

Josie slept.

And I held her.

I held her as I thought about everything Alex and I had talked about. I held her as I replayed the moment I'd turned around and seen Josie, my beautiful Josie standing on the balcony with a look of horror and confusion in her sea-colored eyes. I held her as I saw her curled up in the corner of the shower, her entire body shaking with her sobs, and it killed me. Sliced right through, cutting me wide open, to know I wasn't there for her when she learned her mother had died or that I hadn't been able to protect her from Hyperion. I'd made so many mistakes, countless ones. I did not do right by her.

But I was going to be here for her now.

Smoothing a hand over her wet hair, I brushed the strands back from her face. The bruises stood out starkly against her pale skin. Rage caused my hand to tremble as I tugged the comforter up to her shoulders.

Alex was probably going to cut off my balls the next time I saw her. Well, that was only if she got to mc before Josie was back to . . . to herself.

Gods.

Of all the moments for Josie to wake up and find her way outside, it had to be right then. First, I needed to explain to her what she saw outside. Then I'd explain it to Alex, but I wasn't sure how Josie could accept this—accept this new reality.

Josie

When I opened my eyes, I didn't know where I was.

The room was dark and I was lying on something soft, which didn't make any sense to me, and—oh my *gods*, I was naked under a sheet. I was on a bed and I was *naked*. A hundred horrible fears poisoned my brain. Had Hyperion—? I couldn't even finish the thought. My heart leapt into my throat as I realized my arm was resting against a hard, warm surface that felt an awful lot like a chest.

Panic exploded like buckshot racing through every cell. My body moved before I could slow down and process anything. Jackknifing off the bed, pain flared all across my body as I threw my legs off the bed. I toppled forward, my knees cracking off the stone floor. Eyes wide, I scanned the dark room as my heart thundered in my chest. *Where am I? What is happening?* The form on the bed—the body on the bed—moved, sitting up.

I scuttled across the floor, my palms slipping off the smooth stone. A scream built in my throat, but I couldn't get enough air in my lungs.

"Josie?"

Stilling at the sound of the voice, I drew my knees up. I *knew* that voice. Seth. It was his—that deep voice that was musical in quality, slightly accented. But that didn't make sense, because how could I be here with Seth? Unless everything had been a nightmare—no, no what had happened wasn't a nightmare. It had been real.

The shape on the bed suddenly moved closer. Feet landed on the floor and took a step toward me. A strangled sound left me as fear overrode my senses. *I can't do this anymore. I can't do—*

The shape froze. "It's okay, Josie. You're here with me. You're safe."

That voice—it had to be Seth, and I'd heard that word before. *Safe.* Alex had told me that when I . . . when I woke up earlier. I struggled to push the cobwebs of sleep and confusion aside.

"Seth?" I whispered.

"Yes. It's me. It's just me and you in here. I'm going to turn on the light. Okay?" he asked, and when I didn't respond, he turned. I heard a click a few seconds later, and buttery soft light flooded the room. No longer in the darkness, the events of the last couple of hours rushed to the surface.

Seth stood in front of the bed, his arms at his sides. He was bare-chested and was wearing a pair of loose sweats. Blond hair fell in a mess of waves over his forehead and curled over the tips of his ears.

I *remembered.*

He'd found me in the shower and he held me while I cried. I wasn't in that horrible room anymore. I wasn't being dragged from the dank cellar to serve as a battery pack for Hyperion or Cronus. I was here with Seth. I remembered seeing him outside on a balcony, embracing another woman.

Sucking in a shallow breath full of pain, I curled my arms around my knees to try to hide my nudity. Not that Seth hadn't seen it all and then some, but I was uncomfortable and overexposed.

Especially with the way he was staring at me.

His amber gaze roamed over me, and even though most of all the private parts were hidden, I knew he was seeing the network of bruises and red marks—the bites and torn, frayed skin. I knew this because of the way his striking face was tight and drawn. It was in the way he spoke next.

"Josie, babe . . ." Seth's amber eyes glimmered as he crouched in front of me, not coming any closer. "I . . ."

As he trailed off, I squeezed my eyes shut. What was I doing? Other than sitting on his floor naked as the day I was born? My throat felt raw as I forced my tongue to move. "I woke up and I didn't remember where I was. I thought I was still back *there*. I'm . . . I'm sorry."

I didn't hear him move, but my eyes flew open when I felt his hand land gently on my arm. "You do not need to apologize, *psychi mou*."

Psychi mou? Seth had never called me his soul before.

Sorrow filled his brilliant amber gaze. "Let me get you something to wear, okay? And then we'll move on from there. If you want to stay right where you are, we can do that. If you want to go back to the bed, then that's the plan. You let me know what you want to do, and we'll do it."

Glancing down at my bruised knees, I nodded jerkily.

Seth was still for a moment longer and then he rose, stepping around me. I kept my eyes closed until he returned and soft cloth was draped over my shoulders. The last thing I really needed at this moment was to fully process the fact I was naked on the floor with my arms around my knees.

A girl could only take so much.

Forcing my eyes open, I avoided Seth's gaze as I shoved my arms through the sleeves of an unbelievably soft and fluffy robe. He tugged the belt forward and I reached down, gathering the sides of the robe closed.

Seth secured the belt. "What do you want to do now?"

A flush crawled across my cheeks. "The . . . the bed."

Before I had a chance to stand, Seth slipped an arm under my knees and easily lifted me up in the air. In a few heartbeats, he had me back on the bed, propped up against a mountain of pillows. Sitting next to me, he quickly rearranged the bottom of the robe so that it covered my legs.

"Let me get you something to eat," he said.

I shook my head. "I'm not hungry."

His chin tilted to the side. "You said earlier you weren't . . . you weren't sure when the last time you ate was. You need to eat."

"I know," I answered wearily, peering up at him. Seth looked so different to me with his expression full of concern and trepidation. I couldn't remember if I had ever seen him like that before. "I'm just . . . Not right now."

The muscles along his shoulders stiffened. "Josie, you really need to eat something."

Nodding absently, I toyed with the edges of my belt. There was so much floating around in my head, but there was something just out of reach, lingering in the recesses—something important that I needed a reminder about.

"Do you know what woke you up?" Seth asked.

My fingers tightened around the edge of my belt. "I think I was having a nightmare. I thought I was back . . . back there when I woke up." The next breath I took scalded my throat. "And I just freaked out."

"It's okay. And it's totally understandable—" He picked up my hands, sucking in an audible breath. "Josie, your skin is like ice."

Skin like ice.

I withdrew my hands, curling them against my chest. I'd felt skin like that—skin that was cold and didn't feel weird. A memory wiggled free. I'd crawled across a floor on my knees to check the pulse of Lauren—of the bound demigod. She'd been dead. "Oh my *gods*," I whispered, lifting my gaze.

"What?"

"Oh my *gods*," I repeated as more memories resurfaced at a rapid clip. "I saw the demigods—the missing demigods. One of them—her name was Lauren. She was . . . she died while I was there." Horror filled me as I remembered the feel of her skin and her starved, abused body. "They did horrible things to her, Seth. Horrible things and she died—" My voice broke off, and I swallowed hard. "She died in a room with a dirt floor."

"Josie," he said, voice gruff.

"She had to have been starved and beaten. She was covered in dirt and bruises." I had to keep going, because I had to get the words out of me. It was like lancing a blister. "I thought . . . I thought I was going to become her. You know? I mean, she'd been there for months and months. I can't even imagine—" I sucked in a sharp breath as a sound came from the back of Seth's throat. "They left her in the room with us even after she'd died."

"Gods." Pain flickered across Seth's beautiful face as he took my hands again, folding his around mine.

"And when they finally came for her, they . . . She was dragged out of the room. Just dragged across the floor like she was nothing more than a piece of trash." Tears blurred my vision and then my body jolted at the realization. "Mitchell—Mitchell is still there, Seth. We have to get him." I pulled my hands free once more and started to rise from the bed, but Seth blocked me with one strong arm. I turned wide eyes on him. "Mitchell is still there."

"You need to keep sitting." Seth's voice was too level, too calm.

I stared at him. Keep sitting? "You don't understand. We have to go back and get him. Seth, he was in bad shape, and I hadn't seen him in—I don't know how much time passed, but he won't survive much longer."

If he was still alive, but I couldn't bring myself to think that.

Seth gently turned me so that my back was once again flush with the small mountain of pillows. "I get what you're saying, but you're not going back there."

I opened my mouth.

"You are in no shape to go anywhere right now. I'm not saying that to be an ass, but the last thing you need to be doing is roaming around, let alone putting yourself in danger." Those amber eyes seemed to glow. "You need to be right where you are, resting and getting better."

"I'm fine," I denied, my hands balling into fists.

His brows flew up. "Have you seen yourself, Josie? There is barely an inch of skin that isn't bruised. You're exhausted and can barely stand, and I can't feel—" He cut himself off.

"Can't what?"

His gaze searched mine. "I can barely feel any aether in you, Josie."

My stomach churned. "They . . ."

"I know why, Josie. I see the bite marks." Those eyes turned luminous and a jolt of electricity filled the air. "Right now, all you need to be concerned with is getting better. That is all. Please."

A couple of moments passed before I could speak. "I can't just sit here and pretend that Mitchell doesn't exist."

"I'm not asking you to do that."

"Than what are you asking me to do?" Reaching up, I knocked a strand of hair back from my face. "They have him, and trust me, he will not survive much longer."

Seth didn't respond.

"If you won't let me go, then you can go back to where you

found me. You can try to find him and get him—"

"No."

Stunned, I blinked and then drew back. "Please. *Please*. I can't just forget about them—about Mitchell. You can't ask that of me. We have to help him."

A muscle flexed along his jaw. "I don't expect you to forget about him."

"Then you can go and look for him," I argued, ignoring the roiling sensation in my stomach. "You can do that and I can stay here."

"Right now, they have no idea where we are, but we're not warded against Titans or any other god. I'm not leaving you. Not again. You're my number one priority. You are what I'm focused on." His gaze met mine. "You're all that matters."

Frustration rose like a swelling river within me. It mingled with the very real pain that had settled into every joint and muscle, giving way to the terror that still hummed under my skin. "But you already left me!"

Seth flinched as his back stiffened.

I wanted to take back those words, but I couldn't and I couldn't stop what came out of my mouth next. "You left me already. You left me, Seth. So I wasn't all that mattered to you a few weeks ago, so how can I be all that matters to you now?" Needing space, I scooted over. Seth went to block me again, but I shoved his arm away. "Don't."

Something akin to pain flickered across his face as he pulled his arm back. I stumbled off the bed, my skin feeling like it had been stretched too tight. I walked a few feet away and then stopped, standing on trembling legs. I closed my eyes as I tugged the hair back from my face. I wanted to feel bad for saying that to him, but it was true. He left me, and I couldn't just forget about Mitchell. My life wasn't more important than his.

"I deserved that," Seth said, voice low. I opened my eyes, but didn't face him. "I did leave you. And I wasn't there for you when you found out about your mom or when Hyperion came for you. I let you down in the worst possible way. I cannot say I'm sorry enough. I'll never be able to make up for how I failed you."

My throat burned. "You . . . you didn't know what happened."

"That doesn't matter in the end. You needed me and I wasn't there." His voice deepened, turned ragged. "I will never—"

"Don't," I repeated, unsure of what I was asking him to stop. Exhaustion tugged at me, like I hadn't slept in years. Emotionally spent, I was mentally drained as I slowly faced him. Unsteady on my feet, I swayed slightly. My gaze flickered to his. "What is important right now is Mitchell. They still have him, and if we don't do anything, he will die, Seth. We can't let that happen."

His jaw hardened. "I will think of something, Josie. I'm not saying I'm not going to do anything, but until you've healed, I cannot leave you."

"Seth—"

"No." The one word brokered no argument. "You were held captive for days, Josie. You were nearly drained of all your aether. Gods know all of what happened to you there."

"I'll be okay," I said.

You can get mad at me," he said, rising from the bed. He stood like he was prepared to do battle. "You can hate me for this, and I wouldn't blame you, but I will not leave you unprotected again."

18

*J*osie had argued with my decision not to leave her until she gave in to the exhaustion that was clearly etched into every movement and drawn into the shadows under her eyes. She'd made it back to the bed, and as soon as her head hit those pillows, she was out.

I'd laid down beside her, not intending to fall asleep since I was turning over in my mind everything that she'd said. I got why she wanted to rescue this Mitchell—totally understood it— but that didn't mean I was going to leave her. Nothing against Alex or Aiden, but they hadn't been able to stop Hyperion before. They wouldn't be able to do it again.

The Titan could show at any moment.

You already left me.

Her words cut right through me, because it was the cold, harsh truth. I had left her, and she had *suffered*. When she woke earlier, she hadn't even known where she was, and she had thought she'd been in bed with one of those *fuckers*? Gods. The rage burned through me like lava, and the helplessness that I felt was like a bitter poison in my blood.

I would not fail her again.

Hours passed as I sat beside her, and I must've dozed off, because when I opened my eyes, faint sunlight was seeping underneath the heavy curtains and slowly trekking across the stone floors.

Lifting my head, I looked down at Josie. She was still asleep, but some of the color had returned to the unmarred patches of skin. That was good. I had to keep telling myself that, because every time I looked at her, I wanted to blow shit up.

Like, entire countries.

Her hair had fallen back over her cheek, so I took care of that, tucking it behind her ear. I sat up and glanced at the door. Carefully, I eased away from Josie and fixed the blanket as it started to slip off her.

Walking across the bedroom, I cracked open the door, and as I expected, I found Basil waiting outside. He stood between two statues, hands clasped loosely together. Only the gods knew how long he stood out there.

I needed to get him a cellphone or something to pass the time with.

"How is she, Kýrios?"

"Sleeping again." I leaned against the doorframe. "Can you bring up some food? Nothing too heavy. She hasn't . . . she hasn't eaten recently. When she wakes up, I want her to eat." I'd be damned if she refused food again. "I'd get it myself, but I don't want to leave her. I am not hungry, so just food for her."

"Of course." He stepped forward, obviously happy to have something to do. "I will bring up some rice and soup. That should work well."

"Thank you."

Basil smiled brightly, bowed, and then he was off. I stood there for a moment and then closed the door. I turned around.

The air punched out of my lungs like it had earlier when she woke from a nightmare.

Josie was awake.

Not only that, she was sitting up, clutching the blanket to her chest. Her eyes were wide, and there was a faint flush of pink on her unbruised cheek. Her gaze was on my face and then it dropped to my bare chest and stomach. The pink in her cheeks heightened. This time was nothing like the last time she woke up.

Relief almost cut my knees out from underneath me, and I actually *stumbled* forward a step. "You're awake," I said, realizing how stupid that sounded because she was, in fact, awake. And she had been awake earlier.

Her throat worked. "I was dreaming, and I thought . . . I thought that this was a dream."

Gods.

That killed me all over again. "You're really here, Josie. You're really safe now."

Her eyes shut for a moment and she clutched the blanket tighter. Pain flickered over her face and when she reopened her eyes, there was a glimmer of tears. I moved to her without thinking. Within a heartbeat, I was sitting on the side of the bed, next to her.

Josie jerked, eyes widening. "That . . . that was fast."

Fast was an understatement. I remembered that she had no idea what I was now. We hadn't gotten the chance to talk about any of that. "How are you feeling?"

She hesitated for a moment. "I don't know." Her gaze flickered to the curtained windows. "How long have I've been asleep?"

"A couple of hours."

Her forehead creased. "You . . . you haven't left, have you?"

"No." I took a deep breath. "I know you're mad at me. You want me to—"

"I'm not mad at you," she said so quietly that I thought it was my imagination at first. "I mean, I . . . I want you to try to find Mitchell. I'm not giving up on that. I just . . ." She slowly shook her head. "I'm just not mad."

I stared at her in disbelief. "How can you not be mad at me? You should be furious. You should—" She should hate me. I couldn't bring myself to say that out loud. "I don't know how you can't be angry."

"Maybe I will be again later." A tremor coursed through her as she lowered her hand to the blanket.

My chest hollowed. "Are you in a lot of pain?"

"Not too much," she said, lowering her gaze to the bed-spread. Her fingers tightened around the edge of the blanket.

"I see the bite marks. I can tell you were fed on a lot. You're bruised." I paused. "All over." Anger beat at me, and I worked at keeping my voice level. "Did he—did they—do anything to you I can't see?"

Her eyes squeezed shut, and I barely had a wisp of re-straint left. Outside, there was a flash of intense white light and then thunder boomed. Her eyes flew open. "You mean, was I . . . raped? No," she said, fingers twisting the blanket. "Hyperion . . . he threatened it, but he didn't—didn't get the chance. For the most part, he was disgusted by me."

I didn't feel much relief. Some rapists didn't have to like or even be attracted to someone to rape them. It wasn't about any of that, and all I could hope was that Josie wasn't hiding something. It was obvious he'd found other ways to torture her and he had, but some of my violent anger cooled. There'd be no storm outside. "There is a lot we need to talk about."

Josie stared at me a moment and then her gaze flickered

around the room. "I . . . I don't know what is happening." She swallowed hard. "When I woke up earlier, I was confused and . . . I just don't know what is happening."

All I wanted to do was gather her into my arms, but she didn't sound right. There was something missing from her voice and she had the look of a cornered, confused animal. I had the suspicion she needed some space right now. Probably would be wise of me to sit in one of the numerous chairs in the room, but I couldn't make myself move.

So I sat very still. "I'll fill in as many blanks as I can for you, but I have Basil grabbing some food for you. He'll be coming up here shortly. I want you to eat this time."

Her brows rose. "Basil? Like the plant?"

I smiled faintly. "Basil means kingly in Greek. He's a half and a servant here."

She blinked slowly. "You have half-blood servants here?"

"Yes, but it's not what you think. When I first got here, I told them all to leave. They didn't listen," I explained, wanting her to understand. "None of them are on the elixir. They are all here out of free will."

Confusion increased in her brilliant blue gaze. "But why would you have servants?"

"That's kind of a convoluted story that I will tell you, but there is something more important I need to say."

She shifted and winced.

"You okay?"

Josie nodded. "I'm just . . . sore." She seemed to war with herself and then lifted her gaze to mine. "I'm guessing Hyperion is still alive."

"Not for long," I promised, one I fully intended to keep.

"Then how am I here and not there, in that—?" She trailed off with a sharp breath. "I'm so confused."

Gods. She'd been through a lot, too much. I started to rise. "This can actually wait. I don't—"

"No." One cool hand wrapped around my wrist in a surprisingly strong grip. I looked down at her. "I'm fine. You can talk."

My gaze held hers and then dropped to the bracelet around her slender wrist. Reaching down, I lifted her hand to my mouth. I kissed her palm.

Josie's breath caught and then she pulled her hand free, folding her fingers around the blanket once more. "You . . . you really need to start talking."

"I do." I took a deep breath, inexplicably nervous. I couldn't remember the last time I felt so much anxiety. Actually, I could. It was the last time my mother held a party here. I'd wanted to hide, because I knew she was going to pull me out, do the dog and pony show, pretending to actually care, pretending to be proud. Everyone would stare at me, afraid but curious.

"Seth?"

Shaking my head, I focused on her and said, "I know I said this before, but I have to say it again. I'm sorry. I'm sorry for leaving you in Malibu."

Several moments passed, and I began to fear that she wouldn't say anything. "Why?" she whispered. "Why did you leave me after . . . after everything we've shared?"

"I thought I was protecting you from what . . . what I've become," I explained. "I fed off you without you knowing. I saw how horrified and disgusted you were, and you had every right to be."

"I was shocked," she said, lifting one hand to brush back her damp hair. "And yes, I was . . . I was pissed. What you did was wrong, but we could've worked through that. You didn't give us a chance."

"I know," I agreed, leaning toward her. "I know I didn't

give us a chance, but I thought I was doing the right thing. Especially after Atlas, and what I've become."

"The God Killer?" she asked.

I nodded. "When I came to and realized what I was, it . . . Fuck, it freaked me out, Josie. I didn't know what I was capable of or what I was going to do. That's no excuse. I get it. But I freaked out, and I have never, Josie, *never* been more sorry about anything I've ever done. *Anything*."

Josie's chest rose with a deep breath. She started to speak, but there was a quiet knock on the door.

"It's most likely Basil." I rose but paused. "Are you okay with him coming in here?"

"Yes."

I went to the door, opening it. Basil stepped inside, his gaze focused on the floor. The scent of herbs filled the room. "Would you like me to place the tray on the bed, Kýrios?"

"Sure." I followed behind him, my gaze fixed on Josie.

A look of curiosity filled her features as Basil carried a large silver tray toward the bed. He placed it beside her. "I've brought you soup, Kyría, and steamed wild rice with a hint of light sauce."

Josie gaped at him, and despite everything, a small smile curled the corners of my mouth.

Basil lifted the lids, revealing two large bowls. "I've brought water, but if you would like some other type of refreshment, I would be more than happy to retrieve it for you."

"Water is fine," she said, glancing at me uncertainly before looking back at Basil. "Thank you."

"My pleasure, Kyría." He bowed and then backed away from the bed. "May I be of any other service?"

I shook my head. "That will be all."

Basil bowed once more and left.

Josie now gaped at me. "Did he . . . did he just call me 'lady' and you 'lord'?"

The smile went up a notch as I returned to her side, picking up the bowl and spoon. "They're kind of 'old school' around here."

"Okay," she said, but she was eyeing me with disbelief.

"There's a lot we need to go over, but I want you to eat as much of this as you can first." I dipped the spoon in the soup, loading it up with broth and what appeared to be some sort of noodle. "Open up."

"Are you actually going to hand feed me?"

I glanced down at what I was doing and felt my cheeks heat. "I guess I am."

"I can feed myself."

"I know, but I want . . . I want to do this." And I did. "Besides, you're busy holding the robe closed over your very, very glorious breasts."

Josie's face flushed red and her eyes narrowed. "Don't talk about my breasts."

Another grin pulled at my lips. "But I can look at them?"

"No," she shot back.

Another grin snuck free. "I'm not sure I can promise not to look." I moved the spoon to her mouth. "But I'll try."

Josie watched me for a moment, her look indecipherable, but she opened her mouth. I got about half a dozen spoonfuls of soup in, and half that amount of rice, before she said, "I saw you. You realize that, right?" She leaned back from me. "I saw you out on the balcony, and unless that was a really realistic nightmare, I don't get what's happening here."

"Please eat some more first."

Anger flashed across her face, and I was thrilled to see it. Anger was better than despair and desolation. "Seth—"

"I will explain everything to you. *Everything*," I promised. "But I need you to be better—healthy and whole, and I . . ." My throat suddenly felt thick. "I came back to you—after I left. You weren't at Gable's house. You were somewhere else. I didn't mean to, but I couldn't stop myself. You were sleeping."

Her eyes widened. "I thought I felt you. I chalked it up to a dream, but it *was* you?"

I nodded.

"How in the world?"

"I'll get to that," I said. "When I left you, I told myself that I'd never see you again. Obviously I hadn't held myself to that. I came to you after I left, and then I tried to find you again. That's how I learned what had happened. I didn't—I didn't even know what happened until then, and when I heard that Hyperion had taken you, I have never felt so helpless. I've never felt such terror before, because I couldn't find you. I didn't know *how* to find you. I could've lost you—lost you in the worst possible way, but I didn't. You're here, and right now, I just want to help make you better. To get better, you need to eat, because you told me earlier that you didn't remember the last time you ate. Please let me do this."

Josie started, and for a second, I thought she was going to deny me, but she nodded. When I lifted the spoon again, there was no hiding the way my hand trembled. We nearly finished off the bowl of soup and rice in silence, stopping only when she swore she could neither eat nor drink anymore. I removed the tray, placing it on the table by the door.

She was still holding the robe to her chest when I came back to her, and it was hard not to think of the fact that she was nude under that.

"I was coming after you," she said, and I already knew that, but I kind of loved hearing her say that. "Even though the whole feeding off me was so . . . so wrong, I was going to come after you. That was my plan. I was going to stand next to you. I was going to fight for you. Prove that you . . . you are worthy of how I feel for you." Her voice was raspy. "And after everything, I finally see you, and that—that was all I wanted—was to see you, and I found you with another woman."

My heart cracked all over again at her words and the tears building in her eyes. "It wasn't how it looked."

She coughed out a harsh laugh. "Really?"

"I know how that sounds," I continued. "I truly do, but it is the truth. Her name is Karina and she is the high priestess here."

"High priestess?" she repeated.

"That's a part of the convoluted story I need to tell you—she's a big part of it, and gods know, it's a messed-up story, but I was not *embracing* her. There is absolutely nothing between us. Nothing. There never has been. There won't be."

"Don't lie," she whispered. "I saw you. You had your hands on her. You were *touching* her—"

I shot forward, moving faster than she could track. Carefully clasping her cheeks, I guided her gaze to mine. "It wasn't like that, Josie. I swear to you. It could never be, because I love you, Josie. I love *you*."

19

*M*y heart slowed and then sped up. I'd thought Seth had told me that only once before, when he believed I was asleep, and sometimes I wasn't even a hundred percent sure I'd heard him say that then.

But he really said that now.

Seth said those three short words that meant everything.

Well, "I have cake" was also three short, powerful words, but hearing Seth say he loved me was like a thousand hopes and dreams come true at once.

Part of me wanted to spring out from under the covers and tackle-hug him. The other half was frozen in so much confusion and trepidation. I didn't truly understand what was going on. Maybe it was because I was so damn exhausted, since even upon waking and eating, I was tired down to my bones. But it felt like only hours ago I was huddled on the cold dirt waiting . . . and wanting to die rather than face another second with Hyperion or the rest of the Titans. I still didn't even understand how I'd gotten here or how we were going to help Mitchell if

Seth refused to let me look for him or leave my side.

And I wanted to celebrate what Seth was saying. He was finally telling me how he felt, but I couldn't erase the image of him and that beautiful brunette.

"Josie?" His gaze searched mine, and I realized I hadn't spoken.

I took a shaky breath. "I've . . . I've waited forever for you to say that."

A slow smile started to creep over his lips. "And I should've said it forever ago."

I wanted to smile back at him, but all I could do was stare at him. There was so much we needed to talk about—that I needed to focus on. My thoughts were all over the place, and I was feeling so much—too much. And I was naked. Like, legit naked under the robe that was too big and kept slipping off my shoulder and gapping in the front. And I vaguely remembered Seth hauling my sobbing, naked butt out of the shower, and helping me get in the robe when I'd jumped out of the bed and fell on the floor naked.

Concern filled those amber eyes. "Josie, please say something. Anything."

I needed to say something. "If you love me, then why . . . why did I see you outside with her?"

Seth was still for a moment and then lowered his hands to the space between us. "I think I need to start at the beginning."

"Yeah." I tucked the blanket under my arms. "I think that would make the most sense."

Rising from the bed, Seth walked toward a cabinet. Despite everything that we needed to talk about and all that had happened to me, I couldn't stop my gaze from roaming over all the exposed skin. He'd been shirtless earlier, but I hadn't noticed *him*. I did now. The defined pecs. The tightly coiled abs. The

sweats hanging low enough that they showed off those inden-
tations on either side of his hips. Even his back was amazing.
Long, lean and muscled.

Why couldn't he be wearing a shirt?

But it was Seth, so of course not.

"My whole life, I've had this . . . this unexplainable draw to
aether. It always called to me, even before I awakened as the
Apollyon." Bending down, he grabbed a bottle of water out of
a mini-fridge hidden in the cabinet. Turning, he faced me. "It
got worse when I became the Apollyon, but I never understood
it. Other than the pures and halfs who got addicted to aether
and turned into daimons, I didn't know anyone else who could
feel what I could feel. When Alex awakened, she didn't feel that
way. I always thought there was just something wired wrong in
me, you know? But I . . . I understand now."

Walking back to the bed, he sat beside me. Unscrewing the
lid, he offered the open bottle of water. I took it. "There was
this . . . this voice inside me when I became the God Killer,
guiding what I was doing. I know that sounds crazy, but that
was how it felt. Like everything inside me had been building
to that moment or leading me to that moment." He paused,
frowning. "You need to drink, Josie."

In a daze, I took a decent gulp of water.

Appearing to be satisfied, he said, "You know, now that I
think about it, I wonder if Ares knew the truth. He wanted me
to become the God Killer. Through me, he sought to control the
other gods, but I . . . I cannot be controlled."

My eyes widened, because he said that without an ounce of
arrogance. It was just a statement of fact. A truth bomb deli-
cately detonated. Seth couldn't be controlled now.

"I guess he didn't realize what I would become once I was
the God Killer." The muscles in his shoulders tensed as he

shrugged. "Who knows, though? Anyway, I didn't understand fully what was happening. That's why I left, and I know that's not a good enough excuse for leaving you. It will never be, but I was . . . I was afraid that I would hurt you. That I wouldn't be able to control myself."

Hearing him admit that he was afraid was always a shock, because Seth didn't seem scared of anything.

I took another drink of water.

"Do you remember the nymphs that had helped us outside of your grandparents' house? One of them has been around on and off. His name is Ewan. He rarely makes any sense." A wry grin appeared on his lips. "But he was the first to tell me I was not just a God Killer, but a god."

I almost choked on the water. "What?"

"A god," he repeated, his amber gaze latching onto mine. "I'm a god, Josie, and I'm not saying that to be funny."

Shock rendered me speechless as I stared at him. Part of me wanted to laugh, because it sounded legit crazy, but I was a demigod and that had also sounded crazy at first.

"I didn't believe it at first. Even when I could do things I hadn't been able to do before, it still sounded ridiculous to me." Seth shifted closer, catching a strand of my hair. His fingertips brushed along the curve of my cheek as he tucked it back behind my ear, causing me to shiver. "But it is true. Somehow, and for some reason, this was what I was always meant to be. The Appointed God. The God of Life and Death." He laughed at that as he lowered his hand. "There's even a temple here."

I blinked. "A temple? For you?"

He grinned. "For me."

"Holy crap," I whispered, and that was the best I could come up with. Seth was a god—a god that was *worshipped*.

"The woman you saw me with outside? She is the high

priestess. There are several priests and priestesses here."

At the mention of the woman, I tensed. "And they do what? *Service* you?"

His eyes flashed. "Not in the manner in which you're insinuating."

"I'm not insinuating anything."

One brow rose. "The whole 'being a god' thing actually ties into the whole 'you seeing me outside with Karina and feeding' thing."

The plastic bottle crinkled as my fingers tightened around it. Honestly, I hadn't fully processed Seth being an actual god, but the shock was wearing off. I knew deep down I wasn't going to be happy with what he was about to say.

"I'm not making this up to justify anything, because it sounds like something an addict would say, but I . . . I have to feed," he explained quietly, his gaze never wavering from mine. "It's how the gods are gods. For them, when they're on Olympus or in the Underworld, they are surrounded by aether. It's how their powers are fueled. And it's why I've always been drawn to it."

"That makes sense," I said after a moment. "That's why the Titans were feeding—"

"I'll never do that to you," he responded urgently. "I would never force you to go through that." His gaze dropped to my arm and then to my wrist. The sleeves of the robe had fallen back, and I suddenly wanted to shove both arms under the blanket. "Feeding is not like it used to be for me. None of it is the same. Beforehand, I got . . . I got buzzed off it, but now . . ." He shook his head. "It's like breathing air. If I don't do it after a while, I need to. It doesn't get me wired up or high. It's just the way it is."

I glanced down at the half-empty bottle I held. Taking another drink, I then leaned over and placed the bottle on the nightstand. "It didn't hurt when you did it before. I didn't even know that you'd done it. It was nothing like . . . nothing like what Hyperion and Cronus did."

"It doesn't have to be painful, but that doesn't matter now. I would never take that from you. Never again," he swore, and my stomach dipped, because he said it in a way that left no doubt in my mind that was what he fully intended. "Josie?"

A moment after he said my name, I felt the tips of his fingers pressing gently under my chin. He lifted my gaze to his. "I will never let another thing hurt you again. *Never.*"

The protective vibe was . . . it was sweet, and seeing the fierceness in his gaze, was also, well, hot, but I couldn't rely on him to protect me. I couldn't rely on anyone, and that wasn't because he hadn't stopped Hyperion. I was still, no matter what was done to me, a powerful demigod. I didn't need protection.

Well . . .

That wasn't exactly true. Right at this moment, I couldn't fight off a bed bug, which reminded me of something. I glanced down. "These bands—they're blocking my abilities."

"What?" Seth took my right hand in his. He frowned. "I tried to take them off, but they won't budge."

"I don't know if they will come off," I admitted, and my stomach turned over heavily. "Hyperion said they were made of Cronus and Zeus's blood. That they were what was used to entomb the Titans."

"Hell," he muttered, sliding a finger over the band. "We'll figure out how to get them off. Someone has to know." His gaze flicked up to mine. "This might be why you're not healing as fast as you should."

"I guess." Being drained of my aether and not being fed any sort of regular meal also probably had something to do with it. Closing my eyes, I pushed those thoughts away before they crowded everything out. I slipped my hand free from his. "How did I get here?"

His features tightened. "I tried to locate you, but I couldn't feel you anywhere. Dammit," he growled, sitting back. "I didn't even know until I went to Malibu just to make sure you were okay." Looking away, his gaze fixed on the gauze-shaded door. "Then I went to the University. Saw Marcus and Luke—"

"Luke and Deacon are okay? Gable?" When he nodded, relief washed over me.

"Everyone is okay. They are at the University—well, everyone is there except Alex and Aiden. They ended up coming here to tell me you'd been taken."

"Oh." I was surprised.

"They'd already left for the island when I went to the Covenant. When I learned you'd been taken, I kept looking for you. The whole god-thing allows me to . . . to sense out people. It's how the gods can pop in and out, but you were blocked from me, just like the demigods had been blocked."

Seth could now appear and disappear at will? Why didn't I get a cool ability like that?

"It wasn't until yesterday, when I was trying to sense you out and I felt you. Gods." A muscle flexed in his cheek. "I found you in these woods. Perses—I don't know if you know who that is."

"I know him," I murmured, hitching the blanket up further.

Seth closed his eyes. "I'd helped free Perses, along with Alex and Aiden. I guess once he realized who you were to me, he thought to repay me and freed you."

"He did?"

His gaze drifted to mine. "You don't remember that?"

"I remember . . ." I remembered being taken to Cronus again, and he looked younger than he had the last time. He no longer appeared ancient. Skin smoother, black hair sprouting through the silvery white, and muscles replacing frail bones and tissues. I remembered being held down and him feeding—pulling and pulling from me until my vision turned black and there was nothing. There was more—fragments. "I remember Perses coming to me, but I . . . I think I passed out before we left the room."

Seth was staring at me and he looked like he wanted to ask me something, but changed his mind. "Well, he brought you out, and that's how I found you."

Holding the blanket close, I shivered as I recalled him being the one to hold me down. "I guess that was nice of him, but I won't be thanking him anytime soon."

"Thanking him will never be necessary." Seth's voice was sharp. "He's dead."

My chin jerked up. "What?"

"I killed him for what he took part in."

I gaped at Seth. There wasn't an ounce of remorse in his tone or expression, but I . . . I didn't care that there wasn't, because I wanted to kill Perses. I wanted to kill all of them for what they'd done to me—to Lauren, and would continue to do to Mitchell.

"I'm glad," I said, meaning it. Seth exhaled heavily, and we sat there for a couple of moments. "Okay. Wow. So, you're a god now that apparently can take out Titans easily. That's pretty amazing."

"It is." A half-grin appeared. "I mean, I've always thought I was god-like, so it's not that big of a change."

"Ha." I raised a brow. "Wait. If you're a god, then that means the other gods can't tell you what to do now, right?" Hope sparked deep in my chest, spreading through me like a wildfire. "If you're a god, then they can't kill you and you won't be spending your afterlife working for Hades."

He nodded, his eyes lighting to a tawny gold. "No, they can't control me any longer and Hades is going to have to find a new toy to play with."

"That's so good. Oh my God, that's such great news." It was so amazing I almost started to cry like an overly emotional toddler. "Seth, I'm so happy to hear that."

His entire expression softened. "It's possibly the best part about all of this. Well, next to the ability to will myself from location to location," he teased, and then those thick lashes lifted once more. "I . . . I have a future, Josie."

My mouth dried. A future. Something Seth had never planned on having. Something that I'd hoped to overcome, but never knew how. Now Seth had a tomorrow, a next month, and so on. There was nothing stopping us from—

I cut those thoughts off, because it was all . . . everything was too much. I thought about my mom and . . . and I just didn't want to think.

Seth and I stared at one another, and the silence stretched out. The air practically hummed by the time he looked away, swallowing.

"I need to use the bathroom," I whispered, and then flushed, because Jesus, was there a better mood killer than that?

Nodding, he rose from the bed and gave me space to gather up the robe under the blanket and make sure I wasn't flashing him as I scooted out of the bed.

Wholly aware of his gaze on me, I slowly made my way to the opulent bathroom, closing the door behind me. After using the bathroom, I washed my face, wincing at how the bruised and raw skin stung. By the time I was done, I was exhausted again, and my reflection showed it.

I looked like I'd been riding on the hot-mess express all night.

Dismissing my appearance since there wasn't a damn thing I could do about it, I tightened the oversized robe around me and left the bathroom.

Seth stood by the bed, holding a pale pink and blue cloth. "I had Basil bring you a smaller robe, but we will have clothing for you in the morning."

Glancing at the door, I shuffled over to him. "He was here?"

He nodded.

"That was quiet . . . and fast." I took the new robe from him.

Seth smiled narrowly. "Basil is . . . well, he's pretty useful." He stepped back and then turned away from me. "Let me know when you're done."

My mouth dropped open.

He wasn't going to ogle me and make some sort of sexual comment? *That* was far more surprising than him being a god.

There . . . there was a time when Seth wouldn't have turned away. He would've stared, and the intensity of his stare would've felt like a caress. He'd said he loved me. He promised to protect me, but he was standing there now with his back to me, spine rigid.

Unsure of what to make of what was going on between us, I let the larger robe drop. Seth's head fell back, and I stared at him a moment too long, feeling my skin flush hotly.

It was probably a good thing that he wasn't looking, that he was thinking about my modesty. While the mere thought of his bare skin pressed against mine nearly swept my legs out from under me, my head was still all over the place.

The new robe was thin and silky soft as it slipped over my arms. Cinching the belt around my waist, I was relieved to see that it reached my knees and wouldn't fall off my shoulders or gap in the front. I cleared my throat. "I'm decent."

Seth slowly turned around and his gaze roamed over me. My breath caught at the stark hunger in those stunning eyes.

Well, he definitely still wanted me.

And I still wanted him.

My gaze dropped to the band of his pants.

I'd always want him.

"Yeah," he said, and that was all he said. I wasn't even sure what he was responding to.

I moved forward, stepping around him. I climbed into the bed, tugging the blanket over my bare legs. Heart thumping, I lifted my gaze to his. "I'm . . . I'm tired again." That might've sounded lame, but it was true. My body felt like it was weighed down with lead.

He hesitated and suddenly he didn't look like a god—a powerful being with no match. He stared up at me through thick lashes, and he looked like a man about to ask for the world. "Can I stay with you?"

I wasn't expecting that question.

Seth inched closer to the bed. "I don't think I can leave your side, Josie."

My heart was going to crawl out of my chest, and in an instant, the past and present collided. I loved Seth. I would always love him.

Loving him didn't mean I wasn't disappointed in his choices—that those choices hadn't hurt me. Loving him didn't mean he could keep making those choices and I would keep forgiving him. Loving him meant that I knew from the first moment that I fell for Seth that he was complicated—that loving him wouldn't be easy. Loving him . . . Well, it meant that I was willing to fight for him.

And loving him meant he had to be willing to fight for me.

"If you stay, you *stay*. You can't leave me again," I heard myself say as I held his gaze. "If you can't promise that and mean it, you can't stay with me."

He moved as quick as a bolt of lightning. One second he

was standing next to the bed, and in another, he was only an inch or so away from me, bent at the waist, his hands planted on the bed, beside my hips. "I will never leave you like that again, Josie. You will never have to fear that. I swear to you."

My lips parted. So many words rose and died on the tip of my tongue. I stopped thinking—thinking about everything. Scooting over, I lifted the covers for him. Seth didn't hesitate for a moment. Within a blink of an eye, he was in the bed, his body curled so he was facing me. There were a few inches between us, but my heart was pounding like there was nothing separating us.

Before . . . before everything happened, there wouldn't even be a scant inch between us. Seth was a very physical person. A cuddler. But maybe he worried that he'd accidentally hurt me by holding me close. Or maybe he sensed that I . . . that I wasn't ready for that kind of closeness.

He was silent as he placed his right hand in the space between us. My gaze fell to where his palm was flipped up, waiting. My heart started thundering against my ribs. Closing my eyes, I reached down and placed my left hand over his.

Seth curled his fingers around mine and he held on.

20

"You sure you're up for this?"

Josie was standing on the tips of her toes, trying to see over my shoulder. Basil was out in the hallway, waiting to be of some sort of service, so he was just standing there.

Really needed to get him a computer with an internet connection.

Her blue eyes darted to mine only briefly. "Yes. I feel better."

I studied her closely. She only looked marginally better. The bruises had faded a shade or two. The patches of clear skin were still too pale and the heavy shadows under her eyes were present.

She didn't look ready.

Josie bit down on her lower lip as her gaze found mine again. "Seriously. I'm okay. I can leave this room."

After she fallen asleep beside me, she'd woken up a few hours later, like she had before, in the throes of a nightmare, struggling and screaming. I'd held her through it, smoothing my hand up and down her spine and whispering in her ear until she quieted and fell back to sleep.

I didn't think she remembered.

I did.

Hearing those screams was something I'd never forget. They'd embedded themselves deep inside me. Unable to fall back asleep, I'd lain there fantasizing about slowly, painfully dismembering every single Titan with only a rusty butter knife.

"You can't keep me in this room," she said, crossing her arms.

Despite how dark my thoughts had turned, I was thrilled to see that she was a little more like her old self this morning. "You do realize that I could easily keep you in this room."

Her eyes narrowed. "I'd like to see you try."

That was hot.

Hell, everything about her was hot. Josie had slept through the rest of yesterday and all night, waking only for that nightmare. When I'd woken up this morning, which had only been about an hour ago, I'd done so with a raging hard-on. Kind of felt like a creep about it, but I couldn't help it. After the nightmare, I dozed back off holding her close. She'd gotten turned around and her ass was pressed against my dick, and I was a male, so it happened.

All right. It wasn't just because I was a male.

I'd *missed* her—missed looking at her, listening to her voice and her laugh, and I'd freaking missed touching her. Gods, had I ever missed touching her. Even right now it took everything in me not to have an arm around her shoulders. I wanted her under me and I wanted me *in* her. I wanted to lock her in this room for a month and that desire had nothing to do with making sure she was well-rested.

But I did hold back, because I knew Josie wasn't ready for any of that. I still wasn't one hundred percent sure she was being honest about all that had happened to her during her captivity.

Even if she was, she'd been through some shit and then she'd come to me, and the first thing she'd seen was me feeding. The last thing she needed was for me to be all over her like a boy who just discovered he had a functional dick.

Sighing, I stepped aside and extended my arm toward the door, bowing. "After you, *Kyría.*"

Josie shot me a narrowed-eyed look that brought a slight smile to my lips. The black linen pants and tank top Basil had scrounged up were a size too small. Not that I was complaining. The thin pants hugged her ass quite nicely. I was enjoying the view, but in the back of my head, I was stressing about how Josie hadn't said she loved me in return yesterday. That had not gotten past me unnoticed. Her steps slowed as she entered the hallway and stared at Basil. She seemed to hesitate, obviously unsure of how to handle him.

I joined her. "We're going to take a quick tour of the house."

Basil nodded. "Your other guests are currently in the kitchen, Kýrios. I explained that we have staff more than willing to make them breakfast, but they insisted on doing so themselves."

"That's fine. They can have free run of the place."

He nodded. "Additional clothing for the *kyría* should be arriving by this afternoon."

"Perfect." I grinned down at Josie.

She was staring at Basil with wide eyes even as the half bowed and walked off. She turned to me. "That is so weird. Like, really weird. I mean, it's like having a butler. He's like always there, just waiting to do stuff for you."

"He has to be bored out of his mind. I don't really have him do much. Same goes for any of the staff here. Using them as servants doesn't . . . sit well with me even though they seem to want to be here."

Her head cocked to the side, causing her long hair to tumble over her shoulder. "But you grew up with servants, didn't you?"

I nodded. "This entire house used to be filled with them." I had to touch her, so I placed my hand on her lower back, urging her to take a step forward. "This is the third floor. There are only a few bedrooms up here," I explained, ushering her down the hall. "If you go in the other direction you can go out on the balconies. They circle the entire home."

"Wow." Her gaze darted over the closed doors that used to lead to my bedroom and to my mother's. "Does anyone use these rooms?"

"No. They are closed off." Steering her away from those rooms, I led her down the wide hall, toward the spiral staircase that emptied into the atrium on the first floor. "The second floor is mostly guest bedrooms. There's also a living room that no one used when I was younger and I'm assuming no one uses now."

Josie's gaze was bouncing all over the place as we descended the stairs, bypassing the second floor. She was fascinated with the statues and paintings of the gods. By the time we reached the main level, she appeared thunderstruck. "Okay. Why in the world would you guys need a house this big? I mean, it was just you and your mom, right?"

"People who have money like to show off the fact they have money." I led her toward the back of the house, passing several white-clothed staff who'd paused to bow deeply, causing Josie's face to flush. "My mother would have a lot of parties and the . . . guests would stay for several weeks, months even. That's the library to your right. Main living room is to your right beyond that. A theater room connects off of it."

"A theater room?" she mumbled, shaking her head as we neared the hallway that led to the kitchen and the scent of frying bacon. "When you say 'guests,' you say it like they weren't really guests."

I shrugged as we crossed into the sunroom. "They were mostly other pures and ... lovers." A wry grin appeared. "Mother got around."

Her stare sharpened as she trailed her fingertips over the wide leaf of one of the many potted plants situated among the comfy, oversized chairs and chaise lounges. "So your mom had a lot of lovers?"

Nodding, I stepped in front of her and opened the door that led out to the shaded patio. "This way leads to the courtyard. Would you like to see it?"

"Yes." She followed me out into the balmy breeze. "Your father was one of her lovers."

"That's how I was made."

Her eyes rolled. "Well, duh." She glanced up at the churning ceiling fans. "Did you father stay here?"

Wondering how we got on the topic of my parents. I didn't respond as I stepped off the patio and into the bright sunlight. I headed down the marble pathway, making my way into the middle of the courtyard.

"Seth?"

Glancing over my shoulder, I saw that Josie had stopped beside one of the many stone benches. "My father was a half."

"I know that." She touched a pink flower. "But did you know him?"

I turned and walked back to where she stood. Talking about my parents was the last thing I wanted, but if that was what Josie wanted to talk about, that was what I would do. Part of me figured she was focusing on it so she wasn't thinking about what she had just gone through.

"My father wasn't a Sentinel or Guard. He was a servant here." Taking her hand, I threaded my fingers through hers. "He worked outside, on the grounds. He was never on the elixir. But even if he had been, I doubt it would've stopped her." Disgust filled me. "She didn't care if someone was of sound mind, but I think she liked the halfs better when they weren't highly medicated. Messing with them . . . was more fun that way."

Her gaze dropped to our joined hands and lingered. "That . . . sounds terrible."

"She was pretty terrible."

Her shoulders rose with a deep breath and she lifted her gaze to mine. "You didn't answer my question."

Truth was, I'd never honestly answered that question a day in my life. I'd told Alex once that I hadn't met my father and didn't know his name. That had been a lie, and looking back I didn't even know why I had lied about it. Then again, I lied about a lot of things back then. "I used to sit in my bedroom and watch him tend the flowers in the garden every afternoon, after lunch. From there he'd disappear out further on the grounds and I wouldn't see him again until the next day. I didn't know he was my father at that point, but maybe on some kind of weird biological level, I did, and that's why I watched him."

"Maybe," she said, her gaze searching mine.

"I didn't look like him. He was dark-haired and fair-skinned. I take after my mother."

"She must've been beautiful."

"She was." Lifting Josie's hand, I kissed the tip of her pinky and was pleased when the blue of her eyes deepened. "Most halfs were brought before the Council at a very young age to determine if they would train to be Sentinels or Guards or go into servitude. Not me. Everyone already knew what I would be."

"Of course," she murmured.

I grinned. "All the previous Apollyons' eyes turned amber after they awakened. But I was born with them, so we always knew I was the Apollyon. I'd known that my father was a half long before it became common knowledge that was how an Apollyon could be made." Which was another thing I had withheld from Alex. "I knew for a long time."

She stepped closer, her bare feet brushing mine. "How did you find out?"

"He told me."

Her eyes widened with surprise. "Seriously?"

"I was eleven. My mother had just dragged me out of my bedroom and paraded me through one of her many parties. She was very proud that her bastard son was the Apollyon, so that was quite regular. I was showed off, oohed and awed over, and then sent back to my room. That night was different, though."

Josie's brows knitted. "Why?"

Shifting, I lowered our hands so they hung between us. "I hadn't gone straight to my bedroom like I normally did. I'd gone outside into this courtyard. I don't even know why. Maybe it was fate." Lifting my gaze to the towering house, I could see the bedroom window I spent the bulk of my time looking out of. "I'd sat on one of these benches, feeling quite miserable and most likely daydreaming about smashing all her precious statues inside when the man I often watched from the window approached me. I wasn't particularly pleasant with him, but he didn't seem to mind. He sat beside me, and he told me his name was Kristos."

Josie was quiet as she stared up at me.

Something occurred to me and then I chuckled. "Gods. You know what his name means in Greek? The anointed. Fucking fate. Anyway, he told me the truth—that he was my father. I didn't want to believe him at first. I liked the idea of my father being this . . . badass Sentinel and not this gardener. I know that's wrong, but I was an ass as a kid."

"Do tell," she murmured.

My lips quirked. "I said some . . . pretty horrible things, because I was, well, like I said, an ass, and he didn't seem to hold it against me. He'd been patient, even understanding of my attitude. I guess he'd known how things were in the house. He told me that he was proud of what I would become." I laughed, and it sounded harsh to my own ears. "But he didn't want that kind of life for his son."

"Wow." Her eyes were wide. "What else happened?"

"Well he left, and unbeknownst to us, we'd been spied upon. Mother had eyes and ears everywhere. She was none too pleased about all of it. She sent me to the Covenant in Britain the next day. I never saw him again."

Josie slowly shook her head. "Do you know if he's still around here? If—"

"He's dead. Died protecting my heartless bitch of a mother. How cruel is that?"

"Oh my God," she whispered, squeezing my hand. "Seth—"

"Come." I tugged on her hand, cutting her off as I looked away from the growing pity in her beautiful blue eyes. "There's something I want to show you."

She hesitated a moment, but then let me lead her through the maze of blooming flowers. She sucked in a soft breath as we neared the edge of the courtyard and saw the sweeping marble archways. Walking out from under them, I knew the moment she saw the temple.

"Holy moly," Josie whispered, stopping abruptly.

The temple was quite a sight, all polished marble columns and smooth stone. Large titanium braziers burned at the entrance of the closed doors. Several priests and priestesses stood outside, their amber-colored clothing billowing in the breeze. They all moved in unison, six of them. Three males and three females dropped to their knees and bowed until their foreheads nearly touched the floor.

Dropping my hand, Josie stepped forward and then stopped again. "This is *your* temple?"

"Yep."

"And those are some of *your* priests and priestesses?"

"Double yep."

Josie lifted her hands wordlessly. Sun glinted off her hair, and I knew she had no idea that she looked like a goddess standing before the temple. Several moments passed. "I don't even know what to say. Have you gone in there?"

If she asked to go inside, I would for her, but only for her. "I haven't. Do you want to?"

Josie was silent for a moment and then she turned to me. "Not yet." Walking back to where I stood, she glanced over her shoulder. "It's just a little too weird for me right now."

Relieved, I chuckled. "You and me both."

"I'm surprised you're not reveling in all of this."

"I don't need this—any of this," I admitted, voice low. Her gaze swung to mine. "I just . . ."

"What?"

I stepped into her, crowding her space when I knew I probably shouldn't, but I was unable to help myself. "I only need you, Josie."

Her sharp inhale echoed in my ears.

Heat invaded my cheeks. Shit. Was I blushing? I cursed under my breath. I wasn't ashamed to admit what I did. It was the damn truth, but I really didn't need an audience.

Aware that the golden guards by the doors were within hearing distance, I took her hand once more and walked her around the temple, out to the cliffs that overlooked the glistening sea. Neither of us spoke for several moments as she took in the view.

"It's really beautiful here, Seth." She gazed out over the ocean, focusing on the white sails off in the distance. "I know this place doesn't have the best memories for you, but it's stunning—the house, the island, and even the weird temple."

I laughed at the last part. "Yeah. It is beautiful. Even more so now."

She glanced up at me and gave a slight smile. "You're full of charm today."

"Just speaking the truth," I replied. "You getting hungry?"

She nodded. "I'm always hungry."

"Glad to see your appetite is back."

"I don't think anything could permanently affect my appetite."

"We can head back. Seems like Alex and Aiden are making breakfast." The wind was stronger here, tossing her hair across her face. I caught the strands, smoothing them back. "If we make it in time, we can steal their food."

Josie's laugh was hoarse, but it was the most amazing sound to hear. I stared at her a moment and then started to head back but stopped. "Can I . . . can I ask you something?"

Her hand was still in my other one. "Yeah."

My heart started thundering in my chest, and I knew this question could wait. It should wait, but the idea of going another minute or hour not knowing was going to drive me crazy.

So I took a deep breath and opened myself up in a way I'd never done before. "Do you still love me?"

21

tark vulnerability churned in Seth's amber eyes. I couldn't believe he was asking that kind of question—that he even thought he needed to. A tiny part of me wanted to punch him—punch him with love, of course.

I'd be lying if I said I wasn't wary. Seth had whispered his love to me before and told me everything would be okay, but then he had left. He'd shut me out more than once. None of that had changed the way I felt for him, and maybe that made me a little crazy, but the world I now lived in was insane.

But I felt so . . . so raw, inside and out.

"I know what you're thinking," he said, his gaze searching mine. "And not because I can read your thoughts."

"Thank God for that," I muttered.

A brief grin appeared and then disappeared. "I've let you down." When I opened my mouth, he raised his hand. "I have, Josie. More than once I've . . . I've pushed you away. I've made the wrong choices. I know I haven't come even close to being the kind of man you deserve, but I'm going to change that."

Oh.

Oh.

"You'll never have to doubt me again," he said, voice low and determined. "I'd die before that happened again."

There was a swelling sensation in my chest like I was an un-tethered balloon that could lift off the ground and float away. Tears blurred my vision as I drew in a shaky breath. "I wouldn't be standing here if I didn't love you, Seth. I wouldn't have let you sleep in the same bed with me last night if I didn't," I said, my breath catching. "There's a lot I don't really understand right now, like, for example, the whole 'you're a god' thing. I mean, I get it. You're a god." Slipping my hands free, I wiggled my fingers. "Yay! You seem the same—well, you're more mellow, but I like that, and I love you whether you're a god or a normal human being. And yeah, there's a lot we need to still figure out. Like that whole feeding thing, because I am so not okay with you getting all super close with a woman who looks like she could double for Angelina Jolie, and—"

Seth moved so fast I didn't even register what he was up to until I felt his lips on mine. I sucked in a startled gasp. It felt like an eternity had passed since the last time he'd kissed me.

Just the tips of his fingers cradled my cheeks as his mouth gently moved over mine. He appeared fully aware of the split in my bottom lip, and was careful to not injure it further. His kiss was tender and so sweet, bringing a wave of fresh tears to my eyes. My hands went to his chest, and I could feel his heart pounding under my palm. My lips parted, and the kiss deep-ened, sending my pulse racing as the tip of his tongue touched mine.

I was immediately lost to him—to the feel of his lips, to the touch of his hands, and to his taste. I was lost and a part of me never wanted to be found.

He made a raw, hungry sound as his fingers glided down my throat and over my shoulders. "Say it again," he ordered huskily.

Dazed with desire, I opened my eyes. I knew what he meant without any further explanation. "I love you, Seth."

Seth kissed me again, and this time if he hadn't circled his arm around my waist, I probably would've fallen right over, because this kiss left me breathless and yearning. If he had tried to tug me down on the sandy grass and strip off my clothes, I probably wouldn't have stopped him. I would have been tearing at his clothes just as frantically.

But it was Seth who stopped, lifting his mouth from mine once more. "Sorry," he said, voice thick and sexy. "I just . . . I just had to kiss you."

Leaning in, I rested my head against his chest and sighed. "I'm not complaining."

Seth's deep chuckle sent a warm shiver across my skin. "I hope not."

I met his gaze. "We're in this together, right? For real? No more making decisions that you think are for the best without coming to me. You won't leave me again, because if you do, I don't think I could forgive you for that. Not anymore."

"I'm not leaving you. We're in this together, Josie." His gaze searched mine. "If there is anything in this world, there is us."

Closing my eyes, I let out a soft sigh. So much was going on in my head. I hadn't forgotten about Mitchell or what had happened to Lauren. I missed my mom and Erin, and when it was quiet, I thought about those long, terror-filled hours in that dark, dank room. My head was a mess.

But having this—having the issues somewhat resolved between Seth and me cleared up some of the space in my head. A little of the tension eased from my muscles, and even though there were still so many problems, I had Seth.

And Seth had me.

He pulled me against him so our bodies were flush, and I could feel his arousal against my belly. "I missed you." He curled one hand through my hair and he rested his chin atop my head. "I missed you when I was with you."

Looping my arms around his waist, I closed my eyes. "How did you miss me when I was with you?"

He was silent for a moment. "I don't know. It's hard to explain, but I guess I wasn't . . . I wasn't entirely me, so there was a part of me that wasn't actually there."

I lifted my head and stared into his eyes. "And you're completely here now?"

"I am." His lips brushed my forehead. "For the first time in my life, I'm actually *me*."

* * *

We stayed out on the cliffs until my stomach rumbled so obnoxiously loud that people on the other side of the island could've heard it. Seth had laughed like it was the funniest thing ever, and while I debated hitting him again, he took my hand, leading me back inside.

Seth and I stopped at the same exact time as we entered the kitchen. My first impression was that the room was ridiculously huge, with pale gray countertops and multiple islands. I had no idea why anyone would've needed a kitchen of this size unless they were hosting their own reality chef show, but it wasn't so much the kitchen I was staring at.

It was Alex and Aiden.

They were in the middle of the room, near a multiple-burner stovetop. It looked like they had been in the process of making eggs to go with their bacon, but the eggs remained in a bowl, uncooked, whisked and frothy. It also appeared they'd forgotten everything except each other.

Alex was sitting—barely—on the counter near the stove. Aiden's hips were pressed between her thighs, and one of his hands was somewhere under the loose tank top Alex was wearing. She was grabbing the back of his head with one hand and the other had Aiden's shirt balled, tugging it up. Their mouths and hips were practically fused together.

Oh my.

Heat invaded my face as I glanced up at Seth. His brows were raised. "I think they're about to make a baby," I whispered. "And maybe eggs."

Seth snickered as Aiden stiffened and then slid his hand out from under Alex's shirt, dropping his palm to the smooth countertop. His forehead pressed against hers, and what I could see of Alex's face was blood red.

"I would like to be able to eat food out of this kitchen again," Seth commented. "And actually use the counter to prepare food."

"Shut up," Alex growled. "As if you know how to cook food."

Seth smirked as he swaggered forward, picking up the forgotten bowl. "I am quite the chef, among other things." Passing a pointed look at Aiden, he leaned against the counter. "Unlike some."

Aiden turned his head, scowling. "Just because you're a god doesn't mean I won't punch you."

"Just because you're a guest in my house doesn't mean I won't drown you in the ocean."

"Oh dear," I murmured, wide-eyed.

Ignoring Seth's threat, Aiden pushed back and looked at me as Alex hopped off the counter. "It's good to see you up and moving around," he said. "How are you feeling?"

"I'm good." I inched into the kitchen. "Just a little tired."

"You look so much better," Alex said, and it was probably a lie. She walked over to me and gave me a quick, tight hug. She drew back a few inches and whispered, "Is everything okay with you and Jackass over there?"

"I can hear you," Seth replied, dumping the eggs in a heated skillet.

"I don't care," Alex sang back.

"Yeah." I nodded and smiled. "Everything is . . . It's good."

Relief flickered through her warm brown eyes. "I'm happy to hear that." Wrapping her arm around mine, she guided me toward the island with several high-back chairs surrounding it. "Believe it or not, we were making everyone breakfast."

"Sure looked like it." Seth picked up a spatula.

Aiden turned around with a sigh. "Would you like anything to drink, Josie?"

I stopped. "I can get it."

"I'm closer," he said, walking toward the fridge. He peered inside. "Well, the options appear to be limitless. What would you like?"

"Um, orange juice?" I sat down.

Alex climbed up on the seat next to me as Aiden searched down a glass. "We talked to Deacon and Luke last night. They're relieved to hear you're okay."

"I'm happy to know they're safe at the Covenant," I told her as Aiden placed a glass of OJ in front of me. "Thank you."

He nodded. "They're not exactly safe. They left yesterday to search down the demigod in Canada."

My gaze darted to Seth. He was flipping the eggs, and it was more than weird to see him doing something so domestic any other time, but knowing that he was a god now made it all the more . . . fascinating to watch him fiddle at a stove. I imagined he could just whip up omelets out of thin air or something cool like that. "Will they be okay? The Titans are still searching for the other demigods."

"They'll be as safe as any of us are." Aiden rubbed at his brow. "I'd prefer that they'd stay at the University where at least there are wards, but Deacon isn't . . ."

"A kid anymore?" Seth finished for him. He raised a brow when Aiden frowned. "What? Deacon wants to help. And he has Luke. He's not going to let anything happen to your brother."

Aiden snapped his mouth shut as he stared at Seth. "That was almost . . . reassuring. Are you feeling sick?"

Seth rolled his eyes.

I smiled a little and then took a sip of orange juice. My stomach twisted uncomfortably at the acidic burn. "Has anyone heard anything from . . . from Apollo or any of the gods?" A sharp pain lit up my chest at the mention of my father. What a dickhead. Seriously. "Before I was taken, I thought . . . I thought I saw furies in the sky."

"There weren't any furies that I saw, and they are kind of hard to miss." Alex propped her chin on her fist. "No gods, either. Not a damn thing, but that's not really surprising. Whenever the world dons its crazy pants and gets ready to throw down, they all disappear."

Aiden was still staring at Seth with a mixture of wonder and confusion.

"They probably won't come anywhere near us." Seth lifted his left hand and several plates flew from the cabinet, settling gently on the counter like something straight out of *Beauty and the Beast*.

"Show off," muttered Alex.

He looked up through thick lashes and grinned in a way that replaced that dull ache in my chest. "The gods know what I am. They know I can end them. So they're going to stay far, far away."

"And are you planning to do that?" Aiden dumped slices of bacon on each plate. "End the gods?"

Seth shrugged a shoulder as he scooped up some eggs. "You know, I haven't decided."

I raised a brow as I glanced down at the bacon. My stomach grumbled with hunger, but it also churned unsteadily.

Seth's gaze flickered to mine. "There are one or two I really would like to straight-up murder."

Knowing he was talking about my father, I simply widened my eyes as I took another drink. The queasiness increased.

"Well, maybe you should try to control your murderous impulses," Aiden suggested. "You never know when the gods might actually be useful."

Seth snorted as he placed the last of the eggs on a plate. "That is just as likely as you actually being useful."

One side of Aiden's lips kicked up. "You know, I think you have a crush on me."

Seth simply smiled in return, and it was a bit of a creepy, hide-your-kids kind of smile that actually reminded me of Apollo, and that really made it even more weird.

"It's like the *Twilight Zone*," murmured Alex, her eyes big. "Watching them work together on *anything*, even when it's just eggs and bacon."

I laughed under my breath.

Aiden's lopsided grin spread as he picked up two plates and brought them over to where Alex and I sat. In a few minutes, Seth was beside me and Aiden was next to Alex.

"Supposedly I don't have to eat food anymore." Seth held up a piece of bacon. "But there is no way I'm going to stop eating bacon."

I stared at him. "Really? You don't have to eat anymore?"

Seth nodded as he bit down on the crispy slice.

What the hell? I was a full-blown demigod and I still had to eat.

"You're a freak," Alex said.

Thrusting a fork full of eggs into my mouth, I decided it was best at the moment to not dwell on how different Seth was now.

We ate in silence for a few minutes. The eggs were amazing, fluffy and buttery, and they seemed to settle my stomach down. I could eat an entire skillet of them, and bacon was always delicious as long as it was crispy and greasy.

"So," I said, clearing my throat. "What's the plan?"

Aiden frowned. "The plan?"

"Yeah. What are we doing now? I'm here and I'm okay." I'd forced the last word out, because I wasn't sure how okay I truly was, but hey, I was alive. And it wasn't like anything was going to wait around for me to get my shit together. "What are we going to do about Mitchell?"

Aiden's dark brows snapped together. "Mitchell?"

"Yeah, the demigod that . . ." I trailed off, looking at Seth. "You haven't told them, have you?"

"Haven't exactly had the time," he replied, putting down his other slice of bacon. He continued before I had the chance to respond. "The plan is for you to stay here, to heal, and then after you heal, you're going to continue to stay here."

Slowly lowering my fork, I raised my brows. "Nice of you to include me in this decision you've already made."

"You're welcome. And just so you know, I've made a couple more decisions," Seth tacked on, and I preemptively put the fork down before I turned it into a weapon. "You're not doing the whole search-and-rescue mission. We have to figure out how to get those damn bands off your wrists. That's the plan."

"Uh-oh," whispered Alex.

Aiden leaned forward, resting his arms on the counter. "Seth sort of has a point."

"Holy shit, someone record this," Seth said.

Aiden's eyes narrowed, but he ignored Seth. "You need to get better, Josie. You need to heal."

"I get that, but what then?" I looked around me, my gaze settling on Alex before I twisted toward Seth. The sharp motion did not sit well with my stomach. I guessed the food hadn't helped. "I'm not just going to sit here and do nothing for the rest of eternity. The Titans are still out there, and I wasn't the only demigod Capri Sun they were keeping prisoner. They already killed one of the demigods, and if we don't do something they'll kill Mitchell. He's still there."

Alex straightened. "You saw them?"

Shooting Seth a look that promised we'd so be discussing this later, I focused on Alex. "Yes. One of them was named Lauren. She . . . she died. They drained her and left her to die."

"Gods," Aiden muttered.

I took a deep breath and ignored the rapid twisting my stomach was doing. "Mitchell was in bad shape. He's not going to last much longer. We have to get him out of there."

Seth's jaw locked down.

"We're not leaving him there to die." I scowled at him. "Did you really think that I'd be okay with that?"

Topaz eyes met mine. "No, I don't expect that. I know you don't want to hear this, but if he was in such bad condition, he may not be alive."

"We don't know that," I argued. "We can't give up and not—" A bitter knot moved up my throat and I slapped my hand over my mouth. "Oh God."

"What?" Seth was immediately off his stool, standing in

front of me.

Alex and Aiden faded together into the background as my stomach heaved. I slid off the stool. "I . . . I think I'm going to be sick."

"Vomit sick?" Surprise filled Seth's face.

"Yeah—oh God." I swallowed, and immediately regretted it. "Where's a—?"

Seth wrapped an arm around my waist, and it felt like only a second passed before I was inside a bathroom. Pulling away from Seth, I dropped to my knees and lifted the lid of the toilet.

Stomach heaving, all those eggs and bacon came right back up. Gagging, I clutched the sides of the toilet. My eyes watered and it just kept coming and coming. Vaguely, I was aware of cool hands on my forehead, scooping my hair back.

Finally, after what felt like an eternity in a fresh circle of hell, there was nothing left to throw up. "Oh God," I moaned.

"You all done?" Seth asked.

I winced. "I think so?"

Seth gently tugged me back from the toilet. I heard it flush and then I was cradled in his lap, my cheek resting on his shoulder as I concentrated on taking deep, even breaths. Several minutes passed as he rubbed the center of my back. Holy crap, I threw up. I couldn't even remember the last time I had puked. When I was a child?

There was a knock on the door and I heard Alex ask, "Is everything okay?"

"Yeah," Seth called out. "Just give us a few moments."

"How are you feeling?" He smoothed my hair back off my clammy forehead.

I forced my eyes open. "Better. Stomach's a little . . . wonky."

"We need to get some water in you. Do you think you can handle that?"

"I think so. Oh man." I tipped my head back. "That was so, so gross."

Seth's gaze found mine. Concern etched into his striking face. "Josie, you're . . . you're a demigod. You shouldn't be sick."

I stared at him, unsure of how to respond to that, because I had obviously just gotten very, very sick. "Maybe I just ate too much after not eating a lot?"

"I don't know." Seth didn't sound like he thought that was the case. His gaze dropped, and I followed to see that he was looking at the bands on my wrists. "Maybe."

If the bands were blocking my abilities, could they be slowing down how quickly I could recover? Could they be making me sick? My poor stomach dipped.

Could they be making me mortal?

22

Once we exited the bathroom, the breakfast had sort of fallen apart. I kind of felt bad, because threatening to vomit all over the counter had probably killed their appetites. But once Seth got some water in me, I felt a hundred percent better.

The bracelets around my wrists hadn't tightened, but they felt like they were going to cut off my circulation. The feeling was all in my head, but what if they were making me mortal—susceptible to viruses and serious injuries? I was going to keep that suspicion to myself, because Seth would wrap me up in bubble wrap if that idea occurred to him.

Then again, his hawkish gaze alluded to the fact that he probably already suspected the same.

A small army of staff had appeared out of nowhere to clean up the kitchen, so we ended up in the largest living room I'd ever seen. I curled up in a comfy, overstuffed chair, my feet tucked under me. My stomach was feeling pretty stable and no one was really looking at me like they were waiting for me to hurl again, but tension had crept into the airy room. Alex and Seth were arguing about something, but I wasn't sure what exactly. I was tired after touring the house, eating the large breakfast, and vomiting my guts up. I wanted nothing more than a nap, and that was a wee bit concerning, because I'd been asleep more than awake recently, even when Hyperion had a hold of me.

Sighing, I looked up and saw that Seth was watching me from across the room. My stomach hollowed as I remembered the kiss from the cliffs. He probably wasn't thinking about that since he had just been holding my hair back while I prayed to the porcelain god.

His amber eyes hooded, and I felt my cheeks flush in response. Okay, he most definitely was not thinking about what happened in that bathroom. Good to know he wasn't repulsed.

Alex sat on the loveseat and leaned back, clapping her hands over her stomach. "Man, I think I have a food baby."

I coughed out a tired laugh and then something occurred to me. "Can you two . . . have kids?" The moment I asked the question, I cringed, because whoa, that was a private thing to stick my nose in. "I'm sorry. I shouldn't have asked that. I—"

"It's okay." Alex grinned as she knocked her hair back from her face. I swore I saw a faint pink splash across the heights of Aiden's cheekbones. "We honestly don't know. I mean, I'm not a normal demigod. Neither of us are, so we don't know if one day it could happen. We haven't been trying, but we . . ." She trailed off, shrugging.

But they also probably haven't been using protection.

"The mere idea of you having a child actually frightens me," Seth commented dryly.

"You and me both," Alex muttered under her breath.

Folding my arms across my waist, I snuggled into the cushions. Seth hadn't been sure if that could happen for us, so he'd always used protection. Well, except for that one time. My nose wrinkled. Before Seth had left me, he'd found me in the library, and I was pretty positive he hadn't used a condom.

My stomach dipped and then roiled slightly as I tried to figure out when my last period was. Not that I was seriously worried about getting pregnant, because it was seriously unlikely, and not because I sincerely believed I couldn't get pregnant from one episode of unprotected sex. With my luck, that was a hundred percent feasible, but after everything with Hyperion . . . ? There was no way a pregnancy would've survived that.

Ugh. I shifted in the seat, uncomfortable with my train of thoughts. I was way too young and things were way too crazy to even entertain the idea of popping out a baby Seth.

A baby Seth?

My eyes widened.

I might puke again.

Seth walked behind my chair and placed his hands on my shoulders. "You okay?"

Tilting my head back, I smiled despite the fact my thoughts were on an extended trip through Crazy Land. "Yep," I said. Pushing those really weird thoughts aside, something occurred to me that I hadn't thought about. "We may be facing a really big problem—bigger than we realize. To entomb the Titans, six demigods needed to be brought together and whatever wards were binding their abilities would be removed. They still need their icons, but I know where they are," I said, knowing they were stashed in the library and guarded by Medusa. "I was unbound because my—because Apollo did it himself and that weakened him, so I doubt the other gods will do that. There're not six demigods anymore. Only five."

"So that means the gods have to do what Apollo did for you," Aiden said.

"And how likely is that?" Alex asked. "Especially if it weakens them?"

"Then we don't worry about entombing the Titans." Seth

shrugged a shoulder. "I take care of them like I did Perses."

"Seth, we can't . . ." I trailed off, because I could tell by the look on his face he wasn't hearing it and I really didn't have the energy to argue over it. I had no idea if five demigods could stop the Titans.

What if the only choice was to kill the Titans?

Luckily there hadn't seemed to be any ill effects from taking Perses out. Yet. But with the other Titans? There had to be.

"I want to ask you a couple of questions." Aiden sat beside Alex and leaned forward, resting his arms on his legs as he eyed me. "Are you okay with that?"

Without even looking at Seth, I could tell that he tensed. "Yeah. Of course."

Behind me, Seth sighed.

Aiden smiled faintly. "What can you tell us about the Titans? Anything would be helpful for us to better know what we're dealing with."

Inhaling deeply, I unfolded my arm and reached up, tucking a piece of hair behind my ear. "I only saw a couple of them. It was mostly Hyperion and a woman whose name was really hard to pronounce up until Cronus somehow figured out they had me."

"Cronus? Okay." Aiden's eyes darkened to thunderclouds. "What can you tell us about him?"

"He wasn't what I expected. He was old, like really ancient. Kind of like Gandalf the Gray, but way older." I began to tell them how frail Cronus was at first and how he couldn't even sit up without help. I skimmed over the whole feeding part, but they were able to fill in the blanks when I explained that he'd appeared stronger the next time I'd seen him. As I spoke, Seth came around and sat on the arm of my chair. His jaw was so hard it could cut marble. "I only saw two other Titans. One I think was called Oceanus. He had a bright blue Mohawk and he . . ."

"He what?" Aiden prodded gently.

My gaze dropped to my wrists. "He was the one feeding off Lauren—the girl who died. Mitchell had said he . . ." Biting down on the inside of my cheek, I paused. "Oceanus just needs to die."

There was a gap of silence, and then Alex asked, "Who else?"

"There was Perses, but yeah, he's no more, apparently." I glanced at Seth. He smiled. Alrighty then. "There was also this female Titan. Her name is super hard to say, but I think it's Tet-something. Tethys?" I cringed. "I don't know, but she wasn't very pleasant. I know Hyperion referred to her at one point as his sister, but then they were practically eating one another's faces at one point, so that was weird."

Alex's lip curled with revulsion. "And you didn't see any other Titans?"

I shook my head. "I was alone a lot towards the end. But not in the beginning."

"Who were you with?" Seth asked, his voice too quiet, and when I looked at him, his eyes shone like topaz jewels.

"The other two demigods." I looked over at the others. "When I first saw both of them, I really thought they were dead. Barely moving or breathing." A shudder worked its way through me as I recalled seeing them for the first time. "They've been there so long."

Alex rubbed her arm with her hand. "And you said that this Mitchell was still alive the last time you saw him?" When I nodded, she continued. "Were you all kept in the same place?"

"I think I was eventually moved to some other part of the place. It was like an old, abandoned warehouse. We were kept underground in what felt like a basement." I paused, because there was something I was forgetting. It lingered in the back of my head, just out of reach. "Wherever the warehouse was, it was really hot, so if it was in the states, it had to be somewhere in the south. There was absolutely nothing around it except trees."

"How did you know there was nothing around it?" Aiden inclined his head.

"Hyperion took me outside sometimes. He had me sit in the sun." I lifted my hand, touching the cut in my lip. "I always looked around to see if there was anyone or anything around. I didn't even hear traffic. I tried to escape once. That obviously didn't work out."

"Okay." Aiden sat back, his face a shade or two paler. I didn't want to look at Seth. "I know you don't want to think this, but do you really think Mitchell could still be alive?"

I sucked in an unsteady breath. "I hope so. To die alone, in a place like that, after what was being done . . ." I couldn't finish. My throat sealed right up. I'd truly believed that I would die there, just like Lauren.

"All right." Seth rose and took my hand. My eyes flew up, but before I could protest, he lifted me up out of the chair. "I think that's enough for right now."

I opened my mouth, but Alex was nodding. "We're going to check in with Deacon and Luke to see if they have any news."

"I'll also call my contacts in the communities," Aiden added.

"Awesome." Seth's reply was curt as he led me out of the room.

Stopping the moment we hit the hallway, I pulled my hand free. "Hey, what was all of that about?"

He turned to me, his jaw locked. A moment passed and I thought he was going to speak, but then he moved. One second we were standing outside the living room and the next I was in his arms, my front pressed to his, and we were standing outside, under the warm sun, sand between my toes and the ocean only a few feet away.

"Holy crap!" I pushed away from Seth and stumbled back. Spinning around, I took in the scenery with wide eyes. "Holy crap!"

"I don't really have to walk anywhere anymore."

"No shit!" I whirled, facing him. He'd done that when I'd gotten sick, but I'd been too focused on holding it together to really process that he had popped me from one room to the next. "How about warning me next time?"

A sheepish grin tugged at his lips. "But then I'd miss that look on your face."

"What look?"

"Like you want to kick me and kiss me at the same time," he answered.

My eyes narrowed. "I do not look like I want to kiss you right now. I probably look like I want to vomit on you." I pressed my hand to my lower stomach. "Holy wow, that's a nifty . . . and lazy talent."

"But fast."

It was that.

"Are you feeling sick again?"

I shook my head no. "Why? Why bring me out here?"

Seth walked over to me. "It hadn't occurred to me, and it took a couple of moments for it to sink in, but it makes sense."

"What?" Wind picked up strands of my hair and blew them across my face.

"You said Hyperion took you out in the sun. Did he ever say why?"

For a moment, I didn't get where he was going with this, and then it came to me. "He did! He said it helped replenish the lost aether. I totally forgot about that."

Anger flashed in his brilliant eyes. "Probably because your father is the Sun God. I should've thought of that as soon as I had you back here."

"Why would you think of that? I didn't even remember and I should have."

"You've had a lot on your mind."

"So have you."

"Pisses me off that Hyperion figured that out before me," he grumbled.

"Well, Hyperion has been around for a long time, so . . ." Taking in my surroundings, I shuffled toward the ocean and then sat down in the sand. "And I forgot, so there's no point in being hard on yourself."

Seth dropped down beside me and was quiet as I leaned forward and rolled up the hem of my pants, exposing my blindingly pale calves. Then I stretched out my legs, letting the cool, frothy water tickle my toes. "Are you going to make me stay out here until . . . ?"

"If I could make you stay out here forever, I would, but at least until you start . . ." His brow creased. "Until you start to feel right."

I stopped wiggling my toes. "Yeah, we're going to need to talk about the whole staying here forever part, but first, what do you mean until I feel right?"

His shoulder brushed mine as he stared out over the ocean. "Remember when I told you before that I could barely feel aether in you? Yours has always been strong—almost as strong as a god's, but like I said before, I can barely sense it now."

"Oh. Yeah." I bit down on my lip and then winced when I bit the cut in my lip. "That's . . . not good."

"It's like a light. Normally you're a beacon to me, but you're flickering now." Seth turned his head toward me. "You're weak, and I don't mean that to be insulting, but it's the truth."

"I will get better," I told him.

"I know, but I don't want you risking your life again. Not even for that demigod."

I forced myself to remain patient as I explained what I felt was obvious. "I cannot forget about him, Seth. You don't understand. I know just a little bit of what he's been through, and that's enough to not be able to walk away from this. And I can't stay here while everyone else goes out there and risks their lives."

"Why not?" he shot back. "Haven't you already lost enough? Sacrificed enough, Josie? You've lost your grandparents and then your mother. Your friend Erin? Who knows if she's really alive? Apollo could've lied about that also." He shot to his feet, pacing. Over his shoulder, I saw thick, gray clouds form. "You've had to leave college and your friends. Your whole life has been turned upside down. You were held captive, not once but twice. You've given *enough*."

My heart started thumping as tears pricked my eyes. "So have you, Seth."

He stopped. "And look at me. I'm a god. No matter what I've given up, it sure as hell paid off in the end for me."

"That doesn't change what you've had to go through and sacrifice. You made that deal with the gods for Alex and Aiden without knowing you'd become a god one day and the deal would no longer mean anything."

Thrusting a hand through his messy, golden hair, he growled low. "None of that matters. We're not talking about me. You've done enough, Josie. Let me finish this."

"Finish this how?" The clouds were racing across the blue skies.

Dropping to his knees in the sand beside me, he clasped my

cheeks with his hands. "I can end the Titans. You and the other demigods won't have to face them."

In my chest, my heart twisted. "Seth—"

"And I'll free Mitchell," he continued. "Even though I really don't care about him, and I know that is an asshole thing to say, but I only care about you."

"That's not true." I wrapped my fingers around his wrists. "You care about Alex and Aiden."

His brows rose. "Only because I'm supposed to."

"Seth," I replied flatly.

"Okay. It would suck if something bad happened to them, especially Alex. She will always be important to me," he admitted, and where I used to feel jealousy at hearing that, I no longer did. Somewhere along the way, I'd accepted the special place in his heart that was reserved for Alex. "Aiden? Well, I wouldn't exactly miss him."

"Seth."

"But you? If something happened to you again?" Lighting shot between the clouds, lighting up the sky in brilliant white. "I would burn this fucking world to the ground and then I would destroy Olympus."

Closing my eyes, I didn't dare doubt what he said. "I know. I know, but you can't kill the Titans. We have to entomb them, and I have to help."

"I don't care about entombing the Titans."

Sliding my hands down his arms, I dropped my hands and opened my eyes. "You *do* realize that we have to live on this planet."

Seth popped forward, kissed the tip of my nose, and then drew back, lowering his hands. "Killing the Titans isn't going to destroy the whole world. I mean, shit. I killed Atlas and there were just a couple of earthquakes."

"A couple of earthquakes that freed zombie daimons and probably killed some innocent people."

He looked at me like he wasn't sure he knew where I was going with that statement. Good news was, the clouds were already breaking up and blue peeked through once more. "Nothing has happened with Perses."

"Maybe it's because he's not, I don't know, super important, but we can't be responsible for hundreds, thousands, or millions of deaths," I reasoned. "I just can't stay here and pretend like nothing is happening outside this beautiful island."

Cursing under his breath, Seth sat back. We were at a stalemate. I understood his protective urge. I fully got it. And he had to understand why I couldn't sit around here forever. Neither of us truly wanted to budge, though.

"You're tired," he said after a moment.

Surprised, I looked up at him again. "Can you feel that too?"

A half-grin appeared. "No, but you just . . . you look tired, Josie."

"Gee. Thanks."

He chuckled under his breath as he leaned over, brushing his lips along the curve of my cheek. "You look tired, but you're still the most beautiful woman I've ever seen."

"That sounds a lot better."

Kissing my temple, he pressed his forehead against mine. "How about I make you a deal?"

"Depends on what the deal is."

He reached across me and placed his hand on my hip. "We are trying to find out where the Titans may be. Aiden has people he knows in the pure communities checking to see if there has been any pures that have gone missing. We're not sitting here and doing nothing."

Then why did it feel like I was doing nothing but vacationing on a Greek island? Sighing, I flopped onto my back. "Okay. So what's the deal?"

"You stay where it's safe until we at least figure out how to get the bands off," he offered, stretching outside beside me. His thumb moved along my hip, inching my shirt up. "You don't have your abilities right now. You're as weak as a mortal. If you went out there now, it would be, frankly, stupid as hell. At least let us figure out how to get those bands off."

I didn't like it, but he had a point. With my powers blocked, I was more hindrance than help. "Fine."

An almost painfully stunning smile appeared on his face, warming his otherworldly beauty. "Is it a deal then?"

"It's a deal, *Sethie*."

23

*T*he following evening, Josie fell asleep on the couch while waiting for Alex and Aiden to come back in after Aiden received a call from one of the communities in Georgia. They'd only been gone five minutes, and she was already fast asleep.

Sitting at her hip, I brushed her hair back from her cheek. Her skin was too cool. Jaw working as frustration rose inside me, I looked over at a nearby cabinet. Lifting a hand, I willed the door open and tapped into the air element. A soft, thin blanket flew across the room. I snatched it up and then twisted back to Josie, draping it over her body.

Restlessness stirred within me like a slow-moving storm coming ashore, a sure sign that I would need to feed in the next day or so. I could probably go longer, but I didn't want to let my levels slip. Not when Josie was in such a vulnerable state.

My gaze dropped to those damn bands. We had to get them off. Since the gods had created the damn bracelets, I suspected only they could remove them.

Drawn by approaching footsteps, my gaze flickered to the

doorway. A second later, Alex popped her head in through the doorway. I held up a hand. Turning back to Josie, I bent over and kissed her cheek. She didn't stir as I rose and joined Alex just outside the living room.

"What's going on?" I asked.

Alex peeked into the living room once more. "She's asleep again?"

Rubbing a hand across my chest, I nodded. "She fell asleep about a minute after you guys walked out of the room."

Concern pinched Alex's features. "She hasn't gotten sick again, has she?"

"Not since this afternoon." I glanced into the living room as one of the white-robed servants bowed and then passed by in the hallway. Josie had eaten a late breakfast this morning and was sick again. She hadn't vomited, but she'd been rocking cold-green for a while. "It has to be those bands on her wrists. I . . ." I trailed off, because what could I say? There was something wrong with Josie and there wasn't a damn thing I could do about it.

Alex placed a hand on my arm. "We'll figure something out."

"So I'm guessing we haven't heard from Marcus?" Last night, I'd had Alex call her uncle to see if he'd heard of these types of bands before. He hadn't, but he had access to the massive library with a ton of ancient texts. There had to be something about the bands in there.

She shook her head.

Aiden rounded the corner, slipping his cell into his pocket. "You know I've been checking in with communities in the southern states. I just heard back from one outside of Atlanta. Other than sporadic daimon attacks, they haven't noticed any suspicious missing persons." He leaned against the wall, crossing his legs at the ankles. "I also heard back from the communities in Phoenix and Scottsdale. Thought to check this out since Josie said it was really hot."

Alex tilted her head to the side with a slight frown. "There are trees in Arizona?"

Both Aiden and I turned and looked at her. He raised a brow. "Yes, babe. There are trees in Arizona."

She rolled her eyes. "I know there are trees, but she said it was *heavily* wooded."

Aiden's lips twitched. "There are a couple of national forests there."

"Huh," Alex murmured. "Learn something new every day."

I shook my head. "Anyway, any leads there?"

"No, but I did speak to one of the guards in Baton Rouge. They haven't had a lot of missing pures, but interestingly, they've had what I suspect were shade attacks."

That was something. "Where there are shades, there are Titans nearby."

"The thing is, though, that Josie said she felt like she was kept in a basement of some sort," Aiden said. "I don't think a lot of homes or businesses there would have basements."

"Maybe it wasn't a basement," Alex jumped in. "Maybe it just felt like one to her."

She had a point. "It needs to be checked out, but I'm not leaving Josie. She's not going to like hearing that, but that's not going to change."

Alex's eyes narrowed. "You might want to try to discuss it with her in a less dickhead way, and she'd probably be more understanding."

I shrugged.

"You could pop me there, couldn't you?" Aiden asked. "Would only take a few seconds. Then I can see if I can catch me a shade and . . . convince it to talk."

That was doable.

Alex shifted from one foot to the next. "Wait. I don't like this."

Aiden opened his mouth.

"You have no idea if the Titans are there are not, and I'm not doubting your badassery or anything, but the place could be teeming with shades. You can't go alone." She faced me. "Can't you poof me there, too?"

"I can, but that would mean Josie would be here unprotected." I folded my arms. "I don't care if it's even for a couple of seconds. That's all it would take if they figure out where we are."

Alex looked like she wanted to push the issue, but wisely snapped her mouth shut.

Pushing off the wall, Aiden glanced into the room Josie was sleeping in. "I have to call them and let them know I'm coming in. Give them a chance to put a team together for me. Probably makes sense to wait a few hours."

"Works for me." Turning to Alex, I could tell just by the tight lines of her face she was barely keeping her mouth shut. "Can you do me a favor? Stay with her in case she wakes up?"

Her brows eyes formed into thin slits. "I remember what happened the last time you—"

"Alex," I warned.

She sighed. "Yeah, I can keep an eye on her. Where are you going?"

I arched a brow. "I have something I need to do."

"Like what?"

Aiden circled an arm around Alex's shoulders. He drew her in so she ended up face-planting his chest. Over her head, he shot me a look that said I owed him.

Nodding curtly, I pivoted around and walked past the staircase, spying Basil waiting by the entryway to the kitchen. "Have you seen Karina?"

"She is in the temple, Kýrios."

Gods.

"Do you wish me to retrieve her?" he offered.

Considering Alex was right down the hall and had eyeballed Karina like she wanted to body-slam her into the ocean, that wouldn't be wise. "I'll go to her."

Basil nodded.

Since walking was overrated, I pictured the courtyard outside and a second later there I was, standing just outside the courtyard. Flames rippled from the titanium urns. A priest and priestess stood on either side of the closed doors.

Exhaling heavily, I stared at the sandstone temple, at the invincibility rune above the doors. The last thing I wanted to do was go in there, but I hadn't approached them about the bracelets yet. I needed to feed soon, but it didn't feel right bringing Karina into the same house as Josie. Then again, keeping Karina out here kind of felt like I was doing something shady.

Really was a lose-lose situation.

Each step I took toward the temple felt like I was walking through muddy water. I reached the wide steps and felt a charge of energy roll down my spine. I swallowed back a curse when the two by the door bowed. Willing the doors open, I caught sight of the inside of the temple for the first time.

Cool air that smelled of frankincense washed over me. The inside was wide and open. No statues or odd religious artifacts decorated the walls. There were closed doors in the back, leading to the rooms where I assumed the priestesses and priestess resided.

Only one person was in the temple.

Karina stood before a white altar set upon a raised dais, and boy was I wrong. That was definitely a weird thing in the temple. A single candle cast its glow from the center of the altar. Beside it was the source of the smell. Incense burned. Beside the candle appeared to be a silver dagger much like the ones that the Covenant used. I didn't want to know why they had one of those or what they used it for.

She bowed deeply at the waist. "Kýrios, I've been waiting."

And yeah, that was fucking creepy.

"What do you think of the temple?" she asked, clasping her hands in front of her. As usual, her dark hair was piled atop her head in a startling, intricate fashion.

I looked around. "It's . . . pretty unimpressive."

She tilted her head. "Have you've been inside many temples, Kýrios?"

"Nope. This would be the first."

Karina gave a faint smile. "Then I can assure you that this is rather impressive by comparison."

I was going to have to take her word for it.

"Do you wish to feed now?" she asked.

Something clenched in my chest, and I found myself shaking my head even though I had planned on doing that. "Not . . . not right at this moment."

A look of understanding crossed her face and she nodded. "As you wish."

Well, this was a freaking awkward as hell conversation. "I've come to see if you know anything about these . . . bands that are circling Josie's wrists. The Titans placed them on her to block her demigod abilities and they will not come off. I think they are preventing her from recovering completely and are making her sick."

"Kyría is ill?"

"I . . . I think so." I stepped forward, stopping a few feet from the high priestess. I could feel the aether in her—I could practically see it glowing brightly within her veins. "She's a demigod. She shouldn't be ill."

"No, she should not. I do not know these bands, but I am sure one of the Olympians would."

Frustration spiked. "Even her father is not answering our calls."

Picking up the skirt of her dress, Karina stepped down from the dais. "You should try summoning him again."

I held back a curse. "That would be useless." And catastrophic, because when Apollo inevitably ignored my summons once again, I was going to want to blow something big up.

"Did you know that temples are like conduits to Olympus?" she asked. "The gods can hear your prayers much more clearly here." She stopped beside me. "Especially if you shed a little blood over fire."

My eyes narrowed. "What?"

"You should try it." She breezed on by. "I will await outside."

Turning, I watched her glide across the temple floor and out the door. My gaze moved upward, to the open panel that let the sunlight in. What she had just said sounded absolutely insane, but what could I lose in trying?

If the Olympians created the bands, then Apollo had to know how to get them off. Going to him for help made me want to punch myself in the nuts, but I was willing to do anything for Josie.

Striding across the floor, I stepped up on the dais and approached the altar. I seriously doubted this was going to work, but I picked up the dagger anyway. Spill blood over flame? Shaking my head, I drew the dagger down the center of my palm. A thin line of blood welled up. Fisting my hand over the flame, I squeezed until a few drops of blood seeped out of my hand.

My brows lifted. "What the hell?"

The blood was red, but there was a blue sheen to it. And it shimmered.

My fucking blood *shimmered* now.

Inhaling raggedly, I watched a few drops of blood hit the flame. Fire sizzled and crackled. Drawing my hand back, the smoke turned black and then gray. Cursing under my breath, I lifted my gaze to the ceiling. "Apollo? If you can hear me, you need to get your ass down here now. Your *daughter* needs you."

I waited.

Nothing.

Closing my eyes, I shook my head. What was I thinking? He wouldn't even come for his own—

A burst of pure power filled the temple, coasting over my skin like I had touched a live wire. My eyes flew open as the back of my neck tingled.

"You called?"

24

The sound of Apollo's voice filled me with warring emotions. I was relieved that he finally, finally had answered because maybe he could help Josie. I was also infuriated by his mere presence.

I turned slowly, facing him, and there he was.

Apollo stood in the center of the temple, his all-white eyes glowing like two fucking light bulbs. There was a time, a very brief moment in time, when I'd actually reluctantly respected Apollo. That time occurred once when he was masquerading as Leon, a pure-blooded Sentinel. There might had been a time after I knew what he was, like when he made sure Alex had been taken care of when Ares had broken every bone in her body.

Right now, I wanted nothing more than to knock his head off his shoulders.

"It's about time," I said, jaw clenched. "Got to admit. Kind of surprised you had the balls to show up."

Apollo lifted his chin. "You cannot harm me inside a temple."

"So, what? You basically get to yell 'safe' in a temple?"

"If we were playing a game of tag," he replied. "Then yes."

My hands curled into fists.

"The blood you shed on the flame nullifies our abilities while in the temple. I cannot harm you and you can only stand there and pout. And by the way, do not doubt whether or not I have the balls to do anything."

There were so many things I could say in response to that, but there were more important things to discuss. "Where in the fuck have you been? Your daughter was captured by Hyperion. Your daughter, Apollo. Do you even know what he—" I cut myself off as I took another step forward. "I summoned you. Alex summoned you. Where were you?"

Apollo held still. "Where were you, *Seth*? The last I checked you weren't there, either."

"Oh, trust me. I know exactly where I've been and why I've been there. And I also know exactly the huge-ass fucking mistake I made when I left Josie. I did it because I thought she would be safer away from me. That's no excuse. I'll never regret anything more in my life. But you . . . How could you not know what was happening to her? How could you not *feel* it?"

A muscle flexed along his jaw. "Nothing I say will change it, will it?"

"Fuck no!" I shouted. Outside, thunder rattled the temple. My abilities might have been temporarily blocked in here, but a storm was coming outside. "We summoned you and you ignored our calls. Your daughter was missing and you had to know what that meant—who had her. And you ignored us—ignored *her*."

Apollo turned his head, looking away.

There was so much more I could rage at him about. The fact that he'd lied about her mother. How he'd never treated Josie like a damn daughter whenever he was around her. How he'd unbound her powers without explaining what that entailed. I could keep going for a fucking eternity, but I had to focus. "Josie is not doing well."

His head sharply swung in my direction. Now I had his attention.

"But you might even know that already. That wouldn't surprise me."

"Proceed with caution," he warned.

I smirked. "Aw, thought we can't hurt each other?"

"Doesn't mean we can't try."

"Like to see you do it," I replied coldly. "Because I'm learning that what I can throw down will make what you can do seem like a kid playing with a water gun."

Apollo's nostrils flared. "What's wrong with my daughter?"

Hearing him say the word "daughter" had me seeing the world in amber. But pissing Apollo off and having him run away without getting what I needed wasn't going to help Josie. So I really needed to slow my roll.

I drew in a deep breath. "She isn't recovering as quickly as she should. She's been physically sick, and I can barely feel any aether in her."

Apollo glanced at the door and for a moment I thought he was going to leave the temple, but he briefly closed his eyes. When they reopened, there were irises—eyes as blue as the sea. They were identical to Josie's with the exception of the pupils. His weren't black. There were white, and that was some weird-looking shit right there.

"When she was being held by the Titans, they placed these bands on her wrists to block her powers," I explained.

"Shit," Apollo said.

That didn't sound good. "So you know of these bracelets?"

He nodded curtly. "Those bracelets are fashioned in Tartarus to entomb the Titans. They mute the effects of aether. They may slow down healing if her injuries were . . . were significant enough." He frowned slightly. "They shouldn't make her sicker."

"Well, they are. We need to get them off of her now."

"Only Hades would have the ability to unlock them."

"Then can we get Hades's ass up here and do it?"

"None of the other gods will come near you or Josie. They will not risk it."

Anger hummed under my skin. Fucking cowards. "Bring him to this temple and I can bring Josie here."

"They will not risk it even inside this temple or any temple," Apollo replied. "They do not trust you. They do not trust what you are and aren't capable of."

"And you do?" I retorted.

Apollo's gaze leveled on me. "I simply know you're capable of anything. I could take Josie to Hades—"

My jaw locked down. "Not going to happen."

"You'd refuse aid for her?"

"I will refuse the idea of her going anywhere with you by herself," I shot back. "Do not think I've forgotten how Hades wanted to take out Alex."

"This has nothing to do with Alex."

"But it shows a long history of you guys making shit choices." I unclenched my hands. "I will not leave Josie unprotected, even with you. Figure something else out. Those bands have to come off."

A strange look flickered over Apollo's expression. It was strange because it almost looked like pride, but that made no sense. He was probably constipated. "I will go to Hades and see what can be done."

Disbelief thundered through me. "How could you be unaware of what has happened to her? What she's going through? Or do you just not give a fuck?"

"Do not question how I feel about my daughter or what I would do for her," he cautioned, his voice eerily low and calm.

"You do not understand. You couldn't understand."

Yeah, that sounded like a whole load of bullshit. "At least I can admit that I made a mistake by leaving her. You can't even acknowledge that you weren't there for her."

Apollo closed his eyes and looked like he was counting under his breath. When they reopened, he still appeared to want to hit me. Too bad. "You made the right decision."

My brows flew up. "What?"

Those creepy-ass eyes met mine. "Leaving her was the right choice at the time. You showed a level of . . . restraint I never believed you were capable of."

Was Apollo complimenting me?

"You left to protect her. There is no fault in that."

I had no words.

None.

Apollo stepped back, his gaze traveling to the altar on the raised dais. "I will go to Hades. I will make sure he assists us one way or another." His gaze settled on me again.

If he was waiting for me to thank him, he was going to be waiting for an eternity to hear that. But there was something I wanted to ask him. "Did you know? Did you always know what I would become?"

He sighed heavily. "I am the God of Prophecy."

"That's not really an answer."

Apollo was quiet for a moment and then said, "A prophecy is never guaranteed to play out like it has been seen. Not every aspect of fate is written in stone. I had foreseen the rise of the Appointed One. I have foreseen what is to come, but it still can change."

"You know, a heads-up about this whole god thing would've been great."

He smirked. "What would it have changed?"

"If I had known what I was to become and what I could control, I wouldn't have left Josie."

"And do you plan to keep feeding off your priestesses without her knowing?" He volleyed back, proving that he'd been keeping an eye on this. "Or will you feed off her?"

Fury punched me straight in the chest, and I stepped up to Apollo, going eye to eye. "Or maybe I will take up residence in Olympus and not have to worry about feeding. I'm thinking the place could use a little redecorating."

Apollo's eyes flipped all white. "Is that a threat?"

I smiled tightly. "I guess we'll just have to wait and find out, won't we?"

His expression locked down, his features impassive as he started to fade out. "We just might."

Josie

I was dreaming again.

Part of me could recognize that—a very distant part of me knew that I wasn't really standing at the University. I was at Seth's home. I knew that, but I could feel the warm breeze on my arms and stirring my loose hair. I could see the tall, marble statues that lined the courtyard as the stranger with blond hair and bright blue eyes stepped forward, taking my hands in his.

"Hi there," he said.

I could hear someone crying behind me as he turned my hands over so they were palms up. "It's time, don't you think?"

"Time for what?" I asked, confused.

The stranger smiled boyishly.

Jolting awake, I sat straight up. The soft blanket slipped down and pooled at my waist as I glanced around the room. My head pounded like someone had taken up residence inside my skull and started banging on a set of drums.

"Hey, you're awake."

I jerked around, spying Alex at the entryway to the living room. She was holding a mug in her hand. "Yeah, I . . . I am."

She came into the room, her long ponytail bouncing with each step. "How are you feeling?"

"Okay." Pushing the blanket aside, I dropped my bare feet to the floor. "Actually, I have one hell of a headache."

"Can I get you something for it, Kyría?" Basil announced without warning. He'd suddenly appeared in the doorway.

My eyes widened, as did Alex's. I hadn't even heard him come into the room. "Um, thanks. That would be great."

Basil bowed and quickly disappeared. I looked at Alex. "Is he like a ninja ghost or something?"

She giggled. "I think so."

"Where is everyone?"

"Aiden is making a few phone calls." She dropped into a nearby chair. "We might have a lead on where you were held."

"Really?"

She nodded as she sipped what smelled like coffee. "There is a community of pures that have reported what seems like shade attacks. They're outside Baton Rouge. Aiden will . . . he will be heading there tomorrow morning. Seth's going to poof him there. He'll try to catch one of them and get it to talk."

"He's going by himself?"

"Yep. I am not too happy about it." Alex leaned to the side, placing the mug on the table beside her. "Not that I don't think he can't take care of himself, but it's . . ."

"I get it," I told her. "It's dangerous. Why aren't you going with him?"

She raised a brow. "For me to go, well, Seth would have to poof me there, too, and that would mean you'd be by yourself."

My brows lifted. "I can be by myself."

"I know, but—"

"Seriously. Aiden shouldn't be doing this by himself and leave you here to worry about him because I can't be alone for two seconds." Trying to assuage my headache, I rubbed at my temples. It really didn't help. "Where is Seth?"

Alex's gaze flickered away as she shook her head. "I'm . . . not sure."

My eyes narrowed. "Why do I have a feeling you do know where he is?"

Before she could answer, Basil returned. I dropped my hands when I saw that he held a jar of something that smelled minty. There was no aspirin. No water.

Basil smiled down at me. "This is peppermint oil. When applied to the temples, it works to reduce the pain from headaches. You will find that it is far better than a chemical. May I?"

"Okay," I whispered, glancing at Alex. She'd picked up her mug and all I could see were her brows raised over the rim.

Basil tapped some of the oil onto the tips of his fingers before gently rubbing them against my temples. The oil was cool but heated quickly. The brief massage did feel good. If it didn't work, I'd at least smell good. Like Christmas. That's what it reminded me of.

"Thank you," I said.

"Is there anything else you need, Kyría?"

I shook my head, a little uncomfortable with the idea of someone just waiting to go do things for me. Actually, I was a lot uncomfortable with it. Basil bowed neatly and then left the room. I had a feeling he was lingering out in the hallway.

"Back to Seth," I said. "Where is he?"

"I'm right here," Seth answered.

I jumped at the sound of his voice. He'd literally popped out of nowhere and was now standing in the center of the living room.

"Holy daimon nuts!" Alex shrieked as coffee sloshed out of her cup and onto the front of her shirt. "Jesus. That was not necessary."

Seth's grin grew to epic proportions.

"It really wasn't," I told him, placing my hand over my thumping heart. "Just because you *can* poof in and out of rooms does not mean you *should*."

"But it's so much fun."

Alex was patting at the front of her shirt. "Gods, you're going to be just as bad as freaking Apollo."

"That's actually kind of insulting." Seth joined me on the couch. He tipped his head to the side. "Why do you smell like . . . Christmas?"

My lips twitched. Sometimes it felt like Seth and I were playing in two very different ballparks. Other times it was like we shared the same mind. "I had a headache and Basil gave me some peppermint oil."

"I'm kind of surprised you know what Christmas smells like," Alex muttered. She sighed as she looked down at herself. "I smell like a coffee shop now."

Seth touched my arm. It was a gentle brush of his fingers, but it sent a tight shiver dancing over my skin. "How are you feeling?"

"Fine." Since he'd almost given me a heart attack, I wasn't really paying attention to my head any longer. "I'm glad you decided to pop yourself into the room. We need to talk."

Seth glanced at Alex. She smiled broadly back. His eyes narrowed.

"You're not letting Aiden go by himself to check out the shades," I told him, and when he opened his mouth, I kept going. "It takes you how long to pop people back and forth? Seconds? I'll be fine for a few seconds." Even though I believed that, a icy trickle of fear climbed down my spine. I hated the feeling. "You're going to take Alex."

He stared at me a moment and then looked over at Alex again. "Did you talk her into this?"

She rolled her eyes. "Yes. Because she doesn't have a mind of her own."

I glared at him. "It was my call. And it's the right call."

Seth leaned back, popping a booted foot on the edge of the coffee table. "I'll think about it, but I need to tell you—"

"Don't try to distract me." I twisted toward him. "Alex needs—"

"I just saw Apollo," Seth cut in.

"What?" He'd officially distracted me.

Alex lurched forward in her chair. "Where?"

Seth's eyes roamed over my face and then met and held my gaze. "I summoned him in the temple. Apparently, if you shed your blood over flame, you can't hurt another god in a temple. So he showed up this time."

I didn't say anything, because I didn't know what to say. My father had been here, on this island, and he hadn't come to see me?

"I asked him about those bands," Seth said, reaching over and picking up my hand. "He said only Hades can remove them."

"That's good news." Alex clasped her knees. "We just need to get Hades here."

"He's not going to come here, not even if the temple is safe. Obviously the Olympians are lacking in the courage department."

I was still snagged on the fact that my father had been here and I hadn't seen him.

"Because of you?" Alex asked.

Seth didn't even try to hide his little smirk. "Apollo is going down there to talk with Hades. He has to come through."

Alex said something, and I could feel myself nodding, but my entire being felt like it had been stung. All I could think was that he was here and—*Wait*. Maybe Seth hadn't let him see me. "Did he . . . did he try to see me?"

He didn't immediately respond, and I knew the answer right then. I started to pull my hand away, but Seth's grip tightened. He pulled me toward him, and I wanted to resist, but the moment his arm circled my waist, I gave in. I planted my cheek on Seth's shoulder and squeezed my eyes shut against the stupid, pointless burn in them.

Why was I surprised?

"We didn't have a very good conversation," Seth said after a moment. His free hand smoothed over my cheek. "And I think he knew the moment he left that temple, we wouldn't be talking."

I smiled weakly and pretended I didn't know that Seth was actually making excuses for Apollo. Because it wasn't for him. It was for me, and I did appreciate it, but it didn't erase the hurt.

My father had been on the absentee list nearly my entire life. He let my mom sink into mental illness that may or may not have been caused by him. He wasn't there for me through so much, with the exception of one long, lonely summer. He . . . lied to me about my mother dying, and if he'd wanted to see me he would've. Seth wouldn't have stopped him, and even if he had, Apollo could've found a way around him.

The ache in my chest spread, and I didn't even know why it hurt so much, but as I snuggled into Seth and slowly opened my eyes, I realized that Apollo was my father by blood.

And blood . . . blood meant nothing.

25

I wasn't sure what woke me at first, and I was a little surprised that I'd even managed to doze off while Josie had straight up passed out around two in the afternoon. The ever-present concern for her had kept me awake, my thoughts whirling a mile a minute.

Where in the fuck was Apollo?

Three days had passed since I'd seen Apollo—four days since Josie and I had made our deal—and her bruises had either faded into a dull yellow or disappeared completely. Even so, she was still easily exhausted. No amount of sun I had her sit in seemed to make much of a difference. She'd sleep throughout the night, waking once and sometimes twice due to a nightmare, *always* a nightmare, and then she'd be dead on her feet by the afternoon. She'd gotten sick twice in the last three days, once before eating breakfast and once afterward. There was still no increase in her aether. It flickered rapidly within her.

On the outside, Josie was getting better, but on the inside, she wasn't. There was no denying that, and no one, not even the high priestess, knew what to do while we waited for Apollo.

And I swore with each passing hour that if he didn't come through with some way to get these bands off, I would end him the next time I saw him.

The day after I'd seen Apollo, I did take Aiden and Alex to Baton Rouge. They'd called me last night after coming up empty-handed. There had been no signs of the shades. If they had been there, they were long gone now. They wanted to come back here, and since I figured having them around couldn't hurt, I did the poofing thing with them.

Even though I'd only been gone from Josie for about ten seconds each time, I hated it. Didn't like it one bit. The Titans might not have had any idea where we were, but they had to be looking for us.

Blinking my eyes open just in time to avoid a flailing arm, I jerked back and then caught Josie's hand before it connected with my nose. I rose onto my elbow and stared down at her.

A faint sheen of sweat had broken out across her forehead as her head twisted from side to side. Face pale and brow pinched, her chest rose and fell with too-quick breaths.

Another fucking nightmare.

"Josie. Baby," I said, letting go of her arm and clasping her chin. "Wake up. Come on, wake up."

The skin around her eyes tightened and then her lashes fluttered. A couple of seconds passed and those azure eyes were locked onto mine, full of confusion.

"Hey." I trailed my thumb along her lower lip. The cut had healed, leaving her lips lush and perfect once more. I grinned even though my heart thumped painfully in my chest. "You're okay?"

"Yeah. Did I wake you?" she asked sleepily, brows pinched.

Dragging my thumb over her cheek, I kissed her forehead. "You were having a nightmare."

"I was?"

I lifted up and met her gaze. "You don't remember?"

She stared at me for a moment and then sighed, averting her gaze to my shoulder. "I was . . . I was dreaming about being back *there*," she said, and she didn't need to elaborate on where "there" was. "I'm sorry. I—"

"You do not need to apologize." Smoothing her hair back from her face, I guided her gaze back to mine. "Don't apologize for that."

Josie was quiet as she stared back at me, and I didn't know what to say. Comforting her with words didn't come easy, but I wanted my words to bring her ease so she could sleep without being haunted by what she'd experienced.

"What were you dreaming about?" I asked.

The corners of her lips turned down. "Just . . . just being stuck in that place and . . ."

"And what?" I leaned back on my elbow as she rolled onto her side facing me.

"It doesn't matter. It was just a nightmare."

"*Joe* . . ."

Her eyes rolled as she placed her hand against my chest. Her fingers were cool. "Whatever, Apolly-anna." Her nose wrinkled. "Wait. I can't even call you that anymore. No fair."

I chuckled. "What a shame."

She dragged her finger over my chest. "Did you go some-where when I fell asleep earlier? I thought I felt you leave the bed."

Surprise shuttled through me. I had left briefly so I could feed. "I met with Basil for a few moments." Which wasn't en-tirely a lie. I had met with him on my way back. Josie hadn't asked about the whole feeding thing, and I was hoping she wouldn't—at least for the time being while I figured out how to explain that I still needed to feed. "I'm surprised you even noticed me gone. You were snoring so loudly—"

"I was not snoring!" She slapped my chest. "That's insulting."

"It's nothing to be ashamed of," I teased.

She shot me a dirty look. "You're a jackass."

"You love me."

"You're lucky that I do."

My damn heart clenched in response. Fuck. I couldn't help it. I *was* lucky. Hearing her say that did things to me I couldn't even begin to describe.

Reaching over, I tugged on the thin straps of the tank top she was wearing. I knew that, under the blankets, she wasn't wearing any pants, and I struggled not to focus on that little fact. I was behaving myself. Toying with the strap, I thought about what Aiden had told me upon bringing him and Alex back. A community in East Texas had reported a larger than normal number of pures going missing. Hopefully that was our lead and Hyperion would be found nearby. I'd close out the week by turning that fucking bag of dicks into nothing but a smear on the ground. Maybe, if I killed Hyperion, then Josie wouldn't be so haunted, so terrorized.

"You look like you're about to break your brain," Josie said.

I raised a brow, but the smartass response died on the tip of my tongue. "I want to help you."

Her gaze flicked to mine as she placed her palm on my shoulder. "You are."

"Really? I'm not so sure about that. You have nightmares every night, sometimes twice a night. You're still exhausted all the time and you've been sick." I drew in a shallow breath. "I just want to help you. Tell me how I can."

Josie didn't respond for a long moment, and I knew she was trying to think of a way to change the subject. Talking about her time being held captive wasn't something she wanted to do. Couldn't really blame her for that, but I also knew just how badly unspoken words and unwanted memories could fester.

"Distract me," she whispered finally, running her hand up my chest and around to the nape of my neck. Her fingers slid through my hair and then over to my cheek. "Kiss me."

I didn't hesitate.

There was no way I could deny her.

Ever.

Josie

Seth lowered his head, his eyes lit from within by an amber fire. The moment his lips brushed mine, I wasn't thinking about the way the packed, cold dirt floor felt against my skin.

The kiss started off sweet, a little bit of pressure that left me aching for so much more than just a sweep of his lips on mine. When he started to lift his head, I caught him around the nape of the neck and held him there.

"More," I whispered in the space between us.

His chest rose sharply. "Are you sure?"

I started to frown. "Why wouldn't I be?"

Seth's eyes searched mine. "You've been through a lot. I'm trying not to rush you into anything—"

Lifting my mouth to his, I cut his words off. He was startled for a second and held still. I wasn't exactly great at initiating the whole kissing thing, but I touched the tip of my tongue to the seam of his lips and he opened immediately for me. I deepened the kiss, hoping to show him that what I needed right now was for him—*for us*—to be like the way we were before he left, before Hyperion reappeared. Since we've been reunited, all we'd done was kiss. Nothing more. He'd just recently started holding me in bed instead of making sure there was space between us.

And I needed more.

Seth's hand tightened on my shoulder, and I felt the tremble rock his body. I almost held my breath, fearing that he would pull away, but he didn't. He made this sound that came from the back of his throat, a sound that was animalistic and purely sexual as he finally, really kissed me. His hand slid down my arm and found its way to my stomach. "Okay," he murmured. "Distraction is something I excel at."

"I think there are a lot of things you excel at." Thrilled that I wasn't going to have to beg, my bones liquefied as his hand coasted up over my ribcage.

His tongue flicked over mine, and he drew out the kiss until I was practically panting for breath, and only then did he lift his mouth from mine. He chuckled when my fingers tugged on his hair. "Like what? Don't be shy. I love it when you list all the amazing things about me."

His hand slipped over my breast, and I gasped. His nimble fingers made their way under the hem of my top and found the aching peak. "You're . . . you're really good at that."

"But do I excel at it?" he asked, catching the nipple between his fingers and tugging gently.

Back arching, I moaned as I slipped my hand down to his shoulder. "Yeah. Yes."

He dragged the neckline of my top down, exposing the area of his current fixation. "And how about this?"

Before I could respond, he closed his mouth around where his two fingers had been and sucked deep, hard. A strangled cry ripped from me as heaviness filled my breasts and tiny coils formed low in my stomach. Pleasure darted through my veins.

Seth lifted his head and moved to the other breast. His warm breath danced over my skin. "Do I excel?"

"I . . . I think you know the answer to that."

His tongue flicked over my nipple. "I think I need to hear you say that."

My fingers dug into his skin. "You do."

He rewarded my answer with another swipe of his tongue and a quick nip that melted my insides. He rose, his tongue dragging across my mouth as his hand drifted down my stomach and the tips of his fingers slipped under the band of my undies. He stopped as his mouth played over mine, and for a moment, I worried that he wouldn't go any further than kissing and heavy petting. But then his hand moved and one long finger was slipping over the very center of me.

"Oh God," I whispered against his mouth.

"Yes?"

I laughed softly.

"I can already tell this is something you believe I excel at," he said, voice deep and rough.

Running my hand down his muscled arm, I curled my fingers over his forearm. "I do. I really, *really* do."

"Then I suppose I should prove my talents."

Seth did just that, sinking one finger deep inside me. My hips bucked as raw sensation poured into me. His thumb circled and pressed down on the bundle of nerves as he eased another finger inside. His finger moved slowly at first and then he did something with that finger, hooking it in a way that caused me to lose control. No, that was a lie. I never really had control when it came to Seth and to *this*. I held onto his arm as I ground against his hand and clutched at the strands of his hair with my other hand. His kiss swallowed my cry of release.

My body collapsed back against the bed. For a moment I just lay there, letting the sweet aftershocks ripple through my body. He slipped his hand from between my thighs, and with half-open eyes, I watched him lift his finger to his mouth.

Holy crap.

Everything about me clenched. I reached for him, grabbing at the loose pants he wore. He came only so far, stopping as he hovered above me. "You're not done distracting me," I told him.

"Mmm?" He gripped my hip. "That was all about you."

I tugged on him, wanting his body flush to mine, but he didn't budge. "I want this to be about us now."

He kissed me and then made that rough, raw sound again. "What I just did was about us," he said.

I could feel his arousal against my hip, so I knew he wanted this—wanted me, but he was, like I had suspected, holding back. "Seth, I . . . I want you."

His eyes drifted shut. "I will never get tired of hearing that."

"Then let me . . . let me have you, all of you."

Lowering his forehead to mine, he murmured, "*Psychi mou*, I want you to be ready."

"I *am* ready."

He didn't respond, but his fingers brushed over my wrist, over the band. He didn't pull my hand away, but he held it still.

My heart swelled and broke at the same time. "You're not rushing me into something I'm not ready for," I told him. "You never would, because I know . . . I know that I'm always safe when I'm with you."

His forehead slid against mine. "You weren't safe when I fed from you before."

"You didn't hurt me. I didn't even feel it, and it was nothing like what happened when I was with . . . with *them*," I told him. "And we already talked about that. Doing that without my permission wasn't okay. Not by a long shot. But I've forgiven you and you've promised to never do it again without asking. And we've moved past that. I trust you, Seth. I trust that I will always be safe with you," I repeated. "That you . . . you will always make sure of that."

He froze for a moment and then said roughly, "I don't

deserve you."

I cupped his cheek. "See, that's where you're being just plain stupid."

A startled chuckle left him.

"You do deserve me," I continued. "You deserve my love."

No sooner did those words leave the tip of my tongue before his mouth slanted over mine, and I knew he wouldn't stop this time. He wouldn't ask me if I was okay, or worry that I wasn't ready for this. We were so going to do this.

His lips moved down my throat, leaving a trail of hot kisses and tight shivers in their wake. Sensations raced over my skin, my heart sang, and this was better—

A knock on the door jolted me.

Above me, Seth nipped at my throat. "Ignore it."

"Alrighty," I moaned as I reached between us, wrapping my hand around the thick length straining through his loose cotton sweats. He groaned against my heated skin. I held my breath, and then his mouth closed over the top of my breast, and my entire body tensed and then jerked. "Oh *gods.*"

The knock came again, this time louder and more incessant, but Seth was still on the move, his hands shoving the blanket aside. I lost my grip on him.

"Seth!" Aiden yelled. "I know you're in there."

Seth's head stopped about an inch from what was going to be his promised land. "If you do not go away, Aiden, I will physically and gleefully harm you."

"Yeah, I'm going to have to risk that," was the response.

A low growl emanated from Seth as he rose. "I'm so fucking warning you—"

"We just heard from Deacon." Aiden's voice carried through the closed door. "They've found the demigod that was in Canada."

26

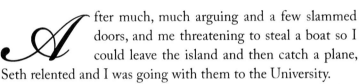fter much, much arguing and a few slammed doors, and me threatening to steal a boat so I could leave the island and then catch a plane, Seth relented and I was going with them to the University.

I appreciated that he was concerned for my well-being, but the Covenant was warded against the Titans, and I would be safe there. And it wasn't like we were driving there. Seth was going to do his super-special transporting thing.

He really didn't see the point in any of us going there, but from what Aiden had gathered from Deacon, the girl they'd brought back with them was not exactly thrilled by what was happening. According to Deacon, she had barricaded herself in one of the dorms and was refusing to come out. Of course, any number of the pures could've busted the door right open, but doing so wouldn't have helped matters. Currently Gable was trying to coax the girl out by relating to what she was experiencing.

There was also the very real chance that they had kidnapped the wrong person since they didn't have Herc to help sniff out the demigod blood, so we all were hoping that the boys hadn't committed a felony. I was curious to how they'd determined that this was one of the demigods.

Plus I didn't want to be left behind like some kind of frail damsel. I refused to allow that to happen. The last thing I needed was endless time alone to dwell over the time I'd spent with the Titans or my mom's death. My subconscious was already doing a bang-up job at that.

And if that wasn't enough to worry about, I was really, really beginning to stress over the whole nauseous and tired thing I was going through. More than once over the last couple of days, I'd tried to seriously figure out the last time I'd had my period. My life had been absolutely insane since I walked into Seth in the stairwell at Radford University. Stress can affect the whole monthly cycle thing, but I was sure I had not had a period in well over a month.

But—and it was a huge but—I'd also been virtually starved while being held by Hyperion. I knew that could affect a cycle. I also didn't think I'd have symptoms of—*oh gods*—a pregnancy so soon after unprotected sex. I mean, it wasn't that long ago, even though it felt like an eternity. It had only been three weeks, give or take a couple of days. I didn't think women had symptoms that quickly, but I also wasn't exactly normal.

And how in the world could a pregnancy last after what I'd been through?

My stomach dipped and rolled every time I seriously thought about the probability of actually being impregnated. I couldn't even process it or what that would really mean.

So, like any normal twenty-year-old, I decided to ride the river of denial and pushed it aside for the time being.

After pulling on a pair of jeans Basil had gotten from somewhere and tugging my hair up in a ponytail, we were ready to go. Seth did the cool god thing, taking Aiden to the Covenant first.

"That is so bizarre," Alex said, shaking her head. "I mean, I thought I'd be used to it by now, but I'm not. It's just so bizarre."

I looked over at her. "But awesome."

"I'm so entirely jealous."

A grin tugged at my lips and then Seth reappeared in front of us, causing me to jump. He smiled as he took my hand. "I'm going to take you next. You ready?"

"Not really." I looked over at Alex, hoping it didn't make me puke. My stomach felt fine today, but then again, I hadn't been poofed anywhere. "It feels really weird."

"Yes, it does," she said with wide eyes.

Wrapping my arm around Seth's waist, I took a deep breath and prepared myself as best I could, which was to close my eyes. "I'm ready."

Seth chuckled. "You look like you're about to jump out of an airplane."

"Shut up," I grumbled, keeping my eyes closed.

He laughed again, and then I felt his breath on my cheek. A heartbeat later, his lips brushed over mine. I gasped in surprise, and he took complete advantage of that, kissing me deeply.

"I'm glad that's not how I got here," I heard Aiden say.

My eyes flew open, and at first all I saw were glowing tawny eyes, and then I stepped back, looking around. I wasn't in Seth's house anymore. We were standing in a large office. I immediately recognized the older man standing by the desk. *Marcus*—Alex's uncle and the Dean of the University. We were at the Covenant.

"Did you forget how I excel at distraction?" Seth murmured in my ear.

I flushed hotly.

Dammit.

He *was* good.

Kissing my cheek, Seth let go. "I'll be right back."

Before I could say a word, he vanished and then suddenly Deacon was in front of me, all blond curls and silver eyes. "Deacon!" I barely got his name out before I was swept up in his lanky arms and hugged until I squeaked. Laughing, I held him just as tightly. "It's so good to see you."

"You have no idea." He rocked me from side to side, and I swore for a second my feet dangled. "Shit. It's good to see you."

The moment Deacon let go, I was enveloped in another hug, and this time it was Luke. "We missed you," he said, then stepped back, still clasping my upper arms. A half-smile formed on his handsome face. "Chicken tenders and fries haven't been the same without you."

"Neither has been watching *Supernatural*," Deacon chimed in. "Luke is all about Sam. I need my Team Dean cohort."

Blinking back sudden tears, I laughed again. These two—I'd only just met them a few months ago, but they were my friends, and I'd missed them. "Well, we need to get some tenders and fries and watch *Supernatural*—oh, and bacon."

The university had amazing bacon. I don't know how they made it differently, but they did.

Deacon nodded empathetically. "We cannot forget about the bacon."

I barely pulled it together as Marcus smiled in my direction. "It's good to see you again, Ms. Bethel."

"Thank you." I swallowed hard as Seth reappeared, this time with a dazed-looking Alex.

She stumbled a step and then shook her head. "Holy crapola, I will never get used to that. Never."

"Try having him randomly pop into your office," Marcus commented dryly.

Seth walked over to where I stood. "But what fun would it be if I announced my arrival first?"

"Indeed." Marcus lifted his brows as he leaned back against the desk. "Now that we are all here—"

"The Army of Awesome reunited at last." Deacon grinned while his brother sighed heavily. "It's been a long time coming."

"We do have a small issue to contend with," Marcus continued.

"Just a tiny one," Deacon added as Alex dropped into one of the chairs placed in front of Marcus's desk. "Our little Canadian demigod refuses to believe that she is what we're saying she is and we are what we're saying we are."

"That's not exactly surprising." Aiden folded his arms. "Most mortals don't even know we exist."

"Yeah, but she's not like most mortals," Luke chimed in.

Feeling a little nauseous all of a sudden, I sat in the chair next to Alex. "How so? Wait a sec. How are we sure she's who we're looking for?"

"That's a good question," Alex said, rising a brow. "Kidnapping is a felony."

"Well, technically, even if she's a demigod, they still kidnapped her." Seth shrugged when we all looked at him. "Hey, I'm just pointing out the obvious here."

Luke turned to Deacon. "You want to do the honors?"

"Of course." Deacon would never turn down being the center of the attention. "Once we got back here with Gable, we had no idea how we were going to find the last two demigods. So I had this idea. Why don't I try to find the librarian?"

Aiden's mouth dropped open. "You went to Medusa? Please tell me you did not attempt to talk to Medusa."

"I just want to add at this moment that she is not an official employee of the university," Marcus stated, and I smothered an absurd-sounding giggle.

Deacon shrugged. "It was a risk I was willing to take. What's the worst that could've happened?"

"She could've, you know, turned you into stone?" Alex suggested, voice pitching high.

"Obviously she didn't see me as threat, because I'm standing here and I'm not made out of stone."

"I would like to go on record and say I had no idea he planned on doing that." Luke slid his narrowed gaze to his boyfriend. "He just went and did it without telling me."

"And it worked!" Deacon reached into his pocket. "All it took was one trip to the library. It's like she was waiting for me—like she knew I was coming. Super freaky if you think about it."

"Seriously? It took me so many times to get her to appear," I muttered, trying not to pout.

"Well, I'm just that special. Anyway, I told her that we were going to find the other demigods and she gave me this." Uncurling his fist, he revealed a necklace that dangled from his fingers. Hanging from an ordinary chain appeared to be some kind of clear quartz crystal.

I leaned forward, squinting. "What is that?"

"It's a scrying stone." He grinned as he cupped the stone in his other hand. "If you're looking for someone and you know what city they're in, all you have to do is hold it over a map and bam! Tells you the exact location. We found our little Canadian demigod working at a bookstore in Thunder Bay."

Hope sparked in my chest. If they used it to find this demigod, then we could use it to find where Mitchell was being held. As soon as the thought finished, I realized the stone would not be able to help us there. We didn't know the city he was in.

I pushed aside that frustration as I eyed the stone. "That's pretty amazing."

"Right?" Deacon slipped it back into his pocket as Marcus pushed off the desk and walked behind it.

"Let's back up for a second. What do you mean she's not like other mortals?" Seth placed his hands on the back of my chair. "What does that mean?"

"I think I know who her godly parent is, which has to do with why she's not exactly normal," Luke said. "She's Demeter's daughter."

Marcus sat in the chair behind the desk as Deacon nodded. "We kind of did the whole stalking her thing for a bit, trying to figure out what was the best way to approach this, when we caught her doing something very interesting after work."

Seth opened his mouth, and I just knew it was going to be something wildly inappropriate. "Don't," I warned.

He smirked.

"She was walking by some old, dried-out bushes. No idea what kind they were." Deacon hopped up and sat on the desk. Marcus sighed. "She stopped and looked around. There wasn't anyone else outside. She didn't see us hiding in the car like complete stalkers."

"Nice," Alex murmured.

"She ran her fingers over the bush and the thing came back to life. Completely," Luke explained. "Went from dead and brown to looking like it was just planted there."

"Demeter is the goddess of agriculture, among other things." Marcus leaned back in his chair, crossing one knee over the other. "Which begs the question of why she is so resistant to the truth considering that is not something mortals can do. It also makes me wonder how she was able to do it. I was under the impression their powers were bound."

I gaped. "What the hell? I didn't have any cool abilities like that. Not at all."

Seth was bent at the waist, so his head was next to mine when he laughed. "Ah, but you're still special."

"Shut up," I muttered crossly. "I still don't have any special abilities like that."

Seth patted my head, and I about swung at him. "So," he said, "is she still locked in a dorm room?"

"Yep." Luke smiled tightly. "She's been talking to Gable through the door, but she won't open it, and other than the water that was in the room, she hasn't had anything else to drink or eat. We need to get her out."

"Then get her out." Seth straightened. "And force some food down her throat. She gets with the program—"

"Or what?" Aiden's eyes darkened to a thunderous gray.

One side of Seth's lips tipped up. "There are no other options, St. Delphi."

"Though his delivery sucks," I reasoned, "Seth has a point. I can try to talk to her."

"Well, while you guys convince this girl that you all aren't crazy and not to press charges, Aiden and I are going to head to Texas." Seth pushed off the chair.

"What?" I looked up at him.

"When Aiden and Alex were in Baton Rouge, they learned about a community outside of Houston that has had some pures disappear," Seth explained.

"And right before we came here, I got a call from a Sentinel that they were tracking what they believed were shades," Aiden added. "Since the Covenant is warded, we're going to check it out."

I was kind of surprised that Seth was willing to leave me here, but also relieved that he trusted that the Covenant was secure.

"So you guys are going now?" Alex asked.

Aiden nodded. "There are a couple of abandoned warehouses about two miles from their community."

She lifted her chin. "So I'm going with you guys."

Behind me, Seth sighed.

"That's not necessary," Aiden returned.

"It's not?" she asked, voice low.

"Oh, man," Deacon mumbled.

As Alex and Aiden descended into a full-blown argument, Seth tapped me on the shoulder and widened his eyes as he nodded to the door. Pushing out of my chair, I followed him to the hallway outside the Dean's office, closing the door behind me.

"Do you think Aiden is going to cave and let Alex come?" I asked.

Seth propped his hip against the wall. "She can be fairly convincing when she wants in on the action, but there really is no point. When they went to Baton Rouge, it was a bust, and even though there are a few places that fit the description of the warehouse you were held in, that doesn't mean we're going to find anything. She doesn't need to go. Neither does Aiden."

"But he wants to help. Both of them do," I reasoned.

"I get that, but they're a liability," he pointed out with a one-shoulder shrug. "They're demigods, but that doesn't mean they can't be seriously injured or killed. I, on the other hand, cannot be killed as easily."

My stomach dipped at the thought of Seth being in danger. "Well, we demigods aren't that easy to kill," I reminded him as the door opened and Marcus walked out, Deacon and Luke behind him. They moved to the other end of the hall, and I thought it was kind of funny that Aiden and Alex had chased the Dean out of his own office. Damn.

"But only Cronus, Hera, and Zeus can kill me, and based on what you've said about Cronus, he's really not a threat at this moment."

"And what about Zeus and Hera?"

Seth grinned. "Pretty sure they spend the vast majority of their time watching old reruns of *Happy Days* and trying to kill each other. They aren't a problem."

"*Happy Days*?" When I pictured Zeus, I saw a middle-aged man with a beard for some odd reason, and now I saw him lounging on a couch watching Fonzie on a massive big-screen while Hera sat in a recliner glaring at him. I shook those images out of my head. "I know you're the ultimate badass right now, but that doesn't mean you shouldn't be careful."

A playful grin teased at his lips. "You know me. I'm always careful."

"Uh-huh," I murmured.

"Surprised you're not demanding to go," Seth said after a moment.

"Do you want me to?"

"No. I'm glad you're not pushing it."

I tilted my head to the side. "We made a deal, and I still have these bands on my wrists." I paused, breathing through another sharp wave of nausea. "And I . . ."

"What?" His gaze sharpened, all playfulness gone.

"I'm good at the hand to hand stuff. I mean, you taught me. So did Luke and . . . and Solos." My heart hurt thinking of the fallen half-blood. "But I'm tired—"

"How tired?"

"Not anything serious," I rushed to assure him. I didn't tell him that I felt sick because I knew, if I did, he wouldn't leave. "I just know that I'm not up to a hundred percent, and even though I want to help and I hate staying back, I know . . . I know I need to stay. Going out there with these damn bands on my wrists and feeling like I do would be the stupidest decision ever."

His eyes searched mine, and then he nodded. "Thank you."

Before I had a chance to ask him what he was thanking me for, Aiden stepped out into the hallway. Based on the messy dark hair and the swollen appearance of his lips, I was guessing he and Alex had argued, and then made up.

"Ready when you are," he called.

"And Alex?" Seth asked.

The tips of his cheeks flushed. "She's agreed to stay behind."

"Uh-huh." Sliding his hand to the nape of my neck, Seth kissed the center of my forehead and then his lips found mine. The kiss was intense, flipping and twisting my insides into a pleasant, heady mess. My hands found their way to his chest and my fingers curled into his shirt. As he lifted his head, I wished we had enough time to go somewhere private and finish what we'd started in his bedroom.

"Be back soon," he said, kissing the corner of my lips.

I nodded and nearly slumped against the wall as he let go of me. He swaggered down the hall to where Aiden waited. Goodness, that was a kiss. Snapping out of the daze, I stepped forward. "Seth?"

He looked over his shoulder.

"I love you."

Seth's response was immediate. The smile that raced across his face was wide and beautiful, and the look he sent me turned my insides to goo. He didn't take his eyes off me as he placed his hand on Aiden's shoulder.

A second later they were gone.

Grinning, Deacon strode forward, hands in his pockets. "Ready to meet our *guest*?"

27

*W*e made a pit stop in the weapons room before we went to Texas. Although I really didn't need them, I grabbed two daggers and a belt mainly because the daggers were fun to use.

Aiden hooked on a set and also grabbed one of the Glocks that was loaded up with titanium-capped bullets. His demigod abilities, much like Josie's, weren't infinite. He'd eventually tire out.

I, on the other hand, pretty much just wanted to stab something.

"You ready?" I asked, amused by the fact that we were actually working together again. "I don't want to be gone too long."

"Understandable." Aiden walked over to where I stood but stopped. His steady gaze met mine. "What's the plan if we come face to face with a Titan?"

If only we'd get *that* lucky.

One side of my lips kicked up. "Kill them."

Aiden crossed his arms as an eyebrow rose. "That's not exactly a plan. The gods—"

"I really don't care what the gods want."

"Killing the Titans causes pretty catastrophic consequences," Aiden reasoned just like the good saint that he was. "We might've gotten lucky with Perses, but we have to take that into consideration. Our actions impact the lives of innocent people, Seth."

I wondered if saying I really didn't care would make me sound like an ass.

His eyes narrowed. "I can tell what you're thinking. You have to care about this."

"See, that's the thing, Aiden. I don't have to do anything I don't want to. I'm not you," I told him. "I'm not here to save the world. That's not who I am. I will never be that."

A muscle ticked in his jaw. "Then what are you?"

"You know what I am." I cocked my head to the side.

"A selfish, arrogant prick?" he replied blandly.

My smile spread. "There is only one person I truly care about. Only one person I would go to the ends of the earth to keep safe. You're not that person. It would be wise to remember that."

Aiden lifted his chin as his eyes flashed silver. "You need to remember that I would do anything to keep Alex safe, and if killing Titans put her in danger, then I will do whatever it takes to stop you."

"I think you will *try* to stop me," I corrected helpfully. "Look, what do you want me to say, Aiden? What would you do if Hyperion had gotten hold of Alex and did those things to her?"

His lips thinned.

"I know what you wanted to do to Ares. I know what you wanted to do to me," I pointed out. Aiden looked away. "I'm not completely irresponsible, contrary to popular belief. If there is a way to entomb those Titans without putting Josie in harm's way, I'm all for it, but I will not let Hyperion live. There is no convincing me otherwise. So if you have a problem with that, then you should probably sit this one out, because if I come face to face with him, he's a dead motherfucker."

A moment passed and Aiden said, "That I can understand." His gaze lifted to the ceiling. "Hyperion is the god of heavenly light—one of the pillars of earth. The east, I believe. Not sure what taking him out would do."

Whatever his death caused was worth it to ensure that Josie never had to live in fear of his return. Cronus was also on my to-kill list, but I wasn't sharing that at this moment.

Aiden drew in a shallow breath. "I don't agree with you nine out of ten times, but this . . . this thing with Hyperion, I understand. If I'd had a chance to kill Ares, I would've taken it."

My gaze met his. "And if you'd had a chance to kill me, you would've taken it."

"Yes. Yes, I would've."

"Glad we're on the same page." I clapped a hand down on Aiden's shoulder. "Let's go."

I didn't wait for Aiden's response, taking us to the location where the Sentinel Aiden had been in contact with had told us to meet. Within seconds, we were in the sticky, murky air of Houston.

"Gods!" a deep male voice boomed in shock from behind us.

Turning around, I smiled as I eyed the group of Sentinels. "Yes?"

The Sentinel in the middle, the one who had spoken, took a step back. His eyes were wide as the sun glistened off his deep brown skin. The other three Sentinels looked like they were close to passing out.

Aiden moved to stand beside me. "Torin?"

He nodded. "You warned me that he . . . he was a god, but I

just wasn't prepared for that." The half glanced in my direction. "You're really a god."

My smile kicked up a notch.

One of the Sentinels behind him blanched.

Aiden sighed. "Yes, he's really a god. And yes, he can do all the cool god things, but we really have limited time. So, if we can get the shock and awe out of the way, that would be great."

I slid Aiden a long look. "Well, that takes the fun out of everything."

He ignored me. "What do you have for us, Torin?"

Torin appeared to snap out of his shock as he ran a hand over his closely cropped dark hair. "As you know, we have had quite a lot of pures go missing recently, but we've had few daimon attacks."

"We've actually barely seen any daimons," another Sentinel spoke up, a younger brunette who barely looked old enough to be out of the Covenant. "So that right there was suspicious."

"We have mandatory escorts in place when the pures leave the communities. It was on a recent shopping trip that we learned we were dealing with shades. They'd possessed several mortals that attacked one of our groups," Torin explained, resting one hand on the handle of a dagger. "There was only one survivor. They confirmed what happened."

"So why are we on this roof in the baking sun of Houston?" I asked.

The female Sentinel strolled forward, walking past us to the cement edge of the roof. She easily hopped up. "See the office building three blocks down? The tall one with the pyramid-shaped roof?"

"Yes." Aiden followed, squinting.

"As we told you, we've been tracking what we believe to be the shades. Other than their . . . smell, it's not easy identifying them if they want to blend in," she said, turning to the building. "We're pretty positive that's where they've been holing up."

"Is it an active office building?" Aiden asked, and of course, he sounded concerned. "Are there mortals working in there?"

"Yes." Torin joined the female. "That's why we've been holding off. Looks like the upper two floors are actually penthouse-type rooms. The rest is office space. They're in this building, surrounded by what appears to be mortals who aren't possessed and probably have no idea what is going on."

"Plus, those mortals those shades are riding are innocent," the girl tacked on. "If they haven't hurt those bodies, the mortals can be saved if we can get the shades out of them."

"And that's stopped you because . . . ?" I asked, genuinely curious.

All the Sentinels turned and looked at me. Not Aiden. He just stared at the building, probably weeping inside because he knew what I already knew. There was no helping those mortals.

"I hate to break it to you guys," I said. "This isn't an episode of *Supernatural.* Once the shades get into the body, the mortal is as good as dead. There is no coming back from that. You're not saving them from shit."

The girl turned to us, her face paling. "There's no exact proof of that, because the shades—"

"Because the shades almost always kill the mortals before they leave the body," Aiden answered, turning to face us. "We need to get in there and see what we're dealing with."

Torin nodded. "That's why we're here. We're your back-up. And if we can save those mortals in there, we're going to try to. We're not going to let them die."

I smirked but said nothing. If they wanted to think we needed back-up and that they could play superhero to a bunch of already dead mortals, then whatever. I strode forward and leapt onto the edge. The buildings were tucked up against one another, all the way to the office we needed to get into. I could easily pop myself to the building, but then I'd have to wait for the rest of them, and I knew better than to think I'd actually wait. I looked over at Aiden, saw that he was gauging the distance between the rooftops. It would be a series of impossible jumps for a mortal to make, but not for us.

Not for trained Sentinels.

"Let's do this." Torin backed up a few steps and then took off running. His booted feet launched off the ledge. He vaulted over the gap, landing on the roof of the next building in a roll. He popped up and took off again, moving faster than the mortals on the ground could track. The other three Sentinels followed.

Aiden was next.

He did the same, taking several steps back before he got a running leap. He got more air then the rest, and he landed in a crouch before springing back up and going for the next building.

I didn't need to run.

Muscles tensed. Power lit up every cell. I kicked off the ledge. Warm air whipped over my body. I landed in the center of the second roof just as Aiden cleared it, hitting the third.

We hopscotched our way three blocks up, finally reaching the building—some kind of bank—next to the office building. The female Sentinel was on the ledge, crouched between the letters of a large neon metal sign. She'd pulled a pair of binoculars out of the small backpack she wore.

A sheen of sweat covered Torin's forehead as he stalked toward the edge. "See anything, Kia?" he asked. She held up a hand as she scanned the building. Torin faced us. "There's a lobby on the main floor. Office spaces every floor up until the last two. She's looking for one of the shades we'd been tracking."

Aiden made his way up to the sign and knelt next to Kia. He said something to her as I walked over to the other edge. The building looked like all the rest, a modern-day stone fortress built with cement and glass, but there was a certain aura of darkness clinging to the gray stone. Maybe it was the godly senses kicking in, because I knew without a doubt that there were shades inside.

"Got them. They're on the top floor," Kia said, lowering the binoculars. "There's at least—hell, at least twenty that I counted. They're with the shade we were tracking. Some of them may be humans, but they're acting kind of weird."

I raised a brow. "Can you elaborate on the weirdness?"

"Can I see?" Aiden asked, and was rewarded with the binoculars. "Yeah, there's a whole bunch and most of them are just kind of . . . lying around. On the floors. A few appear to be awake. They got a . . . Hell." Aiden lowered the binoculars, exhaling roughly. "I think they've got regular mortals in there."

"How can you tell the difference?" Torin asked.

Aiden looked over his shoulder. "They've got them tied up."

I snickered, unable to help myself. "Well, that would definitely be an indication."

Handing the binoculars back to Kia, Aiden rose. "I'm assuming the elevator will take you from the lobby to the top floors, but do you need a special access code to get to those rooms?"

"Yeah, so we're going to need to get a key card," Torin explained while Aiden nodded away. "There's a small maintenance room off the lobby that has all the keys. We grab them and then head up the elevator. From there . . ."

Turning away from them, I scanned the glass windows in front of the top floor. Yeah, I didn't have the fucking time for walking into the lobby and finding some damn key. I squinted at the glass floor to ceiling windows. There was no way all of our asses, dressed in black and carrying guns and daggers wasn't going to draw some unwanted attention. We'd have to use compulsions. Someone would probably scream before we got the chance. I'd get annoyed. Then someone would end up going splat.

"It's that section of windows right there?" I asked, cutting into their conversation. "Correct?"

"Yes." Kia rose. "That appears to be some sort of living room."

"Cool." I faced them. "Can you guys keep a secret? Like, a really big secret that I'd kind of have to kill you if you shared level of secret-keeping?"

"Seth," Aiden sighed with a roll of his eyes.

The Sentinels exchanged looks, but Torin said with a shrug, "Yeah, I guess so."

"Good." Smiling, I pivoted around and lifted my hands. A surge of power rushed the room. "Because I'm about to straight up murder some people. See you on the flip side."

Aiden started forward. "Seth—"

It was too late.

Centering myself, the blue sky around me faded out and was replaced by high white ceilings, slowly churning fans, and several still, musky-smelling mortals.

Jackpot.

28

"How has everything been going here?" I asked Deacon as we walked toward the dorms. The last time I'd been at the University, it appeared as if a war was brewing between the pures and halfs.

The halfs had been through a lot and it had only been a matter of time before they started fighting back.

With his hands in his pockets, he glanced up at the cloudless blue skies. "It seems to have calmed a bit since Luke and I got back. I think a lot has to do with Marcus's no tolerance policy. A lot of pures have been expelled."

"Good," I said, meaning it. Some of the pures had been doing terrible things.

"And a lot of other pures have been standing side by side with the halfs." We climbed the steps and Deacon reached the doors first. He looked over his shoulder at me. "I'm hoping things continue to change, because the old way was one giant dumpster fire."

"Agreed."

We hit the common area of the dorm and passed a group of

students who were sitting on the couches. I realized at once that we were walking down the same hall that Seth and I had stayed in before.

Halfway down, Deacon stopped and faced me. "Before we do this whole meet-and-greet thing, I want to know how you're really doing."

I drew up short. "I'm doing fine."

He cocked his head to the side. "Josie, you were taken captive by a psychotic Titan who had a major bone to pick with your father. How would you be doing okay after that?"

A shaky laugh escaped me. "Well, I'm as okay as I can be, I guess."

His gunmetal gray eyes met mine. "I was really scared for you. We all were."

I swallowed hard. "I was scared for myself," I admitted quietly. "I didn't think . . ." I shook my head and drew in a deep breath as I reached up, tugging the band out of my hair. "I didn't think I'd ever see anyone again."

Deacon stepped, curling an arm around my shoulders. He pulled me in, and I went, circling my arms around his slim waist. "I said it before, but I'll say it again. I'm glad you're here. And if you need anyone to talk to, you got me. Don't forget that."

I squeezed my eyes shut against the sudden burn. "I won't."

"Good." He kissed the top of my head and then drew back. "Now, let's go coax this girl out of her room."

Smiling weakly, I nodded. We started back down the hall, and I discovered that she had been placed in a room about five doors down from where I had stayed. I pulled myself together as we stopped in front of her door. It was important that we got her to understand what was happening here so she didn't end up like Mitchell—like me.

"I know someone's out there," a voice from the other side of the door came. "I can hear you breathing."

Frowning, I looked at Deacon and raised my brows.

He grinned and murmured, "Heavy breather."

Rolling my eyes, I leaned against the wall. "Hi. My name is Josie. You're Cora, right?"

"Yes. That's my name." There was a pause. "If you're not here to let me leave, then you need to go away."

I was guessing now wasn't a good time to ask why the town she lived in was named Thunder Bay. I was curious as to how it had gotten such a badass name.

Placing my hand on the door, I drew in a shallow breath. "I know you're probably freaking out. I've been there. For real."

"So, you've been kidnapped and told that you're a demigod?" she fired back.

"Actually, yes." I glanced at Deacon. "I don't like to use the word 'kidnapped', but when I was found, I didn't believe anything that was being said either. But it's true. All of it. And I know it doesn't seem that way, but we're the good guys and you're safe here."

There was a long stretch of silence and then, "Is that guy out there?"

"Deacon is here with me."

"Hi!" Deacon chirped. "I'm one of the guys who kidnapped you."

My eyes widened as I looked at him. He just shrugged.

"Not you," came the response. "The other guy. His name is Gable."

"No, he's not here," I answered, wondering where he was since I hadn't seen him yet. "Do you want to talk to him?"

There was another gap of silence. "No."

"Josie is the daughter of Apollo," Deacon said from where he'd positioned himself on the other side of the door. "But she doesn't have any cool abilities like you do."

I flipped Deacon off.

"I don't have any abilities!" the girl shouted.

"That's not what I hear." Closing my eyes, I tilted my head against the wall. "I hear you can bring dead plants back to life. That's really cool."

"And also something that mortals can't do," Deacon pointed out. "But we've already had this conversation."

"Deacon is right, though. I don't have any special talents," I said, and Deacon snorted. I ignored him. "Well, I can control the elements, but that's like nothing."

A couple of moments passed. "You said your name is Josie, right?" The voice was closer to the door.

"Yes."

"Gable mentioned you. He said you'd been taken by . . . by freaking Titans."

"I was. I got free. I was lucky, but some like us weren't as lucky. I know you don't feel this way now, but you should know how lucky you are that Deacon and Luke got to you first. If you've seen what I've seen, you wouldn't doubt that for a second." Opening my eyes, I found Deacon staring at me. "Nothing they've told you is a lie. The Titans were looking for you, and if they found you, you would . . ."

"Would what?" she asked.

Lowering my gaze to the floor, I said, "You'd wish you were dead."

About a minute went by and I was afraid she was going to ignore us. "I couldn't always bring plants back to life."

Deacon pushed off the wall, his face sparking with interest. I was guessing this was new info. "You couldn't?"

"No. It started a couple of weeks ago. I found out by accident. I knocked over an old flower that I had in a vase, and when I picked it up the damn thing came to life," Cora said, and then she laughed. "At first, I just kind of ignored it. Because, come on. Then I did it again, a day later. I reached down to pluck up a dead dandelion and those little white wispy things came right back to life." Another brittle-sounding laugh emerged. "I feel like I'm going crazy."

I had no idea why that ability had started to show recently. "You're not."

"That's not all."

"It's not?" Eagerness filled Deacon's voice.

"I can tell things. Like when someone is sick. They have this grayish glow to them, like an aura. I thought I was having vision problems," she said, and the more she talked, I had to wonder how she thought she was a normal mortal. "And I know when women are freaking pregnant! At least I think I do. And by the way, that got me fired."

I blinked slowly.

"Do tell," Deacon murmured, eyes glittering with interest.

"So I was working at the indie bookstore and my manager came into work one morning, late as usual with her husband, and when I looked at her stomach, I could see this little ball of light that for some reason, in my head, was shaped like a baby! A freaking fist-size ball of light shaped like a baby."

Deacon and I exchanged looks.

"So what else would I do? I blurted out that she was pregnant," Cora continued on from the other side of the door. "Little did I know, her and her husband had hit a major dry spell, and if she was pregnant, it couldn't have been her husband's."

"Oh my," I said.

"Yeah, *oh my*. So she fired me that afternoon." There was a thump from the other side of the door that I really hoped wasn't her head. "Of course, I learned to not just blurt out random hallucinations real quickly."

Deacon grinned. "Smart move, but it probably wasn't a hallucination."

Cora's sigh was audible through the door. "This is real, and you guys aren't going away, are you?"

"This is real and we really don't want to leave you," I said, pushing off the wall. "You have to be hungry, right? We can get food and answer all the questions you have."

There was no immediate response, but then I saw the door knob starting to turn. Stepping back, I crossed my arms over my stomach. I had this nearly overwhelming urge to run away before the door opened. If she could see a baby in a belly . . .

Okay.

I was being stupid.

I was not pregnant.

Uncrossing my arms, I hoped the smile that I fixed on my face wasn't as creepy as the one Deacon was rocking.

The door cracked open slowly, and then I saw the girl that Deacon and Luke had technically kidnapped. She was about my height and was absolutely stunning. Raven-colored hair hung in tight, springy curls all the way to her breasts. Her skin was a deep, warm brown that was a startling contrast to eyes so pale they were somewhere between gray and blue.

"Hi," I said, giving her a little wave.

Cora turned from Deacon and looked at me strangely, her light gaze dropping to my stomach. Her brows shot up and then she squeezed her eyes shut as she pinched the bridge of her nose. "I'm not crazy. I'm not crazy."

I stood as still as a cat in front of a hellhound.

Glancing over at Deacon, it didn't appear that he had noticed anything weird, but I was seconds away from freaking out.

Okay.

That was more than just a little weird.

Cora moved aside, holding the door open for us. I forced a smile as I stepped inside the dorm room, hiding the fact that I wanted to find the nearest corner and start rocking in it. She either saw that I was sick—sick from the bands—or she saw something else.

Something that looked like a baby-shaped ball of light.

"We have a lot to talk about," Deacon said, closing the door behind us.

Cora glanced nervously between us, and I made sure the smile was still planted on my face. "We do."

And as soon as we got done there, I needed to find Alex.

* * *

About an hour later, I walked out of Cora's room and headed toward the lobby. Deacon was still with her, and she'd calmed down a lot, but was still understandably mind blown by everything.

My stomach had settled and I no longer felt like I was about to spew vomit everywhere, but there were tiny coils of tension deep in my belly for a whole different reason.

I knew I was probably being dumb, but I needed to take a pregnancy test just to set my mind at ease. The last thing I wanted to do was share the fact that I was most likely overreacting like a mofo, but I had no idea where I could get a test. I doubted they carried them in their university bookstore.

Or maybe they did?

Then again, I remembered hearing that many of the students were given birth-control shots.

That was something I probably should've looked into.

Anxious and jittery, I hurried through the common area. A few of the halfs looked in my direction, but no one really paid me any mind as I pushed open the doors and spied Alex.

She was leaning against one of the columns, talking to Luke and a dark-haired half-blood I had sort of gotten to know before we'd gone to retrieve the other demigods.

"Hey," Colin turned with a smile, his blue eyes as bright as I remembered. "Holy crap, I was wondering if I was ever going to see you again!"

"Hi." I gave him a little wave. "How have you've been?"

Colin gave me a quick one-armed hug. "Perfect. I hear things have been a little crazy for you guys."

"Understatement of the year," Alex chimed in, and I wondered if she knew that Colin totally idolized her and Aiden.

"Yeah, that's the truth," I commented.

"Glad to see you're doing okay." He glanced at Luke. "I heard things got . . . a little rough."

Pressing my lips together, I nodded as I forced my arms across my chest. "I'm doing good."

"How did things go with Cora?" Luke asked, stepping around Colin.

"She finally opened the door and let us in. She's starting to come around. I mean, she believes us now," I told him. "But I think we need to proceed with baby steps so we don't overwhelm her."

"Baby steps?" Colin's dark brows lifted. "And you left her in there with Deacon? He's probably lighting things on fire for her."

"Shit. You're so right." Luke sighed. "I better go check on them."

Before Alex followed Luke, I tapped her arm. "Can I talk with you for a moment?"

"Sure." She pushed away from the column as she brushed her long ponytail off her shoulder.

"Sorry," I said to Colin, feeling bad that I had busted in on the conversation. "I didn't mean to interrupt or steal her."

"Nah. It's cool. I was going to try to follow Luke. Like to meet another demigod," he said, grinning. "It's like you guys are popping up everywhere now."

"Tell me about it," Luke said, motioning Colin to follow him. "Let's go make sure Deacon hasn't traumatized Cora."

"More than you all did when you kidnapped her?" Colin clapped a hand down on my shoulder as he passed me by.

"Look, it wasn't really kidnapping." Luke opened the door. "It was more like witness relocation against her will. Totally different."

Their conversation was cut off as the door closed behind them. Alex raised her brows. "How much do you want to bet they'll have that girl rocking in a corner somewhere?"

"Or marathoning *Supernatural*. There's no in-between."

Alex laughed. "True." Her eyes squinted as she looked up at the fading sun. "So, what did you need to talk to me about?" Concern briefly flickered across her face. "You haven't heard from Seth—"

"No. Nothing like that." My stomach dipped as I glanced at the doors. "Can we walk and talk?"

"Sure." Curiosity now filled her gaze.

I kept my arms crossed as we walked off the wide steps and started along the incredibly impressive marble walkway. The amount of money they had to have spent just to lay the pathways on the campus could probably have fed a small country.

Several knots had formed in my belly. I couldn't believe I was actually going to have to say these words. Especially to someone who had more than once made out with the guy who could possibly be my baby's daddy. Granted, I'd moved way past having a problem with that, but still—awkward. I just didn't know who else to go to.

"Josie?" Her quiet voice snapped me out of my thoughts. "You're starting to worry me."

"I'm sorry. I don't mean to. It's just that . . ." I took a deep breath and pulled my big-girl undies up. "Do you know where I could get a . . . a pregnancy test?"

Alex tripped over her own feet. Throwing out a hand, she caught my arm before she went face-first into the pathway. Her wide-eyed gaze swung in my direction as she straightened. "Um. I . . . Wait. What?"

Cheeks burning a thousand shades of red, I glanced around. No one was near us. "I think . . . I think I might be pregnant."

Her lips parted, forming a complete circle. Several seconds passed while she looked like a fish out of water.

I started to get super uncomfortable.

Alex seemed to recover, blinking once and then twice. "I'm sorry. That just totally caught me off-guard. Was not expecting that."

"You and me both." Lifting a hand, I pushed the hair out of my face. "I mean, we used protection except for that one time and I . . . Well, I don't know if I'm just being crazy or what."

Alex faced me. "I'm assuming you have real reasons to suspect the whole pregnancy thing?"

I nodded, deciding I really didn't want to get into the whole Cora thing. "I just need to know if I am or not. Do you know if there is any way to get one here?"

"You'd have to go to the infirmary to get one."

I cringed. "Seriously?"

"Yeah." A look of sympathy crossed her face. "They don't sell the tests in the stores here because they like to keep track of who's getting pregnant. Completely barbaric and an embarrassing violation of privacy, but unless we can leave here—which wouldn't be smart—you'd have to get one done in the infirmary."

"Oh, sweet baby Jesus," I murmured under my breath.

Alex squeezed my arm. "Do you want to go now? I'll go with you."

What other choice did I have? Resigning myself to what I had to do, I sighed. "Yeah. I'd like that."

She smiled tightly and then we started walking again, this time back toward the main buildings. "It would make sense."

I glanced at her.

"You being sick," she explained. "Maybe it's not just the bands on your wrists."

Feeling like I just might pass out, I was silent for a couple of minutes. "I just . . . I don't know how I could be after what went down with Hyperion."

Her sharp gaze found mine as we neared the square, one-story building that housed some of the training rooms and several nursing stations.

I looked away, focusing on the bronze-colored double doors ahead. "I fought him," I said, pushing past the messy knot forming in the back of my throat. "I fought back and I . . . I didn't win those fights."

"I get it." Alex reached down and took my hand, squeezing it. "I get what you're saying."

Wetness rushed my eyes and I blinked it away. "So I'm probably just overreacting."

Alex let go of my hand and reached for the door. "Maybe." There was a pause. "But you're a demigod and Seth's an Apollyon—or was. I have no idea what that would make a kid, but it's probably a very strong one."

I opened my mouth, but I had no words, because I hadn't even begun to think about what kind of kid could be inside me—a kid that had a demigod and a god as a parent.

"Or it could just be weird cycles? That's possible. I mean, who hasn't thought they were pregnant before?" She tried to sound reassuring, because I figured the panicked expression on my face was pretty obvious. "I thought I was pregnant once and it turned out I had two lesser gods living inside me."

I stared at her.

"Not that I'm saying you have gods inside you, but you know, it could be anything. Anyway . . ." She opened the door. "Let's find out."

In a daze, I followed Alex inside. I was too anxious to do much speaking as Alex found us a nurse and we were escorted into a small, minty-smelling room. There were no chairs in the room, only an examination table, and I didn't want to sit on it since that seemed all too official.

The nurse, a pure-blood dressed in pale blue scrubs, closed the door behind her. She was an older lady with what I thought were pretty amazing amethyst-colored eyes. Turning to us with a clipboard in hand, those odd eyes bounced nervously between Alex and me.

I imagine she hadn't been in the room with two demigods before.

Her smile was full of uncertainty. "How can I help you two?"

I started to look at Alex, but then I realized that I seriously needed to grow up and ask for the test. "I'm not a student here. I'm—"

"I know who you are—who both of you are," the nurse spoke up. "I'm sure everyone at the University is aware of who both of you are."

Having no idea if that was a good thing or not, I exhaled roughly. "I think I might be pregnant, so I was hoping I could take a test."

The nurse's expression didn't change one iota. "Have you had the symptoms of pregnancy?"

I nodded. "I'm late and I've been . . . sick." I didn't feel like it was necessary to even bring the issue of the bands on my wrists into the equation. "I've had unprotected sex. Once," I tacked on like that made a difference. "I really would like this to be private. I mean, the whole doctor-patient privilege thing still works, right?"

Alex snickered. "Privacy at the Covenant? Not likely, but I have a feeling she's not going to want to piss off Apollo's daughter."

The skin around the nurse's mouth tightened. "When I took the oath, I did so for everyone I treat. I am not—"

" . . . like other pure-bloods," Alex finished for her. "Got it. So this conversation and its potential results won't leave this office?"

Damn girl, I thought.

"Right." The nurse put the clipboard down. "We can do a simple urine test and then go from there. How does that sound?"

"Sounds good?" I said, glancing at Alex. She nodded.

The nurse reached into a cabinet and pulled out a small plastic cup with a lid. She scribbled "Jane" across the piece of tape. "Ready?"

I was showed where the nearest bathroom was, and I did the whole pee in the cup thing. That cup of potential doom was placed in a little window and then I went back to the windowless room where Alex was waiting.

Leaning against the wall, I smacked my hands over my face. It sort of hit me right then that this was really happening. There was a good chance I was pregnant and I was going to figure out what the hell that meant other than being pregnant. "I can't believe this is happening."

"Seth . . . doesn't know, does he?" Alex asked.

"No," I said from behind my hands. "It wasn't something I really thought about until recently and I didn't want to get him . . . worried?" I didn't know how Seth would react. I didn't know how I would react if that test came back positive. "I don't know what he'd do or even think. It's not exactly something we've talked about."

Alex wrapped her fingers around my arms and pulled my hands from my face. "Honest? He's probably going to be as shocked as you, but Seth loves you, Josie. He really does, and that is something amazing."

My heart did a little jump. "I know."

She gave a little shake of her head. "I don't know if you really do." Dropping her hands, she drew in a deep breath. "I never believed that Seth was capable of loving anyone more than he loved himself, but he does with you. And because of that, you shouldn't be afraid of telling him if that test comes back positive."

I tipped my head back against the wall. "Even if he's a hundred percent okay with this, how can we do this? There is so much screwed up stuff going on right now, and I . . . I just don't know."

"You'll figure something out. Trust me," she said. "You will, because you'll have to."

She was right, because we *would* have to figure it out. I lowered my chin. "If this comes back positive, please don't tell anyone. I'm going to tell Seth, but I don't want this getting around."

"Of course not," she replied. "Obviously I'll keep my mouth shut, since I just threatened a pure-blood if she ran her mouth."

I laughed nervously, but every single muscle in my body locked up as the door opened and the nurse walked in. I searched her expression for any hint, but it was impressively blank. Still, my heart was pounding like I'd run up several flights of steps.

The nurse, whose name I realized I'd never asked for, propped her hip against the counter and loosely folded her arms. "When we do urine tests, we usually repeat them more than once if we get a certain result to ensure accuracy, so we repeated the tests."

"Okay," I whispered as blood began to roar in my ears.

"It's positive," the nurse said. "You're pregnant."

29

Seth

Standing before the shades, I quickly counted them. There was definitely more than twenty. More like thirty. A few of them looked like they'd played chicken with a car and lost, their flesh torn and patchy in some areas. Shades didn't want to let go of their mortal bodies. Even when the mortal had died, they rode the flesh until nothing was left.

It smelled like the River Styx had thrown up in here, and then a few hellhounds had come in and taken a dump. In the back, against a low wall that led to a bare kitchen, were the tied-up mortals.

They didn't look very alive.

I clapped my hands together.

Heads jerked up. Eyes of all different shapes and colors widened.

"Hey," I said, smiling. "My name is Seth. I have a few questions."

Dark shadows leaked through the whites of their eyes like ink into water. A low hissing sound radiated from all corners of the room, like the air being let out of several balloons. They rose at once.

"I'm glad to see you guys are going to be so helpful."

A blonde that appeared to have run face-first into a blender charged me. Reaching down, I unhooked one of my daggers. I didn't have to do much. Just lifted the blade and stepped to the side.

She impaled herself.

A second later, black smoke poured out of her gaping mouth, shooting into the air. It billowed across the ceiling, seeking a way out.

Lifting my hand, I shoved a couch across the room. It tipped up on one side, blocking the door. Smiling, I turned as another shade barreled down on me. This one was a little fresher, but it too ended up on the floor.

Glass shattered behind me. A second later, Aiden landed in a crouch. Torin hit the floor in a controlled roll. Unfortunately, that controlled roll went right through some splatter. Sucked for him.

Aiden popped up and was immediately swarmed by the shades rocking the mortal bodies. They went after him like daimons jonesing for aether. As Torin rose, wiping off the blood and other stuff, I was sort of offended that the shades didn't want to play with me anymore.

A shade went flying back as Aiden delivered a brutal punch that might have—gods' bless his pure soul—killed the mortal if it wasn't already dead.

"Ah, I think you've got it covered." Raising my hand, I pushed Torin back toward the wall, away from one of the free-roaming shades. "And you," I said. "You really shouldn't have followed Aiden."

Dipping down, Aiden took out the legs of one of the shades.

He lurched up and looked over his shoulder, dark brows slamming together. "Seriously?"

I grinned, crossing my arms over my chest as I stayed back from the melee. "Wouldn't want you to get out of practice." When Aiden cursed and whipped back around, I laughed. "Hey, I'm just looking out for your best interests."

Torin attempted to peel himself out of the corner I'd put him in, but I shook my head. "You wouldn't last long with these bastards. Sorry. You're going to just have to watch." I paused. "And remember that secret you promised to keep."

He opened his mouth, but I pivoted and grabbed the closest shade. Spinning it around, I shoved the blade deep into its chest. The shade escaped, along with all the ones Aiden was taking down. They were crawling across the ceiling, aiming for the broken glass.

Then, a thought occurred to me. I'd seen a furie grab hold of one before. She actually ate the fucking thing. I was not trying that, but I was a god now, so I wondered if a hit of akasha might take the bastards out.

Tapping into the power, I lifted my arm. Whitish-amber light powered down my bicep and erupted out of my palm. The bolt smacked into the mass of shades flowing through the broken window. Akasha washed over the mass, and an eerie howl filled the room. The group of shades warped and rippled as the shadows expanded and then ruptured, spraying the windows with inky blotches.

"Huh." I laughed. "Well then."

"We need one alive," Aiden reminded me. "Try to remember that."

Stepping to the side, I grabbed the blond closest to me. He threw his head back and opened his mouth. Nothing came out. He snapped his jaw shut and glanced down at the hand I had wrapped around his throat.

The shade couldn't escape.

"What do you know? Looks like you're stuck in the body now." I laughed. Interesting. Must be another new god trait. I lifted my gaze. "Guess you're fucked."

The shade let out a roar of anger. "No. I guess this body is fucked."

Without any warning, it wrenched its head to the right. The crack of its neck was like thunder. "Gods." My lip curled as its inky eyes slid back to mine. The head hung at an odd unnatural angle. "That was unnecessary."

It laughed. "It was fun."

"Yeah. You need a fucking hobby."

Torin slammed another shade into the floor, shoving his blade into its chest as he lifted his dark gaze to Aiden. "There's no helping them, is there?"

"Nope." Aiden kicked another back.

"So what are you doing here?" Lifting the shade up, I turned and slammed him into the wall. "You're out there catching pures and bringing them to the Titans? They're nearby, aren't they? Not in this city, I bet. But close."

The shade coughed out a guttural laugh. "What do you think?"

"I think you're nothing but a little bitch boy for the Titans."

Black blood seeped out the corners of the shade's mouth. "They got to eat, too, you know? To get all big and strong."

"Uh-huh." I stepped in, placing my other hand against his chest. Heat poured out of my palm. "Where are they?"

His lips peeled back, revealing tar-stained teeth. "You'll never find them."

"Oh, I think I will." I dug in with my palm. "I'm going to ask you one more time. Where are they?"

The shade stiffened as I pulled in the element of fire, and I felt Aiden draw closer. "I know who you are," it said, jerking as the front of its shirt began to smoke. "I know that we had something that belonged to you."

Everything in me stilled. The world became quiet. "What did you say?"

The shade moaned low, its voice gurgling as more blood spilled out of its mouth. "I . . . I used to stand out on the porch and watch Hyperion drag that blonde bitch into the house. Her screams made me hard. I miss her."

Rage roared to life, mingling with all the heady, powerful aether inside me. The air around me crackled. Those inky eyes met mine and then flared wide. I didn't look away as the shirt burned away under my hand or as the skin bubbled. I didn't blink a damn eyelash as blood and tissue gave way and the shade slumped to the floor.

Exhaling deeply, I briefly closed my eyes as I twisted my neck from the left to the right. I opened my eyes, but I still wanted to destroy something. I wanted to take this whole gods-damn building down.

"What did he say to you?" Aiden asked.

Curling my hands into fists, I stepped back from the heap of burnt clothing and melted flesh. "He was *there*."

Aiden didn't have to ask what that meant. He knew.

"The Titans are here. They're in Texas."

Josie

"You sure you're going to be okay?" I stood in the doorway of the room Seth had been given the last time we were here, dazed by what felt like an out-of-body experience. I found myself nodding at Alex's question.

We'd walked back to the dorm in silence. At least, I think we did. If Alex had spoken, I hadn't heard her. My mind was still back in that minty-smelling room.

I was pregnant. *Pregnant.*

The nurse had taken my blood to just confirm the stick test results. I quickly learned that pregnancy among the pures, and I guess the halfs since the Breed Order had been abolished, was like a mortal pregnancy. Apparently the blood test would give me a better understanding of how far along I was, but I knew I couldn't be more than three weeks unless one of the condoms Seth had used before had broken. That was possible, I guessed.

But the problem with that was, according to the nurse, it wasn't common to have noticeable symptoms so early on. Some women did. Then again, I wasn't mortal and I wasn't a pure-blood. The nurse admitted that pregnancy for a demigod could be something entirely different.

There definitely weren't any "Expecting Demigod Mothers" pamphlets in the room.

The blood results would be back tomorrow, but I already knew deep down what they'd confirm. I was pregnant.

A look of doubt had crept into Alex's expression. "Do you want me to stay with you until Seth gets back?"

"Thank you, but no. I need . . ." I trailed off as my stomach took a dive to the floor. What did I *not* need at this point? I was pregnant. I was actually impregnated by Seth. There was a fetus inside me that could be mortal, could be a demigod, or could be an actual god.

Hell, the baby could be a minotaur for all I knew.

So I needed a lot of things, but only one thing at the moment. "I just need to be alone for a little while. I need to process this."

"I understand." Alex popped forward and gave me a quick, tight hug. "It'll be okay. Especially once you talk to

Seth." She stepped back, but stopped. Her gaze met mine. "Congratulations."

I sucked in a soft breath. A knot plugged my throat as a flutter took root in my chest. From the moment the first thought of being pregnant popped into my head and right up to Alex saying congratulations, I hadn't thought of being pregnant as a good thing. Mainly because I couldn't even let myself truly think about it.

"Thank you," I whispered, and I meant it.

Alex smiled and then gave me a little wave.

Closing the door, I turned and walked past the sitting area, shuffling into the bedroom. The bed had been made and the room was neat and orderly. Thankfully there were no creepy portraits of my father or any other god in this room.

I'm pregnant.

"Oh *gods*," I whispered.

Stopping at the foot of the bed, I tugged up my shirt and exposed my belly. It wasn't flat, but it had never been flat in my entire life. My stomach looked the same as it did before.

But there was a baby in there.

Dropping my shirt, I started to press my hand to my stomach but stopped. I turned and plopped down on the bed. Running my hands over my face, I shook my head for the hundredth time.

How was this going to work?

I had no idea what this meant for a demigod and a god—none whatsoever. Like, would I carry this baby for nine months? Would it come out like Seth, with a baby six-pack and the ability to control things with its mind?

And we had Titans gunning for us—gunning for *me*. My heart turned over heavily as I lowered my hands to my lap. If Hyperion found out I was pregnant? God, he would . . .

I couldn't even let myself think about what he would do—what the other Titans would do.

None of us were safe, and bringing a baby into this was crazy.

Because once I got these bands off my wrists, I would have to fight the Titans. Seth wanted to kill them all, but that could have horrific consequences. We needed to entomb them, and that meant I needed to fight alongside the other demigods.

How could I do that while being pregnant?

How could I not fight?

But even if I was just a mortal and didn't have the whole Titan thing going down, I was nowhere near mentally or emotionally ready to pop out a child. I was so not mother material.

I was only twenty.

Seth was only twenty-two.

We loved each other, but we hadn't been together long and there was so much we were still trying to work out. I didn't even know if he wanted kids.

I didn't even know if *I* wanted kids.

Kind of late to be thinking of that now.

A strangled-sounding laugh escaped me as I lowered my gaze to my stomach. My breath caught, and I did it. I placed my hand on my stomach. It felt normal, but . . .

But I was pregnant.

And this baby . . . *gods*, this baby wanted to be born, because I don't think if I was mortal, or if this child was mortal, it would've survived everything that had happened. My fingers splayed across my lower belly. Somehow I knew that this kid was going to be strong.

"You're a little fighter, aren't you?" I said to my stomach, and then I flushed beet red, because I was seriously talking to my stomach.

My lips twitched as I lifted my gaze to the beige wall. I needed to start Googling this whole pregnancy/baby thing.

The space in front of me suddenly warped and then, without any warning, Seth was standing there.

Yelping, I jerked my hand away from my stomach as I nearly slid off the bed. "Holy crap!" Jumping up, I smacked him—smacked him *hard* on the chest. "A warning would be—"

He caught my hand, and all I saw was a flash of golden eyes a second before he hauled me against his chest. His other arm circled my waist and then his mouth was on mine.

Seth kissed me like he was taking his first breath of fresh air. It was deep and scorching. Sensation rushed over me, pouring into my system and pushing everything aside. Kissing Seth was like finally waking up from a deep, endless sleep, and when he lifted his mouth from mine, I made this sound I barely recognized and which caused Seth to chuckle.

"Missed you," he said, pressing another kiss to the corner of my lips.

Sliding my hand to his shoulder, I rested my forehead against his. "You haven't been gone that long."

His nose brushed mine. "Long enough."

I shivered in his arms, relieved that he was back and okay. It was strange, knowing that there were only three beings in this world that could take Seth out and still worrying about his safety. "Aiden's okay?"

"Of course." Seth chuckled again. "Not like I'd leave him there."

Leaning back, I raised my brows.

Seth's grin twisted my stomach into pleasant knots. It was just so damn . . . devilish. "Ye of little faith."

"Uh huh."

His hand slid up my spine, tangling in my loose hair. "How

are you feeling?"

"Good," I said, taking a breath. I needed to tell him about the whole pregnancy thing, but this was also important. "Find out anything?"

"Yes." He kissed the center of my forehead and let go. "I think you were definitely held in an area east of Houston."

Hope smacked through me as I sat down on the edge of the bed. "Did you find the warehouse?"

Running a hand through his hair, he shook his head. "No, but we did find shades, and they're definitely there because of the Titans."

I folded my hands in my lap. "How do you know?"

"Turns out I'm more awesome than I previously realized."

"Oh really?"

"Yep." Still grinning that ridiculously sexy and often infuriating grin, he said, "We caught one. And it turns out that being a god means I can actually stop the shade from leaving its body. That meant we were able to get some info out of it."

I really didn't want to think about how they went about that. "What did you learn?"

A coldness settled into those deep amber eyes. "The Titans are in Texas. Or they have been."

Everything was bigger in Texas. A hyena-sounding giggle almost escaped.

The shade knew of you," he explained, and I tensed. "You said you were kept near a wooded area. Aiden and I learned there's a place called Piney Woods not too far from there. We're going to start scouting out areas in that location."

Like before, there was something just on the fringe of my subconscious that I couldn't quite pull forward. "I feel like . . . like I'm forgetting something—something I saw. It's right there, but I just can't remember it."

"It'll come to you."

I nodded as I inhaled roughly. My pulse started to pick up as I peeked up at him. Seth was going to be a dad.

Oh my *gods*, I was going to be a mom.

But he was going to be a *dad*.

A really hot dad—like the kind you saw with a baby that made your ovaries go boom. Except my ovaries apparently already went boom.

Holy crap, what was I thinking? I did not need to be thinking about him as a hot dad, because he didn't even know he was going to become a dad. I needed to tell him.

Anxiety rose in my chest, causing me to clasp and unclasp my hands. "This is all . . . good, though. At least we have a general idea."

"Right," he replied, his eyes warming to a tawny glow as he watched me. "How did things go with the kidnapped demigod?"

"Um, good. We got her to open the door and Deacon was going to get her some food," I said, looking away when his gaze caught mine. "She understands that we're here to help her. So that's a few steps in the right direction."

"Cool." Seth reached down to his hips and I saw that he had daggers. "We can head back to the island if you want."

We so needed to stay, at least until tomorrow—well, wait. I had no idea how safe the whole poofing thing Seth did was. I guess it was okay, because he'd done that quite a few times. "Can we hang here for a little bit? It's safe, right?"

Seth nodded.

"When did you get the daggers?" I asked.

"Made a pit stop in the weapons room before we went to Texas. I guess I really don't need them, but they're fun to use."

"Oh, that's smart. Not the fun part, because that's a little creepy, but the grabbing them part." My heart was racing so fast

I thought I'd be sick. "When are you going to head back out?"

He unhooked the daggers. "Soon. Was thinking about checking out Piney Woods tomorrow."

That was good, because we needed to find Mitchell. I just hoped we weren't too late. But if Seth was going back out there tomorrow, should I tell him about the whole baby thing? He could come face to face with one of the Titans. Being distracted was the last thing he needed.

It could be deadly.

I sucked in a sharp breath. If Seth came face to face with a fully energized Cronus, what would happen?

"Hey," Seth said, drawing my gaze to his. "What's going on?"

Wiping my damp palms against my knees, I forced a casual shrug. "Nothing. Just got a lot on my mind."

Seth placed the daggers on the dresser. His hands dropped to the belt that had held them. "You sure you're feeling okay? You're looking a little flushed."

And I was feeling like I was going to laugh and cry and throw myself face-first onto the bed. I opened my mouth, but nothing came out.

Unhooking the weapons belt, he draped it over the dresser and then crossed the small distance between us. "Look, you need to be honest with me if you're feeling unwell. I need to know—I *want* to know."

Mouth dry, I shook my head and tried once more to say something, anything, but nothing came out but inaudible sounds. What was I doing? How could I not tell him? Even though I had no idea how he would react, how he would feel about this, I couldn't keep it from him. It was too big. Too important. This involved both of us.

This involved our future . . . if we had one.

A frown pulled at his lips as he stood in front of me. Seth

knelt, placing his hands over mine, effectively stopping me from rubbing the skin right off. "Josie," he said, his concerned gaze searching mine. "What is going on?"

"I . . . I have to tell you something important."

His brows knitted together. "Okay."

"I really don't know how to tell you without just saying it." My breath caught and it felt like my heart was going to jump out of my chest. "I'm pregnant."

30

I choked out a laugh. "You're . . . Wait, *what?*"

Josie's ocean-colored eyes were wide and her cheeks a faint pink. "I'm . . . I'm kind of pregnant. I mean, I'm not *kind of* pregnant. I don't think you can be *kind of* pregnant."

The half-smile faded.

"Alex went with me, because I honestly had no idea where to find a pregnancy test, and yeah, that was a little awkward. Anyway, turns out they don't just sell them here. You have to go get one done. So I did the whole pee-test thing and when they get a positive response, they repeat the test. Both tests came back positive, so I'm pregnant—pregnant with your baby." She winced. "You probably figured that last part out already. The baby being yours part."

My lips parted on a sharp inhale.

"That's why I've been nauseous and puking," she continued in a rush. "I guess the bands are making me heal slower than I should be, but I don't think they are causing the tiredness and everything else. And I didn't think it was that—you know, me being pregnant until I realized a few days ago I hadn't had my period."

Josie is . . .

I stopped breathing as her words settled through the shocked fog that had invaded my brain. A hundred different thoughts erupted in rapid succession.

"I thought it was just stress, but then—well, I went down to one of the infirmaries, like I said, and got the test." She folded her hands together, pressing them against her breasts. "And yeah, it's positive."

I'm fucking sure my heart stopped for several beats as I stared at her from where I was crouched. My head tilted to the side as I slowly understood what she was telling me. Josie was . . . pregnant with my child?

A surge of unbridled emotion whirled through me, a wild mixture of acidic fear and brilliant joy—the kind of fear and joy I'd never in my life experienced. The emotions were so raw and so powerful I could barely make sense of them, could barely think around them.

Josie's lower lip trembled. "Please say something, because I've been freaking out pretty much all day, and now you're just staring at me, not talking."

I hadn't said anything? I needed to. I need to say a lot, but as I started to rise, I realized my knees were strangely weak. Like they were devoid of all muscle and bone. Somehow I lost my balance. I actually stumbled back and I went down, landing on my ass. The daggers rattled on the dresser behind me.

"Oh my God!" Josie jumped and reached for me. "Seth!"

Stunned that I *actually* fell over, I looked around the room as if there was some pint-size apparition that had just taken my legs out. Of course, there wasn't shit. My knees had given out.

"Seth . . ."

Lifting my gaze to her, I finally got my tongue to work. "You're pregnant?"

Josie pulled back, clasping her hands together. She nodded. "Yes." Her chest rose with a deep breath. Those beautiful eyes—eyes that were like two polished sapphires—glistened with unshed tears. "I'm sorry," she whispered.

I jerked. I mean, my entire body jolted.

She was sorry—sorry about being pregnant with my child? My brows flew up, and for a small instant that icy terror poured into my chest. How could I be a good father? After everything that I had done—everything I *would* do to keep Josie safe. My hands were dirty, but they'd soon be soaked in blood. Was that why she was sorry? Because she knew I was probably the last person in the world who was fit to have and raise a child?

But I'd give up my life for my child.

Josie sat back down, her throat working as she squeezed her eyes shut. "I know this is a surprise. It . . . it shocked me. It had to be that one time—right when you left. We didn't use a condom. I know we're not ready for this, but I was hoping we . . ." Trailing off, she shook her head as she pressed the tips of her fingers to her mouth.

Then it struck me.

She thought I was unhappy with the news, and she had good reason to believe that, because I was sitting on the godsdamn floor like a dumbass.

Snapping out my stupor, I flew to my feet and grasped her hands. I startled her and those damp lashes lifted. "I am *not* sorry," I told her. "I could *never* feel sorry that you're having my child."

Her eyes widened and she whispered, "What?"

I brought her hands to my chest as I hauled her up to her feet. "I was . . . fuck, I was shocked. I was not expecting you to say that. At all. But I am *not* sorry."

Josie's chest rose against our joined hands. "You're not? You're okay with me . . . with this?"

"How could I not be okay?" I shook my head as my heart pounded a mile a minute. "Gods, Josie, I was shocked enough that I just fell over on my ass, but I love you—I will always love you. That means I will love our child."

I couldn't believe I just said those two words. *Our child.* But the moment they left my tongue I never knew anything else could feel so right. I knew, in that moment, it was true.

A tremble rocked her body. "But how . . . how can we do this? We're not ready—"

"We'll get ready," I told her, meaning it. Gods knew she was right. We were the furthest thing from ready, but we would get there. "I don't have a doubt in my mind that you'd make—" My voice thickened and became hoarse with emotion. "—you *will* make a wonderful mother."

"Oh my God," Josie cried, planting her face into my shoulder. "I can't believe you just said that."

"Why?" Was she crying? Letting go of her hands, I curled one arm around her waist and then gently guided her head back up with the other. "*Psychi mou*, are you crying?"

"I don't know," she said, sniffling. "I just . . . I was so afraid you would be unhappy and I'm scared, because I don't know if I would be a good mom. I mean, I can't even remember to brush my teeth every night, and I'm going to be responsible for another person? We are so young—like too young. I mean, we can live for, like, eternity and I don't even know what this baby is going to be and there's so much crazy going on right now."

Chuckling hoarsely, I smoothed away her tears. "I could never be unhappy and you have no reason to be scared, Josie. We're . . . we're in this together. I know there's a lot of crazy, but you're not in this alone."

Josie blinked rapidly as she stared up at me. "You're really . . . you're really okay with this?"

"We're . . . we're having a baby, Josie. How could I not be okay with that?"

She let out a throaty sound and threw her arms around me. "I love you. I love you," she said, repeating the three words over and over.

It hit me again, almost taking my legs right out from under me once more. This meant everything would change and we needed to seriously talk about what that meant, but right now, all I could focus on was this . . . fuck, *this* beautiful moment I hadn't thought I'd ever experience.

"I'm going to be a father," I said, sort of dumbstruck by the mere realization. I could feel my lips curving into a smile—a smile I couldn't stop even if I wanted to. "I never . . . It's not something I've ever thought about." I brought my hand to her cheek. "I just never thought it would be in my future. Probably because it wasn't until recently that I even *had* a future, but I never . . ." I laughed in shock, only because it was rare when I was actually speechless. "I'm going to be a dad."

Josie smiled as she nodded. "You . . . will be an amazing father. No child would ever be more loved, more safe."

Her beautiful face blurred as stark emotion punched a hole right through my chest. Who knew hearing those words would have such a intense impact? But they did. And my own eyes felt oddly damp. My knees felt weak again and my body . . . my body reacted strongly and without thought.

Lifting her up, in one powerful lunge, I had Josie on her back, and all that glorious hair was spread out along the bedspread. I hovered over her, my fist punched into the bed beside her head and my other hand gripping her hip. My heart was a battering ram against my ribs as I stared down at her.

"I love you," I said, my voice shaking—my fucking hand trembling as I slid it over, resting just below her navel. "And I love this . . . this child already." Shocked at the truthfulness in that statement, my breath got lodged in my throat. My gaze lifted to her in a dazed wonder. "Neither of you will ever want for anything. I promise you that."

And that was a promise I would kill to keep.

And die to ensure.

Josie

A sharp pang of raw emotion sliced through me. There was so much fear and confusion warring inside me, but what had started as a tiny speck of happiness had erupted into the purest, brightest joy.

We were in this together.

And Seth was okay with this—he was more than okay.

I knew this, because I saw what he was feeling in those tawny eyes. Seth was as overwhelmed as I was, but he wasn't freaking out. He was diving head-first into this really unexpected development and he was *welcoming* it.

Seth was happy about the fact I was going to have his child.

I didn't know what I expected from him, but not this—not the *tears* I knew I saw crowding his eyes. I looked down and saw his hand on my stomach, the touch so reverent and gentle I was seconds from breaking into sobs.

But the unbridled emotion whirling through me like a cyclone chased away the doubt and the fear that I guessed was common even for people who weren't newly unbound demigods impregnated by newly appointed gods.

Reaching up, I touched his smooth jaw, then dragged my fingers over to his lips.

He pressed a kiss to them. "We're going to be okay. We're going to be more than okay."

Oh God, my heart imploded into goo.

There was so much we needed to discuss and figure out, but I didn't want words right now. I wanted Seth, only him, with nothing between us.

Lifting myself up on my elbows, I brushed my lips against his, and he seemed to know exactly what I wanted, what I needed.

Seth settled between my legs as he pressed me back down into the bed. We kissed like it was the last time we'd ever get the chance. We kissed like we were starving for one another, and we were. Our hands were everywhere. His hands slid up the curve of my waist. My hand slipped under his shirt. And we kept kissing, breaking apart only so I could tug his black shirt off and he could pull mine off. The shirts fell somewhere on the floor. His boots came off next. Then my sneakers.

I ran my fingers down his defined pecs and over the tightly coiled ridges of his abs. His golden skin felt like silk stretched over steel. My fingers fell to the button on his pants, and he didn't stop me this time. Oh no, he lifted his hips as I popped the button free and dragged the zipper down. He inched one strap of my bra down my arm and then the other. He hooked a finger between the cups of my bra, and with a quick flick of his wrist my breasts were exposed.

And we were still kissing, our tongues tangling as he shifted sideways, shoving his pants and the tight boxer briefs down. His nimble fingers made quick work of my jeans.

Seth rose above and then scooted down. He caught my jeans and then my panties, quickly dragging them off. Within seconds, I was completely bare, and it felt like an eternity since there had been nothing between us.

His hands coasted up inside my legs and then over my hips. My heart thundered and my pulse pounded as a delicious ache filled me. He was still for a moment above me, his head bowed and locks of blond hair fell forward, shielding half his face. I reached for him, clutching his forearm as he lowered his head.

Seth kissed my stomach, just below my navel.

My breath caught at the sweet gesture. "Seth . . ."

He peered up at me with luminous eyes. "This," he said, voice thick as he smoothed a hand over my stomach. "This is a gift. It is nothing less than a . . . than a miraculous gift."

Tears blurred my eyes, and oh *gods*, I was going to start crying again. All I could do was reach for him, and he came to me. The bare skin of his leg dragged over mine. I whimpered as I felt him hot and hard against my thigh, searing my skin.

His heated gaze roamed my face and then lower, over the taut tips of my breasts. His stare was like a physical caress, eliciting a sharp swirl of shivers. Then his gaze moved even lower and his lips parted, his lips moving as if he were searching for words and was coming up empty. When those thick lashes lifted and his gaze pierced mine, I saw that awe again.

"I love you," I said, curling my hand around the back of his neck. "I love you so much."

Seth made this partially animalistic sound that caused my blood to turn to molten lava. Heat spread into the very core of my being. I pulled his mouth down to mine and I kissed him like I was drowning, and I was.

We couldn't wait.

There was no need for long, lazy caresses or drugging, hazy kisses. I was ready. He was ready. I needed him. He wanted me. I shifted my hips as he reached between us with one hand, guiding his rigid length to me. He whispered those beautiful words against my lips as he pushed in, his size, his hardness stretching and burning in the most exquisite way.

Back arching, I kicked my head back as a keening sound escaped me. Seth caught my chin, forcing my gaze back to his. He held my stare, and I couldn't look away. His mouth hovered over mine as he slowly, maddeningly pushed in, inch by nerve-wrecking inch.

"Seth," I gasped out, lifting my leg and hooking it around his hip. He went deeper and deeper until there was no space between our hips, until we were one.

He groaned my name in the air between our lips. "I can't . . . I need you—need this now."

"Don't wait," I whispered. "Don't."

Seth rumbled out a curse and then his hips started moving. Each thrust, each retreat sent bolts of electricity through every cell. My body quivered as my anticipation swelled. I wrapped my arms around him, digging my heels into his legs. Every place he was hard, I was soft.

Panting in shallow, uneven breaths, I held onto him as his thrusts quickened, losing all rhythm. He dug his arm into the bed and lifted me up. He moved as hard and fast as I'd ever felt. His lean body covered mine as his hips pounded in and out. His breathing became ragged, and everything . . .

Everything became frantic.

Our hands were clenching and clutching. Sweat beaded on my skin. I was rising up and being pressed back into the mattress, taking each thrust and reaching for more, always more. My name dripped from his lips. Soft cries parted mine. Tendrils of pleasure coiled tightly. My nails grazed his skin as I rocked against him. A curling, burning heat seared my skin.

I couldn't take it.

My body exploded.

Pleasure thundered through me as inaudible sounds filled

the room—sounds I don't think I'd ever made before. Each lunge of his hips went deep and then deeper, over and over, and then he planted himself deep in me, his mouth claiming mine as I felt him jerk and spasm. A storm passed before he stilled, and I held onto him, held onto all that this meant as sweet aftershocks rattled me to the very core.

Dragging his mouth from mine, he lifted his head. His eyes locked with mine. He said nothing. There wasn't a need for words. The corner of my lips tipped up. His did the same, and we just looked at each. We just . . . watched each other.

Then Seth eased onto his side, slipping out of me. My hands slid down his arms as he rested his forehead against my breasts. Our legs were tangled. Our breathing and hearts slowing. Neither of us moved for several long moments.

"You okay?" He pushed the tangled, damp strands off my forehead.

"Yeah." I turned my body into his. "That was . . ."

"Everything," he murmured against my cheek.

Yes. That was everything.

"Gods, Josie." He wrapped his arms around me, fitting me to the side of his body. "You've . . . you've made my life."

I smiled broadly. "That sounds impressive."

"It is."

Nestling against his chest, I pressed my cheek to where his heart raced. Seth reached down, tucking my leg between his. He shuddered, and I felt his lips brush across my forehead. Tears filled my eyes, because I was finally . . . I was finally where I was meant to be.

But it was more than that, so much more.

Seth gently shifted me onto my back, easing half his body onto mine as if he sought to shield me. His hand moved from my lips, trailing down the center of my body. It came to a stop over my stomach. His fingers splayed, and my heart jumped as I lifted my gaze to his.

The line of his jaw was soft, his touch even more so. "You know what?"

"What?"

One side of his lips quirked up. "You're going to be my very own MILF."

I blinked. For a moment, I didn't think I heard him correctly. "And I'm going to be your DILF."

My mouth dropped open. "I can't believe you just said that."

Seth grinned as he gave me a lopsided shrug. "It's true."

I stared at him and then I turned, laughing as I threw my arm around his waist. "You're so . . ."

"Amazing? Perfect. Sexy? A beast?"

Giggling, I shook my head. "You're insane."

"Insanely in love with you." Gathering me against his front, he folded his arms around me. "Josie?"

Having no idea what he was about to say, I murmured, "What?"

Seth coasted his hand down my spine and then back up to the nape of my neck, where his fingers curled in a possessive, protective hold. A heartbeat passed and then he said, "Thank you."

31

*S*eth traced invisible patterns on my skin, a circle over my upper arm and what felt like a cross along the line of my shoulder, and other times it felt like he was playing tic-tac-toe with himself along my back.

We were lying on our sides, facing one another. Seth had pulled the blanket up to our waists. Well, he hadn't used a hand to do so. The blanket sort of just moved on its own.

I really missed being able to do all those cool things, but I was trying not to think about the bands.

"So Alex knows?" he asked.

"Yeah. It was weird with her being there, but it was nice of her to be there for me." I was busy circling my finger around his nipple. "I was really freaking out. Being pregnant isn't something I . . . I planned on."

"Really?" he teased.

Grinning, I lifted my gaze. His eyes were closed, and those impossibly long lashes fanned his cheeks. "I never even thought about wanting kids. It just wasn't something I thought about."

"I never thought about it either," he admitted, his finger trailing up my arm. "Never seemed like an option."

Up until he reached his god-hood or whatever you wanted to call it, Seth hadn't had a future, so that made sense. I bit down on my lip as I studied the striking lines of his face.

Sometimes, as shallow as it sounded to admit, I got a little lost just looking at him. I could remember what I thought the first time I'd met him. His beauty had been so cold, almost unreal and untouchable. Not anymore. There was a warmth there, a softness that couldn't be denied.

I flattened my hand over his chest, feeling his heart beat strongly. "I'm . . . I'm scared."

His lashes lifted and his hand stilled on my arm. His gaze searched mine. "Josie . . . *psychi mou.*"

I loved it when he said that. *My soul.* That broke me in the very best ways every time. "I know it's common, right? I mean, I guess most expecting . . . moms are. I just don't know if I'm doing things right." I glanced down at my belly, wishing I could talk to my mom or my grandmother. "That I'll mess up. It's just scary."

"I'll be here." Seth cupped my cheek, drawing my gaze to his. "You're not going to be alone in this."

"I know." A few moments of silence stretched out between us. "I'm surprised that I'm still pregnant after everything that happened. This baby . . ."

"This baby is a fighter. Can we be surprised?" A half-smile formed. "You're a fighter."

"So are you." How could he not realize that?

"Both of us are," he corrected, smoothing his thumb over my lower lip. "But I was born into a life where fighting was first nature. You were thrust into this. In a way, you're stronger than most Sentinels."

I wasn't sure about that. I was scared witless by the fact I was pregnant. I had no idea what giving birth was going to be like, and I seriously doubted it would be a fun thing to go through. Raising a child, being responsible for a little being, was terrifying because I knew there was a good chance I'd drop it once or three times. And that's not even acknowledging everything else going on.

But I liked that he said that, because his vote of confidence did help. "This kid is going to be . . . Man, what is this kid going to be?" I asked, curious. "A demigod? A god?"

He kissed the tip of my nose. "I don't know, but we'll figure it out, and either way it will be all good."

Drawing back, I stared at him. "How can you be . . . be so calm?"

"Calm?" His brows lifted. "I'm just better at hiding my panic."

"You're panicking?"

He slid his hand around the back of my neck. "I'm . . . I'm scared, too. Having a kid is seriously some uncharted territory. Everything . . . everything has changed, Josie."

My breath caught. I had a feeling I knew what he meant.

"Today is nothing like yesterday," he said, his gaze searching mine intently. "And later tonight, when we go to sleep, it will be nothing like last night. Everything that we do, every decision that we make going forward, will change because of this."

I drew in a shallow breath, but it got stuck.

"Nothing is just about us anymore. I don't mean that there still can't just be an us," he said, threading his fingers through my hair. "But the big decisions, we can't just think about us."

He was right, and I knew that. "When have we ever even gotten a chance to think about just us?"

Seth opened his mouth, but then what could he say? I was right. We hadn't had the chance to be selfish in our relationship. We probably wouldn't for a long, long time.

"And the world is not going to stop just because I'm pregnant. The Titans aren't going to just call a time-out, and the gods? How long are they going to stay out of this and out of our lives once the Titans are taken care of?" I asked, squirming as my unease rose. "Nothing outside this room has ceased to exist, and it won't. We still have to find Mitchell. We still have to take care of the Titans and anything else that comes our way. That hasn't changed."

Seth's eyes darkened to a chilled topaz. "But we will have to make some changes."

I raised a brow. "We?"

"Yeah." A grin softened the hard look. "Both of us. Probably in ways I don't even know yet."

"Pregnant or not, I still have to help. I have to entomb the Titans," I said quietly. "I know you don't want to hear that, but you can't just go and kill them all."

His lips pursed, and I could just tell he wanted to ask why not, but he didn't. Seth didn't say anything as he tipped my head back and kissed me.

And those kisses turned deep, becoming something infinitely more, leaving me breathless and wanting. I ended up on my back and Seth's wonderful, talented hands were between my legs and his tongue and his teeth replaced those devious fingers of his.

Within moments I was lost to the touch and the taste that was all him. Our bodies were fused together and we were twisting and tangling. I was in his lap and then I was on my knees and his arm was pinned under my breasts.

There was no rush this time, no scrabbling of hands and frantic thrusts, but this release, when it came, was no less powerful than the one before. But afterward, as we lay in each other arms, our bodies heated and damp, our breath mingling and hearts pounding, the questions lingered.

How could I walk away from my duty?

How could I put my—*our*—unborn child in danger?

I didn't know.

I didn't know if there was a right or wrong answer.

But I knew I would have to choose.

And I also knew I may not even have a choice.

* * *

I dozed as Seth continued to make little designs with his fingers, this time across my stomach because I now lay on my other side, my bottom tucked into his hips. I woke every so often to the feel of his fingers dancing over my skin. I'd wiggle against him and was immediately rewarded with a kiss to my cheek or my neck. I don't think he slept, but I was tired, so I drifted in and out.

A feeling of . . . peace had seeped into my muscles, and while I lay in his strong arms, all those concerns from earlier retreated outside the room. It was just him and me and . . . the future we were making.

But I still slipped into a dream.

A nightmare.

No longer in his arms, I was on the ground. Rough, broken asphalt dug into my palms and scraped my knees through the dirty, torn jeans. My hair hung in my face in thick clumps.

I was back there, outside the warehouse, and I could feel *him* beside me, waiting and watching. My mouth opened but there was no sound. *This isn't real. This isn't real.* I kept repeating that over and over, because I knew, deep down, I wasn't in that warehouse anymore. I just needed to wake up. I had to—

My head was wrenched back. Panicked, my arms pinwheeled as I fell backward. My wide gaze swung over the trees, over the truck sitting by the garage bays. I landed on my ass. The bright sun was blotted out by a tall figure.

Oh no, no, no.

Jerking upright, I gasped for air as I threw my arm out. The beige walls came into focus, but I wasn't seeing the walls. I didn't feel the bed under my naked skin or Seth beside me.

Part of me was still back at the warehouse, outside in the almost empty parking lot. There was *something* there—something I saw, something I needed to see again.

"Josie." Seth was sitting up, holding onto my arm. "You okay?"

I still saw the thick trees ahead of me. I could feel the hot sun beating down on my skin, the beads of sweat running down my face. I sucked in a shrill breath as pressure filled my chest and expanded. "I had a . . . I had a nightmare. I was back at the warehouse."

"Babe." He scooted behind me as he wrapped an arm around my waist, hauling me back against his chest. The other circled me, and I was in his arms, far away from that place of hell. "You're safe." He kissed my temple. "You're never going to have to experience anything like that again."

Leaning into him, I closed my eyes. "There was something I saw while there. I know it. Something outside—" I saw the woods again, the tall, never-ending trees. The needles on the ground. The cracked pavement and the box truck . . ."Oh my *gods.*"

"Josie?"

Pulling away from him, I twisted around. I climbed onto my knees, grasping his shoulders. I didn't even care that I was naked. "I remember something!"

"What?" His gaze dropped to my chest, because, well, he was Seth.

"Pay attention." I shook him.

A playful grin appeared. "Sorry. You're fucking gorgeous and

I really—"

"Focus." I smacked his shoulders. "I saw something outside the warehouse. I can't believe I didn't remember it until now. But there was some kind of truck outside—a box or delivery truck. It had a name written on the side of it. MILLS AND SONS. If the truck belonged to that warehouse . . ."

Understanding flashed across Seth's face. "Then we have a way to find the warehouse."

32

As Josie took a shower, I changed into a pair of tactical pants that had been left behind and pulled on a shirt. Walking away from the bathroom and not joining her literally took every ounce of free will I had in me.

I wanted nothing more than a round three and four and ten with her, but I needed to fill Aiden in on what Josie had remembered, and she needed to get some food in her. So I had done the responsible thing, showered first and left Josie to hers.

Hair still wet, I pushed it back out of my face and walked into the small sitting room. Halfway through, I came to a complete stop as my stomach did a drop, like it hit my feet.

Josie was pregnant.

Lifting my gaze to the ceiling, I was rooted to the floor. Ever since she'd told me, those three words floated in and out of my thoughts on an endless cycle, and each time it was like the first time hearing it.

There was a rush of emotions—the happiness blew my mind. Like I'd said to Josie, I'd never even thought about having kids, to be honest, so it wasn't like I didn't want them. It just wasn't a *thing*. Never in a hundred years would I have thought I'd actually be happy about that, but I was. I was fucking thrilled.

I was fucking *blessed.*

But gods, what I felt almost knocked me on my ass again. Closing my eyes, I exhaled roughly as I leaned over, pressing my palms into my thighs.

I was never a praying man.

I didn't believe the gods answered prayers. Knew for a fucking fact that they didn't care enough to do so, but in that moment, I wanted to pray. I want to pray that this was real, that this was really happening.

It seemed too good, too beautiful.

Gods, it didn't seem like I'd deserve not only Josie but a child as well.

And that was terrifying for a whole shit-ton of reasons.

Because there was fear. Fear that something would happen to her, happen to the baby—to both of them. Fear that I would somehow fuck up, because I had no idea how to do the whole parenting thing.

Not to mention I was seriously probably the last person on this earth anyone would trust a small child with. Less than an hour before I found out I was going to be a father, I sort of melted a guy from the inside out, *so* . . .

But that was *my* baby, in *my* girl.

That changed everything in a manner of seconds.

Straightening, I let out a shaky laugh and found myself smiling at . . . at fucking nothing.

I need to get my shit together.

One way to avoid fucking this up was making the world safe for Josie and for our child.

Walking out of the room, I looked down the hall, and a

totally different smile appeared. Sensing out Aiden, I zeroed in on his presence. A heartbeat later, I was in another sitting area, in a room several doors down.

"Hello," I said.

Aiden flew up from where he was sitting on the couch.

"Dammit!" Alex shrieked as she nearly slid off the arm of the couch. "Oh my gods! Now you're going to do that too?"

"Not cool." Aiden's eyes were like thunderclouds. "Not cool."

"I thought it was pretty cool."

Alex gaped at me, and then she spun around, picked up a small throw pillow, and threw it at me.

I snatched the pillow out of the air and tossed it back to the couch. "I hope I wasn't interrupting."

"We were just talking," Alex answered, glaring at me. "If not, you'd be missing two eyeballs."

"That's not the only thing he'd be missing," Aiden muttered.

I winked at him. "I'm actually here with some important news. Josie remembered something about the warehouse."

"And here I thought you were just popping in because you missed us." Alex sat back down on the couch. "What did she remember?"

"She saw a delivery truck of some sort outside the warehouse where she was kept," I told them. "She remembered that the truck had writing on it. MILLS AND SON."

"Hell. That's big. If that truck belonged to the warehouse, we should be able to look it up." Aiden glanced around the room, frowning. "I'll grab Deacon's laptop and see what I can find."

"Let me know."

"If it turns out to be the place, are you leaving right away?" he asked.

Odd question. "Gods know if Josie finds out, she's going to want all of us to go there, but I need to get some food in her and . . . and yeah. We'll see what happens from there."

Aiden eyed me as he nodded. "Sounds good."

I started to say something, but my gaze slid to Alex. She was staring at the wall over my shoulder, her lips pressed together and her cheeks expanded like a puffer fish. My eyes narrowed. Her gaze flickered to me and then quickly darted away.

Sighing heavily, I folded my arms. "Something you want to say, Alex?"

Oddly mute, she shook her head.

"Really?"

Gaze still trained on the wall, she nodded.

I looked over at Aiden. What was the likelihood of her not saying something to him? Probably somewhere around next to impossible.

Aiden dropped his gaze, and then I saw it—the twitch of his lips as if he was trying not to smile.

"You told him," I stated.

The air Alex was holding in her mouth popped out as her gaze swung around to mine. "I didn't mean to! I just sort of blurted it out, but it's Aiden. I had to tell Aiden."

"She had to tell me," he agreed.

Actually, she didn't.

"I will not tell anyone else. I swear, and I do feel bad for saying something to Aiden, because I told Josie I wouldn't. I hope she's not mad at me." Alex squirmed on the couch, her forehead creased. "I'm sorry for saying something, but . . ."

I couldn't find an ounce of anger in me. And then it hit me with the force of a hurricane. I *wanted* people to know. What the hell? I didn't even know what to do with that.

"But you're . . . you're going to be a father," she finished in a whisper that sounded so awed.

I blinked slowly, unfolding my arms. "Yeah. Yeah, I am."

Alex clasped her hands together. "I am *made* of questions right now."

"You and me both," I replied dryly.

"Are you . . . are you happy—?"

"I'm fucking thrilled," I cut in, and then I sat down in the chair. "I'm shocked." My gaze flitted from Alex to Aiden. "I'd never been more shocked in my life. I actually fell flat on my ass when she told me." I felt warmth hit my cheeks. "It's . . . it's crazy timing with everything going on. But how could I not be happy? I love Josie. I already . . . I already love this child."

Alex's smile raced across her face. "I think I might cry."

"Please don't," I said, glancing at Aiden.

Staring at the floor, he dragged his hands down his face. I tensed. Every muscle locking up as I waited for Aiden to go into a lecture about how I needed to really think about things, be a better person. Like, "stop melting people" kind of shit and wanting to kill the Titans.

Alex leaned into him, placing her hand on his leg. For a moment I didn't get it. Then I remembered. Fuck. I'd forgotten. Alex had once believed she'd been pregnant and, knowing Aiden, knowing how I felt upon hearing the news, he would've felt like me.

Holy shit.

Alex hadn't been pregnant. It had been Ares's doing. He had his sons invade her to mess with her head. I hadn't known he'd planned to do that, but that didn't change a damn thing in the end.

I couldn't even imagine how I'd feel if that turned out to be the case after feeling all of this.

I couldn't even imagine what he was feeling—what Alex was feeling.

"I'm sorry," I said roughly.

Aiden's chin jerked up. Our gazes met, and he knew. Yeah, he knew what I was apologizing for. His throat worked on a hard swallow.

Beside him, Alex cleared her throat. "I really am happy for you, Seth. I know it's crazy timing and you weren't planning for this, but you're happy with it, and so is Josie, and that's all that matters."

But it really wasn't all that mattered, because what Josie had said earlier was right. The world wasn't going to stop turning. Not at all.

"I can't believe I'm saying this, but you're going to do good." Aiden smiled slightly as he nodded like he just realized he'd agreed with himself. "You're going to do more than good, Seth."

I stared at him, unsure if he was having some kind of medical emergency.

"He's right. That kid will want for nothing." Alex leaned back, her lips pursed. "Wait. Does this mean your kid is a god? I have no idea. I need to find some books on this."

"Not sure if there are books on this, Alex." Aiden turned his grin on her.

"All right," I said, standing. "This convo is over."

Aiden rose. "We really are happy for you, Seth. I still want to punch you in the throat, but I am happy for you."

"Uh-huh." So, knocked off-kilter by their words, I actually walked out of the door instead of taking the cool way out.

* * *

After ensuring Josie about a hundred times that Aiden was looking into the name on the delivery truck, we grabbed food from the cafeteria. She wanted to go outside, and I had no problem with that. Who knew if the whole sitting in the sun thing was helping with the bands and the pregnancy, but it couldn't hurt. There was at least an hour or so before the sun went down.

I wanted to take her back to the island, but we wouldn't have the blood results until tomorrow. Although Josie was fairly confident nothing was going to change in those results, she wanted to stay.

Honestly, I think she missed everyone and wanted to be at the Covenant, and if that was what she wanted, then we'd be here. For now, she was probably safer here.

But I'd have to go back in a couple of days to recharge. I wasn't thinking about that. Kind of like pissing on your own parade right there.

Carrying our trays outside, we walked to the courtyard, passing through the vine-covered gates. Josie led the way, heading past the benches. She roamed until she found a pretty large patch of grass, then sat down, placing her tray in front of her. I'd loaded her plate up. Fries. Chicken tenders. A salad, because she figured she should eat some sort of vegetable. A bottle of water and a soda. A side order of strawberries.

The early evening sunlight glinted off her bowed head, turning all the shades in her hair into spun gold. Its length fell over her shoulder, brushing her thigh as she bent forward to pick up the can of soda.

She lifted her chin. "You going to join me?"

"I was thinking about just standing here and staring at you some more, to be honest."

She grinned as she popped the lid to her soda. "Well, that doesn't make me uncomfortable or anything."

Laughing, I sat beside her. My plate just had a burger on it. I wasn't hungry, obviously, but how could I pass up a burger? "I thought you liked it when I stared at you."

"Not when I'm about to stuff my face full of food." She dug into the fries first. "It's weird that I still have to eat as a demigod, but you really don't have to eat as a god."

"I don't make the rules," I murmured, hoping she didn't connect the dots back to the fact I did have to feed. "Have you been sick at all today?"

She shook her head. "Just nauseous this morning. I'm kind of surprised I'm having symptoms already. I hope that doesn't mean I'm going to spend nine months puking my guts up."

My eyes widened as I picked up the burger. "You and me both."

"I also have no idea if I'll be pregnant for a full nine months."

That reminded me. "By the way, Alex told Aiden."

Her lips twitched. "Of course she did."

"You're not mad?"

She shook her head and then took a drink. "Aiden's the love of her life. I doubt there's a single thing they don't share. People are going to find out eventually. I just didn't want him to find out before I told you."

I smiled at that. "We should keep the news to people we really trust. We don't need the news getting out there to those we don't want to find out."

Josie nodded in agreement as she moved on to the tenders, dipping the crispy pieces into ranch dressing.

"Anyway, I think Alex is going to be searching for books on pregnancy. She wants to know if we're having a god or not."

Her hand froze halfway to her mouth. "Those are some words I never thought I'd hear before."

I chuckled as I glanced over at her. Her levels of aether were still low and the lights flickered. Was it the bands or the baby? Speaking of the bands, where in the hell was Apollo?

And what in the hell would he do when he found out Josie was pregnant?

That should be interesting.

Sensing an approach, I glanced up to the gate. "We're about to get company."

A few seconds later, Alex and Aiden entered the courtyard, and right behind them were Luke and Deacon.

"We'd figured you be out here," Alex said, carrying a small paper bag. As she came closer, I could smell the buttery popcorn. "So, we're interrupting you."

"We're not just bothering you," Deacon said. "I've got—"

Catching his gaze, I shook my head. If they were out here, that meant they'd found out something about the warehouse. I didn't want it brought up in front of Josie. I didn't want her to know, because I fully planned on taking care of business without her knowing.

She'd be pissed.

But a safe and angry Josie was better than an in-danger one, because even though she had the bands on her wrists, she would want to be involved since it had to do with this bound demigod. She'd forgot our deal and I'd rather have her yell at me afterward than before.

I also didn't want her to worry, because she would. She knew that, if we found Mitchell, it was likely we'd find a Titan. Hell, the damn bastards could just be waiting for us to figure out where Josie had been held.

Luckily Deacon caught my stare and clamped his mouth shut. I glanced over at Aiden, and he seemed to read the silent message I was sending his way.

"You've got what?" Josie asked.

"I've got a . . . a story to tell you?" Deacon said, his brows lifted high.

Luke frowned.

"You do?" she asked. "About what?"

"About, um . . . Well, did you know that the guy who played

John Winchester who was on *Supernatural* is now on *The Walking Dead* and he plays this guy who pretty much bashes people's heads in with a bat? Sam and Dean must be so proud of their dad."

Josie blinked slowly. "I . . . I didn't know that."

"Yep." Deacon dropped down beside her. "Maggie used to be on *Supernatural* too."

I didn't quite know if that was a good save or not, but hell, whatever worked.

"Where's Gable?" Josie asked, picking up another fry. "Is he with Cora?"

Deacon stretched out his lanky frame as Luke sat on the nearby bench. "Yeah. Colin's with them too."

"How's she doing?" she asked.

"Better every hour," Luke answered, leaning back as he crossed his arms. "We still have that other demigod to find."

"That one's in Britain, right?" Aiden sat down next to Luke, and I guessed no one was leaving anytime soon. "The haunted town."

"Gasp!" Deacon waved his hands. "You actually remembered that?"

"How could anyone forget?" Alex sat in Aiden's lap. "It's all you talked about the whole drive back to the Covenant."

"Dude, who wouldn't be excited?" he exclaimed, shaking his head. "It's an entire town that's supposedly haunted. Like, if I'm not scared to death when I go there, I'm going to be disappointed."

"Who said you were going there?" Aiden asked, wrapping his arms around Alex's waist.

Deacon groaned. "Can we not have this conversation again? I'm going to get the other demigod before they get . . ."

I looked over at Alex. She kept glancing at Josie like she was seconds away from bursting into a torrent of questions. I was surprised she hadn't blurted anything out yet. Though I figured Deacon and Luke would discover what was going on.

Tuning them out, I focused on Josie. She was looking at the roses with a strange, almost perplexed look. I nudged her shoulder. She glanced over at me. "What you thinking about?"

She smiled as she ducked her chin. "Nothing. I just . . . I was dazing."

I looked down and willed her plate closer to her. "You should eat more."

"Look at you, being all godly and not even touching the plate," she said.

Chuckling, I leaned into her. "Just imagine how creative I can—"

A fissure of energy rolled across the courtyard, rising the fine hairs on my arms. Everyone felt it. Grabbing Josie's arm, I launched to my feet as ancient, bronze-colored doors appeared just in front of the gateway. Runes were carved into the metal—runes and symbols that represented the Underworld.

"What the . . . ?" Aiden was already on his feet, as were Alex and Luke.

I stepped in front of Josie as the doors opened, prepared for anything to come through those doors.

Mist rolled out, creeping over the grass and roses. Then a form appeared, and as the heavy mist retracted a blond boy I hadn't seen in a long, long time strolled forward.

That I was not prepared for.

Stunned, I dropped Josie's arm. What in the world?

"Caleb!" Alex shrieked, causing Josie to jump. "What are you doing here?"

He grinned in her direction. "Long story, but first, there's something I'm here to do." His bright blues eyes focused on us.

"Something really important."

Gods, he looked like the last time I'd seen him alive, all messy hair and a big smile. He started toward us, and out of instinct I blocked Josie.

Caleb's smile spread, reaching his eyes. "I'm here because of Apollo."

"What?" Alex whispered in a thick voice.

"Let me see her," Caleb asked. "I can help her."

There was a part of me that didn't trust him—trust anyone when it came to Josie's safety, but that damn girl had stepped around me. I looked down as Caleb reached over and took Josie's hands in his.

"Hi there," Caleb said, turning her hands so they were palms up. "It's time, don't you think?"

"Time for what?" she asked, that strange look settling into her features again.

Caleb smiled, and Josie gasped. My heart about fucking stopped in my chest.

"Oh my *gods*," Josie said, pulling her hands free as she stumbled back.

Spinning, I reached out and wrapped an arm around her. Blood drained from her face as she stared at Caleb like she'd seen a ghost. But that was impossible, because Josie had never met Caleb.

He'd died before we met her.

"I've seen you before," she whispered.

I swung toward Caleb. His brows were pinched together. "Sorry." He looked over at Alex. "But we've never met before, and I just need to ho—"

"But we have," Josie insisted, lifting her startled gaze to mine. "I've *seen* him before—I've *seen* this in a dream. Oh my *gods*, I get it. It wasn't a dream. None of the dreams have been dreams."

"What?" I clasped her cheeks, confused as all hell. "What are you saying?"

Josie then did the damnedest thing, considering she was so pale. She smiled—smiled wildly. "I *am* special."

"Um, yeah . . . yeah you are." I was starting to get worried.

Alex shifted closer to Caleb. "What is she talking about?"

"I have no idea," Caleb said.

"You don't get it." She gripped my wrists. "Some of the dreams I've had—they weren't dreams. They're *prophecies*."

33

*H*oly crap, I *was* special!

I just hadn't known it.

Well, I wasn't as special as Cora, who could bring plants back to life, and tell when someone was sick or pregnant, but I had been having *prophecies*. And it made sense. My absentee father was the god of prophecy among many other things.

"Josie, what are you talking about?" Seth's amber's eyes were full of concern.

"I saw this—I saw him coming to me in a dream. Just like I saw Atlas, but didn't realize it was him," I explained, slipping free of Seth's gentle grasp. "Every time, right before and after I'd have those dreams, I'd get headaches. Remember the headaches?"

"Yeah, I remember them." Seth dropped his hands to his sides.

I whirled around. Everyone was staring at me like I'd grown a third boob out of the center of my forehead, and no one seemed to care about the gaping doors that appeared out of nowhere—doors to the Underworld that were still wide open.

"I saw you!" I said to the boy who had to be a year or so younger than me. "You walked up and took my hands. And you—" I faced Alex. Her cheeks were damp. "You were crying in my dream."

"I'm so damn emotional," Alex said, wiping at her cheeks. It was then I remembered who this boy was. Deacon had told me about him—about Alex's friend who'd died in a daimon attack. Caleb. "It's just different seeing him up here."

Spinning back to Seth, I threw up my hands. "I know this sounds crazy, but I'm positive that's what's happening. If only my . . ." I trailed off, lowering my arms. If only my father was around to fill in the blanks, but this boy had said his name. Turning away, I faced him. "You said my father sent you?"

"Yeah," Caleb responded. "He's been in the palace—Hades's palace, and let me tell you, those two threw down like cray."

Seth was by my side. "Is that so?"

"Yep. Like, it was so bad that Persephone threatened to leave if Hades didn't agree to whatever Apollo had demanded, and I don't know, but that screws up the seasons or something," Caleb explained. "And then I was summoned to the palace."

"Why did they summon you?" Alex asked the question that was obviously at the forefront of everyone's mind.

"He figured that, since I was already dead, Seth couldn't really kill me." Caleb shrugged as my jaw popped open. "I think it's also because Seth wouldn't want to hurt me, right?"

"Right," murmured Seth.

Deacon was standing. "Damn, it's good to see you. Really is, but why would they send you up here?"

"Because none of the gods will come near me," Seth answered rather smugly.

"Bingo," Caleb agreed. "So they got this idea to send me up

to take off those things—those bands on your wrists."

Now what he'd said in the dream—in the *prophecy*—and a few moments ago made sense. "You . . . you can remove them?"

Caleb extended his hands again. "That's what they tell me."

I started forward, but Seth stopped me. "Wait. How do we know that this isn't a trick?" he demanded. "No offense, Caleb, but they could be using you without you even knowing."

"Do you really think that?" Alex asked, sounding stunned. "That Apollo would use Caleb to harm his own daughter?"

"Damn," Luke muttered. "That would be beyond messed up."

Pressure expanded in my chest as I looked over at Seth. "He wouldn't."

His jaw hardened as he stared down Caleb. "How do you remove the bands?"

"I just need to touch him," Caleb explained. "See, Hades had placed his hand on my head and said some weird, magical mumbo-jumbo. Told me that all I needed to do was take her hands and move my fingers over the bands. They'd unhook."

"And that's all?" Seth demanded.

I really couldn't believe Apollo would agree to anything that would harm me. Granted, I wanted to drop-kick him, but he was my father. He'd weakened himself to unbind my powers.

"I know what you're thinking," Seth said in that freaky way that made you think that he was reading your thoughts. "It's not Apollo I'm worried about. It's Hades. There's always a catch with him."

"Well, there *is* a catch," Caleb said.

I stiffened. "What do you mean?"

Caleb glanced at Seth with a sheepish grin. "Hades wants me to put the bands on you."

"What?" I gasped.

"Oh shit," Luke said under his breath as Alex stepped forward.

Seth crossed his arms. "Is that so?"

"Yep. I looked at him like he was crazy, because I'm not quite sure how he expects me to put the bands on without you noticing." Caleb shrugged like it was no big deal. "And I'm pretty sure if Apollo had normal eyes when this was going on, he would've been rolling them."

"Wait a second," I jumped in before Seth could do something stupid. "You're expected to free me but turn around and bind Seth's abilities?"

"Expected to? Yes. Am I going to do so? Nope."

Alex reached Caleb's side, tipping her head back so she could meet his gaze. "What will happen if you free Josie and don't do what they ask?"

"Come on, Hades has to know that Seth isn't going to stand there and let me slap those babies on him. So, what I was thinking, you could just hit me with a god bolt and send me back that way," Caleb suggested. "Then, at least I'm not lying when I say Seth stopped me."

My mouth dropped open.

"What?" Alex demanded. "He is not hitting you with a god bolt!"

"This has gotten really weird," Deacon murmured.

Seth tilted his head to the side. "Not like it's going to kill him or anything."

Caleb nodded.

"It's still going to hurt!" argued Alex.

"Actually, when you're dead, it just feels like a quick zap."

My jaw was now on the ground. "Have you . . . been hit with a god bolt before?"

Caleb snorted. "Persephone and Hades are sore losers when

they play Mario Kart or when they lose at anything. I've been zapped more times than I can count."

"Alrighty then," I murmured.

"But I *am* here to help you. I can remove those bands." Caleb twisted toward Seth as he spoke. "Just let me spend a couple of minutes with everyone before you send me back, okay?"

Seth appeared to consider this. "You can have as much time as you want."

"Thank you." Sliding Alex a coy look, Caleb grinned. "Told you there was always hope."

Alex's lips pursed while Seth's eyes narrowed. I had no idea what that was about, but Caleb took my hands in his. It was only then that I realized that a dead person was holding my hands.

A legit dead person.

I tried to keep my expression blank as he turned my palms up. My gaze flickered over his shoulder, to the gateway. There was nothing but a dark abyss beyond the doors, but I couldn't help but wonder—if I walked through them, would I be able to find my mother?

It was too much of a risk—for me and for the child I carried.

Caleb smoothed his thumbs over the thin bands. I held my breath. Nothing happened at first. I glanced up at him, and he gave a little shrug. One side of his lips curled down. "It should—"

A soft *click* interrupted him, and a second later the bands slipped off my wrists. Caleb let go of my hands, quickly catching them as a jolt of what felt like electricity shot through my veins.

Gasping, I took a step back as I lifted my hands. A white tint filled the veins of my hands and flowed up my arms. I could feel the warmth under my skin, washing over me. My attention shot to Seth.

His eyes were luminous as he stared at me. He could see this—the aether following the network of vessels, pumping my body full of light and power. And I could feel *it*.

It was like stepping under cold water first thing in the morning. My body was thrust into shock, kicking my pulse and heart rate up. A rush of pins and needles started at my feet and hit every inch of my body. A final pulse of heat invaded my insides, centering around the scar Apollo had left behind on the center of my chest.

And then it was all gone, except . . .

Except I could feel the aether in me. Sucking in a sharp breath, I turned to Seth. "Do I . . . Can you see it now?"

"Yeah." Amber eyes glowed as he stared at me—at my stomach. He looked like he might tip over and fall on his ass again. "Yeah, I can see it. Can you use it?"

There was only one more way to make sure that I was back to, well, what the new normal was. Focusing on the can of soda on my tray, I lifted my hand.

Luke backed up. "Oh jeez."

Ignoring him, I tapped into the air element. The can shook and then lifted straight up. I snatched it out of the air, sloshing brown liquid over my hand. My gaze flew to Seth's. "I'm back."

Seth reached over, taking my free hand. He tugged me toward him. I was careful to not spill my drink on him. Wrapping an arm around my waist, he tilted his head toward Caleb. "Thank you, man."

"Yes. Thank you," I said to him.

"No problem." Holding the bands in his hands, he grinned. "Not often I get to actually be helpful. Kind of like old times."

My heart tugged as I saw Alex's face crumple a little. She made a sound that sounded like a squeal and then grabbed the blond boy, pulling him in for a hug. Within seconds, Caleb was surrounded by her, Deacon and Luke. Aiden joined them, too.

I guessed Alex and Aiden got to see Caleb when they were in the Underworld, but I supposed it was different to see each other here, where everyone was actually . . . sort of alive.

As the happy reunion took place, Seth pressed his cheek to mine. When he spoke, he did so in a low enough voice that only I could hear him. "How are you feeling?"

"Good." I knew what he was asking. "I feel the same, but just not as . . . as tired, if that makes sense."

"It does." He kissed the space below my ear. "I now understand what I saw flickering when I looked at you."

I turned my cheek to his. "What do you mean?"

The breath Seth took, I felt. "Remember when I said the aether looked like it was flickering in you? It wasn't *your* aether I'd been seeing. You must've been nearly depleted, because I can still see the part that's flickering. I think . . . no, I know it's the baby."

"What?" I drew back, gaping.

His eyes were soft as he kept his voice low. "I can still see it. I see your aether and I see the . . . I see the baby's."

My lips parted, but I didn't have the words. Emotion crawled up my throat. He could see the aether in our child? That was . . . Wow. I really didn't know how to process that. "Does it . . . does it look good? Like, okay?"

"I think so." He placed his forehead against mine. "I mean, it has to be."

And I suddenly wanted to cry—cry happy tears.

So I face-planted his shoulder.

Somehow Seth got the can of Coke out of my hand and it went somewhere, who knew where, and then both of his arms were around me. "I'm not usually this emotional," I said into his chest, repeating the same thing Alex had said mere minutes before.

"What?" he asked.

My voice was still muffled but I continued anyway. "It's just that . . . you can see it and that just makes it all the more real."

His hand pressed into my back as he whispered my name into my ear. "Sometimes I have no idea how your brain words, but I love you," he said, his grip tightening. "I love you with every ounce of my being."

There was no stopping my smile. No matter what, this was a beginning.

34

Before I zapped Caleb back to the Underworld with a god bolt, I pulled Deacon aside while Josie sat with Luke and listened to Deacon regale them with tales of the Underworld, Nintendo edition.

He had the info that I needed.

The name of the warehouse was in fact an abandoned warehouse just outside Piney Woods. That was where Josie had been held, along with the other two, and it was most likely where I would find Hyperion.

Something told me that if he sensed me, he would come. He was a dumb motherfucker like that.

"What are you going to do?" Deacon asked as he glanced over at the group. "Do some scouting? Free the demigod?" He paused. "Call out Hyperion and kill him?"

I shrugged a shoulder.

Deacon tipped his head back. "You don't have to tell me, because I'm sure I already know."

"Is that so?"

He nodded. "I don't blame you for it."

I started to ask him what he wasn't blaming me for, but I stopped as my gaze landed on him. Those silver eyes were far too observant. Sometimes I forgot just how tuned into things Deacon was. We all did.

"Just make sure you come back," he said, looking away—looking at Josie. "She doesn't deserve to be left again."

"I know," I said, following his gaze. "And I will come back."

* * *

Kissing Josie on the cheek, I closed my eyes and forced myself out of the bed. It was a hard thing to do. The warmth of her bare skin against mine and the taste of her on my tongue was a lure that was hard to resist.

But I had to, because there was something I needed to take care of before she woke.

I changed quickly, leaving the daggers on the dresser. I would not need them. Not for this. Before I left, I allowed myself one more long look at her.

She was so beautiful to me.

Curled on her side with her hands snug under her cheek and her long hair sprayed out across the pillow, she looked like an angel to me. And she really was my own personal angel. I knew if she was awake and knew of my plan, she would advise me against it. Josie might even manage to sway me. After all, she was a calming presence when I wanted to Hulk-smash the world, but I didn't need to be calm.

I was going to end Hyperion.

The world could call me selfish and reckless. I simply did not care. Whatever the consequences for taking out Hyperion would be worth it.

I wasn't like Apollo. I wouldn't sacrifice the only people I cared about to protect the many.

I was doing this for Josie.

I was doing this for our child.

Because I would not allow her to live one more day in fear of Hyperion and I sure as hell would not allow my child to grow inside her and to be born, forced to live with that kind of terror.

Exhaling slowly, I willed myself out in the hallway and immediately swallowed a groan.

Aiden stood outside the room he shared with Alex, arms crossed against his chest as he leaned against the wall. He was dressed as a Sentinel, daggers and all, and I knew he was ready.

Walking toward him, I glanced over my shoulder, and then my gaze settled on him. He opened his mouth. "No," I said.

His eyes narrowed.

"You're not going with me."

Unfolding his arms, he pushed off the wall. "You're going to that warehouse and I'm going—"

"To make sure I play well with others?" I cut him off. "I'm going to find the guy named Mitchell."

"Yeah. Like you really give two shits about that guy," he said, and well, I really couldn't argue that. Aiden squared off with me. "You're going because you hope it'll draw out Hyperion."

I raised my brows.

Aiden seemed to take a deep breath. "Either we got lucky with Perses, or we just don't know what that fallout is, but Hyperion is one of the first twelve Titans. There is no way that taking him out isn't going to do something really bad."

"I feel like we've already had this conversation," I mused.

His eyes turned quicksilver. "Hyperion is the god of wisdom—"

I snorted.

Aiden was undaunted. "He is the god of wisdom, watchfulness and light. Now the first two things probably aren't going to be a big deal, but the light part? I'm guessing his death will have some impact on that."

Staring at him, I worked a kink out of my neck. "So, I'm guessing you want to hear me say I care, but I'm also guessing you already know that I don't. *So*, can we please end this conversation? I've got shit to do."

"I know you don't care," he replied, voice flat.

"Look, I get that you're about saving the world and shit, but we already had this conversation. You and I both know that if Hyperion did that shit to Alex, you'd be gunning for his ass. Just because those shoes aren't on your feet right now, don't think for a second I don't know what you'd be doing."

Aiden looked away, because he couldn't deny that.

"I cannot allow you to come with me. If Hyperion got a hold of you and you ended up dead, I so would not want to deal with Alex."

His turned back to me and he raised his brows.

"You will be a liability, because Hyperion can take you out."

"And he can't take you out?"

I smiled as I shook my head. "No."

A flicker of emotion shot across his face. Looked a lot like unease. For what? I wasn't sure.

"If you really want to be a help, then watch over Josie for me," I told him. "If she wakes up and I'm not back yet, tell her I will be. I don't want her to worry. That's what you can do."

Aiden looked like he was going to argue, but after a moment, he nodded. Knowing that he would do exactly that, I took myself away from the Covenant. I didn't go to Piney Woods first. I went to the island—to just outside the temple.

It was daylight as I climbed the steps and entered the temple, finding who I was looking for.

Karina stood by the alter, her hands clasped together as if

she was waiting. Just like with Basil, I really felt like I needed to get them each an iPad and introduce them to Snapchat or something. "Kýrios?"

I strode toward her, arms loose at my sides but my knuckles bleached white from how tight I was clenching my hands. "I need to feed."

* * *

Powering up seemed like the smart thing to do. I was going to need everything in me as I focused in on the location Deacon had told me earlier. It took seconds to travel back around the globe to the run-down piece of crap of a warehouse.

The moment the building came into view I knew it was the right place.

I don't know, but the place just gave off some creep vibes. The busted out windows and dirtied exterior walls screamed "serial killer hide-out."

Crickets chirped off in the distance as I approached the front doors. Moonlight shone down, lighting my path. Wrapping my hands around the handle on the industrial door, I tapped into the fire element. The metal heated up under my grasp and the internal gears melted. The door slid open.

Dust stirred as I walked inside, my booted feet echoing off the warped floors. It was dark inside, but my vision adjusted quickly. Forgotten work benches and pallets were scattered across the floor. Mice scurried for their hidey holes, their claws clicking as they chittered.

Based on what Josie had said, she had been kept below ground. I searched the main floor, keeping my senses on high alert. I neared the back of the building, spying a closed door that didn't look like it led to any offices.

This door was unlocked.

Opening it, I was immediately surrounded by the damp musky scent and a sickly-sweet stench that did not bode well. Shit. I headed down, already knowing what I was going to find.

Moonlight crept through a small window, casting faint light over the small, dirt-packed room. Water dripped from the ceiling, an old busted pipe. In the corner, there was a mass of clothes . . . and something else.

"Fuck," I muttered.

Walking over, I knelt down. The first thing I saw were two goldish bands circling bony wrists. The skin was patchy in spots, and I realized he was lying half on his back, half on his side. His eyes were eyes, wide and glazed over. Mitchell was dead.

And he'd been dead a while.

This was going to hurt Josie, and I hated that. She would blame herself, thinking that if she'd remembered the name on the box truck sooner, she would've been able to save him. But from the looks of it, this guy'd never had a chance.

Sighing, I leaned back. Scanning the dank room, I shook my head. Josie had been right. No one deserved to die in a place like that.

Well, I *did* know of one person.

A trickle of awareness skated over the back of my neck and a slow smile inched across my face.

Laughter broke the silence, and then Hyperion said, "I knew you would come."

I lifted my gaze up the damp wall and slowly rose.

"I waited. Took you long enough," Hyperion taunted. "Did you have to work up the nerve?"

With my back to him, I tilted my head. "Oh, yeah. I was so scared."

"You should've been, you little bitch."

I laughed as I felt the deadliest element known to man and

god stir deep inside me.

"You can't even look at me, can you?" Hyperion laughed. "You may have the other Titans scared, especially since you took out Atlas and then Perses, but I know what you are."

Fury hummed over my skin. "And what is that?"

"You're just a supped-up God Killer and that means I can kill you," he said, chuckling. "But I'm not going to kill you fast. I'm going to keep you down here just like I did with your pretty girlfriend."

Akasha snapped alive, wrapping itself around the volcanic anger swirling inside me.

"I'm going to feed off you," Hyperion continued. "And I'm going to go find that blonde bitch again and then I'll gut her right in front of you."

Power crackled along my knuckles. "Is that a promise?"

"Oh, yeah it is. But not before I have a little fun with her," he said, chuckling. "Then when you're begging for death, I'll hand you over to Cronus and he'll reward me by giving me Apollo."

"Well then." I said, turning around. Hyperion stood near the doorway. "I was planning to kill you slowly."

Hyperion grinned. "Yeah?"

"Yeah," I said, nodding. "I was going to drag it out, cut little slices into your skin, turn you into a living fucking coloring book. You know they're all the rage now. Then slowly burn you from the inside out, but not before I cut your dick off and shoved it down your throat and hang your balls around your neck like a noose."

"Sounds like a fun evening."

"It would've been, but, you see, I've matured," I said, smirking as I took a step toward him. Hyperion tensed, and my smirk grew. "I'm not going to drag this out. I'm not going to take pleasure in turning you into a weeping mass of flesh and broken bone." I paused, dipping my chin as I felt pure power rippling up my spine. "But I am going to take great pleasure in killing you."

Hyperion's lip curled. "You aren't going to do anything. You're not absolute."

"Then give me your best shot." I lifted my arms.

He didn't have to be asked twice. Shooting across the room, he cocked an arm back. A second later, his fist slammed into my jaw, knocking me back several inches. I didn't raise my hands or even try to stop him.

The pain actually felt good.

Like I needed to feel, because there was a part of me that deserved the first punch and then the second. I welcomed the fiery bite, a retribution for the pain I'd caused Josie. And when I hit the ground with the third punch, the air rushing for my lungs was a pittance for the pain I was most likely going to cause a whole lot of innocent people by the end of the night.

The kick in the stomach was enough.

Hyperion loomed over me, bloody fists at his sides. "You're not going to fight back?"

Spitting out a mouthful of blood, I laughed coldly. "You're a dumbass."

He blinked.

I tipped my head back, smiling up at him. "I'm just playing with you." Popping to my feet, I slammed my hands into his shoulders, knocking the Titan across the room and onto his ass. "Now you're going to die."

35

*L*etting the purest, strongest power take over, I lifted my arm. Amber light lit up the room as a bolt of godly akasha whirled down my bicep. The world tinted white as I let the bolt of absolute power go.

It shot across the small room, smacking into Hyperion's chest. He'd tried to move. He tried to dart to the side, but he wasn't fast enough. I was done playing with him. That was it. It was over.

The fucker was going to die.

And it was like Atlas all over again.

A look of pure astonishment washed over Hyperion's face as the whitish-amber light pulsed. The same dumb motherfucking look that said he couldn't believe I just punched out his immortality card as he stared down at the gaping, glowing hole in the center of his chest.

Outside, lightning slammed into the ground and thunder cracked the sky wide open. The smell of burnt ozone filled the tiny room. Hyperion went down on one knee, the impact splitting the floor. I kept up, pulling every ounce of deadly power from within as he fought back, throwing out an arm as if to stop the stream of akasha. Air crackled and popped as the very fine network of veins lit up under Hyperion's skin.

I lowered my arm. "I *am* absolute."

He opened his mouth, but there was no sound as the light in his veins expanded, bled through the vessels and washed over his body. The light pulsed once more and then it was an explosion of fireworks that shook the ceiling and the floor—the entire building.

And then there was nothing but scorched earth remaining.

"No!" a female voice shouted.

I spun around. It was her—the female Titan. Power rippled over my skin. My chin dipped down as I stalked toward her. "Too late."

She screeched as she drew back. Her screams ripped through the air as she spun in a dizzying circle. Black smoke surrounded her body as I summoned the absolute power once more.

She flew to the side, a mini funnel of rage crashing through a wall. Plaster exploded, pluming into the air. The female Titan was gone, most likely to alert the rest of the crew that their days were numbered.

Jaw working, I turned back to the spot where Hyperion had stood. A weight lifted from my shoulders. Wasn't like we didn't have the other Titans to worry about, but this one . . . yeah, this one had needed to go.

The charred floor had changed. Tiny specks of glowing red embers flickered. Closing my hands into fists, I walked over to the spot and stared down, brows knitting together. The flecks looked like—

"What have you done?"

My back stiffened. There was no denying who stood behind me. "Awful brave of you to show up after the Titan who captured your *daughter* is no longer in the picture."

"I warned you once about questioning my loyalty to my daughter," Apollo shot back. "I will not warn you again."

I faced Apollo, ignoring his threat. "I think it's pretty obvious what I did."

"Do you have any idea what this could cause?" Apollo stepped toward me. "He needed to be entombed."

"He needed to die!" Power crackled in the air around me. "Do you know what he did to Josie? There was going to be no entombing for that bastard. I will not have her living in fear. I will not have our—" I cut myself off.

"You will not have your *what*?" he demanded, and then he sucked in a sharp breath. I had no idea if he'd guessed the truth. I sure as hell wasn't going to confirm it, because I didn't trust the bastard. The god's all-white eyes snapped electricity. "You may be a god now, but you need to understand that your emotions cannot rule you."

"Oh, that's really funny coming from you."

His chest rose. "With godhood comes great responsibility—"

"Did you rip that off from Spider-Man?"

Anger tightened his features. "Is everything a joke to you?"

"Yeah." I looked around the room. "Mainly you?"

He exhaled roughly. "If my daughter didn't love you . . ."

"What?" I threw up my arms. "What would you do, Apollo? Turn me into a bush that smells like cat piss? Really? Don't you think that's a little played out? I'm not—"

Apollo moved faster than I could track.

One moment he was standing in front of me, and the next he had a hand around my throat and my back into a wall. Dirt filled the air as he leaned in, getting all up in my face. "You test every strain of my patience," he growled as his fingers dug into my windpipe.

"This is my I-don't-give-a-fuck face, in case you're wondering."

"You best learn quick who you're speaking to, Seth."

Wrapping a hand around his wrist, I bared my teeth. "And you best learn real quick who you're messing with." Slamming my free hand down on his, I broke his hold and threw him back.

Apollo caught himself as shock splashed across his face. His wide-eyed gaze met mine as I came off the wall.

"There's only one reason why I won't kill you," I warned, stalking toward him. "But that does not mean I will not bring you to an inch of your death."

A muscle thrummed in his jaw as several moments passed. "Do you have any idea of what you have begun? The chain of events you have started?"

I opened my mouth, but I really didn't have an answer.

"Do you not remember what Ewan had said to you?" He straightened as he referenced the nymph. Apollo shook his head. "You better be ready."

A cold shiver curled done my spine. "Ready for what?"

"There will be consequences," Apollo said. "There will be consequences for what you have done tonight."

"Aren't there always?"

He lifted his chin as he stepped back. "Not like this, Seth. Not like this."

Josie

I knew what'd happened the exact moment I woke. I realized my bed was empty and the world was shaking. It was like some kind of instinctual knowledge told me what happened.

I was going to kill Seth.

Okay. I wasn't going to kill him, but I was most definitely going to hit him.

Throwing the covers off, I shot to my feet and grabbed my clothes off the floor, hastily pulling them on in case the entire

Covenant came down on my head. I rushed from the bedroom and through the sitting room. Throwing open the door, I drew up short, coming face to face with a silver-eyed demigod.

"Where is he?" I demanded. My heart pounded painfully in my chest.

Aiden glanced up at the flickering overhead light. "You know where he went."

I cursed under my breath as a doorway down the hall opened and Alex stumbled out, blinking rapidly. She threw her arms out as a tremor rocked the hallway. "Oh gods, this is not a normal earthquake, is it?"

Aiden sighed. "I'm going to go with no."

She lowered her arms. "You let him go?"

"Didn't really have a choice," Aiden replied dryly. "Think you forgot the whole Seth-is-a-god-now thing."

Alex stopped, frowning. "You're shirt's inside out."

Of course it was.

Doors all up and down the hall opened and I spotted Deacon and Luke. I drew in a sharp breath as I stepped back. The flickering light steadied. "How long ago did he leave?"

"You miss me already?"

Gasping, I spun around. Seth stood in front of the door. I didn't think. Cocking back an arm, I punched him in the stomach as hard as possible.

Seth grunted out a laugh as he bent at the waist. "*Gods.*"

"What did you do?" I demanded, and then I really saw him as he straightened. There was a faint bruise on his cheek. His lip looked raw and his shirt . . . his shirt was charred at the hem. "What happened to your face—your clothes?"

"Don't worry, my perfect face will heal," he said, grinning in a way that looked like it would hurt.

I shook my head. "Seth. . . ."

The grin slipped from his face. "I had to, Josie."

"But you didn't," I whispered, but . . . but who was I kidding. Did I for one second truly believe that Seth wasn't going to go after Hyperion? No, I didn't. I closed my eyes. "Hyperion is dead?"

"Yes. So are quite a few charbroiled daimons that eventually climbed out of a hole in the ground." A few seconds later, I felt his hands on my cheeks. Aware that we had audience, I stiffened as he leaned in, resting his forehead against mine. "I know you're probably pissed and even disappointed. I'm sorry for that. He could not live. Not now. There was no way."

I shuddered, torn between being relieved that Hyperion was gone and horrified by the possible repercussions. What was going to happen? Hyperion was a big deal. Then I remembered. My head snapped up and my eyes opened. "Mitchell? Did you—"

Seth shook his head. "I'm sorry. He . . . he didn't make it."

"No," I whispered, refusing to believe it. "He was alive. He had to be."

His tawny eyes searched mine. "*Psychi mou*, he had been gone for a while."

Tears crawled up my throat. I don't know why it affected me so much, but it did, because saving Mitchell was important. He hadn't deserved what was done to him. And to die like that? It was so wrong.

Seth said something, and then the next second we were back in the room, on the bed. I was in his lap, and his arms were tight around me. "I'm sorry," he said. "It is not your fault, Josie. You couldn't have changed the outcome."

I wasn't so sure about that. Maybe if I'd gotten my head together quicker I would've remembered the box truck.

"Please." He tipped my chin up so our gazes met. "This is

not your guilt to carry. Hyperion did that to him. The Titans did. You are not at fault."

Repeating those words over and over in my head didn't change how I felt and beyond the bitter sadness of discovering that Mitchell had died, how in the world were we going to entomb the Titans now? Seth could not keep killing them. God only knows what was happening out in the world even though the tremors here had stopped.

I took a deep, shaky breath. "What's going to happen now?"

He folded his hand over my cheek as a shadow crossed his features. "I know things aren't going to be easy. I don't know everything that is going to happen, but I know one thing."

"What?"

"You will not have to fear Hyperion or any Titan. Our child won't have to worry about things not being okay," Seth said, splaying his other hand across my lower stomach. "Because we're going to end this. We're going to make it okay for this child."

"Together?"

Seth's lips brushed the curve of my jaw. He stopped to press a kiss to my pulse and then said, "Together."

Closing my eyes, I wiggled closer to him. I didn't want to think about how we were going to stop any of this. Right then, I just wanted to focus on us—on what we both had been feeling earlier, because that had been warm and wonderful.

Maybe that made me a terrible person. There was so much death and I knew there would be more. Things were happening outside of this little piece of the world. We had no idea what was going to happen in the next hour. The world could try to come crashing down on us and all those we cared about. We'd fight it. We'd fight it for each other, for our child, and for our friends. And tomorrow, I was probably going to hit Seth again.

I was probably going to be angry that he'd gone after Hyperion. But I was still going to love him, so we were going to deal with that.

Right now . . . we just had *right now*.

Seth's lips found mine and the kiss was soul-deep. There was always something about the way he kissed me. Like it was the first and last time. There was no hurry, no rush. If he'd never said he loved me, this kiss told me he did.

But he *had* spoken those words.

My arms tightened around his waist as I rested my cheek against his chest. Seth's hand smoothed up and down my back, following the line of my spine, and my eyes started to drift shut again when something occurred to me.

And then I remembered.

Sucking in air, I drew back as tension clamped down on my chest. I'd been having prophecies since Apollo had unlocked my abilities. Most of them had served as some kind of warning of what was to come.

"Josie?"

My gaze swung back to Seth's as an icy sense of disbelief invaded my veins. It hit me then that I had seen more than just Caleb in my so-called dreams. I had heard more than just Atlas's warning that he was coming for us, that one of us would die. I'd seen something else. I'd seen it more than once, and I knew it hadn't been a dream.

I'd seen my own death.

Just like Atlas had come and had ended Solos's life and how I'd seen Caleb standing before me when I'd never even met him, I knew that this prophecy would come to pass, too.

And just like Seth had promised. He had no idea, but we were to face that *together*.

Acknowledgements

First and foremost I would like to thank my agent Kevan Lyon and foreign rights agent, Taryn Fagerness, for always doing everything possible to get my books into as many hands as possible. A big thank you to my old school editorial team you whipped The Struggle into shape and Christine Borgford, at Type A Formatting who did her formatting magic. I also would like to thank Drew Leighty for being the most awesome Seth that I could ask for and Brooke DiTullio for gracing the cover as Josie. Also a big thanks to Okay Creations for creating the cover and E.J. Photography for taking the amazing photos.

None of this would've been possible with the support or friendship of Stacey Morgan, Stephanie Brown, Hannah McBride, Sarah J Maas, Andrea Joan, Laura Kaye, Jillian Stein, Liz Berry, Jay Crownover, Kathleen Tucker, Cora Carmack, Jen Frederick, and many, many more. Of course, thank you to my family and to Loki… and Diesel. Not sure why I'm thanking the dogs, but don't question me.

And finally, thank you, the reader. Many of you have been with this series since the very, very beginning all the way back when. Some of you started off only with Seth's journey. Without any you, there would be no point to this. Every reader, every reviewer—thank you!

About

JENNIFER L. ARMENTROUT

Jennifer L. Armentrout is the # 1 New York Times and International best selling author who lives in Martinsburg, West Virginia. Not all the rumors you've heard about her state are true. When she's not busy writing, she likes to garden, work out, watch really bad zombie movies, pretend to write, and hang out with her husband and her hyper Jack Russell named Loki.

She writes young adult contemporary, science fiction, and paranormal romance for Spencer Hill Press, Entangled Teen, Disney Hyperion, and Harlequin Teen. Don't Look Back was nominated as Best in Young Adult Fiction by the Young Adult Library Association. Her book Obsidian has been optioned for a major motion picture and her Covenant Series has been optioned for TV.

Under the name J. Lynn, Jennifer has written New Adult and Adult contemporary and paranormal romance, including the # 1 New York Times best seller Wait for You. She writes for HarperCollins and Entangled Brazen.

For details about current and upcoming titles from
Jennifer L. Armentrout,
please visit www.jenniferlarmentrout.com

CPSIA information can be obtained
at www.ICGtesting.com
Printed in the USA
LVOW11s0043150417
530767LV00002B/18/P